Keepers

CHUCK BOYER

Chuck Boyer
11/24/17

INFINITY
PUBLISHING

ISBN 978-1-4958-0977-4 Paperback
ISBN 978-1-4958-0891-3 eBook

Published December 2015

INFINITY PUBLISHING
1094 New DeHaven Street, Suite 100
West Conshohocken, PA 19428-2713
Toll-free (877) BUY BOOK
Local Phone (610) 941-9999
Fax (610) 941-9959
Info@buybooksontheweb.com
www.buybooksontheweb.com

Disclaimer

"This is a work of fiction. Names, characters, places, and incidents are the products of the author's imagination or are used fictitiously. Any resemblance to actual events, locales, or persons, living or dead, is entirely coincidental."

Dedication

"This book is dedicated to the children who have suffered the uncertainties of foster care and to the many dedicated foster parents, caseworkers and advocates who have helped them along that most difficult path."

CHAPTER 1

Stan Iverson stepped out of the rain and into the Fifth Street Bar in Oldtown, Ashton. The tavern was devoid of the hardscrabble crowd normally imbedded around clusters of tables or propped up by the bull-nosed counter. He strolled to the far end of the dimly lighted bar. It offered a clear view of incoming patrons and easy access to a backdoor exit. His choice was more professional habit than personal preference. A career cop until a couple of years ago, Iverson retained many of the habits and behaviors he'd acquired as a law enforcement officer. Awareness and control, traits common among successful cops, were tools kept in good working order by the former Sergeant.

Iverson removed his sodden coat and placed it and himself on adjoining bar stools. He stared at the cornucopia of multicolored liquids on the shelves behind the bar and contemplated their efficacy. A stiff drink was his self-prescribed antidote for yet another day of sieving through the self-indulgent and overly-inflated problems of others. His self-inflicted career move from city cop to private detective was not going as planned.

The only other customer in the seedy saloon sat at the opposite end of the bar. He looked worse than Iverson felt. Like Iverson, he'd been out in the rain before finding refuge in the bar. Water droplets trailed down his long, black overcoat finding temporary residence among the peanut shells scattered on the wood-plank floor. His crumpled hat rested on the bar's counter and rainwater pooled in its creases. Iverson studied the man carefully. He shivered like a Chihuahua and had one hand clasped tightly around a bottle of Budweiser. His other hand clenched a pen whose tip moved slowly on a page of a small notebook. Iverson wasn't planning on getting to know him.

The Fifth Street Bar was one of the few businesses still operating in the Ashton neighborhood known as The Brubaker. The district was the city's original area of settlement and was once a proud and vibrant neighborhood. Land and timber barons had built mansions in the foothills. Commercial ventures and housing sprung up below them to service the workers the construction companies and lumber mills employed. The timber industry crash ended the prosperity. The wealthy shuttered their doors and herded their money to more profitable pastures. The Brubaker, for all intents and purposes, died. The city bestowed the district a nom du temp of Oldtown to add a measure of quaintness to the neighborhood in hopes revitalization would follow. It didn't. The Brubaker was broken. So were its inhabitants.

Stan Iverson, however, had roots in The Brubaker. Of the many shuttered, disfigured and abandoned houses remaining, Iverson had called at least three of them home at some point in his childhood. A visit to the Fifth Street Bar, as cheerless and derelict as it was, was a visit home. Dave, the ancient, gray bearded bartender and proprietor, approached Iverson with a fresh bottle of beer and a slip of paper.

"These are both courtesy of the gentleman over there," Dave said and nodded in the direction of the bar's only other patron. Iverson took the bottle, set it on the bar's scarred summit and moved his gaze toward the man at the far end of the bar. The man was hunched over the counter and staring at the endless rows of intoxicating liquids.

"Give him my thanks," Iverson said. He unfolded the small piece of paper and read the short message it contained. "I'll give you $50,000 to kill me. Tonight!"

Iverson read the unsteadily penned lines at least five times before he realized his eyes weren't deceiving him. He called Dave over.

"Who is that guy?" Iverson asked.

"No clue," replied Dave in his typical brief-speak style.

"Ever see him in here before?"

"Nope. Is there a problem?"

"I'm not sure," Iverson replied hesitantly. He chose not to reveal the contents of the note.

Iverson sat quietly for another five minutes, occasionally affixing his gaze toward the man who had just offered him a significant amount of money to kill him. Who was this guy? What did he really want? Was this a joke? He contemplated leaving both the tavern and the questions behind but the intense curiosity that had made him a good cop required an explanation.

The man's fixation with the array of booze remained steady and the mirrored backdrop to the bottles provided

Iverson with only a distorted glimpse of his face. He swiveled slightly on his barstool and redirected his scrutiny onto Iverson. His eyes, dark and penetrating even in the bar's dim light, held a sad resolve. A slight nod conveyed an invitation to join him. Iverson returned the nod, considered the summons and accepted it. He approached slowly and purposefully and conducted additional inventory of his bar mate before stopping a few feet from the man's four-legged perch.

The man looked old, but Iverson got a sense that he wasn't. A few strands of gray hair darted about above his ears but what else remained on his head was remnant brown. He had a corrugated forehead and the beginnings of crow's feet migrating from the corners of both eyes. A collection of scars peppered about his face were trying to hide behind more than a few days of coarse stubble. Iverson reckoned his bar mate had had a hard life no matter how long it had been lived.

"Excuse me," Iverson submitted, "but I thought I should at least thank you for the beer."

The offering was met with a throaty grunt and a slight bow of the head. Iverson took a long swallow of the gift beer and pushed the conversation forward.

"What's with the note?" he asked. It was part question, part demand.

"Can't read English?" the man asked gruffly.

Iverson detected an accent but wasn't sure of its origin. But he *was* sure that he wasn't in the mood for a scolding from a stranger making bizarre requests in a bar.

"I read English just fine, thank you," Iverson replied tersely and turned to go back to his stool.

"Wait," the stranger said. "I'll explain. Please sit down." He patted the crackled vinyl top of the seat next to his.

Iverson paused while considering the invitation. He disregarded the bar stool and buttressed his frame with an elbow on the bar. "You've got five minutes," he said curtly.

"I'll take it," replied the stranger. "I'm sure my request took you a little off guard."

"It's not every day that someone asks me to kill them."

The man smiled slightly and with effort. Iverson guessed it was not a frequent bearing.

"It's the first time I've asked," the stranger explained. "I should tell you right off it's a serious request."

"And I suppose you might imagine that I'd have a few questions," responded Iverson.

"I hoped you would."

"Good. Three come to mind immediately and the clock's ticking so I'll start. What's your name?"

"That's actually a complicated question, but I'll start simple. Call me Gabos."

Iverson looked perplexed.

"It's Croatian," explained Gabos.

Iverson lolled his head back slightly. "The accent," he reasoned out loud.

"Yeah," Gabos validated. "Never did get rid of it. Never wanted to, really."

"Okay," Iverson said. "Gabos what?" Iverson inquired.

"That's where the complications begin."

"Complications?"

"I've had quite a few last names."

"Then I guess you get to choose."

The man smiled again, this time more easily. "Horvat," he said. "Gabos Horvat."

"Fine by me," Iverson sanctioned. "Next question, Gabos Horvat. Why do you want me to kill you?"

"The answer to that question would take time; a lot of time, Mr. Iverson. Unfortunately, my time is short and our time limited. Suffice it to say, I need to die."

Iverson swayed back and took a hard look at Gabos Horvat. How and why did he know his name and why did he need to die? Questions that begged answers.

"Okay," Iverson finally said, "I'll move on, but I reserve the right of return."

"We're on your clock, Mr. Iverson."

"Why me?" Iverson continued. "Why did *I* get the note?"

"Because you have the skills and tools to both end and expose my miserable existence." Horvat bent forward and nodded in the direction of where Iverson holstered his .38 Colt revolver. He then added grimly, "My story needs to be told."

"And what story would that be, Mr. Horvat?"

"I'd like your commitment to honor my request before I get into that."

Iverson reflected briefly, and then said, "I can't promise to kill you, Mr. Horvat. Your request is more than a bit unusual and no doubt has more than a few obstacles, the least of which would fit into a legal context. As you appear to know something of my employment history, I will assume you also know that I normally tread on the legitimate side of the law. Killing you, whether you solicited it or not, would most definitely fall on the other side and I am inclined to reject offers steering me in that direction."

Horvat sloshed down the remaining beer in his bottle, set the lone soldier in front of him and looked directly into Iverson's eyes. "I suppose that's true," he said. "But, Mr. Iverson, there is this. Without doubt my life will end before the next sun rises and I am offering you an opportunity to expose a dark and dangerous secret. I want the world to know what happened to me and I'd like you to craft my epitaph. If you decline, then I will die anonymously and many others will die needlessly. The choice is yours."

Horvat shifted his intense stare away from Iverson, slumped over the bar and laid his head on craggy, fisted hands. It was Iverson's move and he wasn't sure if he wanted to know any more about Gabos Horvat. They sat in silence while Iverson's five minute time restriction expired. His professional instincts told him to push forward, his personal ennui wanted him to head back to his bar stool. Then again, he reasoned, he'd been sitting on that stool silently bemoaning the tedious monotony in his life. He couldn't have it both ways. Horvat was interesting if nothing else and he could use something interesting in his life right now.

"Okay," Iverson finally said. "You've tapped my curiosity and secured my attention . . . the brief version. I promise nothing and your death wish is definitely not on the immediate menu. If that's not acceptable, our conversation will end here."

"Let's get out of here," Horvat said brusquely and rose to leave.

"And go where?" Iverson asked.

"I've got a squalid little room in the hooker hotel a couple of blocks from this palace. We can talk there. It's private except for the resident rodent population and I've got notes you'll need."

Iverson balked. Following a complete stranger who had just solicited him for his own killing to a cheap motel room in The Brubaker couldn't possibly be a good idea.

"You coming or not?" Horvat demanded. Iverson sensed an effort to intimidate.

Iverson answered, "Not sure." His instincts were conversing again.

"Look," Horvat said, "I don't have the luxury of time. You either trust me or you don't. I can appreciate your hesitancy but please understand this. My death will occur with or without your assistance. I'm only trying to make it meaningful and on my own terms. I know this sounds dramatic, and it's certainly odd, but I can't help that."

Iverson looked at Horvat and the intimidation had disappeared. It had been replaced with a matter-of-fact calmness. Iverson sensed, although he didn't know why, that he was being honest. The investigator in Iverson pushed forward. He nodded and followed Gabos Horvat out the door and into the rainy, cool night.

CHAPTER 2

Fifth Street was deserted. The steady rain curtained down and left small reflecting pools scattered in the cratered sidewalk. Horvat pulled his coat collar up, sucked in a deep, damp breath and turned north. Iverson followed and they walked slowly among The Brubaker's relics. They said nothing. Horvat walked briskly and resolutely ... all the time a few feet in front of Iverson. Gabos Horvat apparently had need for neither companionship nor conversation from the person he'd chosen to kill him. The cold, bitter night mirrored its human spirit.

Iverson's avocations demanded a vigilant approach to the many dangerous situations he'd visited and this night was quickly morphing in that direction. His well-trained senses were alert to anything out of the ordinary ... a challenge under any circumstance, but one made even more difficult in The Brubaker. Faint lighting revealed long abandoned buildings with skeletal shelving stocked with the remains of cut-rate merchandise and semi-mummified foodstuffs. The buildings and the dimly lit alley ways between them provided perfect hiding places for those working the fringes of Ashton society. The Brubaker had a grim present and no future.

Iverson saw nothing out of The Brubaker's ordinary until he noticed a car slipping out from one of the side streets. The presence of a car wasn't unusual, but the fact that its headlamps were not lit, was. It slowed as it approached. Horvat stopped and took a tight hold of Iverson's right arm.

"I found you too late," Horvat whispered. The words conveyed a sad resignation.

"What the hell does that mean?" demanded Iverson.

"It means it won't be you that ends my life." Horvat replied calmly. He unearthed a small Manila envelope from an outside jacket pocket and handed it to Iverson. "Keep this in a safe place, Mr. Iverson. A very safe place."

"What's this?" Iverson questioned.

"I don't have time to explain. It'll make sense later."

Iverson folded the packet and hurriedly stuffed it into the back pocket of his Levis. Horvat watched the maneuver carefully. He then grabbed Iverson with both hands, flung him forcefully onto the street and walked directly toward the approaching vehicle. Iverson lost his balance, slipped on the street's moss coated curb and landed awkwardly on hard asphalt. An audible thud accompanied his skull's collision with the pavement.

Iverson propped himself up with a wobbly arm and fought to regain focus. Through blurry eyes he saw Gabos Horvat, arms folded, standing defiantly in front of the idling, dark sedan. Two men in dark trench coats emerged from their car carrying what appeared to be shotguns. They walked slowly and decisively, stopping ten feet from Horvat. No one spoke. Iverson instinctively knew that these men knew each other. The absence of any form of emotion indicated their acceptance of the inevitability of this encounter and Iverson's collision with the road rendered him powerless to affect it. The deafening discharge and blinding flash were simultaneous.

The strangers strode slowly and silently toward Horvat's motionless body. Once there, one of them bent over and checked his pulse at the carotid artery. Apparently satisfied they had completed their task, they surveyed the landscape for unwanted bystanders. Unfortunately, Iverson had fallen, quite literally, into that category and he was located in seconds. The killers stepped confidently toward him while simultaneously reloading their weapons. Iverson attempted to get up but the impact with the pavement had scrambled his synapses and neither his brain nor his feet found useful traction. He slumped back to the ground and looked for possible cover. His blurred vision saw none.

The first blow Iverson felt was against his left temple from the butt of one of the men's guns. It sent Iverson sprawling and left him spread face down on the wet pavement. The second strike was administered to his ribcage and the weapon was the cowboy boot worn by the second predator. The blows stunned Iverson but he was still conscious. He had to buy some time or he'd be laying on a slab at Ashton's morgue.

His tormentors took a moment to reassess the landscape and Iverson exploited their surveillance break. He rolled quickly and painfully to an abandoned car and quickly slid beneath its undercarriage. The two men followed silently and slowly, apparently confident that their prey had only delayed its certain demise. They methodically paced the perimeter outside the car while Iverson turned on his back, reached across his battered ribcage and drew his weapon from its leathered sheath. He then quieted his body, reacquired sensory input and left his fate to instinct and experience.

Abruptly the footfalls stopped. They began again but moved away from Iverson at a quickened pace. Iverson heard two car doors slam and a car speed off, tires spinning on wet, slick pavement. More footsteps approached. Iverson's pulse quickened.

"You all right?" someone directed under the car.

"Hell no, I'm not all right," Iverson managed. "Who the hell are you?"

No voiced reply came, but Iverson recognized the tattoos on the two very large arms that reached into his retreat and roughly jerked him out from under the car. It was Dave the bartender. He loomed over Iverson.

Iverson sat up, propped his back up against the wheel well of the old vehicle and scanned the area for the dark sedan. Seeing it nowhere, he labored, "the other guy ... Horvat?"

Dave nodded towards the motionless body of Gabos Horvat. "Not sure, but he ain't movin'," Dave reported. "I called 9-1-1 when I heard the gunshots, then came running with Bouncer. Damn sure didn't expect to find you. You sure you're okay?"

"Bouncer?" Iverson queried with effort.

Dave nodded toward the sawed-off shotgun that normally was stationed behind the bar but now rested on a rusted out fender of the derelict vehicle. Iverson quickly made the connection between Dave, Bouncer and the hasty departure of the sedan and its occupants.

"Help me over to Horvat," Iverson said resolutely. He made an attempt to stand. He failed.

Dave knew Iverson well enough to know he'd crawl if he had to so he helped the ex-cop up and offered his shoulder for support. They reached Horvat and Iverson clutched Dave's arm, bent forward and assessed the damage. Horvat had dropped face upward, his arms and legs splayed outward onto the pavement. Raindrops ricocheted randomly around the contorted expression on his face. His jacket lay open faced and blood was slowly saturating his shirt at multiple locations. If he wasn't already dead, the unabated seepage mined by multiple shotgun pellets assured that he soon would be. Iverson dropped to one knee, bent over and pressed his ear to Horvat's chest. He heard a shallow heartbeat.

"Get some . . ."

"Already coming," Dave interrupted.

Iverson scraped off his coat, laid it over Horvat's body and sat down on the wet pavement to await medical help. He tried to tell Dave something but whatever it was, it didn't evolve to spoken form. His head throbbed and warm, red liquid escaped from his ear and ran down his cheek. The last thing he remembered was the faint sound of sirens in the distance.

Chapter 3

The man named Kant waited patiently in a dark, shadowy corner of an unnamed alley. The persistent rain had left his clothing damp and his body chilled. He was at this miserable place, not out of personal choice, but out of duty. He was there to kill someone. He had never met his intended victim and would have no reason to kill him other than that he had been told to do so. He'd received the identification, description and location of his target earlier in the day and had not requested a reason for the kill. It was simply an order and he had been trained to follow orders without question or hesitation.

Kant finally spotted his target exiting The President's Hotel in downtown Portland. It was exactly nine o'clock and the target was precisely on time. The middle aged man wore a dark, gray overcoat and a brimmed hat to deflect the rain. He surveyed the landscape outside the hotel, swung a long, tasseled scarf around his neck and descended the hotel's stone-stepped entryway to the sidewalk. He walked with an air of confident importance.

At his distance, Kant wasn't able to make out distinct facial features but he was certain this was the man he was supposed to kill. He'd been given specific information as to the man's whereabouts and the time that he would be leaving the hotel. There was no other human traffic on the hotel's perimeter and none within the marble and gilded walls of the hotel's foyer. He knew the man would be walking to his favorite poker pub a few blocks away and that he'd have time to affirm his judgment. Still, he didn't want to make a mistake. Mistakes weren't tolerated.

Kant stepped out of the alley, filled his lungs with a deep breath of cool air and tracked the unsuspecting man from the opposite side of the rain slickened street. He calculated the distance to the neon sign broadcasting the target's destination and altered his pace to be able to intercept him at the point he'd chosen to accomplish his task. The identified kill spot, reconnoitered hours earlier, provided both dim lit cover for the murder and a ready escape route once it was completed.

Kant moved stealthily towards his victim while maintaining constant vigilance of the public and fluid landscape. Absolute attention to detail was essential. Witnesses were not allowed and getting caught was not an option.

Kant's training had provided the skills he now employed, skills that were now second nature. That training had also instilled in him an emotional detachment from the process. Kant, in fact, had not had emotions of any kind for as long as he could remember. There was a time when he felt saddened by the act of killing but it was an inexplicable sadness for himself as much as it had been for the lives he had ended. Those feelings had gradually dissipated and eventually they were replaced with a singular submission to duty. He had relinquished all emotion. In essence, he existed in isolation from the traits that made him human.

Kant quickened his pace, crossed the street a block ahead of his target and walked casually toward him, the gap between them contracting with each step. One hundred feet from the entrance to The Full House pub, at a point where the street intersected with another of Portland's web of alleys, Kant hailed the man and asked for directions to an invented location. While the man pondered the question, Kant completed his final analysis of the man's identification. Six feet two inches tall, blue-green eyes, light brown hair with emergent gray strands around the temples, mid-fifties and, most importantly, a small crescent shaped scar above the left eyebrow. Satisfied he'd found his intended target, Kant muted his prey with a swift and well-placed blow to the throat that immediately collapsed the man's trachea. The target grabbed his throat, crumpled to his knees and gasped for air.

Kant scanned the area. No one had witnessed his attack. He gripped his prey with powerful arms and dragged him forcibly into the alley and dropped him onto the cobbled stone surface. He watched as his wide eyed victim flailed violently; grunting and gasping in a desperate quest for air. Kant removed the scarf from around the man's neck, twice-wrapped it around his head and over his mouth to muffle the sounds and waited dispassionately until the man grew still. He then extracted the man's wallet from the inside pocket of his suit coat and ripped the expensive watch from his wrist. Both were items he had no personal use for and would quickly discard in an appropriate place. Finally, he knelt next to the target and checked both the carotid and radial pulse.

Kant found no evidence of a beating heart. He moved the man adjacent to the bricked wall of the alley and propped him into a sitting position. He tied the scarf back around the target's neck, returned his hat to its proper perch and straightened his shirt and coat. Kant stepped slowly back from the lifeless body and took one last look. Satisfied that his task had been completed according to plan, he merged into the shadows of the alley way and stepped away from another death.

Chapter 4

Iverson awoke to fast moving, fast talking people and the hum and beep of machines. He was in the Emergency Room at Ashton's Valley Christian Hospital. A blue cold pack covered the top of his head and another was secured to his chest with several wraps of white tape. The bulk and buzz of activity in the room, however, was not directed towards him.

A drawn, semi-opaque curtain separated Iverson from the main activity in the ER. He shook the fog from his head and slowly navigated to a position that allowed him to slightly push back the curtain and observe the activity next to his cubicle. A team of green clad, masked and gloved people swarmed over the man who had asked Iverson to end his life.

"Massive blood loss," said a heavy set woman who tamped snow white towels onto several areas of Gabos Horvat's body and removed those turned crimson. Another nurse strategically inserted a needle into his right arm, withdrew bright, red liquid into a plastic ampule and rushed out of the room. A yellow garbed man replaced the departed blood runner and stuck tendrilled patches to Horvat's chest, stretched the confluence of wires to a central connector and plugged it into a droning machine.

A blood pressure cuff was wrapped around Horvat's arm, inflated and connected to an apparatus whose neon line displayed intermittent blips. A short, pear shaped nurse swiftly and quietly placed a shiny metal tray on a bedside table, removed the clear plastic wrapping covering it and inventoried the instruments exposed. Still another shrouded worker guided a clear, plastic tube down Horvat's throat, attached a large bag to the tube and began to squeeze air into his lungs. Long-necked poles with curved, hooked summits were wheeled to either side of the bed and plastic bags were hung from the catches. Their contents rapidly began a journey through flexible tubing to veins in Horvat's arms.

Gabos Horvat uttered no sound while the myriad intrusive procedures were levied on his damaged body. Iverson watched, frozen in his own silence, as the ER staff completed their efficient routines. That silence was abruptly interrupted.

"Gloves!" ordered the man striding into the room. He snapped on the fingered latex seconds later and quickly turned his attention to those areas on Horvat's body still oozing blood. He examined the wounds gingerly with his fingers, then, with one of the instruments provided from the tray, carefully burrowed into a wound and lifted something out of Horvat's motionless body. Once removed, it was discarded into a metal container with a sound like lug nuts hitting a hubcap. Additional probes into more holes produced the same result.

"Vitals?" the doctor demanded.

"BP seventy over thirty-five. Pulse forty," reported the tech manning the battery of machines cabled to Horvat.

"Hang a liter of Ringers and dextran," the doctor ordered, "and get two units of O-positive ready. Vitals again!"

"BP sixty over thirty. Pulse forty."

"Damn it! Start the blood," he ordered, "and tighten that cuff."

"He's leaking from a lot of holes, Doctor," reported one of the nurses.

The doctor shot a quick look of irritation to the nurse. "No shit!" he barked. "I don't need to be told the obvious. There're at least a dozen bleed points you can quick-patch while I tie off the two artery incursions gushing the most blood. Think you can handle that?"

"Just tell me where to start, Doctor."

The doctor did a quick inventory and listed a hierarchy of the wounds for the nurse to attend. He then took two instruments from the table-side tray and returned his attention to his own tasks.

"Vitals?" he demanded again.

"BP sixty over thirty. Pulse forty."

"At least we're holding," the doctor assessed. He moved decisively around the bed, stopped abruptly and fixed on Iverson's unwanted surveillance and raised the bushy eyebrows above his deep set eyes. An attentive nurse recognized the implicit signal and pulled closed the drape between Iverson and Horvat.

Iverson eased back onto his heap of pillows and stared at the ceiling. He remembered the packet Horvat had given him and his instruction: "Keep it very safe, Mr. Iverson." He searched his pants pockets, found the packet and stuffed it into his underwear next to the family jewels. It was the safest place he could think of. Moments later, a somber and silent orderly wheeled him out of the ER and into an adjoining room where a plump nurse in a starched, white uniform tended to his wounds, wounds that now seemed trivial.

"Is he going to make it?" Iverson asked the nurse.

"Who?" she asked, without making eye contact.

"Gabos Horvat. The man next door."

She stuck a needle in Iverson's arm and plunged an amber liquid into his soft muscle. "I'm afraid I don't know who you're talking about, sir."

Iverson jerked his head up. "Really?" he asked sarcastically. "You do work here, right? There's a guy full of buckshot next door. Half the hospital's staff is in there working on him, and you don't know who I'm talking about?"

"I'm afraid I don't, sir. Why don't you just lay back and relax. The sedative will begin to take effect in a few minutes."

"I don't want to be sedated, godamnit," Iverson argued. "I want to know what's happening with Gabos Horvat."

"I'm not aware of a Gabos Horvat at this hospital, sir. Now please, just lay back and relax."

Iverson could feel the muscles in his body going limp. He tried to right himself on the bed but his brain had ceased communicating with the rest of his body. His head collapsed into a pillow and he saw the nurse smile as his eyelids closed and his consciousness escaped.

CHAPTER 5

Stan Iverson's eyes opened and grudgingly let in the hazy daylight filtering in through the slatted blinds covering the windows in his room. It took him a few minutes to recall where he was and why he was there. He braced himself up in bed and looked around at the small, sterile chamber that encased him. His head throbbed and his shoulder ached. Movement in any direction initiated pain and elicited a muted groan. The events of the prior evening slowly trickled back into his consciousness and he wondered if Horvat was alive and, if he was, what kind of shape he was in. Then he remembered the nurse and her denial of Horvat's existence. He needed some answers.

Iverson put his feet on the cold, linoleum floor and started to get up when a tall, thin man in a bleached white coat entered the room. He had a long nose, beady eyes and glossy, slicked back hair.

"I don't think that's a good idea," the man stated tersely.

"What's not a good idea?"

"Getting out of bed. You've suffered a pretty severe head wound, not to mention assorted contusions and abrasions."

"And just who the hell are you?" Iverson demanded.

"I'm your doctor, Mr. Iverson."

"My doctor? Really? My doctor's name is Stern. He's short, fat and has maybe three strands of hair on his head. You don't look much like him."

The man laughed a semi-patronizing laugh. "I'm Doctor Jenkins," he said, "the doctor assigned to your case. You do remember being admitted to the hospital last night, don't you, Mr. Iverson?"

"Yeah, I remember. I also remember coming into this establishment with a guy named Gabos Horvat. You wouldn't happen to know anything about him would you?"

"No, I'm sorry I don't. I just came on duty a couple of hours ago at which time I was handed your case. Apparently you came to us through the ER. Your chart indicates that you may have been in some kind of scrape."

"Yeah, some kind of scrape," Iverson repeated mockingly. "Look, I want to know about the other guy that came into the ER with me. Where is he?"

"I've looked over the ER reports from last night, Mr. Iverson, and nothing indicates that someone was brought in with you. You were placed under some pretty heavy sedation last night and sometimes people dream quite extravagantly under drugs."

"I didn't dream it, Doctor," Iverson asserted. "And if your reports don't show that someone was admitted with me, someone with multiple gunshot wounds, I might add, then you either have very bad reporting procedures or someone is not telling the truth around here."

"Come now, Mr. Iverson."

"Don't give me that condescending crap, Doctor. I know what's real and what isn't. I came into your hospital last night after getting into an altercation with two men with shotguns. The man I was with, Gabos Horvat, was shot. I saw him shot. I later witnessed a number of your comrades working on him in the ER while I was behind a curtain. It sounded to me like they weren't sure he was going to make it. I want to know if he did."

"The records show . . ."

"Fuck your records!" Iverson barked. "Horvat was in your emergency room. You can deny that if you want to, but he was there."

"Calm down, Mr. Iverson. You don't need to be raising your blood pressure. Not with your head injury."

Jenkins was right about that. Iverson's head felt like it was about to explode. He lay back down and took a couple of deep breaths. The doctor did some doctor things. Listened to his heart, took his blood pressure and told him again to relax.

"You need to rest," Jenkins said, "or you'll be spending more time in here than I'm sure you want to. I'll go check those ER records again, just to be sure, but not because I doubt their accuracy. I don't expect to find anything different than what I've already told you, but I'll check. In the meantime, get some sleep, Mr. Iverson. That's an order!"

Chapter 6

The boy named Tomas finished his day's work and was directed back to the old house. The Keeper opened the heavy wooden entryway and Tomas shuffled silently and dutifully through the spotless cooking area and toward the doorway that lead to a windowless cellar. He opened the door and descended the dimly lighted stairway, pausing briefly on the last step to hear the familiar turn of the key that sealed him into his subterranean home. He trudged stoically down the hallway to a porcelain washbasin, stripped off his clothes and relentlessly scrubbed layers of dirt and grime from his body. Satisfied that he was appositely clean, Tomas turned, walked back up the hallway and entered a dreary side room. He lowered himself onto a single bed, switched on a lamp sitting on a three legged table and opened the book he'd been given the week before. The evening meal would be available at the usual time and Tomas would be tested on the book's contents and graded on his personal hygiene. Success on both accounts would reward him with food. Failure would result in hunger.

Tomas had been living at this home for six months. To the best of his recollection, he'd lived at three other homes during his sixteen years. All were timeworn buildings. All were far away from civilization. That was the plan.

Each home had different people in charge. Two of them. A man and a woman. The Keepers. Tomas had never attended a school, had never seen a movie and had never witnessed the machinations of a city. He had no brothers or sisters. He'd never had friends. He didn't consider this odd or different. It was simply the way it was.

Tomas' education had been overseen by the Keepers. Early Keepers taught him to read and write. Later Keepers presented mathematics and science. All Keepers attended his physical needs. They kept him sheltered, clothed and fed. They also stressed two things above all else: an unquestionable belief in an all-powerful God and strict obedience to the Keepers who did his bidding.

Weapons and martial arts training began when Tomas was twelve. Small arms, handguns and rifles, were mastered through hours of practice and daily animal hunts on the acreage surrounding the homes. Each time Tomas achieved proficiency in a weapon, a new one was added. Every time he moved to a new home, the training was intensified and the weapons upgraded. His toys were made by Glock, Ruger and Remington, not Hasbro or Mattel. He didn't play with G.I Joe. He was G.I. Joe. He was becoming a skilled killer.

Chapter 7

Iverson heard voices but wasn't sure if they were real. He forced his eyes open and saw three men dressed in middle class suits speaking in hushed tones and discussing something he couldn't hear. When they realized the patient was awake, their discussion ended. One of them left the room and the other two walked slowly and purposefully over to Iverson.

"Stan Iverson," engaged the taller of the two, "I'm Agent Frantzen from the FBI. My friend here is Agent Dulles. We'd like to ask you a few questions." He was about forty-five, well-constructed and with dark, deep eyes set above strong cheek bones. His salt and pepper hair was cropped short and contrasted with his heavy, unruly eyebrows. His voice had a mellifluous quality.

While at the Ashton Police Department, Iverson had worked with the FBI on numerous occasions. Although he'd never actually had any dealings with Frantzen, he'd heard of him. He had a reputation as a loner which meant he was someone other agents didn't want to work with. Dulles was a name he'd not heard before.

Iverson stared at the two men, deciding whether or not to be cooperative. "Quid pro quo?" he queried.

"That depends," replied Frantzen.

"On what?" asked Iverson.

"If your questions are reasonable and if I'm authorized to answer them."

"Fine," Iverson responded. "I'll trade answers for answers."

Frantzen paused, and then paced the room for a few seconds before responding. "Sure, why not," he finally said.

"Ask away," Iverson prompted.

"Do you have any idea who attacked you?" Frantzen asked.

"Not a clue."

"How many were there?"

"Two."

"Could you identify them if you saw them?"

"Not sure," Iverson replied.

"Well, could you or couldn't you?" interrupted Dulles. He was about the same age as Frantzen but in contrast to the athletic looking detective, Dulles was short, squat and had a rounded slab of a face. Thick lensed glasses perched precariously on his pug nose and they shielded nervous, beady eyes. Iverson figured he'd taken a few too many punches.

"I told you I wasn't sure," Iverson insisted.

An obviously distressed Dulles sucked some air, turned and walked away from Iverson's bed.

"He's had a bad day," explained Frantzen. Dulles shot him a cold look of disapproval.

"I'm not exactly having the time of my life," countered Iverson.

"No, I'm sure you're not, Mr. Iverson. Why do you suppose you were attacked?"

"Why *we* were attacked," corrected Iverson.

Frantzen stared at Iverson, then looked over at his partner. Dulles presented no opinion as to the direction Frantzen should take.

"Someone else was attacked?" Frantzen asked meekly.

It was a lame question and a second-rate attempt at getting Iverson to release more information. Iverson wasn't going to play that game.

"Okay, fine, Agent. I was alone. But tell me, Agent Frantzen, why are you and Mr. Magoo over there talking to me if there isn't something more going on here than me getting mugged?"

Frantzen eyeballed Iverson intently. He didn't offer an answer. Dulles motioned for Frantzen to join him in the corner of the room and Frantzen complied. They spoke briefly out of Iverson's earshot after which Frantzen left the room and Dulles approached Iverson.

"Let's be frank, Iverson," Dulles said in a semi-threatening tone. "I don't have time for games."

"Meaning what?" Iverson asked.

"You know exactly what I mean, Iverson." The conversation's formality had been abandoned. Iverson smiled and decided it was time to revisit their deal.

"Quid pro quo, Agent, remember? Maybe we'll both get something we want. I believe it's my turn."

Dulles took a moment, decided his intimidation approach hadn't worked and relinquished control of the conversation's direction. "Fine," he said indignantly. "Go ahead and ask your damn question."

Iverson adjusted his position in the bed and asked, "Just who are you, really, Agent Dulles?"

Dulles blew out a loud sigh. "We told you, Iverson," he said impatiently, "we're FBI."

"Frantzen might be FBI, but you're definitely not," Iverson countered. "Just who is it that signs your paycheck?"

Dulles backed away from both the question and the bed. The puffy tissue around his mouth tightened and the words coming out of it were more deliberate.

"It doesn't matter who I am," Dulles proclaimed. "What matters is what your friend Horvat told you."

Iverson took both Dulles' new demeanor and the conversation's turn to Gabos Horvat in stride. He was glad to have reality surface.

"And why might that be so important, Agent? And who is it that wants to know?"

"You have a lot of questions, don't you, Iverson?"

"It's my business to have a lot of questions. It's also my business to find answers."

"Well, I'm afraid I'm not the answer man, Iverson. What I am is the messenger, and the message for you is to leave this alone."

Iverson knew a threat when he heard one.

"I don't respond well to intimidation," Iverson cautioned. "If you'd done your homework, you'd know that."

Dulles' face tightened and flushed crimson. "Don't play games with me, Iverson," he huffed. "You don't realize who you're dealing with here."

"So help me out with that, Dulles. Who exactly *am* I dealing with?"

"I can't answer that."

"Who is Gabos Horvat?"

"I can't answer that either."

"Is Horvat alive?"

Dulles ignored Iverson and it was obvious that the conversation was headed nowhere. Iverson sensed Dulles was about to walk out of the room and he hadn't learned anything.

"Okay, Dulles," Iverson entreated, "let me try an easy one. Does Gabos Horvat, or at least the man I knew as Gabos Horvat, exist?"

Dulles' face slackened and he walked a small half-circle to the other side of Iverson's bed. "Yes," he finally said, "the man you call Gabos Horvat exists."

"Is he still alive?" Iverson quickly added.

"Barely."

"Is Horvat ..."

"Look, Iverson," Dulles interrupted, "I'm the one asking the questions."

"That's not our arrangement."

"What?"

Quid pro quo, remember?" Iverson admonished. Dulles' shoulders slumped. "But you're right," Iverson added, "it is your turn."

Dulles reconsidered the arrangement. He obviously would have preferred that Iverson simply buckle to his pseudo authority and dutifully discharge whatever information he had. He nervously checked his watch, walked over to the door and summoned his colleague.

His discussion with Frantzen was brief and one-sided ... Dulles talked and Frantzen listened. Frantzen retreated from the doorway and Dulles returned his attention to Iverson.

"How long have you known the man you knew as Horvat?"

"Before he was shot," Iverson guessed, "about ten minutes."

"Ten minutes!" Dulles exclaimed. "What the hell do you mean ten minutes?"

"I mean ten minutes," Iverson emphasized. "You know, 600 seconds. He bought me a beer and we started up a conversation."

"About what?" Dulles demanded.

Iverson debated briefly with himself the value of full disclosure. He eventually figured *what the hell.* "Mr. Horvat asked me to kill him," he divulged.

The revelation did not surprise Dulles, or if it did, he didn't show it. He paced back and forth at the foot of Iverson's bed for a few minutes, stroked his meaty chin and tried to steal another turn in the conversation.

"What else did you talk about?"

"My turn, Agent," Iverson declared.

Dulles scowled, but acquiesced with a dismissive wave of his hand.

"Who was Horvat? I mean who was he *really*?"

"I can't answer that."

"Can't or won't?"

"Can't. I don't know who he really was."

"Your turn," Iverson said, maintaining the rules of the game.

"What else was discussed at the bar?"

"Not much. As I said, it was a very short discussion. He asked me to kill him, I told him no. He asked me to take a walk."

"A walk where?"

"Quid-pro-quo," Iverson stated calmly. Dulles sighed his acknowledgement.

"Who are you working for?"

Dulles paused, walked over to the room's solitary window and stared out at a view of weathered brick and frayed tarpaper. "I can't answer that either."

"Come on, Dulles," Iverson said with obvious frustration. "You're either government or big business. They're the only ones who make people disappear. I just want to know if it's taxes or profits paying your salary. I'll find out eventually. How about saving me some time?"

"That won't happen," Dulles said bluntly. "There's no point in continuing this conversation; a conversation that never took place. You need to back off, Iverson. If you don't, you'll regret it."

"I told you I don't respond to threats," Iverson countered, "and we've definitely achieved the threat threshold."

Dulles reached full froth. "No more questions," he bellowed. "Just remember what I told you. Forget Horvat. You never met him because he doesn't exist."

"Sure, whatever you say, Dulles," Iverson said calmly. "Thanks for coming by and cheering me up."

"Asshole," Dulles mumbled as left the room. Frantzen was waiting for him outside the door and Dulles hurled a few choice obscenities his way as well before they both left. A few minutes later, Doctor Jenkins returned to Iverson's room.

"Mr. Iverson," the doctor said, "I made some inquiries about the patient you mentioned."

"So what didn't you find, Doctor?"

The physician looked at Iverson with averted eyes. "The entire record of last night's ER events seems to have disappeared."

"Somehow I'm not surprised, Doctor. Any theories as to where they might have migrated to?"

The doctor paused, considering which conversational direction to take. He looked genuinely distraught, a bearing that issued a modicum of hope for his future. He busied himself with Iverson's chart while seeking the most appropriate answer. Iverson waited patiently and strategically. He knew the silence wore more heavily on the doctor.

"I'm sure there's a perfectly logical explanation for all of this, Mr. Iverson," the doctor finally managed.

"Oh, sure there is Doc," Iverson said with unhidden sarcasm. "Hospital records disappear all the time, don't they?"

The doctor raised his narrow eyebrows but offered no verbal response. Iverson furtively slid his hand under the thin, double layers of hospital bed covers and reached down into his underwear. He was searching for the envelope Horvat had given him. It was there. He grimaced, grunted and sat upright.

"Look, Doc," Iverson said, "just sign me out of here and I'll figure this thing out on my own."

"I can't sign you out. You're still under observation."

"Well, I'll just have to observe myself. Either you sign me out or I'll walk out on my own. It makes no difference to me."

Jenkins' mouth opened but his vocal cords formed no rebuttal. He ran his fingers through his glossy mane and nervously shifted his eyes to the tile floor beneath his feet.

"Please, just wait here," the doctor said nervously. "I'll be right back." He didn't wait for Iverson's response and the tails of his unbuttoned white coat nearly caught in the door as he left.

Iverson didn't wait either. He located his clothes, dressed quickly and walked out of VCH. His body ached and each step he took reaffirmed Jenkins' assessment of a need for additional recovery time.

CHAPTER 8

Iverson got two blocks from the hospital, extracted his cell phone from his jacket's inner pocket and called a cab to take him back to his vehicle at the Fifth Street Bar. Standing on the curb and hailing the oncoming Uptown Taxi, Iverson unbuckled his belt, reached down into his crotch and pulled out the crumpled and somewhat damp package Horvat had given him. His actions drew startled looks from two elderly ladies passing by. They stopped abruptly, decoded the moment and shot him looks marked equally with shock and curiosity. Iverson countered with an apologetic smile and waved the envelope in their view in an attempt to explain his behavior. They lingered briefly, returned his smile and hurried on their way having been provided with a week's worth of conversation.

Iverson opened the moist envelope. He found a silver colored key and a hand penned note. The key resembled those used for bank lock boxes. The unraveled note was short and to the point. "Confederated Bank. Box 443. Forge the signature." It was signed by Gabos Horvat.

Iverson read the note three times. Horvat had, for some reason, chosen Iverson as the person to help him. Help him do what, Iverson hadn't yet figured out. But he knew where the next clue was located.

*****

The cabbie returned Iverson to his vehicle. Iverson paid the tattooed hack twelve bucks for the five mile trip. He suspected his meter was rigged, but didn't make it an issue. *Better things to do,* he told himself.

Iverson hopped into his Ford 250 and drove to Ashton's main library; a spanking new building with spanking old books. He parked in the building's back lot; a habit acquired during his years at APD. He cut the engine. He waited and watched. Another habit. His caution quelled, he exited the truck and circled to the front of the building on foot. He trudged up the single flight of stairs to the main entrance, strolled in, and approached the main desk. It was worked by a middle-aged, good looking woman wearing large, circular earrings and a butter yellow dress. *Not your typical librarian,* Iverson thought. *Not in any way, shape or form . . . particularly in shape and form.*

Iverson, noting an absence of a wedding ring, asked the receptionist for a small pad of paper and a pencil. He had both stashed somewhere in his coat pockets but a few extra moments with the woman behind the desk seemed like a good thing. He received a warm smile along with a freshly sharpened number two pencil and a yellow writing pad fixed with more paper than he would need. He made a mental note to frequent the library more often.

Iverson found an unoccupied table, sat down, and practiced Horvat's signature for over an hour. When comfortable with his forgery skills, he purposefully routed himself past the main desk again and was more than mildly dismayed to find that a shift change had returned the library to the care of a more traditional looking librarian. He walked out onto Oak Street and headed to Confederated Bank, three blocks north of the library. As he walked, he passed through Ashton's outdoor mall and its transient, diurnal residents. Ashton possessed its share of homeless and marginalized youth. They clustered in pockets around the mall and its antiquated shops. The entire area, commercially and aesthetically, had endured slow but steady decay since newer and larger shopping centers emerged on the west and east ends of the city. Despite repeated efforts to restore vitality to the area, it had not recovered. Bargain hunters and middle class pubescent teens apparently preferred the sterile confines of stuffy aired malls.

Iverson approached the bank and paused outside the front door. His nerves tingled. He stared at his reflection in the large, spotless window fronting the building. It stared back. *Are you sure about this?* He'd informed Horvat that he worked only the legitimate side of the law. But here he was, minutes away from stealing someone's identity . . . from knowingly and intentionally breaking the law. *Extraordinary circumstances,* he reasoned to the reflection. The rationalization helped, but only a little. Illegal is illegal. Not much grey there. Horvat had sanctioned the action, but it was still a criminal act. *Make a decision, Iverson.* He took a deep breath, opened the door and entered Confederated Bank. Five steps in, he heard his name called.

"Well, Stan Iverson. It's been a long time. How the hell have you been?"

It was Jack Darden, a fellow bar fly from the Fifth Street Bar.

"Hi, Jack," Iverson said nervously. "Fancy meeting you here." Darden was of the perpetually jovial sort that

Iverson had difficulty with. He viewed life through bright blue eyes somewhat obscured by the unruly and immensely curly hairy protruding from both his scalp and his chin.

"How's the gumshoe business?" he asked, much louder than Iverson would have liked.

"It's fine, Jack," Iverson answered with significantly less volume. "Mind if we step outside and talk?"

Darden cocked his head slightly and looked at Iverson inquisitively. "Outside?" he asked. "Why?"

"Well, I'm here on business, Jack, and I'm thinking low-key would be good."

"Oh, some of that hush, hush stuff you private eye types are always involved in, huh, Stan?"

"Something like that, Jack." He was ignoring Iverson's request to relocate and Iverson was getting more pissed than anxious.

"Tell you what, Stan," Jack said, leaning over and whispering, "My silence can easily be bought with a brew."

"Sure, Jack. Sounds fine," Iverson pledged. Darden's breath told Iverson that he'd already jump-started his beer based regimen, but he'd have offered him a Rolls Royce to get him out of the bank.

"Great, Stan!" Darden said with a twinkle in his eye. He lowered his voice to ask, "Six o'clock at the watering hole?"

"Perfect," Iverson replied, calculating there was a good chance Darden wouldn't even recall the conversation.

"Till then," Darden said and waved as he walked through Confederated Bank's ornate glass doors and out onto the sidewalk.

Iverson waved back half-heartedly and let out a long, audible breath. *Composure, Stan Iverson,* he told himself. *Time to get to work.*

Iverson moved toward the sign labeled "Safe-Deposit Boxes" and the arrow that pointed to a middle-aged lady wearing a frumpy dress and a matching expression. He approached slowly.

"Good afternoon, miss," Iverson greeted pleasantly. "I was wondering if you could help me."

"I'll do my best," she replied. The harsh face melted into a cordial smile. Iverson exhaled. "Do you want to access a safe-deposit box?"

"Yes. I'm not too late, am I?"

"Oh no, of course not. We won't close for another hour or so, Mr., uh . . . "

"Horvat," Iverson said quickly. "Gabos Horvat."

"And what is your box number, Mr. Horvat?"

The number! *What's the damn number*? Darden's interruption had loosened it from Iverson's synapses.

"I seem to have forgotten it," Iverson explained lamely. His mental ineptitude returned some sternness to the clerk's face. He quickly searched his pockets for Horvat's note. He found it in a shirt pocket.

"Here it is," Iverson said repentantly. "I apologize for the delay."

Her smile returned. "No problem, Mr. Horvat. If you'll give me the number and sign here on the access request form, I'll retrieve your original signature card."

Iverson glanced at the note. "It's number 443," he said and sat down to sign the sheet of paper the clerk pushed towards him.

Iverson placed the paper in front of him; fully conscious of the shaking hands that he hoped wouldn't be noticed. He spotted the little x where the forged signature was to go and began writing. Fast enough to appear natural; slow enough to allow his hand to trace what he hoped he'd imprinted onto his brain.

"Very well, Mr. Horvat," the clerk said when Iverson had finished. She took the paper and left. Iverson folded his hands on his lap and steadied them. He'd know in a matter of moments if his criminal enterprise had succeeded.

The clerk returned alone, a good sign, Iverson figured. She returned to her seat across from Iverson and compared his forged signature with Horvat's. "Everything appears to be in order, Mr. Horvat," she said. "Shall we go get your box?"

Iverson's held breath escaped through his pursed lips. He'd expected one last step: to be asked to produce a picture ID. He'd even prepared a workable retreat. But the clerk didn't ask. Standard Operating Procedure was obviously not part of Confederated Bank's policy. Horvat had most likely chosen this bank for its *lack* of security. Iverson smiled weakly and stood up, more than simply relieved. "Great," he managed.

His escort led Iverson down a long hallway until they stopped at a gated portal. She unlocked the barred door and they walked a few more feet before stopping at a wall festooned with metal box fronts. The clerk inserted her key into the lock of box number 443 and then looked at Iverson expectantly.

"Your key, Mr. Horvat?"

"Uh, what?" Iverson fumbled.

"Your key. Please insert *your* key in the other lock."

"Oh, I'm sorry," Iverson said, "I was daydreaming, I guess. It's been a long day."

Iverson lifted Horvat's key from his pocket, inserted it into the second lock and turned it counterclockwise. The clerk then turned her key clockwise, opened the lock-box door and slid the long, narrow container out from its berth and on to the long metal counter that encircled the room.

"Would you like a private room?" she asked.

"Yes, I would," Iverson replied. "Thank you."

The clerk unlocked another door across the hall from the wall of boxes and led Iverson into a small, wood paneled room with a modest oak table in the center flanked by two cushioned arm chairs.

"When you're finished, Mr. Horvat," the clerk informed, "just push the button by the gated door. It'll buzz me at my desk and tell me that you've completed your business. I'll pop over and let you out."

"Thank you," Iverson replied. "You've been very helpful."

The clerk left the room and carefully closed the door behind her. Iverson's relief was total when he heard her footsteps move down the hallway. He had done it. He had achieved the status of successful criminal.

Iverson lifted the lid off the box and emptied its contents onto the table. There was a sealed, large sized Manila envelope, three pieces of letter sized paper, folded in half and attached with a paper clip, and another key. *Horvat's hooker hotel?* Iverson wondered. He stored the key in his pocket, sat down on one of the chairs and removed the paper clip from the stack of papers. Unfolded, the papers revealed three hand written letters. The top one was addressed to him.

For Stan Iverson

I write this letter with blind hope. Though we have met, you don't really know me. I don't really know you either. Any discussions we've had have been brief and have probably left you confused or alarmed. I'm sure you question my sanity. I could not blame you. There is good chance I am already dead and that my crimes have been buried. If so, that would benefit only those who hired me many years ago. This letter is an appeal to you to find the truth about the evil they do and that I have done. I have faith, knowing something of you, that you will accept this task. I hope my faith is rewarded.

Iverson laid the handwritten letter on the table, pushed back his chair and stared up at the florescent lights imbedded in the ceiling. It had been an interesting twenty-four hours. A sullen stranger at a bar had asked him to kill *him*. Then he wanted the ex-cop to assume a criminal role and steal *his* identity. And now he was asking Iverson to investigate *his* life. The fee-for-service was good: $50,000. But the chances of banking it were slim. The payer was missing. Quite possibly dead. And since the relationship with Gabos Horvat had begun, Iverson had also had the crap kicked out of him, acquired a couple of new enemies and undoubtedly been added to a few additional shit lists. Never a good thing, but not a big deal either. He was on quite a few already.

A part of Iverson told him to walk out of the bank and forget Gabos Horvat. It'd been interesting. Kind of fun, actually. Except for the trip to the hospital. Not so much fun there. *Move on to something real and less painful.* He rose out of the chair and paced the floor of the sterile cubicle. He stared at the letter. It stared back. His decision didn't take long. He returned to the chair and resumed reading.

War destroyed my homeland and my family. It also, I know now, destroyed my humanity. War does that. It produces heartless men. I am one of those men.

The war must be won so I joined the fight. I was told to find soldiers and I did as I was told. We stole children, gave them weapons and taught them to kill. Sometimes they killed their friends. Sometimes their families. It didn't matter because we also taught them not to care.

Wars end. Winners and losers are declared. Winners get the spoils and celebrate victory. Losers bury their dead and stoke their hatred. They await their next opportunity. The cycle goes on. And on. Or you adapt. America is the land of opportunity. Killing is always marketable. It can be profitable. I was contacted in 1995. They made offers. I accepted. It was easy to sell my soul.

I supplied killers. Someone else supplied victims. I was paid well. But I am old now and very sad. Very ashamed. I have examined my life. It is filled with cruelty, brutality, isolation and emptiness. That is my fate. I can't change what I've done. Maybe I can stop what others intend to do.

Powerful people hired me. We never met and I don't know who they all are. I had my people, they had theirs. Contacts were mostly by phone. Payments were made by wire transfers. It worked for twenty years. So who pulled the strings? How does this nightmare end? These are questions I have asked too late. I am weary. I have become the hunted.

So, Mr. Iverson, I ask you to find the answers. I have done my homework. You are not a random choice. It is a difficult task but you're a capable man. I can offer you a name, Tremaine, and a context of foster care. I will share no more. I must protect my countryman.

It does not matter what becomes of me. More important matters exist. Killers are lurking in shadows, awaiting their orders. It is not their fault. It is my fault. But it is they who must now be found; their carnage stopped; their humanity restored.

Much depends on you, Stan Iverson. Želim ti sreću.

Gabos Horvat

Iverson read the letter again; then once more. He slumped back in the chair and digested the words. As a cop, he'd encountered a wide variety of people. He'd heard countless outrageous stories. He'd had his concept of reality tweaked more times than he could remember. This, however, was different. The real question was whether or not it was believable.

Iverson did a quick review of the suspicious events at the hospital and they gave a measure of legitimacy to Horvat's claims. Horvat had definitely been shot and Dulles, whoever he was, was certainly a dubious character who was obviously hiding something. Then there were the missing hospital records. That couldn't possibly be an everyday occurrence.

Iverson glanced at the other two letters. They were photocopies; signed by Gabos Horvat and addressed to "The Attorney General of the United States." They were dated 2012 and 2013. *A previous cry for help*? Iverson checked the time. It was fifteen minutes before the bank closed. He set aside the letters and opened the large Manila envelope. It contained one notebook. Inscribed on the cover was: "Kill Book I."

CHAPTER 9

Iverson buzzed the clerk. She appeared at the reinforced door a minute later.

"I know you're closing soon," Iverson acknowledged, "but could I make a few copies before I leave?"

The clerked glanced at a wall clock, then back at Iverson. "No problem. I'd be happy to copy whatever you need copied." She held out a hand, expecting the Manila folder Iverson clutched.

"I really need to do it myself, miss," Iverson beseeched pleasantly. "Would that be all right? It's a matter of confidentiality."

The clerk paused briefly. "I guess it'd be okay. The copy machine's over there." She pointed to a large, cream colored copier in a corner of the room.

"Great. Thanks. I won't be but a few minutes," Iverson said. "I promise I won't delay your closing routine."

The clerk smiled a professional smile, turned abruptly and walked away. Iverson headed to the copier.

Iverson extracted the A.G. letters and the Kill Book from the envelope. He ran the letters through the machine's feeder then spread the notebook wide under its top cover and reproduced its contents twice. Finished, he smiled and waved at the clerk and left Confederated Bank and walked the three blocks back to his truck in the library parking lot.

*****

Iverson drove through Ashton's business district toward the city's boundaries. He checked his rear view mirror repeatedly ... a habit ingrained in him via his many years on the police force. He slowly and methodically wended his way through Ashton's paved arteries until he reached rural, country roads. He eventually turned down a gravel road framed by the sagging boughs of Western Red Cedars. Iverson pulled his truck to the edge of the road and turned off the engine. He watched and listened for any sign that he'd been tailed. Satisfied that he wasn't, he continued along the rutted roadway.

Iverson arrived at the old farm house he'd purchased years ago for the price of the taxes owed by its prior tenants. When working for the Ashton PD, and for a while after he'd left, he'd rented a small house in the city to keep close to the demands of the job. But the job demands were now his own. As he eased into his new life, the farm's remoteness appealed to him.

The 1940's building had been left vacant for many years and Iverson had decided only a few months ago to reclaim it from inexorable decay. The place was barely habitable. It could easily have been condemned. Thick clumps of moss covered the warped roof in layers of shaggy green. The rotting porch sagged and the wind whistled a cacophony of notes through myriad cracks in the cedar plank walls. The house listed westward; gravity and decay pulling it toward the setting sun. It was a derelict, but it was home. It was isolated, but so was Iverson. He was taking the private aspect of private detective very seriously.

Iverson exited his car and was greeted by the multi-breed, grungy canine companion his friend Jon Farrell had gifted him when he'd relocated to the farm. Max was a mid-sized mutt; stocky and black except for a few streaks of silver dispersed about his chest and some white specks dappling the backs of his ears. His right eye was perpetually bloodshot and his scruffy tail bent downward about six inches from its tip. He had the run of the farm, patrolled it like he owned it, and rarely sought his owner's company. His preferred sleeping area was an old horse stall in the farm's ramshackle barn and Iverson made sure he always had available food and water nearby. He didn't worry about other critters pilfering the dog's food. Max had an attitude.

Iverson stepped onto the plywood sheet he'd placed over the porch's spongy spots and opened the front door. Surprisingly, Max wanted in. Iverson obliged him. Once in, he examined his owner with penetrating eyes. He circled him slowly and sniffed him noisily. He then herded Iverson through a maze of old newspapers, stacked books and dirty dishes to the singular chair in the room. Iverson collapsed into it and fell instantly asleep.

*****

Iverson awoke with Max sitting contentedly at his feet. His brief but deep sleep had been a welcome and needed respite. Seeing his master awake, Max indicated his desire to go outside and Iverson released the hound. He shuffled into the kitchen, put the fixings for coffee into a 1980's era coffee maker and pushed the brew button. His head ached. His body still hurt from the beating outside the Fifth Street Bar. *Getting too old for this shit,* he told himself. He gulped three aspirins and returned to his chair.

Iverson opened the manila envelope he'd taken from Horvat's bank box. He reread his letter again and then the two addressed to the U.S.A.G. Those letters appeared to be an attempt to interest the highest level of federal law enforcement in what Horvat labeled a "grand conspiracy." Iverson figured he was probably written off as a nut job. He shifted his attention to "Kill Book I" and perused its contents. It was a collection of chronologically ordered dates, the majority of which were trailed by capitalized initials. The dates, fifty five of them, began in 1995 and ended in 2011. Most initials were followed by a lower case notation, "target." A few had a lower case "collateral."

Iverson sat back, gathered his thoughts and pondered what he was looking at and if he should continue looking. Private investigators don't lead the glamorous lives portrayed in movies. Few PI's get rich. Fewer get famous. Iverson didn't need the money. He didn't want the fame. He wanted a case that would motivate him. If it paid well, he'd take the gravy but he mostly wanted interesting players. What he didn't want was to be played. Horvat's story might be true. But it could also be a well-crafted work of fiction. But the possibility of its truth was incredibly magnetic. Horvat was missing. Murder and corruption were potentially involved. Ingredients in a mystery begging for someone to solve it. End of discussion.

Iverson bundled Horvat's paperwork into three identical shares and stashed one in a hollowed out cavity hidden in the closet in his bedroom. He'd found the nook behind a false front when exploring the possibilities of expanding the space to accommodate his clothes. After a review of his limited wardrobe, he'd abandoned the remodel but kept the hiding place hidden. He was glad he did.

Iverson took the other two bundles, stuffed them into an old leather satchel and considered his next move. He still had connections at the Ashton Police Department. He hoped.

*****

Iverson arrived at Ashton's two-story, brick-faced stationhouse, parked near his old space and walked into the building. With the bag containing Horvat's paperwork slung over his arm, he headed toward Desk Sergeant Tom Crupa, a twenty year fixture who controlled access to the squad room. The two shared a few stories before Crupa made the requisite inquiry as to what Iverson's official business was. Iverson briefly sketched out the Gabos Horvat situation, connected it to what he assumed was by now a formal investigation and ended with his hope that he could talk with whoever was in charge of the case. The Desk Sergeant gave Iverson a puzzled look, checked his log notes from the past twenty four hours and then peered at the ex-Sergeant over his thick-lensed eyeglasses.

"Stan," the burly officer said matter-of-factly, "there's no record of an incident involving a guy named Horvat."

"Could you look again?" Iverson asked.

Crupa looked irritated but reviewed the log book again. "Nope," he finally said. "No Horvat. You sure about the name?"

"I'm getting less sure by the minute," Iverson lamented.

"You said you met this Horvat guy at a bar," Crupa offered. "You sure he isn't the byproduct of a few too many beers?"

Crupa had a legitimate point. What he didn't have was Iverson's very vivid memory of the scenes outside the bar and inside the hospital. Iverson also possessed the tangible evidence gleaned from the lock box.

"No, Tom," Iverson assured. "This guy, whoever he is, is very real."

The Desk Sergeant didn't reply. Iverson had a feeling he was gauging his sanity as well as his resolve. "What the hell, Stan," he finally said. "You've earned the benefit of the doubt around here. Go on in and see if you can dig up something useful. Sorry I wasn't more help."

Crupa waved his meaty hand in the direction of the squad room and Iverson offered an earnest thanks and left the Desk Sergeant to his ample stack of paperwork. Iverson walked through double doors and started up the tiered stairwell toward the upper level home of Ashton's detective squad. He paused to catch his breath between the first and second levels and tried to look busy in thought while furtively resupplying his lungs. Fortunately, the foot traffic was light and no one gave him a second glance. Iverson had mixed feelings about that. Not being recognized vs. being recognized as to what he'd become . . . old. He regained his pneumatic equilibrium and made it to The Pen. As usual, the place hummed with activity.

Iverson strode deliberately through the labyrinth of clustered cops looking for a familiar face. The Pen hadn't changed much since his retirement four years ago. The murky green walls still wore the jagged scars created by the forever shifting clay beneath the building's foundation. The ceiling still sagged and the old hardwood floor retained the pockmarks installed by hard soled shoes worn by hard core cops. Despite the current ban on smoking, The Pen retained the residual odor and sullied patina of cigarette smoke ... much of it due to Iverson's still unchecked addiction.

The old building held myriad memories for Iverson, both good ones and bad ones, and he paused briefly to let a few of the good ones linger. His career with the Ashton Police Department had begun thirty one years ago as a beat cop on the lower floor. He'd worked his way through the ranks and up the stairs over the years and ultimately reached Detective Sergeant prior to his retirement. He'd chosen a law enforcement career with hopes of making a difference. Whether or not he'd accomplished that goal, he'd leave to others to decide. He'd had a good run and left the force when faced with a clear reality. Times had changed and he had not.

Iverson resumed his stroll through The Pen in search of someone to enlighten him on the subject of Gabos Horvat. His presence elicited the expected scrutiny from the newer cops but none of them inquired as to his purpose. It was assumed, because he was allowed access to The Pen, he had legitimate business there. It was up to Iverson to figure out with whom to conduct that business.

Iverson worked past the rows of desks manned by junior officers and headed toward The Pen's more seasoned members. It was custom in most squad rooms that senior officers were positioned closer to the Lieutenant's office, usually at the very end of the squad room. The Captain's office, and the inherent politics that go with that position, was sequestered away from the squad room and its drone of activity. This organizational structure served both the need for hierarchical order and chain-of-command communication.

The squad's younger cops, closest to the stairway, were new generation; an odd blend of computer geek and workout junky. Flat screens and water bottles landscaped each desk and the ubiquitous cell phones competed in a discordance of abridged, irritating tunes. Having come from an age of desktop doughnuts and stale coffee, Iverson couldn't help but wonder if new age gadgets and tricked out bodies were producing better cops. Iverson's gloom was interrupted by Cassie Numaga, a former co-worker. Cassie was the first female to achieve the rank of Detective on the Ashton force. Now in her mid to late forties, she was a fixture on Ashton's police force. Her straight, black hair framed a resolute face anchored by the high cheek bones she'd inherited from her Native American ancestors. Alert, dark eyes served as portals to an intense temperament. Numaga had been recruited to provide the department check-offs in a couple of affirmative action categories, but she'd proven to be much more than a useful statistic. Though Iverson had never worked directly with her, he'd had ample opportunity to assess her investigative skills and her ability to navigate a male dominated culture. She'd sloughed off years of crude jokes and outright bigotry thrown her way and focused on the work of being a cop. She did it well. Iverson admired her.

"Just what the hell are you doing here, Stan?" she asked point blankly. "You don't make social calls so you must want something. What is it?"

Iverson hesitated, still uncertain as to the validity and significance of his recent experiences. The Desk Sergeant, in fact, had just suggested that his memory may have been influenced by distilled spirits. But the thought of running it by someone he respected was appealing so he downloaded an abridged but detailed version of the Gabos Horvat story onto Cassie Numaga.

"Damn," Cassie said after Iverson had finished. "That's one helluva story you got there, Stan"

"Yeah, it is," Iverson responded. "I'm just not sure yet if it's fact or fiction."

"Do you suspect the safe-deposit documents to be real?"

"At this point, yeah, I do," Iverson answered as convincingly as possible.

"Then what's your next move?"

"I have to find Horvat."

"Sounds like that might not be too easy. Any ideas floating around up there?" Cassie asked and tapped Iverson playfully on his forehead.

Iverson craned back and grinned awkwardly. "I plan on starting at the hospital unless you have a better idea."

"Stan," Numaga said seriously, "you're not a cop now. You've got no authority and no back-up. If Horvat's story is real, things could get dicey in a hurry. You've already been to the hospital. Your next stop could be the morgue. You're aware of that, right?"

"I am," Iverson replied, "and I'll do my best to avoid that venue."

Cassie paused and gave Iverson a long, hard stare. She then gestured down a hallway split off from the main area of the squad room.

"Have a seat in IR-1, Stan," Numaga said. It was more an order than an invitation. IR-1 was the first of the three interrogation rooms that lined the passage. All were glass-fronted, windowless rooms used to question, coerce and intimidate those suspected of being involved in crimes. It was a place where Iverson had frequently employed tactical mendacity in the pursuit of eventual truth.

"Uh, why?" Iverson asked tentatively.

"Because I told you to," Cassie replied sternly. She then added the crooked smile Iverson had seen tiptoe across her face many times before. He hesitated.

"Well?" she asked impatiently.

"Fine," Iverson relented. He wasn't sure what Cassie Numaga was up to but he was enjoying the opportunity to talk to someone about Horvat. She turned and walked away and Iverson headed down the hallway and toward IR-1. He let himself into the interrogation room and sat behind the elongated metal table and in the seat normally occupied by suspected criminals or those who knew them. Two other chairs graced the room, both directly across the table from where Iverson sat. He hitched his chair forward and studied the reflection staring back at him from the two-way mirror opposite his location. "Good God, Stan Iverson," he said out loud. "You've got to start taking better care of yourself."

IR-1 was encased in pale yellow walls anchored by an institutional gray floor burnished by decades of traffic. Two caged fixtures housing low wattage bulbs hung from the ceiling. It was, by design, a dreary, unfriendly and uncomfortable place. And Iverson was uncomfortable. He looked back through the room's large, wire-meshed glass window and watched Cassie Numaga stroll to her desk and sit next to a foot tall wall of paperwork. She made a call of short duration before leaning back in her chair, clasping her hands behind her head and staring up at the yellowed ceiling. She then rose and paced the squad room briefly before disappearing into the Lieutenant's office. She entered IR-1 a few moments later.

"Stan," Cassie said bluntly, "I think pursuing this Horvat case is a good idea."

Iverson appeared puzzled. "Okay, thanks," he responded.

"But," Numaga continued, "to be safe and smart, I'm recommending you take on a partner."

"I'm a private dick, Numaga," Iverson argued. "A *very* private dick. I couldn't afford a partner if I wanted one.

And, even if I could, I don't know anyone who'd want to work with a surly old fart like me."

"I've got someone in mind," Cassie countered quickly. "Someone you know."

"Really?" Iverson asked skeptically. His tone indicated his attitude toward the possibility of a partnership. "Does this mystery person have an identity?"

"Me," Numaga said confidently.

Iverson's eyebrows scrunched slightly and his tone turned serious. "Seems to me you have a job, Numaga."

Numaga countered Iverson's staid realism with a coy smile and a dose of her own reality. "Yeah, Stan, I do. But I've been contemplating a career move recently and I think your visit here today is the sign I've been looking for."

"Sign?" Iverson queried.

"Yeah, sign, Stan," Cassie replied, then added quickly, "It's an Indian thing."

Iverson's mien intensified. He sat back and digested the proposal. Cassie Numaga waited.

"You're serious, right?" Iverson finally asked.

"Dead serious," Cassie replied. "I just checked with Lieutenant Solaras and ran your case and my idea by him. I have to keep him in the loop of what we're doing, but I can clear the next month with comp and vacation time. That should be enough time to gauge our compatibility.

It'll also give me time to decide whether or not I really want to leave the force. You need the help and I need the kick-in-the-butt to make a decision. I see a win-win here, Stan. How about you?"

CHAPTER 10

Kant woke up rested. He briefly reviewed the events of the previous night moving quickly past the kill when judging that his overseer would rate it as efficient. He wasn't concerned with approval, only the satisfaction that he'd completed his task in accordance with his self-employed expectations. The target was cleanly eliminated. There would be no trace of who committed the crime because Kant himself had no trace. There was no record of him in any database. His finger prints would not be found on computer tracking systems. All pictures of Kant had been systematically destroyed. He lived under a fake name in an inconspicuous house leased by an equally fictitious person. Kant was under the radar because the radar had no idea he existed.

Kant showered, dressed and prepared himself for whatever the day might present him. He moved to the home's kitchen, paused briefly then opened the door of a large cupboard. After scrutinizing its contents, Kant chose three bags of powered ingredients from the well-stocked pantry and spooned large portions from each bag into an oversized blender. He retrieved one each of five varieties of fruit from separate bags, peeled and sliced each and added the segments to the dry ingredients. Lastly, he opened the refrigerator, extracted two cartons and poured measured amounts of milky liquid to the mix. Satisfied with the concoction, he tapped the puree button on the machine and counted off thirty seconds before pouring the contents of the blender's glass beaker into a tall ceramic mug.

Kant finished his viscid breakfast, left the kitchen area and walked to a larger room. Exercise machines of various sizes and configurations occupied the area where most homes held couches, tables and entertainment centers. Such items were impractical to Kant. He was not allowed company, a rule for which he was grateful given his social ineptitude. Televisions intrigued him but were forbidden and Kant did not break rules.

The physical workout lasted two hours. Time was equally split between cables, LAT pulldowns, free weight repetitions and, Kant's favorite, Russian Kettlebells. Each piece of equipment was employed to stress every fiber in his body to its maximum limit. It was excruciating physical exercise. It burned his muscles and Kant relished it. The pain provided focus.

Kant left the workout room and walked the hallway before turning left into a smallish, whitewashed room. As with all other rooms in Kant's house, no evidence existed to suggest that he had family or friends. The walls were stark and unadorned. The room was bereft of emotional and physical comfort. No photographs. No art. No collections of things that kindle fond memories. No evidence of a life lived.

Past the door rested a slat-wood desk attended by an erect, metal chair. A pad of lined, yellow note paper resided at the table's left, upper corner and a single, sharpened pencil lay beneath its spine. A cluster of its kin peeked out over the rim of an Oregon Ducks coffee cup. A brown, leather sheathed chair improved an otherwise dismal corner opposite the desk. A small table sat next to it decked with a one bulb lamp and Kant's burner phone.

Kant checked his watch, lowered himself into the chair and waited. The call for his next kill came five minutes later.

Chapter 11

Iverson and his apprentice partner descended the stairs outside the Ashton PD squad room, walked past the now vacant Desk Sergeant's post and stopped outside the door fronting the building.

"You're sure about this, Numaga?" Iverson asked.

"Yeah," answered Cassie, "unless you're gonna keep asking me that question." She placed her hands on her hips and gave Iverson a look of frustration.

"Okay, I got it. No more questions on that topic."

Numaga had arranged to finish the two days left in her work week before taking on her new role as Iverson's partner. The two days would provide her the opportunity to use the department's computers in search of information on Horvat, Dulles and Frantzen. Iverson gave her one of the bundled copies of Horvat's papers for her to review and research if possible. *Four eyes better than two,* he figured.

Numaga and Iverson agreed to meet after her scheduled shift on both of her final two days. The idea was to share information, strategize and get better acquainted. The sessions would launch today, at 5:30 PM, at the Coffee Hut on the south end of Ashton.

Iverson left Cassie Numaga and headed toward the APD parking lot and "Henry," the name he'd christened his truck with. He settled into the faded front seat, lit a cigarette and took a long draw from the filtered Camel. He'd yielded to Numaga's partners pitch because, deep down, he'd wanted the company. His last shield carrying case had involved strangers who'd become friends. Good friends. Iverson, Jon Farrell and Sandra McKinney had visited a dark side of humanity together and had managed to find some light. Jon and Sandra remained important people in Iverson's life but the emotion, adrenaline and challenges had dissolved when the case ended. Farrell and McKinney moved on to new stages in their lives. Iverson didn't. When real life returned, he took a long, hard look at himself. He didn't like much of what he saw. He was getting old. He was unhappy. He was lonely.

Iverson confronted the unhappiness by leaving APD, but private gumshoeing hadn't yet cured his melancholy. He'd become an old dog. New tricks were hard. A brief detour into his past hadn't removed the loneliness. It was a mistake. His ex-wife needed to remain his ex-wife and he needed to be nobody's husband. He didn't do well in relationships involving emotional expectations. His kind of life was best lived alone. *Or maybe,* Iverson considered, *with a no-strings-attached partner.*

Grey-blue smoke billowed from Henry's tailpipe as Iverson turned over the old Ford's surly engine and steered away from the Ashton Police Department. With Numaga on board and focused on gathering information from police sources, Iverson turned his attention to another agency he had familiarity with: Child Protection Services. Given Horvat's reference to foster care, it seemed like a good place to start.

CHAPTER 12

In 1874 America, it was illegal to beat your dog. But it wasn't illegal to whip your child. Mary Ellen McCormack, a self-possessed 10-year-old who lived in the Hell's Kitchen section of Manhattan, changed that. "Mamma has been in the habit of whipping and beating me almost every day," the little girl testified. "She used to whip me with a twisted whip. She struck me with scissors and cut me. ... I never dared speak to anybody, because if I did I would get whipped."

Mary Ellen had been orphaned as a baby. Her father, Thomas Wilson, was a Union soldier who died in the Second Battle of Cold Harbor, in Virginia. Her mother, Frances, boarded the baby with a woman living on Mulberry Bend, on the Lower East Side, while working double shifts as a laundress. When she lost her job, she could no longer afford to care for her daughter and was forced to send her to the city orphanage on Blackwell's Island. A few years later, Mary Ellen was adopted by Thomas and Mary McCormack. Thomas died soon after the adoption, and his widow married Francis Connolly. Unhappy and overburdened, the adoptive mother took to physically abusing Mary Ellen.

Mary Ellen's case was brought by the American Society for the Prevention of Cruelty to Animals because there were no laws protecting her from her mother. It was an era of "spare the rod and spoil the child," and parents routinely meted out painful and damaging punishment without comment or penalty. Sometime in late 1873, the severely battered and neglected child attracted the attention of neighbors. They complained to the Department of Public Charities and Correction, the agency administering the city's orphanages, jails and hospitals. The investigator assigned to Mary Ellen's case, Etta Angell Wheeler, was shocked by Mary Ellen's condition and became inspired to do something.

Frustrated by the lack of child-protection laws, Wheeler approached the A.S.P.C.A. It was a shrewd move. Mary Ellen's plight captured the imagination of the society's founder, Henry Bergh. Bergh recruited a prominent lawyer, Elbridge Gerry, who took the case to the New York State Supreme Court. Gerry argued there was good reason to believe that Mary Ellen would be subjected to irreparable harm unless she was removed from her home. Judge Abraham R. Lawrence ordered the child brought into the courtroom. Because she was a child, her testimony was unusual. It was also pivotal. For both Mary Ellen and for the welfare of children.

Ms. Connolly was charged and found guilty of several counts of assault and battery. Mary Ellen never returned to her adoptive home. In a lifesaving act of kindness, Etta Wheeler, her mother and her sister volunteered to raise Mary Ellen.

Mary Ellen's case led Bergh and Gerry to found the New York Society for the Prevention of Cruelty to Children in December, 1874. It was administered by wealthy, white men who hired middle-class males to investigate largely poor women. Neither a perfect nor a balanced solution, but a start.

Society no longer sanctions child abuse by ignoring its existence. A broad spectrum of laws, programs, diagnostic tools and reporting protocols have been developed to protect children from abuse and neglect. But every day, at least three children die in the United States as a result of parental mistreatment. Many more suffer physical and psychological injury. Still more remain hidden and at risk of great harm.

*****

Iverson parked in the lot behind the building housing those that worked to prevent child abuse. He delayed briefly as thoughts of his past flooded his consciousness. During the course of his cop career, he'd had a few occasions to work with Child Protective Services personnel when children had been the victims of violent crimes. More telling, and certainly more personal, were the occasions when he had been one of those children. He'd had a rough childhood. His mother had died when he was six. The death certificate listed "unknown causes" but Iverson would have substituted "perpetual drunkenness" had he been asked to fill in the paperwork. His biological father had been one of his mother's many random boyfriends; a one and done whom Iverson had never met and had no desire to.

His mother's frequent negligence, a byproduct of her alcoholism, eventually drew the attention of the CPS agency and Iverson began his career as a foster kid. For years he was shuffled back and forth between a litany of strangers and his mother, herself all too often a stranger to the vulnerable child. Inevitably and predictably, his mother finally and fully surrendered to the alcohol. Her death released a flood of conflicting emotions in the young Iverson. Unbearable loss, because a child loves his mother unconditionally; fear because he'd seen what life in foster care looked like, and maybe the most damaging, relief, because that welcomed respite from his mother's anguish would evolve to a guilt that never fully went away. It was the cause of that gnarled knot now forming in Iverson's belly.

Iverson entered the lobby and walked slowly to the reception area. The nature of CPS work involved frequent confrontations with angry and sometimes violent parents, and therefore the two people working behind the counter were enclosed behind high-grade Plexiglas. Though Iverson was acquainted with many CPS staff, the two women behind the barrier were not among them. He peered through the transparent barricade, stooped his body to speak through the slotted opening and stated his business.

"I'd like to speak to a foster home certifier," Iverson said succinctly.

"Your name, sir?" queried the younger of the two women curtly and business-like. She was in her early twenties with a freckled face framed by layered waves of auburn hair. More than a few interspersed emerald green strands made a personal fashion statement.

"Stan Iverson."

"Are you a parent or relative of a child in foster care?"

"I am not," Iverson reported.

The receptionist entered notations on a log sheet anchored in a three-ringed binder. She continued her data collection without looking up.

"Are you registering a complaint, Mr. Iverson?"

"No," answered Iverson brusquely. He was getting agitated but he also was familiar with the routine and sympathetic to the need for the interrogation. CPS clientele, at least the adult segment, tended to be capricious and deceitful people. The agency also had strict rules of confidentiality regarding both the children they were charged to keep safe and the foster parents they contracted to assure that safety. Iverson told himself to be patient.

"What exactly is the nature of your business then, Mr. Iverson?"

"I have some questions regarding a foster home that operated in the early 1990's."

The note taking abruptly halted. The receptionist looked at Iverson over the top of her wire-rimmed glasses.

"Really?" she asked.

"Really," Iverson replied.

"Why?" the clerk asked unavoidably.

"I'm working a case."

"So you're with the Ashton Police Department?"

"No."

"The D.A.'s office?"

"No."

" Are you a CASA?"

"No." Iverson's vagueness was intentional.

"But you said ...," The woman lost her words momentarily, then continued. "How about if I see if a certifier is available?"

"That'd be great," Iverson responded softly. He added a smile.

"Have a seat over there and I'll see if I can locate some help for you." She gestured toward the rows of coupled chairs that lined both sides of the foyer behind Iverson. He nodded his acceptance of the arrangement, offered another appreciative smile and took a seat. The room's only other occupant was an elderly woman whose weathered face bore an anxious countenance. Iverson looked directly but gently into the woman's eyes with an offer of conversation. She caught his glance but quickly darted her gaze to the stack of magazines on the table stationed between them. She chose one at random and buried her attention deep within it.

Iverson abandoned his social intentions, rose and busied himself reading the CPS literature distributed about the waiting area. Parents' rights, agency standards and emergency contact numbers were among the postings festooning the blandly colored walls. Iverson worked his way through a few of them before the receptionist alerted him that a certifier was on her way. Moments later, he heard a familiar voice.

"Well, I'll be damned, it really is Stan Iverson. I'd heard you'd retired and was hoping you'd had the good sense to move to Hawaii."

The voice belonged to Grace Johnson. She was a tall, picket thin woman with a handsome face and piercing blue eyes. She was in Iverson's age bracket. Her tenure and reputation at CPS closely matched that of the old Sergeant's at APD. Her long, silver-grey hair bounced about her shoulders as she approached Iverson.

"Grace, it's really good to see you," Iverson greeted warmly. His sentiment was genuine. Grace Johnson was a known commodity. She and Iverson had worked a few cases together in years past and Iverson found her to be both capable and professional. If there was usable information to be found at CPS, Grace would find it.

"Good to see you too, Stan. What the hell are you doing here? I was told you had some questions about an old foster home."

"I do," affirmed Iverson. "Is there somewhere we can sit and chat?" Grace motioned for Iverson to follow her and they moved to a room adjacent the lobby. A sign on the door identified the space as "Family Visit Area." This was where parents or other family members visited with the children who had been removed from their families due to abuse or neglect. Silent, stuffed creatures and hard, plastic toys littered the room and provided tactile comfort to angst riddled kids. A large two-way mirror and two video cameras provided scrutiny of their dysfunctional parents. Iverson and Johnson took seats in small plastic chairs pulled from beneath a short legged table.

The conversation was brief. Iverson shared what aspects of the Horvat case he felt were pertinent to his request. Iverson also shared with Grace the name Horvat had mentioned in the letter: Tremaine. Iverson thought it likely that it was the name of a provider. Grace Johnson offered to construct, if she could, a list of foster homes operational during the early1990's.

The constraints of confidentiality loomed large and Grace warned Iverson that his new, unofficial capacity would be problematic. Information on foster kids, foster homes and foster care providers is protected. There was a good chance that if Iverson wanted specific names, he'd likely need a signed ROI, a Release of Information form, or a Court order. *Good luck with that,* Iverson thought. He expressed his appreciation for whatever information he could get and for Grace's effort of looking. He got a warm hug from Grace Johnson and left the CPS office.

Oregon's winters normally consist of perpetually gray skies leaking intermittent drizzles. Today was different. The clouds hung dark and thick and the rain beat down hard and fast. Thunder, a rare occurrence in Oregon's low country, was rumbling in the distance. Iverson hurried through the heavy drops ricocheting off the asphalt, hopped into his old Ford and fired up both the engine and another Camel. He glanced in the passenger's side mirror and noticed a dark, late model automobile identical to one he'd seen when he'd left the APD lot. Iverson didn't believe in coincidences. Like the other car, it had been parked at a distance making it difficult to get a read on the occupant and impossible to discern a plate number. Iverson decided that if it was a tail, it would follow him away from CPS. He engaged the transmission, drove off the rain slickened lot and into traffic. The sedan followed.

CHAPTER 13

Iverson headed down Sixth Street and the sedan in his rear-view mirror followed him into the evening's after-work traffic. He drove slowly on the one way street, carefully monitoring the number of motorists between Henry and his tail. He reached a high traffic commercial area of Ashton with stop-lighted, short-blocked cross streets. Iverson timed the signals and turned his old truck left onto Madison Avenue. The two trailing vehicles passed through the intersection but Iverson's calculated pace forced the sedan to hit the red light with cross traffic already moving across the crossing. Iverson glanced back in time to see the angry driver slam his fists into the steering wheel.

Iverson took another left turn into the parking lot of Hurley's Wood Stoves, turned slightly left again and finally stopped when his car fronted Sixth Street and the dark sedan awaiting a light change. He was lighting a cigarette when the driver finally looked in his direction. The initial shock on Dulles' face quickly morphed to anger. Iverson offered him a mock salute and a condescending smile. A horn blared from the vehicle immediately behind Dulles and he subtracted some tread from his tires as he sped through the now green traffic light. Iverson watched until Dulles was out of sight. He checked his watch and realized he was late for the meeting with Cassie Numaga.

*****

Numaga was sitting at a corner table in the back of the Coffee Hut. Iverson acknowledged her with a subtle nod of his head, walked to the counter and ordered a tall Americano and a cheese croissant from the barista. He collected what would most likely be his dinner and joined Numaga who was engrossed in a laptop computer.

"Detective," greeted Iverson.

"Hi, Stan," Numaga returned. "Be right with you."

Numaga completed her laptop task and turned her full attention to Iverson.

"Any interesting developments since we last talked?" she asked.

"I left some questions with a friend at CPS," Iverson replied. "I should hear back tomorrow or early next week."

"What kind of questions?"

"I'm hoping to identify foster homes from the time period Horvat operated in Oregon. How about you? Any luck tracking Horvat on the computer?"

Numaga opened a notepad. "One Horvat found. First name, Urban. Listed in a 1956 Portland Press obit. Died of a heart attack. Apparently in heaven playing chess with previously deceased family members. No other Horvats. You sure about the name?"

"No, I'm not sure. Hell, I'm not sure about any of this, Numaga. This could all be a wild goose chase."

"I don't think so, Stan," reassured Numaga.

"Really?" asked Iverson. "Why's that?"

"The other names you gave me, Frantzen and Dulles, have proved interesting." Iverson's eyes widened.

"Interesting in what way?"

"You said they introduced themselves as Agents Frantzen and Dulles, right?"

"Right," Iverson confirmed.

"And you assumed, since they had those titles, they had to be with the FBI, correct?"

"Well, yes and no," Iverson reported impatiently. "What's your point, Detective?"

"My point, Mr. Iverson, is that the FBI reports no currently active agents with the names Dulles or Frantzen."

"You checked?"

Numaga's annoyed look provided the answer.

"Okay, bad question," Iverson apologized. "But Frantzen *was* an agent. His name was occasionally attached to APD cases. Did the agency say when he left?"

"Yeah, they did. About three years ago. Rumors have him currently selling his services on the open market."

"How do you ...?"

"I have my contacts, Stan," Numaga explained. "Just like you."

Of course she did, Iverson thought. *She's a good cop.* This partner thing would take some getting used to.

"And Dulles?" asked Iverson.

"That's another story," reported Numaga. "There's no record of a Dulles at the FBI. There's no record of a Dulles at any Oregon law enforcement agency, for that matter. I don't know who Dulles is and I don't know where he came from."

A wry smiled waxed onto Iverson's face. "Well that *is* interesting, Numaga."

"Didn't Frantzen tell you he was Bureau?"

"He did. And he introduced Dulles as a fellow agent. But let's keep that bit of fraudulent representation in our pocket. It might come in handy later. Anything else?"

"Nope. That's all I had time for today. More might jump out of the computer tomorrow. How about you?"

"Well, our man Dulles apparently thought it was necessary to keep track of me."

"Meaning?" Numaga begged.

"Meaning he tailed me from CPS and I assume he followed me there from APD after we parted ways."

"How do you know your tail was Dulles?"

Iverson provided details.

"What do you suppose he hoped to gain?"

"I think his employer has been made aware of my contact with Horvat. The tail could indicate that the same employer is interested in knowing who I might be sharing information with about Horvat. I'm thinking they're doing a risk assessment, Numaga."

"To what end?"

"Let's assume Horvat was telling the truth, that this whole affair centers on a high level murder for hire operation. The data in his Kill Book at least hints at that possibility. So if that's the case, there's a lot of money involved. Probably a lot of powerful people, too. People with a lot to lose. People who, if threatened, will take measures to eliminate the threat."

"For instance?"

"Looking at it from a corporate perspective, you'd first identify the threat. Next you assess the potential damage. Last, you choose and implement a solution. I think Frantzen and Dulles are doing part one. They're the grunts. They're running around identifying anyone who's come in contact with Horvat ... and what Horvat knew."

"And then what?"

"Then they pass what they've learned up the food chain and await further orders."

"So who's on the list?"

"Horvat had to be number one. And given my hospital visit from Frantzen and Dulles, I think putting me at number two is a safe bet."

"That's it?"

"Sorry, Detective," Iverson cautioned. "I think you've made the list."

Numaga reflected for a moment. "So if we're the problem, what's their solution?"

"I saw what it was for Horvat."

"Shit," Numaga lamented. "I thought I was taking a vacation."

Iverson nodded and squeezed out a smile. He was liking the partnership.

"But," continued Iverson, "if that's really the case, then we need to be careful who we talk to. At the very least, where we talk to them. We assume the risks willingly, but we shouldn't knowingly pass them on. If we're truly dealing with power, then we're also dealing with greed. Greed has no conscience. We need to be cautious."

Numaga nodded her agreement, took a long swallow of her now cool coffee and changed the topic.

"I heard some interesting things about you from some of your former co-workers." The statement was posed playfully and begged Iverson's participation.

"Who have you been talking to, Numaga?" Iverson requested.

"A good cop never reveals a source, Detective Sergeant, Iverson."

Iverson studied Numaga. Her lips had curled into a coy smile and a mischievous twinkle danced in her dark brown eyes. She was serving a summons to get personal and Iverson wasn't sure he was ready to accept it. He bought some time with a return to the counter for a refill of coffee. He inserted his cup under the Americano label, opened the spigot and flashed back to the advice given to him by a friend. "Live your life well," Jon Farrell had told him. "You only get one."

Farrell's advice had been meant to prompt Iverson to participate in the positive aspects of humanity. It was a foreign concept for someone whose life was immersed in the dark neighborhoods of human behavior. But Iverson also had grown to recognize the toll his work had taken on his life. It had cost him a marriage. It had left him isolated. He'd left the Ashton Police Department hoping things would change. So far, there'd been no discernible success realized on that plan. Maybe, he thought as the Americano reached the rim of his cup, he needed to make a better effort. He returned to the small table and small talk.

"So, Detective Numaga," Iverson inquired, "what lies have you been told about your new partner?"

Numaga's expression bore both relief and approval. "Oh, there's so much to share and so little time." The smile broadened, the eyes twinkled brighter.

"I can help with that," submitted Iverson. "First, filter out opinions from anyone above Sergeant's rank. Too political. Then take the rest of the freely offered bullshit and distill it down to ten percent legitimacy. If there's any truth to be had, it will be found in that ten percent."

Numaga responded with a knowing nod. She understood the dynamics of police department politics and the personality types that drove them.

"Stan," Numaga said seriously, "I did get a lot of ribbing today when word got out about our partnership. I expected that and I get that. A few hard asses warned me about working with you but, for the most part, everybody was positive and wished us well. You were, and still are, very highly thought of at APD."

Iverson, unaccustomed to and uncomfortable with compliments, readjusted his chair and focused a blank stare on the crowd that had gathered in the coffee shop. "There is, however," Numaga continued, "one rumor I wanted to double check with you. One that might affect this case and those of us working it."

Iverson returned his attention to his tablemate and responded. "And what might that be, Detective?"

"I was told you were a foster kid. Any truth to that?"

Iverson was stunned. His history had been carefully guarded and this was ancient history to boot. "I can't see how my childhood has any relevance," he asserted.

Numaga answered. "You've told me that Horvat's crimes are somehow connected to foster homes."

"Yeah, that's true," Iverson acknowledged. "So what?"

"So maybe your judgment is compromised. Maybe your empathy will get in the way of your objectivity."

Iverson placed his elbows on the table and looked directly into Numaga's eyes. "That's totally crazy, Detective. I was in foster care over forty years ago. What happened to me then has no influence on me a half century later."

"You're wrong, Stan," asserted Numaga.

"Really?" Iverson parried. "What makes you an expert on this particular subject?"

"I'm an ex-foster kid too, Stan."

Iverson went silent, pushed back his chair from the table and took a long gulp of his coffee. Numaga re-opened the dialog.

"I'm just wondering if we're the wrong people to be looking into Horvat's case. Our own baggage could make us a liability."

Iverson bristled inside. He'd survived his checkered and volatile childhood and was a self-made, semi-successful adult. He'd buried the bad memories deep and had no interest in resurrecting them. He considered walking away from Cassie Numaga and any re-visitation to a painful past. He decided against it.

"You're missing an important piece, Detective," Iverson posited.

"What's that, Stan?"

"There is no case. Not formally anyway. If we don't try and make sense of Horvat and what happened to him, no one will. No one else will be looking because no one else has knowledge of Gabos Horvat. How do I know that? I know that because I talked to Desk Sergeant, Crupa. He asked me if I'd been drinking. There is no Gabos Horvat case at APD, Detective Numaga."

Numaga sipped some coffee and considered Iverson's logic. "A valid point, Stan," she replied.

"So, Detective Numaga," Iverson continued, "are you in or not?"

"*All* in," Numaga answered emphatically.

CHAPTER 14

The boy named Tomas passed inspection, sat down at the kitchen table and awaited the pre-meal prayer with a bowed head. Food had already been distributed on the worn plank surface in an assemblage of same-sized, same-colored and same-shaped bowls. Steaming hot root vegetables occupied two of the containers and a third vessel held a thick, brown stew. A large loaf of freshly-made bread resting on a wooden cutting board and a thick handled, stoneware pitcher filled with chilled milk rounded out the meal's offerings. The bounty came from the Keepers' farm. Goats and cows produced meat and milk and free-range chickens contributed eggs and poultry. A large, meticulous garden and a cultivated field provided vegetables and grains. Self-sufficiency kept civilization at bay.

The meal was consumed in silence; the only sounds made by utensils scraping plates and food containers being shuffled in a well-practiced routine. The male Keeper kept his coffee colored eyes fixed on his food and smoothly filtered each morsel through the maelstrom of whiskers surrounding his mouth. His podgy partner fingered the pages of a Bible as she ate, her heavy lips moving silently in pursuit of both spiritual and physical nourishment. The gray mood inside the house matched the muted damp dusk encroaching outside it.

Tomas' attention was drawn to a bright point of light coming from the far boundary of the property. It pin-pricked through the kitchen's large paned window and moved slowly and deliberately toward the farm house. As the light grew closer, Tomas' eyes grew larger. The male Keeper observed Tomas' gaze, latched onto its track and followed it out the window. He located the light, pushed back his chair and strode to the roll top desk that occupied a corner of the adjacent room. He mined a pair of binoculars from its bottom, right-side drawer, removed their round, plastic covers and focused his newly enhanced vision on the bright object. Twenty seconds later, the Keeper returned to the kitchen.

"We've got company," he announced.

Tomas checked the oncoming light and saw that the single point had morphed into two. They were the headlights of vehicle wending its way up the long gravel driveway leading to the house. He watched with interest as the illuminated orbs approached, slowed and eventually stopped fifty yards from the front porch. Tomas was filled with anxious curiosity. People didn't come to the Keepers' farm. A delivery truck occasionally came by, but never this late. And when they did, they drove up to the porch, dropped off a package and sped away. No one ever visited. No one ever stayed. This was different. This vehicle had intent. It had purpose.

The Keepers had prepared for this event. They had a clearly defined and well-rehearsed plan and it included killing anyone who threatened their secret. Tomas' existence must never be known. That was the Keepers' main responsibility and they were paid handsomely for their efforts. They stared through the rainy twilight and briefly assessed the incoming risk. The resultant calculation carried an unspoken acceptance of what they needed to do.

Tomas shifted back his chair, rose and walked to the cellar door. The Keepers left the table, walked hastily through the kitchen and into the adjacent room before stopping at large wooden trunk. The male Keeper excavated a chain of keys from the bottom of a pocket, selected one and unlocked the bulky padlock that secured the chest. He lifted the lid and extracted two Remington 870 pump action shotguns and a box of 12 gauge, 3 inch shells. He handed one of the weapons and a handful of ammunition to his partner and stuffed another handful into his left-side pants pocket. He pointed to a window near the home's entryway and the female Keeper silently positioned herself there. The man then approached Tomas and nodded a message the boy understood. Tomas passed through the doorway and descended the stairs. He walked to his room and pulled a small wooden box out from under his bed, slid the lid open and extracted a small caliber revolver. After checking the chamber, he placed it next to him on the bed and waited.

The Keepers peered through the growing darkness in search of their uninvited guest. They saw no movement. They heard no sounds. They repositioned once and then again in a deliberate effort to cover all possible points of vulnerability. The old farm house had three doors and an array of widows spread out over all sides of the house. It was impossible to guard them all.

The intruder waited patiently while the darkness grew and with it, his invisibility. When he knew his movements would be all but untraceable, he confidently approached the house and assessed its weak points. He knew that they knew he was there. He had not attempted hide his presence. There was no need to. He'd brought only one weapon, a Glock 19 with a suppressor and no spare mags. He would succeed or he would fail and failure tonight would be his final act. It wasn't always this simple. He liked that.

The man slowly circled the house probing for a weakness before choosing a tactical position. He monitored the movements within the house, timing the intervals the Keepers remained at their watch posts and mentally charting the pattern of their rotations. Satisfied his intel had provided a workable plan, he checked his weapon and moved forward.

The female Keeper assumed her third rotation post and stared intently out the window and into the now pitch-black night. A whispered voice behind her broke her vigilance.

"I'm sorry," it said.

She turned slowly to the voice and produced a queer smile. It was surrounded by the aura of relief that is felt at the end of a long-suffered sadness. "Don't be," she answered stoically.

The intruder studied her face curiously, curled his bottom lip inward and fired one silent round from the Glock that split the distance equally between the woman's vacant eyes. He caught the body before it hit the floor and rested it gently onto the hardwood surface. He moved to the arched doorway leading to the next room, crouched to his knees and awaited the remaining Keeper.

The male Keeper appeared at the room's threshold, took full stock of what had occurred and knelt at the side of his dead companion. He placed his shotgun next to hers on the floor, lifted a limp hand into one of his own and with the other, beckoned the intruder to complete his task. The man rose from his haunches, strode slowly to the Keeper and used another round from the Glock to accommodate his request. The assassin bent down and checked two pulse points on each of the bodies. Convinced they were both dead, he located a key chain in the male Keeper's pocket, walked to the cellar door and opened it. He set the keys on the plank table and descended down the stairs.

The man turned from the hallway into Tomas' room and eyed the young boy. Tomas had not moved from his bed. He was not afraid. He had been told that this day might come and he knew he would have to make a choice. Tomas' gaze moved from the attacker to the revolver sitting next to him. He gathered it slowly and considered his options. The man in the doorway watched with familiar interest. Tomas calmly shifted his gaze between the intruder and his weapon. He took his time.

"I have questions," Tomas finally stated.

The assailant looked puzzled. Dialogue was unexpected ... quite possibly not allowed. "Questions?" he asked. "What sort of questions?"

"Simple questions," the boy explained.

"Go ahead," the man decided.

"Are they dead?" Tomas asked.

"Yes," answered the man softly.

Tomas looked at the man with penetrating eyes. "Am I you?" he asked.

The man paused. It was a puzzling question but he understood it. "Yes," he finally said. "I am what you will become."

"Thank you," replied Tomas. He slowly surveyed the room around him, smiled the same queer smile that the female Keeper had smiled and then pressed the barrel of his revolver firmly to the temple of his head and pulled the trigger. The intruder observed but made no effort to stop him. He studied the scene briefly, moved to the fallen boy and bent slowly down to check his pulse. He changed his mind halfway there, straightened his back and moved a few steps away from Tomas' body. He laid the palm of his left hand over his chest, felt the pulse of his own heart and mimed a silent goodbye to the boy. The man named Kant walked back up the stairs and navigated his way out of the house and back to his car. He left the farm approximately one hour after he'd arrived. He would report that his task had been completed fully and efficiently. He would not report the feelings he couldn't explain.

Chapter 15

Iverson left Cassie Numaga at the Coffee Hut and headed home. He needed sleep. He also needed a shower and some clean clothes. Numaga had hinted as much. He left Ashton's designated boundaries, drove cautiously on the rain-slickened highway until he saw the battered roadside mailbox that served as his marker to home. He pulled onto the graveled road leading to the farmhouse, made two quick turns and slowed in a corridor of trees. He followed the camber of the road into a shallow pullout established by years of tractor traffic when the farm was run by farmers.

Iverson waited. His vigilance was ingrained. Cops saw things others didn't because they were trained to look. They were trained to be suspicious. There were no coincidences. Dulles' tail that afternoon only reinforced Iverson's belief in anthropologist Jared Diamond's concept of "constructive paranoia." Sometimes paranoia saves your life.

Satisfied he was alone, Iverson continued on the rutted road while revisiting snippets of his conversation with Cassie Numaga. The topic that cycled most acutely through his synapses was the concept of risk and how it applied to those recruited to help solve the mystery of Gabos Horvat. There had been unintended risk purchased at great cost in the case he'd worked with Jon

Farrell. Innocent people had died because of peripheral connections. Iverson didn't want a replay.

Iverson reached the farmhouse, parked Henry parallel to the porch and pushed his tired frame out of the vehicle. Max came running from the barn area and greeted him with pinned back ears and a low growl. Not normal. Iverson unsheathed his Colt, lowered himself behind the truck and eyeballed the property. The hard graveled driveway revealed no evidence of visitors so he scanned the soft, rain dampened dirt bordering the porch for evidence of foot traffic. He saw two sets of large soled, heavy heeled footprints about two feet from the porch's first step. One set pointed toward the house, the other, away. Small traces of the damp soil had trailed onto the porch's planking. Somebody had recently come and gone. *Well, maybe, gone,* Iverson told himself. He looked at Max.

"Where is he, Max?" Iverson whispered. Max didn't answer.

"Big help you are," Iverson said softly. "One of us needs better communication skills."

Iverson studied the house, scanned the adjacent outbuildings and decided he'd secure his backside first. He walked cautiously toward the barn, checking back towards the house frequently. Max followed. They reached the barn and walked its perimeter; four eyes looking, four ears listening, one nose sniffing. Seeing no evidence of an intruder, Iverson stepped through the barn's winged doors and into Max's enclave. He extracted a steel blue Mini Maglite from a jacket pocket and inspected the three horse stalls. Empty. He climbed the ladder to the loft and searched its partitioned storage compartments. No one there. The barn was clear. He moved back outside, his Colt and eyes tracing in all directions. Still, no one.

"Well," he told Max, "*your* castle appears safe. Let's go check mine."

Iverson strode slowly back toward the house, stopping briefly to use Henry's hull as a shield. The rain moved to a light mist. The sky lightened a bit. He strained to see movement inside the house, detected none and moved away from the truck and onto the porch. He put his hand on the handle of the screen door and was about to swing it open when Max growled again. Iverson loosened his grip on the handle and eased over to the window abutting the doorway. He waited, listened then craned his neck slightly to acquire a dim, narrow view of the living room. He heard nothing, saw nothing and moved back to the door. Max growled louder. Iverson grasped the screen door's handle again and the dog latched onto Iverson's left pant leg with his jaws.

"Max!" Iverson blurted before he could muffle his surprise. He kicked at the dog but Max held his grip. Iverson released his hold on the door and retreated from the threshold. He was about to use the butt of his revolver on Max's head when the dog let go. Max placed himself between Iverson and the door, postured a menacing pose and discharged a deep throaty growl through bared, white teeth. Iverson eyed the dog carefully. *Another relationship gone bad*, he hastily assumed.

"Okay, Max," Iverson conceded and backed further away from the door. "You don't want me in the house. I think I get that. What is it that you *do* want?"

Max stopped growling, cocked his head and raised one ear. He wasn't going to make this easy. Iverson moved one step forward and the growl resumed. Iverson retreated again and reviewed his limited list of options. Forcing his way past the dog would undoubtedly result in injuries to both of them. Shooting the dog was considered, then discarded. Probably a bit too extreme and besides, he was actually starting to like the mutt. Iverson chose a more reasoned approach.

"So then, Max," Iverson announced. "I'm thinking the back door is your choice."

Max's expression offered no discernible opinion so Iverson read it as tacit agreement, stepped off the porch and headed to the side of the house. Max followed silently.

They stalked the perimeter slowly. Iverson paused and peered cautiously through the few windows that intersected his path around the building. He reached the back, west corner of the house and scanned the open field behind it. Nothing suspicious was identified in the low cut expanse. He crouched low and approached the house's rear entrance; a stretched and screened porch that the prior owner had added to provide aerated comfort to hot summer evenings. Four steps led up to an aluminum framed door that accessed the portico.

Iverson probed the area with the Maglite, grasped the door's red metal handle and glanced down at Max. The dog presented no sign of disagreement and Iverson interpreted the indifference as sanction to proceed. He swung back the door and stepped onto the porch. Max followed. Iverson moved to the door leading into the house, turned the knob and pushed it open. Max rushed past him into the house. Iverson called him back but the dog ignored him. Iverson waited. He listed and tilted his head forward in search of unfamiliar sounds. He heard only Max's claws tapping the hardwood floors beyond the narrow entryway.

Leading with the Colt and the Maglite, Iverson walked in. He stepped softly past galvanized wash tubs, a quilt wrapped water tank and a hasp clasped freezer. Floor to ceiling shelves, embracing little but dust and a few cans of food, lined the hallway. The ex-cop entered the large kitchen, flipped on a light and swept the area with his weapon. Nothing. He moved forward and systematically searched the two bedrooms and the bathroom. Nothing suspicious there either. *One room to go.* Iverson walked into the living room that took up the front half of the house, flipped another switch and saw Max sitting next to the door ... the same door he'd refused to allow Iverson to walk through.

Iverson walked slowly over to Max and studied the doorway the dog appeared to be guarding. The door looked unchanged . . . almost. A closer inspection revealed an inch wide strip of a dull greyish substance strung along the upper left, upper right and top of the door's wood molding. At the top section's mid-point, the Playdough like material had been balled into a larger globular mass. A small metal cap protruded from the center of the lump. A fine gauge, tautly strung wire extended from the cap to the door's knob and was secured there with multiple turns around the knob's neck and a single tab of black electrical tape.

Iverson recognized the setup immediately. He'd seen it in training films and once at a real time crime scene. The

Playdough was cyclotrimethylene-trinitramine, or C-4, a malleable plastic explosive. The short metal stem stuck in the balled glob was a blasting cap, the mechanism required to ignite the normally stable C-4 material. The wire stretching from the cap to the doorknob was the trigger that would have made it all work. It had been rigged to explode when Iverson opened the front door to the house.

Iverson examined the homespun device carefully. Though he felt reasonably confident in his ability to disarm it, he decided the intelligent choice would be to leave it to the Bomb Squad. He backed away from the C-4, gingerly opened the refrigerator's door and removed one long-necked soldier from a mostly barren shelf. He resealed the fridge door carefully before motioning for Max to follow him. They backtracked through the house and the screened porch. Iverson lowered himself to the second of the three entry steps and Max found a reasonably dry spot of dirt and plopped himself down noisily.

Iverson snatched a pack of Camels from his shirt pocket, shook one from the crumpled package and lit it. He took a draw of smoke deep into his lungs and held the smoke longer than normal before expelling it slowly in a series of perfectly concentric rings. He twisted the top off the bottle, drained its contents with two long pulls and called 9-1-1. With his nerves calmed and help on the way, he pivoted and made a short trip back into the house. He opened the door to the old freezer sitting in the hallway, removed two large steaks wrapped in white butcher paper and tossed them into the microwave to thaw. One for himself and one for his new very best friend.

Chapter 16

The man named Kant lay on his bed clad only in bleached white undershorts. He'd reworked the evening's events in his head numerous times but remained unsure what to make of the feelings keeping him awake. His stomach churned. There was a light headedness likened only to when his personal discipline required an absence of food. Killing had never been uncomfortable. It never left him with questions. This time was different. Why had the Keepers embraced death? Where was their fear? Why did the boy take his own life?

Kant rose from the bed and paced the room. He circled the small space numerous times, angled into the kitchen and busied himself mixing a cocktail of juices, raw eggs and finely sifted grains. The blender whirred while Kant stared at its contents mindlessly. He punched the stop button as his cell phone beeped.

"Task completed successfully?" the caller asked.

Kant didn't answer.

"Kant?" inquired the caller.

"Task completed successfully," Kant affirmed weakly.

"Is there a problem?"

No answer.

"Kant?"

"Yes, sir?" asked Kant.

"I asked if there's a problem," the caller stated irritably.

"No, sir. No problem. There is no problem."

"Details," instructed the caller. "There were three targets. All were eliminated?"

"All three eliminated, sir," Kant confirmed.

"Dead?"

"Dead, sir."

"To be clear, you eliminated all three designated targets?"

"No, sir."

The caller paused, then asked. "All three targets eliminated, correct?"

"Correct, sir."

"You just told me you didn't eliminate all three." The caller's voice was edgy.

"That's correct, sir. I eliminated only two."

"So one remains alive?"

"No, sir. All three targets were eliminated."

Another pause, this one escorted by an audible sigh.

"Okay, Kant," the caller submitted deliberately. "Two targets eliminated. What happened to target three?"

"Self-eliminated."

The caller paused again. "Which target?" he asked calmly.

"The boy," Kant replied softly.

The caller processed the information for a few moments and then moved on. "You have another task."

It was Kant's pause now. He filled his mouth with blended protein and stared at the pallid walls surrounding him.

"Kant?" queried the caller impatiently.

"Yes, sir," Kant replied wearily. "Ready for details, sir."

"You have two targets," informed the caller. "Possibly more."

"Two targets. Possibility of additional targets," Kant repeated. "Location?"

Kant was provided directions, descriptions of both the location and the targets and a window of time the targets could be expected at the location. The call ended.

Kant paced the hardwood floor. Something was eating at him but he didn't understand the nascent feelings. A workout would probably help him refocus. A kill definitely would.

Chapter 17

Dawn broke as Ashton again turned toward the sun. The rain scrubbed sky held remnant clouds flaming pink and purple hues. The city would wake slowly. Its bevy of workers would sip gourmet coffee, munch fresh bagels and peruse the paper delivered to their front door earlier in the morning. They would read nothing of Gabos Horvat or the three people lying dead in a rural farmhouse.

Iverson awoke rested. Sleep had been hard to locate but, once found, had been deep. The attempt to scatter his atoms with coils of C-4 apparently provided subconscious perspective. Death does wait on the other side of the door. The trick is to not open it.

Iverson took a quick shower, scraped off a few days' worth of grey stubble and searched for some clean clothes. He chose a long-sleeved denim work shirt and loose fitted tan khakis from a limited wardrobe. For Iverson, function always outweighed fashion. Cleaned and dressed, he scrambled the last three eggs discovered in the refrigerator and inserted two heels of bread into a toaster. They would be washed down with either water or beer. *Time to restock the pantry.*

Iverson waited for the toast, looked out through the kitchen window and watched Max prowl the area around the barn. The dog had watched with keen interest as the bomb squad secured the house. Their job completed and their presence gone, he'd taken his steak to the front porch, wolfed down its meaty parts and gnawed the bone slowly while keeping tabs on the graveled road. Eventually contented, he'd returned to his pastoral wanderings and the comfort of the barn. *Perfect partner,* Iverson thought. *Loyal and independent.*

Iverson collected his breakfast, sat down in the living room's singular chair and turned on his cell phone. Powered up, he checked the messaging function. There were three new ones. The first was from Cassie Numaga. *Call me ASAP.* The second message was from Grace Johnson at CPS. *Have info. Let's meet.* The third message was from an unidentified source. *Horvat at Harding Grange.*

Iverson stared at the last message. Concise. To the point. He checked for a sender. None. *Burner phone,* Iverson figured. He checked the time sent. 7:15 AM. Harding Grange was about fifteen miles east of Ashton. Iverson was ten minutes west. With morning work traffic, he could be there in forty five minutes. Longer if he picked up Numaga. He called his new partner.

Numaga picked up after one ring. "Stan," she answered eagerly. "I just heard about the bomb. You all right?"

"I'm fine. We can talk about that later. Where are you?"

"At the station. That's how I found out about the C-4."

"I'll be there in a few minutes. Meet me out front."

"Sure," Numaga agreed. "We headed some place in particular?"

"Harding Grange," replied Iverson. He ended the call.

Numaga shrugged her shoulders, grabbed some paperwork off the printer and headed out of the station. Iverson rolled up to the curb ten minutes later.

Numaga opened the truck's door, noted it's vintage and plopped onto the passenger side of the bench. The scent that greeted her was an unpleasant merger of fast food and old cigarettes. An olfactory insult.

"Thrift store special, Stan?" she inquired.

Iverson didn't respond but a smile leaked from his mouth. His new partner was bringing some humor into his life.

Numaga shuffled the debris on the floorboard to give herself some room. "Glad to see you're still whole, Stan."

"That makes it unanimous," Iverson quipped

"Seriously?" Numaga asked. "Who voted?"

"You, me and my dog," tallied Iverson.

"Not sure dog votes count, Stan," reasoned Numaga.

"They do at my house, Numaga," asserted Iverson.

The conversation was a typical cop response. It skirted the seriousness of the attack. The job was dangerous. Every cop knew it. No need to talk about it.

"What's in Harding, Stan?" Numaga redirected.

"It's actually *who,* but I'm not sure it's anything yet," Iverson cautioned. He quoted the text but couched it in skepticism.

"Almost too easy," Iverson argued.

"Gotta check," opined Numaga.

"That's why we're headed to the Harding Grange."

They drove the remainder of the short trip in silence. Numaga dug out a folder from her canvas satchel and leafed through some paperwork. Iverson stared at the road ahead.

They arrived at the Harding Grange at 8:30 AM. It was a 1920's building bordered by fallow farmland where green, untamed grasses danced and waved in the cool morning breeze. Three outbuildings edged the grange hall's perimeter and they listed in various directions. All needed paint. All needed a glazier's attention.

Iverson drove slowly around the complex's perimeter . . . once, twice, and then a third time. They spotted no parked vehicles but the main building and two of the others were large enough to conceal a small truck or car. Each had garage door. Typical grange setup.

The weathered sign above the main hall read, "Harding Grange - Established 1885." The grange movement began in the U.S. in 1867. It was the first national farm organization. Granges were the hub of farm activity when farms were owned and worked by families.

Corporate farming changed that. Grange halls, scattered about farmlands across the country, were where farmers gathered. Grange families were large families. Important families. Powerful families.

Granges promoted the value of farming and raised the status of farmers. They used their collective position as America's food source to sway legislators, impact trade agreements and influence land management policy. Lobbyists in overalls. Granges also advocated for social evolution. They supported women's suffrage a full sixty years before it was legislated and they were the first to help organize post-civil war black farmers. Grange halls hold the echoes of noble conversations.

Iverson drove Henry the entire length of the dirt driveway, K-turned the truck and parked thirty feet to the rear of the smallest building. He and Numaga exited the vehicle simultaneously and drew their weapons.

"One building at a time," Iverson instructed. "Work our way to the hall." He indicated a split circumnavigation and which direction he'd take.

Numaga nodded her agreement. "See you up front," she whispered.

The cop and ex-cop walked the structure's perimeter, checking doors and peering carefully through windows when encountered. They met at the front door.

"Anything?" asked Iverson.

"Clear on the outside," replied Numaga. "A lot of broken windows but no access. Windows are shuttered from the inside."

"Same here," Iverson reported. He looked at the door. Padlocked. But the doorframe was splintering and the hasp was loose. He took a jackknife from a pants pocket, flipped out the longer of two blades and worked it under the hasp. He pried slowly and in short strokes. Worm-holed frame shards dropped to the ground and assembled around Iverson's shoes. The short, rusty screws offered minimal resistance and the hasp and padlock were removed quickly. Iverson exchanged the knife for his Maglite. Numaga followed suit.

Iverson slowly opened the door. It creaked noisily on its rusty hinges. He opened it fully, waited a few seconds and then entered. Numaga trailed. The room was musty and the air stale. Their Maglite beams reflected off dust particles disturbed by the breeze invading through the opened door. Iverson threw his light around. A few wood slat chairs, an old library table, and a chipped-paint bookshelf devoid of books. The floor was covered with stratified dust and the fecal tailings of the mice that were making the derelict structure their rainy day shelter. The floor revealed his and Numaga's footprints, but no others. No one had been in this building in a very long time.

"Next building," said Iverson.

Two more buildings. Same approach. Same results. They moved to the grange's hall.

"More acreage in this one," Numaga noted.

Iverson responded, "More rooms. More doors. More blind spots."

"Want me to call for back-up?"

"And tell them what? We don't have any bad guys. The good guy, if that's what Horvat is, doesn't exist. I doubt they'd take us seriously."

"I'm still on the force, Stan," Numaga said. "They'd have to respond."

"Yeah, they would. But what if it's nothing? We'll have played our help card and you only get one when you're not clocking in every day."

Numaga considered Iverson's assessment. "So how do you want to play it?" she asked.

"Same as the others, slow and easy," Iverson answered. "Expect the unexpected."

The hall had four entry points. A front door, two side doors and large, double barn doors in the rear. Starting in the front, they split up and circled the building, meeting again under the Harding Grange sign. All doors were checked. No access was found. The side doors were dead bolted from inside. The bulky front door had keyed entry and the barn doors were padlocked. Securely. An imposing, long shanked Master Lock hung from a sturdy hasp anchored with hex bolts. This building was maintained and its contents valued.

"Any ideas?" Iverson asked.

"Just one," replied Numaga. She groped a pocket in her cargo pants and produced a multi-toothed key. She inserted it into the lock, turned it ninety degrees left and pushed open the door.

"So you're a Harding Grange member, Detective?" Iverson inquired.

"I am now," Numaga claimed.

Iverson's tilted head revealed his question.

"There's got to be a lot of people needing access to this place," Numaga explained. "Members, maintenance men, cleaning crews, etc. They can't all have their own keys and members *with* keys aren't going to drive all the way out here to let the cable guy in the door. There had to be need-to-know access. I figured they'd stash a key like everybody else does and share its location with people they trusted. They did. And I found it."

Iverson stared approvingly at his partner. "Good job," he appraised.

"Thanks," Numaga responded. "Ready to play 'Where's Horvat?'"

Iverson shook his head and suppressed a smile. "Sure," he replied.

The main hall building, like the others, had shuttered windows. Also like the others, they were shut tight and secured with crossbars. These windows, however, had been recently opened; fresh air allowed in. The floor had been swept and mopped. No dust-cratered footprints. No rodent droppings. The air was heavy and still but the fetid odors permeating the small buildings were absent in the hall.

With Maglites and weapons leading the way, Numaga and Iverson stepped further into the room. Iverson found a light switch, flipped it north, but produced no light. "Breakers must be off," he whispered to Numaga. "See if you can find a control panel."

Numaga focused her light to their right. It revealed a small kitchen area with a large stainless steel sink, a four burner stove and an older, double-door refrigerator. Thick, wood countertops bridged the sink to the stove and beneath them were cabinet doors and utensil drawers. Heavy shelves anchored to the wall adjacent the refrigerator were stocked with number ten cans and boxed food stuffs. A small, bracketed shelf above the stove held spices and a small collection of porcelain farm animals. Two flowery aprons and a pair of tattered oven mitts hung from spikes hammered into the wall. Numaga gave Iverson a nodded *okay* and moved toward the appliances in search of a breaker box.

Iverson went left and scanned the rest of the hall's large room. Folding chairs, a lot of them, were corded four deep and leaned up against the far wall. A few of their kin attended a platoon of tables organized in rows of three. The far end of the room was fully spent on a planked stage and the last of the chairs resided there. A lectern stood near the stage's front termination and steps on either side of the platform helped navigate a rise of about twelve inches. An American flag sentried one set of steps; a Harding Grange banner, the other. A smoke sullied farm mural back-dropped the entire area. Gabos

Horvat wasn't in the room but Iverson's Maglite located three additional doors leading to three other rooms.

Iverson checked the first door. Open. He stepped through it slowly. A flip of the light switch informed him Numaga had not yet found the breaker box. He left the switch in the on position and scanned the space thoroughly with his flashlight's beam. It was a windowless storage room lined with adjustable, metal shelves. A chaos of items filled them. Tools, electronics, paper goods, plastic and metal ware and myriad other items with varied functions shared disorganized space. Nothing of interest.

Iverson moved on to the next room. Another open door, a repeat of the search pattern. This room had windows but they were shuttered tightly. Not even a sliver of sunlight leaked into the room. It had a library feel. An old paper smell. Hundreds of books rested on shelves and lay stacked on the floor. Two sturdy, double-drawered, wooden tables sat in the center of the room attended by high-back, caned-seat chairs. Flex-necked lamps rested on their surfaces.

Iverson moved around the room and read titles on spines. Law books. History books. Almanacs and ledgers. Many were really old books. Yellow paper old. Elongated paper rolls, stacked like cord wood, had their own subdivision in the room. Iverson unfurled one. It was a 1915 map illustrating the legal boundaries of each of the county's farms. *The Harding Grange archives,* Iverson thought. He returned the map, left the library and moved on again. One room to go.

CHAPTER 18

The man behind the polished teak desk took the anticipated call. He leaned back in a plush, leather chair, straightened his silk tie and awaited the news he was expecting to hear.

"Tell me it's done, Vitez Babić," he commanded sternly.

"Not yet, Kralj Kovačić."

"Is there a problem?"

"We haven't heard back from the pjesek yet."

"It's noon." admonished Kovačić.

"Yes, sir, it is," Babić acknowledged. "The location is distant and possibly out of cell phone range. The pjesek is reliable. The targets will be eliminated."

"It's imperative that they are."

"Understood, Kralj Kovačić."

"Call me when it's done."

"Yes, sir."

"And one more thing."

"Yes, sir?"

"One chance only." Kovačić ended the call and made another. "It's Kovačić," he told the man on the other end of the line.

"The agreement was not to call me here," the man barked. "What the hell do you want?"

"We have a potential problem."

"We don't share problems, Kovačić," the man replied tersely. "I take care of my end, you take care of yours."

"This one could affect all of us," Kovačić explained.

The man paused briefly before answering. "So what is it that your small Croat brain can't handle?" he sniped.

Kovačić bit his lower lip hard. He wasn't accustomed to being debased but this American had made it a habit. The fact that it came from a man he despised made it all the harder to digest. If this was Croatia, the man would be dead. He took a deep breath and moved forward.

"The man and the woman remain in play. They are proving to be capable opponents."

"That's your problem to solve, Kovačić."

"I agree. But I thought it best to advise you that it will take additional time and that we might need your assistance."

"You Croats are truly incompetent, aren't you? Houston would have been better off hiring chimps."

Kovačić steamed but kept his bearing. "Fine," he replied. "I'm just letting you know that the risk is still out there. We're working on it, but we might need some help from inside."

"I'm your last option, Kovačić," the man warned. "Don't expect me jump up and do the job you and your band of idiots signed on to do."

Kovačić ended the call without tendering a response. He was beyond angry. He'd kept his cool on the phone because it was business. When the business was done, he'd deal with that man.

Chapter 19

Iverson found Numaga across the room with his Maglite. She turned toward the beam's origin, shrugged her shoulders and went back to her search for the breaker box.

Iverson paused in front of door number three. "Well, Mr. Horvat," he whispered to himself, "it's time to show up." He cracked the door open and thrust a hand in looking for the switch plate. Found it. Flipped it up. Still no lights. *C'mon, Numaga!*

Iverson opened the door wide and scanned the space. Large. Empty. Except for the guy tied to a chair in the center of the room. His head lolled forward, chin touching chest. Pea green, loose fitted clothing clad the limp, motionless body. Iverson recognized the brand. Hospital issue. Gray duct tape, lapped generously around the torso, was the only accessory.

Iverson approached cautiously. He reached the chair, paused and swept the Maglite's beam throughout the room. Just the two of them. He put his Colt on the floor, pushed the man's head back and focused the beam of light on his face. It was Horvat. Iverson took a long look.

Horvat's jaw dropped agape and raspy, tubercular sounds escaped from deep in his throat. His eyes rolled back, opaque and vacant. His face was an abstract of blackish-blue tissue. Red, quarter-shaped markings overlay both temples and blood had dripped from his ears and caked in the sideburn hair beneath them. The pea greens were spattered randomly with small blood stains.

Iverson lowered to one knee, mouthed the Maglite and placed his middle and index fingers on Horvat's right temple. No pulse. He slid the fingers down Horvat's neck to the carotid artery and felt a faint, unsteady beat. He gently cradled Horvat's head in his hands and lowered his chin back onto his chest. The lights went on.

"Do not move," a voice said. The words were articulated carefully.

Iverson turned. Numaga stood just inside the doorway. The man behind the voice stood behind Numaga. He held a Glock 19 with a suppressor attachment.

The man physically prodded Numaga forward. They stopped twenty feet from where Iverson knelt. The ex-cop looked at his Colt on the floor, then back to the man. *Not now*, he decided.

Iverson took the flashlight out of his mouth. "You know this man?" he asked casually. He nodded towards Horvat.

"Can't tell," the man replied.

Iverson said, "I can show you his face." He was buying time.

The Glock holder paused briefly. "Why should I care?" he asked.

"Killing is a tough business. Worse if you kill the wrong people."

Another pause. Longer. "Sure, go ahead," he finally sanctioned. "Slowly."

Iverson reached over and raised Horvat's head slightly. The man with the gun examined the brutalized face carefully. "We've met," he said quietly.

"What's his name?"

"We aren't told names."

"Who's we?" Iverson asked.

No answer. The man nudged Numaga forward, his left hand on her left shoulder. Fifteen feet from Iverson, he torqued his right arm out from behind Numaga and hit her flush on the right temple with the butt of the Glock. She crumpled to the floor in a heap. Iverson jumped to his feet.

"Sit," commanded the man.

Iverson's face flushed. He grabbed his lowered lip with his teeth, bit down and tasted blood. He stared at the man; glanced at the Colt.

"She'll live," the man said casually.

Iverson eyeballed Numaga carefully. No movement. He looked closer and saw her chest rise and fall. He turned his attention back to the man and prepared a quick appraisal. Twenty-five to thirty years old. Six-feet two inches tall and around two hundred pounds. Buzz cut hair. Clean shaved face. Dark, deep set eyes. His muscular frame was covered in loose fitted Levi's and a white, short-sleeved t-shirt. His light tan shoes were spattered with mud. A wide, black leather belt held up the Levi's and Numaga's Sig Sauer rested inside it. Iverson's Colt still resided a tantalizing foot away.

"I need to check her," Iverson said sternly.

"No!" the man said emphatically. "I told you to sit. I won't tell you again."

Iverson lowered himself back down to the floor and onto his haunches. The man moved directly behind him and Horvat and stopped. "I'll take the Colt," he announced. "Pick it up by the barrel and hand it to me over your head. Use your left hand."

Iverson didn't respond.

"Do it now or I'll shoot the woman," the man warned.

Iverson looked at the Colt. Getting to it, pivoting, locating the target and firing accurately would take maybe two seconds. On a good day. If he was young. Which he wasn't. He was fifty-six and a whole lot slower than he used to be. He might get lucky and get to the Colt. He might even be lucky enough to get off a shot. Then again, he might not. The perfect fantasy was an improbable reality. It was more likely he'd stumble, fumble, fall and end up shooting Horvat by mistake. And then the Glock clip would be emptied into him. Him and Numaga. It felt really shitty to be old. He picked up the Colt by the barrel and handed it over. The man circled back and sat down ten feet in front of Iverson. Numaga lay quiet behind him.

"He and I are part of we," the man offered and nodded toward Horvat. "The boy, too."

"The boy?" queried Iverson. "What boy?"

"The boy at the farm."

"What farm?"

"The Keepers' farm."

"Who are the Keepers?"

No response came from the man. They sat through a prolonged silence. Iverson decided to change things up. *Keep talking. Keep it simple,* he told himself.

"My name's Iverson. Stan Iverson. What do I call you?"

"Does it matter?"

"Yeah, it matters. To me, anyway."

"Why?"

"We're given names. Might as well use them," Iverson reasoned. He was stalling, hoping for an opening. He didn't have many options.

The man considered Iverson's philosophy. "Kant," he finally said.

"Just Kant?" asked Iverson.

"Just Kant."

"Okay, Kant," Iverson continued. "I'm usually just Iverson so we can both go simple on the names. Okay?"

"Sure," replied Kant.

Iverson waited purposefully before saying, "Tell me about the boy."

"Boy?"

"The boy on the farm."

"I didn't kill him," Kant said firmly.

"You were told to kill him?"

"Yes. But I didn't," stressed Kant. "I didn't have to."

"Why didn't you have to kill the boy?" asked Iverson.

"Because he killed himself," Kant explained.

"Why did he do that?"

Kant paused again before answering. "He didn't want to become me," he finally said.

"And what are you, Kant?" Iverson asked earnestly.

"I was the boy once," replied Kant. "And now I am a killer. I've killed a lot of people, Iverson."

"Why did you kill them?"

"Because I was instructed to kill them."

"Who instructed you?"

"I don't know who. I get a call."

"From who?"

"The vitez."

"Vitez?" Iverson asked. He assumed it was a person. "Does Vitez have another name?"

"No."

Keep talking. Keep it simple, Iverson told himself again. "Did you know the boy's name?"

"No."

"How did you feel when he killed himself?"

Kant considered the question thoughtfully, searching for the appropriate words. "Relieved," he eventually decided.

Iverson noticed Numaga's right leg move. Ever so slightly, but it moved. "Relieved why?" he asked Kant.

"I didn't have to kill him," Kant explained.

Numaga's left arm moved.

"You didn't want to kill him?"

"No. He was just a boy."

"But you killed the others. You killed the Keepers."

"Yes."

"And many others?"

"Yes."

Numaga groaned. Kant cocked his head backward but didn't look at her. *He heard her,* Iverson thought.

"I have questions," Kant submitted.

"Go ahead," Iverson authorized.

"Am I evil?"

Numaga opened her eyes, acquired her bearings and looked at Iverson. He met her eyes briefly, refocused on Kant and continued the conversation.

"Maybe," Iverson opined. "You know what you've done. You get to decide."

Kant digested the answer and then asked another question.

"Would you kill me?"

Trick question? Iverson wondered. Was it a request or a character evaluation? He pondered the best answer and opted for, "If I had to."

Numaga slowly propped herself up to a sitting position. Iverson knew Kant was aware of her movement but puzzled as to why he didn't react.

"You might have to," Kant said. A small smile stole across his mouth.

Numaga grabbed ahold of a pant leg, pulled upward and extracted a .22 caliber pistol from an ankle holster. She raised the small sidearm to within a foot of Kant's head and spoke coolly and directly to him.

"Drop the Glock and lay the other two weapons on the floor."

Kant did not respond.

"Last time I'll say it," Numaga said more forcefully. "Put the weapons down."

Kant turned slowly toward Numaga, the Glock in his hand, the hand at his side.

"Drop it now," commanded Numaga loudly.

Kant looked at Numaga with empty eyes and raised the Glock. Numaga shot him in the shoulder. Kant staggered back and the gun dropped to the floor. He bent down, picked up the gun and raised it again. Numaga shot another round. This one hit Kant in the chest, knocking him to the floor. He rose up on one elbow, shifted his torso and pointed the Glock at Iverson. Numaga put a third round into his rib cage just below his left armpit. The man called Kant collapsed and fell silent.

Chapter 20

Iverson moved over to Kant, checked two pulse points and informed Numaga that he was dead. Numaga shook her head slowly. "Didn't have to end that way," she said remorsefully.

"He committed suicide, Numaga," Iverson reassured. "You know that, right?"

"Yeah, I know that, Stan," Numaga responded. "Doesn't make it any easier."

Iverson nodded his empathy. Numaga gestured toward the other person in the room.

"Gabos Horvat, I presume?"

Iverson verified her presumption.

"Also dead?" Numaga asked.

"Not yet, but close."

Numaga pulled out her cell phone. "I'll include a request for an ambulance in my call to APD."

"No ambulance, Numaga," Iverson insisted. "Horvat isn't headed to VCH. He's been there and done that.

It didn't work out well for him. For me either, for that matter. You need to call the shooting in, I understand that. But I'll take care of Horvat my way."

"And your way would be . . .?"

"Not exactly the legal way, but absolutely a better way."

Numaga paused, considering her professional responsibilities. Iverson knew what she was thinking.

"You have a decision to make, Numaga," Iverson advised. "A decision that will be made by either Numaga the cop or Numaga the private investigator. It can be a difficult choice. I know. I've had to make them. I had to make one yesterday."

"I'm not you, Stan," Numaga stated realistically.

"No you're not," Iverson conceded. "But you're considering a move from cop to PI, a big change. One I've already made. You may be doing it for different reasons, but we're both coming from and going to the same places. I'm pretty sure you've asked yourself some of the same questions I've asked myself. They're difficult questions. Sometimes there's no answers. I loved being a cop. It gave me an identity. It gave me structure. But I came to realize that it also gave me conflict. The law is always correct, but it's not always right. As a cop, I was compelled to follow the law as it was written. Usually easy. But there were times I had to enforce laws only because they were laws. Times when I felt the law was in conflict with justice. I experienced more of those times as I got older. Either the laws changed or I did. I suspect both.

"So what's your point, Stan?" Numaga asked.

"My point is this. I'm not raking in big bucks or serving clients with Dali Lama morals. I'm also not 100 percent thrilled with my life as a PI. But I do like basing my choices on what I think as opposed to what APD policies dictate. If you can't work with me on that, then we've got a problem."

Numaga took some time to digest Iverson's words. She'd been thinking about the transition from her work at APD for a few years. Thinking about it was obviously different than doing it. Iverson's rationale made sense but it had competition from myriad sources; twenty plus years of indoctrinated protocols, potential legal ramifications and future career considerations being just a few of them.

"What would you do with Horvat?" she finally asked. "He obviously needs medical attention and I'm thinking you taking him home and doing medical magic with kitchen utensils and duct tape ain't gonna cut it."

Iverson broke off a smile. He'd miss Numaga if she opted out.

"I did consider that," Iverson quipped, "but only briefly. I do have a better idea."

"Please share."

Horvat stirred. His head rose, wobbled and fell back toward his chest. He didn't find consciousness.

"I know a doctor who takes special cases," Iverson continued.

"Is he licensed?"

"*She* is."

"Works in an office?"

"As opposed to what?"

"A barn."

"Definitely an office."

Numaga weighed the information and stayed in the game. "Okay, Stan," she reported, "but I have a follow-up question."

"Shoot."

"How did we get here?"

"Huh?"

"We load Horvat into your truck and you take him to your doctor friend. Two down, two to go. I get APD out here and tell them a story about our dead guy there. They'll do their job. They'll check the scene. Inside and outside. They'll notice the lack of transportation on the outside. Their gonna ask me how I got here. How he got here."

Iverson considered the scenario, then asked, "APD knows were working together, right?"

"They do," Numaga confirmed.

"So we work the story around our partnership. I dropped you off here to meet somebody who said he had information on Horvat. You're a good cop. APD knows that. They know I know that. We all know you can handle yourself, by yourself. So I drop you here and leave to follow a different lead. A phone call from you was our plan to return me to the grange to pick you up."

"And the dead guy? How'd he get here?"

"Who knows? Maybe Scotty beamed him down from the Enterprise. You don't have to explain him. He's definitely not going to refute anything you say."

"Okay," judged Numaga. "So far, so good."

"Obviously, the alleged informant was a bad guy. So bad, you had to kill him. Self-defense, which it really was. A couple rounds from the Glock fired into a wall wouldn't hurt that claim. Your end of it shouldn't be an issue. The kill weapon is yours and it's licensed to you. You're not an active cop, but you're still a cop. You're trusted. The shooting will be reviewed per protocol but it will be justified. Ballistics and forensics will support that."

Numaga couldn't argue Iverson's scenario. Set aside the letter of the law, and it made sense. She'd have to omit a few facts, make up a few more in her report to APD and put a few slugs in a wall. But in the end, her story would reflect the meat of what happened. The dead guy was dead because she'd had to shoot him. Divulging that he wanted to be dead was not that important, not in the full context of the case. And Iverson was right about Horvat and Valley Christian Hospital. They misplaced both him and his records once. No telling what they'd do if given another opportunity.

"Let's load up Horvat and get you outta here," Numaga finally said.

"Ready when you are," pronounced Iverson.

Horvat was hauled over to Henry still duct taped to his chair. It was easier that way but it still wasn't easy. Horvat wasn't a small man and he was inert. Passive weight is heavy weight. Numaga unwrapped him and they loaded the comatose Croatian into the passenger's side of Iverson's truck. Iverson hopped into the driver's side and woke up Henry's engine.

"Hey, Stan," Numaga said.

"Yeah?"

"Did the dead guy share his name?"

"Kant," Iverson revealed. "He said his name was Kant."

"What'd you and Kant talk about while I was out?"

"I think we talked mainly about guilt."

"Guilt?"

"Yeah, guilt. The word itself wasn't spoken, but I'm pretty sure that's what our conversation was about."

"Does it lead us anywhere?"

"Not sure. But we're gonna be looking for a farmhouse with three dead people in it."

"Seriously?"

"Seriously."

Iverson gave Numaga a wink, put Henry in gear and left the Harding Grange. He popped a cell phone out of a pocket and tapped a name on a list. Numaga walked back into the hall, called APD and reported her situation. She stashed her phone in her pocket, sat facing the man she'd killed and sang the Paiute Cry.

Chapter 21

Yugoslavia, the Land of Southern Slavs, was created at the end of World War I. Croatian, Slovenian, and Bosnian territories, former members of the Austro-Hungarian Empire, joined with the Serbian Kingdom. The German occupation during World War II created a Nazi-allied Croatian state from these regions but Yugoslavia was reunified at the end of the war when the communists, led by Josip Broz Tito liberated the country.

Yugoslavia broke away from the Soviet sphere of influence in 1948, became a founding member of the Non-Aligned Movement in 1961, and adopted a less repressive form of government as compared with other East European communist states during the Cold War. However, the collapse of communism in Eastern Europe in 1989, the unification of Germany one year later, and the imminent collapse of the Soviet Union all eroded Yugoslavia's political stability. Internal stress swelled rapidly and the tensions ultimately fractured the country.

The varied reasons for the country's breakup ranged from the cultural and religious divisions between its ethnic groups to the memories of WWII atrocities committed by all sides. The single largest contributing factor was the death of the strong armed Tito on May 4, 1980. His death left a power vacuum and years of bloody ethnic battles followed in attempts to fill it. Slobodan Milosevic,

Serbia's president in 1989, was one of the men seeking to expand his influence. He used Serbian nationalism to fan the flames of conflict and enhanced his power through brutal control of local governments and the press. He stripped the neighboring provinces of Kosovo and Vojvodina of their autonomy and absorbed them into Serbia. He replaced the leadership in Montenegro with his allies.

As Milosevic consolidated power in Serbia, elections in Slovenia and Croatia in 1990 gave non-communist parties control of their governments. Slovenia declared sovereignty. Croatia and Bosnia and Herzegovina followed suit. Croatia and Slovenia were internationally recognized in January 1992. Bosnia and Herzegovina soon thereafter. The three countries joined the United Nations on May 22, 1992.

Serbia and Montenegro formed a new Yugoslavia but the international community refused to recognize it. The Serb minority in Croatia declared its own independence and its desire to join Serbia. Serbs in Bosnia boycotted the efforts for Bosnian independence and also aligned themselves with the Serbian regime. Ethnic tensions flared and they quickly escalated to violence.

From 1992 to 1995, Europe witnessed the most horrific fighting on its soil since the end of World War II. The war in Bosnia and Herzegovina claimed hundreds of thousands of lives. Millions lost their homes and they were left with remnant lives and depraved hearts. Men nourished by war sought sustenance elsewhere.

*****

The teak desk sat unattended. Kralj Kovačić paced the thickly piled carpet in an agitated state. In the three years since he'd replaced Kralj Horvat as the leader of the Uskoci, he'd never had problems like this. America had been everything the Uskoks had imagined. It was truly the land of opportunity. Wealth and power seeking more wealth and power. The prosperous have money, but timidity toward murder. The Uskoks were willing to kill, their consciences having been left on the battlefields of Croatia. Need met want. Winners all around. Until now.

Kovačić's intercom beeped. "What?" he asked tersely.

Vitez Babić is here, sir," replied the woman working the outer office.

"Send him in," commanded Kovačić.

Vitez Babić walked through the door, closed it behind him and greeted his boss. He said nothing more. It was understood that the Kralj lead all conversations. The Kralj was the King. The vitez was a knight. Chess characters assigned traditional roles playing a perpetual game of life, death and profit. The vitezovi existed to protect the Kralj. Vitez Babić had not done his job.

"So you have failed, Vitez Babić," admonished the Kralj.

"The objective of the mission was not met, Kralj Kovačić," Babić confirmed.

"And what of the pjesek?"

"He is dead," Babić reported.

"Did he put us at risk?"

"Unknown, Kralj Kovačić."

"Most unfortunate," Kovačić determined.

"It is," Babić agreed.

"For you," the Kralj added.

Chapter 22

Iverson's call was answered by his friend Jon Farrell.

"Well, I'll be damned," Farrell exclaimed. "Sure is good to hear your voice, Sarge."

"Yours too," Iverson said. "But fair warning, Jon, this isn't a social call."

"No surprise there. Social call and Stan Iverson are oxymoronic. What do you need?"

"A doctor."

"Pick up a STD, Sarge?"

Iverson grunted. "Funny, Jon, but I'm not the patient. The comatose guy sitting next to me in my truck is, however, and he needs immediate attention from a doctor willing to do furtive health care."

"Doc Matkin?"

"I'm hoping."

"Give me a brief synopsis of the situation and I'll give her a call and pass it along. She'll decide if she wants to get involved."

"That's all I'm asking."

Iverson relayed a condensed form of Horvat's condition and the reason for it.

"Still got the same cell number?" Jon asked.

"Yeah."

"I'll call Doc and get right back to you," Jon offered.

"Great," Iverson said. "And Jon . . .,"

"Yeah?"

"Thanks."

"No problem, Sarge," Farrell countered. "It'll be a small payment from the IOU bucket. I'll call back as soon as I can." He ended the call.

Iverson wasn't a patient man but he had no choice but to wait. Wait and hope. If Doc Matkin said no, or if she wasn't available, he didn't have a Plan B. The hospital would be a last resort. Despite what Numaga had joked, his farm house and whatever he could muster as a First Aid kit, might be his only good option.

Iverson drove to Hermitage Park, a seedy green area frequented mainly by transients. He parked with a view of the river and watched a fly fisherman slice the air with graceful arcs of lime green line. Horvat didn't stir. His breathing was labored, harsh and sprinkled with moans. His eyes remained closed but leaked a syrupy, reddish fluid from their corners. Salivated rivulets channeled down his chin and onto his pea-green shirt. Iverson located a semi-clean rag behind his seat and tamped the wetness. His phone chirped and identified the caller as Jon Farrell.

"Any luck, Jon?" Iverson asked hopefully.

"She'll see him."

Iverson exhaled heavily. "When?"

"As soon as you can get him there."

"I need a location," prompted Iverson. Farrell provided an address. Iverson knew the street.

"I'm on my way. Meet me there?" Iverson asked.

"Count on it," Farrell replied.

*****

Iverson found the street and checked numbers on buildings. He spotted Farrell's vehicle, sped toward it and parked Henry next to Farrell's Jeep Cherokee. Iverson knew of Doc Matkin's work, but not where she conducted it. Her office was apparently her house. It sat in a venerable neighborhood populated with classic homes. Matkin's home was colored and cut in the Craftsman style. Olive green paint with burnt umber trim covered its geometric angles. The roof was low-pitched, gabled and checkered with east facing dormers . . . welcoming portals for morning's first light. Pyramiding columns of wood framed a porch resting on stacked basalt. The portico boarded white wicker chairs guarding a blood red door. Jon Farrell stood in it.

Farrell hustled down the porch steps and over to the truck. Iverson had already made his way around to the passenger side and opened the door. Jon was shocked by what he saw.

"Damn, Sarge," Farrell blurted. "What the hell happened to your friend?"

"Long story, Jon. Let's get him inside."

They carried Horvat into the house where Doc Matkin waited. "Follow me," she instructed and they trailed the doctor into a brightly lit room in the rear of the building.

Matkin's examination room was a mini-ER. A hard surfaced table and a padded gurney sat side-by-side in the center of the chamber. A bright yellow defibrillator lurked ominously nearby. Paned-glass cabinets surrounded the room and housed packaged, boxed and bottled supplies. Stethoscopes, otoscopes and ventilators shared counter top space with tubes, syringes and shiny instruments in clear-covered trays.

"Put him there," Matkin said and pointed at the table.

Iverson and Farrell gently laid Horvat on the table and retreated. They watched intently as Matkin used blunt tipped scissors to cut away the hospital issue clothes.

"What's his name?" Matkin asked.

"Horvat," Iverson answered. "Gabos Horvat."

"For real?"

"As far as I know."

"Interesting wardrobe," she observed. "Oughta be a helluva explanation."

Iverson's face flashed some guilt. Matkin's smile extinguished it.

"Jon," Matkin coached, "wash your hands and bring me some towels from the counter."

Jon turned and complied without hesitation. *He's been here, done this*, Iverson noted.

"Sergeant," Doc Matkin barked.

"Yes, ma'am?"

"There's a large plastic jug marked disinfectant on the counter next to Jon. Get it, pour a good amount into the basin sitting next to it, and place it on the gurney."

Iverson followed Jon's example and turned to his task without comment. They completed their assignments and the bleached white towels and purplish antiseptic were placed where Doc Matkin instructed.

"Anything else?" Iverson asked.

"One thing only," Matkin responded. "Get out of here and let me work."

Iverson and Farrell withdrew to the anteroom outside the exam area.

"Interesting bed-side manner," Iverson observed.

"Interesting lady," advised Farrell.

Matkin was interesting. Born into poverty but also into a wealth of love and compassion, she used her academic drive to achieve a degree from Harvard's School of Medicine. She'd tried her hand at being a big city physician . . . plush office, mostly faceless patients. But after a few years, she realized it wasn't working. She had a healthy bank account but a bankrupt existence. She ditched it all for a cabin in the woods and resurfaced years later with a different plan. She opened a clinic in Seattle, set her fees low and accepted clients other doctors refused. But the small practice got big and so did the problems. She moved again, this time to Ashton. Smaller town, smaller problems. So far, at least. Helen Matkin and Stan Iverson had both looked into their mirrors. They both saw the need for change and they both took the leap. Matkin did it sooner. Iverson wished he'd had.

Iverson shared Horvat's story with Farrell and his theory as to the causes of his current condition.

"Found yourself another byzantine case didn't you, Sarge?" weighed Farrell.

"If byzantine means complicated, then yeah, Jon, I did," Iverson confirmed. "Another byzantine case and another interesting partner."

"Anybody I know?"

"I doubt it. Her name's Numaga. She's APD."

"Wow!" exclaimed Farrell. "The starchy old Sergeant partnered with a woman. Sandra will be shocked. Shocked and pleased."

Sandra McKinney was Farrell's paramour and he'd met her while working with Iverson. One of the IOUs in the bucket. Farrell probed about Numaga. Iverson asked about Sandra. Doc Matkin's presence interrupted the conversation.

"Is he gonna live, Doc?" Iverson inquired calmly.

"He's still unconscious, but he's stable. He should be in a hospital. Care to tell me why he's not?"

"He was," Iverson explained. "You obviously noticed the hospital issues. We were both wearing them in the ER two days ago. They moved me to another room and moved him to who knows where."

Matkin shook her head. "Where do you find these people, Sergeant?"

"This one found *me*, Doc."

"Were you serious about the name?"

"Gabos Horvat? Yeah, I was serious. It's the name he gave me. He told me he was Croatian; that he'd been in the wars over there."

"He's got the scars to prove it and he'll have new ones now, too," revealed Matkin.

"What'd they do to him?" Iverson asked.

"First off, he's been scatter shot. He's got a lot of holes in him."

"I was there for that part," Iverson contributed.

"He also has extensive blunt force trauma. The marks hint at a baseball bat. I can't tell the scope of the damage without x-rays, but it's mainly to the abdominal area which could lead to internal bleeding and organ damage. The temporal markings and pupil reaction would seem to indicate electrical shock was administered and could be the cause of his comatose state. There's also fresh tracking along one arm so he was either abused chemically or he's a recent initiate to injectable drugs. I'll know more about that when I get the lab tests back."

"Can we get x-rays?" asked Farrell

"I don't have that capability on site but I have a friend who has a friend who has a portable machine. I'll make a call."

Iverson rose from his chair and paced the Spanish tile floor. "What are his chances, Doc?"

"It's hard to tell until I get more information."

"Can you keep him here?"

It was Matkin's turn to pace. She took longer than Iverson.

"You know the drill, Sergeant. I'm required to report suspicious injuries, certainly gunshot wounds. Reporting him probably means hospitalizing him. Am I interpreting the law accurately?"

"Under normal circumstances, yes," Iverson conceded. "But this isn't normal, Doc. Horvat *was* reported and hospitalized regarding the shooting . . . the scatter shots event. I was injured in the same incident and also taken to VCH. I watched doctors treat Horvat in the ER. Two men claiming to be FBI agents came into my room and grilled me about him. The doctors and the alleged agents obviously knew Horvat. Yet the doctors deny his existence and more than likely have dumped any record of his hospitalization. The agents told me to forget him . . . actually threatened me at one point if I didn't. And now he turns up as a zombie. Reporting him once damn near killed him. Reporting him again might finish the job."

Matkin took some time to digest Iverson's story. "So I'm not breaking the law if I keep him here and make no report to APD?"

"It's a judgement call, Doc," Iverson clarified. "But if I'm the judge, I'd definitely consider this a mitigating circumstance."

"Okay, Judge Iverson," Matkin decided, "you've made your case. Horvat stays here. I'll do what I can for him."

"That's all I can ask, Doc. Thank you."

"You can thank me by finding the people who did this . . . quickly."

"That's the plan," Iverson assured.

Iverson's ringtone alerted him. He checked the caller ID, pressed the answer icon and greeted Cassie Numaga.

"Are you calling me for bail money?"

"Fortunately, no," Numaga reported. "Would you have paid it?"

"I'd have thought about it," offered Iverson.

Numaga laughed and moved the conversation forward. "How's Horvat?"

"Not well, but in good hands. Can we meet?"

"Definitely, but give me thirty minutes. I'm finishing up some web work that I'll share when we meet. Got a location in mind?"

"I need some fuel," Iverson established. "Got a favorite eatery?"

"I do," answered Numaga. "It's 'El Sol' down on First Street."

"Good choice," judged Iverson. "See you in thirty."

Iverson looked in on Horvat and gave Doc Matkin a business card and another round of gratitude. Jon walked him out to the curb.

"I owe you," Iverson stated.

"No, you don't," refuted Farrell.

"At least a beer," Iverson argued.

"You buy the beer, I'll cook the food," Farrell negotiated. "At our house."

"It's a deal," Iverson agreed. "As soon as I'm done with this case."

Chapter 23

The King ruled his kingdom but money ruled the King. Kralj Kovačić had knights and pawns but wealthier, more powerful people had the money that paid them. Those people had expectations. They also had a low tolerance for failure. Kovačić never met them in person. He met their emissaries and they met clandestinely. He was meeting one now.

"They're not happy," Dulles informed Kovačić.

"Neither am I," complained Kovačić.

"So how are you planning on taking care of this?"

"Those who didn't perform have been eliminated. The problem will be taken care of by different people."

"Better people?"

"Different people," the Kralj insisted. "A pjesek malfunctioned but the system still works."

"Your system *isn't* working," Dulles rebutted, "and you've got more problems than a busted part, Kovačić. You're killing your own and you're attracting attention. That's unacceptable."

"It will be made right," the Kralj asserted.

"They'll be the judge of that," Dulles retorted. "I suggest you do your job."

Dulles turned and walked away from the meeting. Kralj Kovačić stood thinking; thinking and wondering how they knew what they knew.

Chapter 24

Iverson stopped by the CPS office to see Grace Johnson before he headed to El Sol for his food date with Numaga. The same young lady worked the enclosure as had the previous day.

"Hello again," she greeted.

"Hi," Iverson returned. "Could you let Grace Johnson know I'm here?"

The clerk checked her watch, lifted a receiver from a phone and punched two numbers. Iverson stepped back and waited. He was informed moments later that "Ms. Johnson" would be right down. She was and they returned to the room they'd occupied on his earlier visit.

"I've got good news and bad news, Stan," Grace announced. "Which do you want first?"

"Let's start with the bad and work toward the good," opted Iverson.

Grace moved to the door and closed it behind them. She motioned for Iverson to take a seat, took one herself, and checked her notes before starting her report.

"Confidentiality is a problem, Stan, but it's one we both understand. It protects those that need protection. But it also prevents me from providing you the information you want. I can access it; I just can't share it. Your unofficial capacity complicates things but it would be difficult even if you were still with APD."

Iverson leaned back in his little chair. "So nothing on foster care providers, then?"

"There is one exception," Grace reported, "and that's the good news."

Iverson rolled forward. "I'm all ears, Ms. Johnson."

"The name you gave me, Tremaine, connects to a provider we contracted with in the early 90's. We had to terminate their contract because they were in frequent non-compliance with our reporting standards. They repeatedly violated our policy requiring agency notification of injuries or illnesses incurred by the children placed in their care and they moved at least twice without notifying us of the move. Their license was pulled on September 26, 1992."

"So how are you able to share their information but not other's?"

"We had put them on probation prior to ending their contract. Back then, CPS probation meant a suspension of their confidentiality rights. It was thought it would enable public scrutiny and violation reporting regarding the home on probation. Essentially, the Tremaines were told to prove themselves to the community."

"Did they still get placements?"

"No. No kids without a license. They were told to maintain all CPS certification requirements and resubmit for licensure after their six month probation. If all had gone well, we'd have written a new contract and re-started placements."

"So what happened?"

"They never reapplied for licensure. Certification staff documented numerous attempts to make contact but we never heard from them again. Phone calls, e-mails and and visits to their last listed address turned up nothing. The Tremaine family apparently decided to pack it in."

"So I can have their info?"

"I can provide you the last address we have for them."

"It's a start," Iverson conceded. His disappointment was obvious.

"It's the best I can do, Stan," lamented Grace. She pushed a note with the Tremaine's last known address toward Iverson.

"It's more than I had when I walked in here, Grace," Iverson qualified. "And I truly appreciate your time and effort in getting it for me." Iverson took the note, stowed it in a pocket and walked toward the door. He paused, turned and added, "Really, Grace. This is helpful. It gives me a direction I didn't have before. You've been terrific."

"My pleasure, Stan. I hope it helps." She walked over to Iverson, touched his arm gently and added, "It was nice to see you, Stan. Let's do this again . . . without the business part."

Iverson fumbled his reply. "Uh, yeah, that'd be nice," he stuttered. "Maybe coffee sometime."

Grace saw Iverson's discomfort. "No pressure, Stan," she replied kindly. "You know where I live. At work."

Iverson stumbled out of the CPS office and headed to El Sol.

*****

Iverson walked past the line at the order window and checked the crowd. No Numaga but the restaurant was busy. He returned to the line and waited his turn.

El Sol was an odd contrast: great food, crummy ambience. The building was a rehabbed, retrofitted Tasty Freeze. It lacked signage. It needed paint. The crowds frequenting El Sol sat on plastic chairs and around an eclectic array of thrift store tables that rested on a dirt floor protected from the elements by an old circus tent. Plastic ware and paper cups were self-served. Napkins were supplied in metal dispensers. El Sol's patronage overlooked its aesthetic shortcomings because it offered great food. Food with *real* traditional flavors. Mexican-Mexican food instead of American-Mexican food. Locals revered it; tourists gave it multiple stars.

Iverson closed in on the counter. He watched two aproned, gray haired Mexican ladies roll and punch balls of dough and then flatten the spheres into tortillas in a small metal press. An intense, dark haired boy swiftly and expertly diced onions, tomatoes and multi-colored peppers into small piles and directed his assemblages into containers labeled hot, hotter and hottest. A large metal griddle spat hot grease from marinated meats and the sizzling morsels were married to still warm tortillas. A blur of hands moved rellenos, tacos and enchiladas to a counter where numbers were called and hungry people made happy. It was an orchestrated movement that produced a delightful repast. Iverson's eyes watched approvingly. His stomach growled loudly.

Numaga arrived and slid into line next to Iverson. She ignored the stink eyes directed her way and greeted her partner while examining the daily specials.

"We meet again, Mr. Iverson."

"Around food, again, Ms. Numaga."

"Nothing wrong with that, is there, Stan?"

"Not if it's good food."

"That's why we're at El Sol."

Iverson smiled his response. It was his turn to order and he chose the special. Two carnitas soft tacos, a relleno in white cheese sauce and a Corona. Numaga followed with "Ditto." They grabbed their food, found an open table close to a tent pole, took a seat and shared the dynamics of their day after they'd parted at the grange. Numaga had used her status at APD to tell a believable story and Iverson had found safe haven for Horvat. They were personally unscathed but they'd witnessed some carnage and it could easily have been their own. They debriefed like cops do . . . briefly. They moved on.

"You said you found some information on your computer?" Iverson queried.

"I did," Numaga validated. "I took a look at Horvat's Kill Book, made an assumption that the initials were victims and started a process to find names to attach them to."

"Making a list and checking it twice?"

"I tried that," Numaga deadpanned. "Santa was busy."

"So what, then?" Iverson asked. "We're talking fifty-five sets of initials."

"There's a time frame involved . . . 1995 to 2011. So if I'm on the right track, I've got fifty-five victims in a sixteen year period. That's three and a half victims per year. That's actually an under-the-radar number. It's not abnormal data. Nobody would be thinking conspiracy."

Iverson was busy eating so Numaga continued sculpting her scenario.

"If Kant was a professional killer, and if Horvat ran a stable of Kants, then our initials might represent their objectives. If the killers are still active, then the crimes are unsolved. And Horvat hinted they were active, right?"

Iverson recalled Horvat's letter. *It is they who must now be found; their carnage stopped.* "Yeah, I think he did," he said. "Hold that thought, Numaga. I need another beer."

"Get two," prompted his partner.

Iverson walked to the order window, talked with the old man working it and returned with two more Coronas. "If you're right about active killers, what's the scale?" he asked Numaga.

"Good question. There could be a lot of Kants out there and a library of Kill Books. I'm just getting started but I'll know more when I start getting info back from the PD's."

"What PD's?"

"I've put in requests to PD's from Seattle to San Francisco for data on unsolved homicides, 1995 to 2011. I've only requested names but it's still gonna take time. We're talking about departments that range from metro divisions to rural one-cop shops. Not all of them will have the manpower, technology or the motivation to process my request. Lieutenant Solaras sent the requests from his office so I'm hoping that helps. It'll still take time."

"Solaras?" Iverson queried.

"My time-off deal required I keep him apprised of the case, remember?" Numaga explained.

"Vaguely," Iverson admitted. "Solaras ran the Narcotics Division when I was on the job. Our paths didn't cross much. What's he like?"

"He's a pompous, self-absorbed ass. I think it's a requirement for anyone at the lieutenant level or higher."

"No argument from me on that, Numaga."

"But there's something else disturbing about him. He's mean. He's obviously an angry person."

"Maybe you have that effect on people, Numaga," Iverson quipped.

"Numaga looked at Iverson sternly but sidestepped the comment. "Anyway," she continued, "it's very possible I'll get nothing from the e-mail effort."

"We might not need much," Iverson gauged. "If we can get enough to start seeing patterns or relationships, that could be helpful."

"I'm doing my best, Stan."

"Your best is working out fine, Numaga. Can you laptop your work?"

"Yeah," Numaga answered. "I can also check my phone for e-mails if we're in a service area but I'll need Wi-Fi for any Internet searches. Hopefully I can find an unsecured signal if I need one. What've you got in mind, Stan?"

"A road trip. We need to find a family named Tremaine."

"What about the farmhouse you mentioned?"

"I'm guessing when we find the farmhouse, we find the Tremaines."

"And you expect to find them dead?"

"According to Kant."

Numaga rolled back in her chair, stretched her arms out behind her and opened a yawn. She was spent, physically and emotionally. They both were and the Coronas had congealed their exhaustion. "Tomorrow, I hope?" she pleaded.

"Tomorrow," Iverson confirmed. His fatigue matched Numaga's but he had one last stop on today's ticket. Horvat's hooker hotel was on his way home and he needed to see if the key in his pocket opened one of its doors.

Chapter 25

Darkness met Iverson as he left the El Sol. Low, heavy clouds made the night feel close and threatened to dampen it. Iverson fired up a Camel and Henry's engine and headed toward The Brubaker. His mind was busy with the past day's events and the plan for tomorrow. His new partner, Cassie Numaga, had connected some dots and created some clarity regarding *what* they were dealing with. *Who* they were dealing with was still colored grey. Horvat had answers but he wasn't talking. He might never talk again. But he'd done what he could and asked Iverson to do that which he couldn't. So finding the who would be Iverson's job and finding them soon would be best. They'd already found him.

Iverson pulled into The Brubaker neighborhood and cruised past the Fifth Street Bar. Its dim lighting revealed Dave the bartender and a stooped customer manning the counter. *Business as usual,* Iverson thought. He checked the street repeatedly, both ahead and behind him, and the walkways on either side. He left the main roadway and navigated a network of alleys before settling Henry under a rust coated fire escape bolted to the bricks of The Gleason Hotel. The Gleason was a remnant of The Brubaker's glory days and for years its bricks bore the name of the family that built it. The name was sandblasted off the bricks when family records revealed a history of bigotry. An honest look at the past was replaced by a greedy eye to the future. In the end, everybody was blinded.

Iverson waited quietly, obeying his instincts. He knew the alley. He'd walked it as a kid and driven it as a cop. He also knew where its myriad doorways led and he walked to the one providing a back entrance to The Gleason. In the hotel's heyday, it would have been locked tightly at night and guarded closely during the day. No doorman or lock impeded entry now. Hookers had all-day access via unwritten contracts with pay-per-day rules. Alley access is important in the profession of prostitution. It is back-door work.

Iverson stepped through the door and into the dimly lit hallway. Disagreeable scents flooded his nose and hurried his step. He reached the spacious lobby and slowly surveyed the room. It was unoccupied save for the sour looking clerk seated behind a five-foot counter at the west end of the room. He hadn't yet noticed Iverson's arrival. The hardwood floor was pocked and stained and the rugs strewn on its surface were in similar condition. Clustered chairs gathered around round oaken tables beckoned long-ago days and long-dead patrons. Even their memories had abandoned The Gleason.

The hotel's current business was kept shrouded by the faded and frayed blue draperies jacketing its windows. A young Iverson stared through those windows and had been fascinated with the frenetic milieu inside. The Gleason had been Ashton's early hub for culture and wealth. But the money left, the hotel decayed and a different sort of reputation was now afforded its less gilded guests.

Iverson sauntered over to the counter. The clerk looked up. "You need sumpthin?" he asked gruffly.

Iverson examined the clerk carefully. Oily grey hair was matted onto his scalp and a three-day-old stubble retained remnants of his last meal. His nostrils needed a shave as much as his face. His short-sleeved plaid shirt hadn't seen the laundry in a while and was left opened enough to reveal another carpet of hair. Iverson was thankful the counter concealed what remained of the clerk. *Some things are best left unseen.*

A scattering of magazines shared the counter with a cradled telephone, three pencils in a coffee stained mug and what appeared to be a log book which probably tracked the user fees paid by the hotel's workforce. The magazines' covers revealed that guns and motorcycles ruled the reading habits of the hirsute clerk. Unfortunately, Iverson saw nothing with the prospect of offering him grooming tips.

"I need information," answered Iverson.

"You a cop?" asked the clerk.

"Nope," replied Iverson.

"Then information ain't free."

Iverson pulled the twenty from his pocket that he'd put there in anticipation of this rule of engagement and laid it on the counter. Next to it, he put Horvat's key. It had the number twelve etched on it.

"I'll be heading up to room twelve, but I'd like to know what you know about its recent occupant first."

"You can't just go snooping around a man's room."

"I can, and I will," Iverson snapped. "All that's in question here is whether or not you want that twenty."

The clerk snatched the bill. "Go ahead, ask," he bitched. "I'll let you know when your meter's run out."

"What was his name?"

"We look like a place that takes names?"

Iverson reckoned he had a point. He pressed forward. "Ever see him have visitors?"

"Nope."

"Phone calls?"

"Nope."

Iverson was getting discouraged but it wasn't unexpected.

"Did he go out much?"

"I don't keep track of the comins' and goins' of folks. If they pay, they stay. If they don't, they won't."

"Did he partake of any of your part-time guests?"

The hairy man paused, measured Iverson and answered, "Not that I know of."

Iverson figured the clerk was probably being as honest as he could and asked one last question.

"Anyone else been around looking?"

"Was wondering if you'd ask," the clerk replied smugly.

"And . . .?" prompted Iverson irritably.

"Yesterday, two guys came in asking the same questions. Made damn sure I saw their hardware."

Iverson described Dulles and Frantzen to the man behind the counter.

"Sounds like em'," the clerk confirmed.

"What'd you tell *them*?"

"Same's I told you. Didn't get no twenty, though."

"Then . . .?" Iverson led impatiently.

"Then they went up to twelve," the clerk explained. "Came down thirty minutes later with two stuffed trash bags and left."

"Shit," Iverson blurted. "Have you been in twelve since?"

"Ain't had the time."

Iverson looked at the clerk with relieved disbelief. At least his indolence was good for something. He grabbed the key and walked up to room twelve. The room had been ransacked. What furniture there was had been tossed. A stained mattress stood on its end, its coverings nowhere in sight. Three drawers from a beat-up old chest and one from a bedside table had been removed and whatever contents they might have held had been taken. Nothing that could have been labeled a personal item remained in the room. No shirt, no shoes, no toothbrush. *No goddamned anything.*

Iverson paced the room, his face reddening as his anger and frustration grew. *Should have come earlier,* he scolded himself. He stood in the open doorway, put his hands up over the chipped paint on the top jam and leaned his body through the opening. The tips of his fingers brushed the air vent above the door and a sharp piece of the metal grate scraped his index finger causing it to bleed. He examined the offending vent cover and noticed the grate was missing a screw. He retrieved a chair, positioned it below the vent and climbed atop it. A dime from his pocket served as a flat-head screwdriver and he quickly removed the remaining screw and pulled away the vent cover. His Maglite revealed a brown paper bag tucked into the deepest recess of the air supply duct. He stepped off the chair, grabbed a coat hanger from the closet and lifted the dowel it was hanging on from its thick plastic cradles. He fashioned himself a makeshift grappling hook, stuck it down the metal shaft and snagged the sack. In it he found a large notebook with a title written on the front cover. Kill Book II

CHAPTER 26

In the Paiute language, Numaga means "giver of food," indicating that the holder of the name is a generous person. Numaga was a Northern Paiute leader during the Paiute War of 1860 that centered on Pyramid Lake in what is now Nevada in the United States. He was born around 1830 and said by some to be the son of Chief Winnemucca and either the brother or cousin of Sarah Winnemucca, one of the most venerated and outspoken critics of the treatment of Native Americans.

Numaga was at least six feet tall, a man of physical strength and quiet dignity. A soldier who saw him in August 1860 said: "In appearance he is all that romance could desire, deep-chested and strong-limbed with a watchful, earnest expression of countenance, indicative of graver thought and study than is common to the aboriginal race."

Numaga picked up English while working for several seasons as a field hand for the Mission priests in the Santa Clara Valley of California. Through his intellect, eloquence and courage, Numaga gained considerable stature among the Paiute and was viewed by the whites as their leader.

Early contacts between the Paiutes and trappers and traders were friendly, but the Northern Paiute became more hostile after the California gold rush began in 1848 and brought large numbers of miners and immigrants into their lands. In 1859, news broke that silver had been found in the Comstock Lode in Washoe, a region that would soon become the territory of Nevada. Hordes of miners flooded to the mining center of Virginia City. They cut down pinyon trees to make fuel for ore-processing, destroying the pine-nut orchards that were essential to the Paiute food economy. Hunters and trappers took big game, fish and waterfowl to feed the miners. Ranchers moved into the fertile valleys, cutting off access to places where nuts, roots and seeds had been gathered for thousands of years.

In the late fall of 1859, two miners were killed in the mountains and were found with arrows in their bodies. Their money had been stolen but not their clothing or supplies, making it questionable whether Indians were responsible since the native people did not have a money economy. Major William Ormsby of the U.S. Army asked for help in finding the culprits from Chief Winnemucca whose daughter Sarah was staying in his house to be educated in English. Two days later, one hundred Paiute warriors rode into Carson City led by Chief Numaga. Numaga sent five men to the camp of the Washoe leader Captain Jim to ask him to give up the guilty men, since the arrows had been made by Washoe's. Under protest, Captain Jim sent two men to stand trial in order to avoid reprisals on his people. They were shot dead in Numaga's presence by a mob of angry whites.

The Paiute, Washoe and all other indigenous peoples of the region were threatened by starvation in the winter of 1859–1860. There were growing numbers of fights between whites and Indians. The Paiutes gathered at Pyramid Lake towards the end of April 1860 for a conference on how to deal with the encroachments of the whites. Most of the leaders spoke out for war. Winnemucca, the most senior leader at the assembly, appeared to favor war but refrained from taking a position. Numaga was the only chief who spoke in favor of peace. From his experience with the whites in California, Numaga was more aware of their resources than most of his audience. He agreed that white men had greatly wronged the Indians, but pointed out that the whites would win any war.

"Your enemies are like the sands in the bed of your rivers; when taken away they only give place for more to come and settle there. What hope is there for the Pah-Ute? From where is to come your guns, your powder, your lead, your dried meats to live upon, and hay to feed your ponies with while you carry on this war. Your enemies have all of these things, more than they can use. They will come like the sand in a whirlwind and drive you from your homes. You will be forced among the barren rocks of the north, where your ponies will die; where you will see the women and old men starve, and listen to the cries of your children for food. I love my people; let them live; and when their spirits shall be called to the Great Camp in the southern sky, let their bones rest where their fathers were buried."

War was averted but the conflict simmered. More silver was found and more whites came to get rich. The entitled newcomers took the Paiute's land, destroyed their food and assaulted their culture. The flash point came on May, 12 1860. Five Pony Express employees captured and raped two Northern Paiute women. A band of Northern Paiutes attacked the post, killed the men and freed the women. Major Ormsby collected a force of one hundred volunteers from Virginia City to punish the Paiutes. The Paiutes were led by Numaga. The volunteers were poorly armed and badly trained. They were quickly outmaneuvered and what began as a confident advance turned into a desperate defense. Seventy-six whites were killed and many others wounded in what is now known as the Battle of Pyramid Lake. The defeat by the "savages" infuriated the whites.

Frederick R Lander, of the U.S. Army, was ordered to restore order and protect the white population. He captured five Northern Paiutes near the Humboldt River and offered to exchange them for a meeting with Numaga. They met at Deep Hole Springs on August 21, 1860. Lander opened the negotiation by saying he could relay Numaga's grievances to Washington, but could make no promises. Numaga responded that he was pleased to hear no promises would be made because the whites had never kept any.

Chief Numaga died of tuberculosis in 1871.The Northern Paiutes survive to this day. They have protected lands and an enduring culture. It is likely there would be no Paiute Nation in the present if it were not for Numaga's vision in the past. He is a virtual unknown but he is a prodigious character in the theater of the American West.

Cassie Numaga, Chief Numaga's Great-Great Granddaughter, grew up on the Paiute Reservation near Burns, Oregon. Her biological parents were Native American teens afflicted by a Native American disease: alcoholism. She was removed from their care at one year of age and made a ward of the court. She was shuffled through the foster home circuit in the Burns area, her collection of foster parents mainly being white families with their own white kids. Predictable issues became persistent problems.

Native American children have been victimized for decades. They died in droves when Europeans brought diseases for which the native population had no genetic immunities. Diseases like measles, yellow fever and smallpox. Diseases incubated for thousands of years in an agrarian culture the Americas hadn't had.

After white diseases and expansion had decimated Native American populations and dwindled their lands, there remained what to do with what remained of their culture. The solution focused on children. Killing a culture is like killing a weed. You poison its roots.

The Indian Appropriation Act of 1882 established the Indian School System and the schools moved quickly across the country. Thousands of children, many under five years of age, were ripped from their homes and placed into schools, many of which were sponsored by religious groups. Indian children were forced to attend and government agents withheld food rations and other supplies from Indian families who would not enroll or keep their children in these schools. Students were forbidden to speak their native languages or practice their native religions. They were given new names, told to wear different clothes and required to cut the hair that had carried spiritual meaning. Grueling chores and stiff punishments were part of daily routines. Mental and sexual abuses were prevalent.

Farms benefitted as well from the raid on Indian children. Shipped on trains to labor starved regions, Native American children became family farmhands under the guise of adoption. The Indian Child Welfare Act of 1978 was enacted in large part because of the high rate of removal of Indian children from their traditional homes. ICWA gave back to Native Americans the right to raise their children. ICWA brought Cassie Numaga back to her culture.

Cassie was adopted at age nine by Paiute tribal members. Life wasn't perfect but she was among people who understood her challenges and supported her choices. One of those choices was to follow her interest in law enforcement. She volunteered, took courses at a community college and ultimately was hired by the Burns-Paiute Tribal Police. Another choice was an early marriage. It didn't last, mainly because she'd married another cop and the collective intensity produced constant conflict. But she also had conflict within herself. Her unexplained anger spilled into her marriage and sometimes onto her job. Friendships came and went and they usually went because Cassie didn't know how to trust people. She was now forty-four and had been single for twenty-one years. The last ten were with the Ashton PD. It was where she'd finally found peace.

*****

Numaga arrived home and parked her Camry in the driveway. She sat in her car, eyeballed the house and thought of Max, the Bomb Sniffing Dog. Numaga was a city dweller; her neighborhood typical of middle class Ashton. Her house was one level high spread over a normal city lot. Cream colored trim off-set the mossy green exterior and the red shingled roof bore a brick chimney stack with a black-capped pot. A small roof extension over the doorway was shaded by a trio of native Garry oaks and Numaga had planted the beds encircling them with low maintenance shrubs. The mulched areas fronting the home were thick with azaleas sporting tightly tucked buds awaiting their grand opening.

Numaga exited her vehicle and walked the house's perimeter, peering through windows and checking on doors. *Home on the grange*, she teased herself. She felt the eyes of a neighbor on her back, turned, but didn't see anybody. Satisfied with her due diligence, she inserted a key in the front door lock, turned it slowly and pushed the door open. No explosion! She did a quick look-around before tossing her keys on the top of a small table by the door and storing her weapon in the drawer beneath them. She kicked off her shoes, threw her coat on a couch and collapsed in an overstuffed chair. Sleep came quickly.

Chapter 27

Iverson complained out of bed and worked his way to the coffee pot. The fixins' fixed, he performed what magic he could with a shower and a shave. His thinning hair no longer required a comb. A simple finger fluffing steered in place the strands that remained. He checked the refrigerator and found his breakfast in a carton holding two unborn chickens. The muffins in the bread drawer were well preserved with chemical additives that Iverson ignored. He considered cooking an inconvenience and label reading made it a larger one. After his marriage dissolved, he ate-out or took-out most of the time. He'd never been health conscious and he wasn't about to change his eating habits this late in life. Until that first heart attack, anyway.

The eggs stared back in the pan while four muffin halves browned in the toaster. When the muffins popped up, they were buttered and placed on a paper plate secured in a plastic plate holder. The eggs were trimmed down to their yokes, flipped onto two muffin halves and covered with two others. The "I-Muffin" breakfast was ready.

Iverson chased his meal with a third cup of coffee then tapped Numaga's name on his cell phone. She answered after one ring.

"Ready if you are, Stan," Numaga proclaimed.

"I'll pick you up in twenty."

"Sorry, Stan," Numaga countered. "I've been in your vehicle. We'll take my car."

"Henry's just fine, Numaga," Iverson defended. "And besides, you don't know where I live."

"Henry?"

"Henry, the truck," Iverson explained. "Henry Ford, actually."

"Well, whatever his name is, it's a beat-up, unpleasantly pungent hunk of junk," Numaga argued. "And regarding whereabouts, I believe you don't know where I live either unless you've been stalking your new partner."

Iverson considered Numaga's biting rationale. "Fine, Detective," he begrudgingly agreed. "You'll need directions."

"I'm pencil ready, Sergeant."

Iverson provided Numaga rural route numbers, approximate distances and roadside hallmarks to watch for. She'd been a cop in the area for ten years. It was all familiar.

"Got it," she told Iverson. "I should be there in twenty."

"I'll be waiting outside," Iverson apprised. "There'll be no tour of the facilities."

"Fine with me," Numaga consented. "I do insist, however, on meeting Max."

"He'll be the first to greet you."

Iverson put Kill Book II in the hidden closet cubby with Kill Book I and the original Horvat papers, grabbed the old leather satchel that held the second set of copies and sat on the porch stoop to await his partner.

*****

Numaga arrived in thirty and Max greeted her quickly but coolly when she got out of her car. He was unaccustomed to visitors and the last ones had either planted a bomb or removed one. Not the sort of activity that engenders tail wagging. Max didn't growl but he didn't face-lick either. He circled and sniffed Numaga briefly, sensed she was there by invitation and moved out to pasture. Iverson walked to Numaga's car, watched as Max disappeared into a field of tall grass and took a seat in the passenger's side. Numaga lingered briefly, measured her partner's property then joined him in the Camry.

"Nice spread, Stan," she opined.

"Back tax bargain," Iverson explained.

"Ever get lonely?"

"I've got Max to keep me company."

"He might keep you safe, but he doesn't appear inclined towards cuddling."

"That makes us the perfect couple," Iverson jibed before moving on to the day's business. "Take a left when you get to the road."

Numaga followed the directive and they headed west on Route 126. The weather had improved from the last few days. The rain had backed off and blue patches of sky were peeking out from behind billowy white clouds. They followed the two-track highway for about ten miles until Iverson located the numbers on a post mounted mailbox that matched those given to him by Grace Johnson. He instructed Numaga to turn into a graveled driveway leading to a distant cluster of buildings.

Iverson suggested a slow approach and Numaga crawled forward. A hundred yards from the compound they saw a middle aged man standing in the winged, opened doors of a small barn. He was holding a bow saw and watching the approaching Camry with interest. Numaga steered in his direction and stopped fifty feet short of the man. Both Iverson and Numaga exited the vehicle and unzipped their jackets freeing up access to their revolvers. Numaga settled in by the hood of her car and Iverson approached the man by the barn.

"Good morning," Iverson greeted.

"Mornin'," the man returned glumly.

"You the owner of this place?"

"Who's askin'?"

"Name's Iverson," Iverson offered. "I'm looking for a family named Tremaine."

"The Tremaines don't live here. Used to, but they moved on."

"Any idea where?"

"Last I heard was a place near Notch. Tremaine came by after we was moved in and asked about some tools he thought he'd left. I let em' look around but he didn't find nuthin'. I had some questions about the well, offered him a beer and we talked a bit."

"That's when he told you about the place over by Notch?"

"Yeah."

"Anything about his new place strike you?"

The man paused, reaching for a forgotten conversation and the permission to share it. "He said he walked to the store from his house. We gotta drive ten miles for milk out here."

"Anything else?"

"Nah. It's been a while."

Iverson thanked the man, pulled a small card from his wallet and handed it to him. "Just in case you remember anything else," he said.

"Doubt it," the man responded sullenly.

"Just so you know," Iverson added, "we're not cops. My partner over there and I are private investigators. We're looking for information regarding a case the Ashton PD has no interest in."

"And the Tremaines are involved?" the man queried.

"If we find them, we'll ask them."

"Well, good luck with that," the man said.

Iverson turned to leave, curved back and said, "I didn't catch your name."

"I didn't give it," the man replied curtly. He pivoted and walked into his barn. Iverson returned to the Camry.

"You hear?" Iverson asked Numaga.

"I did," she reported. "The guy's name is Blakely."

"Did I miss a name tag?"

"It was on the mailbox," Numaga clarified. "Under the numbers . . . small print," she added with a smile.

"Good to know," Iverson admitted.

"On to Notch?"

"The Notch Country Store, more specifically."

*****

Iverson and Numaga headed to Notch, a backroads trip trailing the Siuslaw River. The meandering waterway was rimmed by Douglas firs competing for sunlight with Sitka spruce and spatters of vine maples. Their mid-morning shadows hung over the shallow stream as it gurgled along over its freestone bottom. The frenzied froth of sporadic cascades was all that disrupted the Siuslaw's rhythmic and inexorable path to the sea.

Fly fisherman dotted the river's shoreline, protected from the river's cold waters by waist-high waders and waterproof jackets. It was the promise of steelhead that had brought them there; the large rainbows returning after three years in the Pacific Ocean. Two separate runs brought them home to create a new generation of their species. Something deep in their genetic coding told them when and where to return. The runs also triggered the genes of fishermen seeking the thrill of the strike and the play of the line. The scaled and the skinned shared the same panic. So many fish . . . so little time.

Iverson noticed Numaga's laptop sitting on the back bench of the Camry. "I thought you were gonna remote while *I* drove," he recalled.

"I checked my e-mails before I left home this morning. I've gotten a few responses from some rural departments, but that's all so far."

"Any fruit from the tree?"

"Not yet, but it's early. I'll check again this afternoon." They rode for another mile before Numaga asked, "Was that a business card you gave Farmer John?"

"Uh, yeah," Iverson answered meekly.

"Let me see one."

"Why?"

"Why not?"

Iverson hesitated briefly. He wasn't a showy kind of guy. He'd never felt a need to impress people and the cards had been made strictly for a tool to acquire business. But he'd also never had feedback on their design; a design he'd created and printed himself from his Cro-Magnon computer. From what he was quickly learning of Numaga, she'd give him an honest opinion. He leaned forward, grabbed his wallet from a back pants pocket and extracted a card.

"Here," Iverson said gruffly and thrust it at Numaga.

Numaga took the card and waited for a straight stretch in the road before examining it. "Stanley B. Iverson – Professional Investigations" it advertised in deep red ink. A phone number and an e-mail address trailed beneath in smaller, black font. It was printed on sepia toned business card stock.

Numaga handed the card back to Iverson without comment and they continued tracking the Siuslaw. Iverson didn't want to ask, but did. "Your thoughts on the card, Detective?"

"I think it's almost perfect," Numaga appraised.

"Almost?" Iverson questioned.

"I'd only make one change."

Iverson grimaced, faced Numaga directly and asked, "And that would be . . .?"

"I'd add my name next to yours," Numaga said candidly. Iverson returned the card to the wallet and sat back to enjoy the ride. *Maybe not a bad idea,* he thought.

*****

Notch was a tiny hamlet tucked into a small cavity of the Coast Range. Notch had never owned a large enough population to warrant a post office and the accompanying town charter, but outlying farms and backroad travelers kept the Notch General Store alive. It was once a thriving stopover for fully laden log trucks and the hard men that drove them. The kitchen had closed and the menu was altered when the logging retreated. The red vinyl booth seats were replaced with scant tables and chairs and the meals had morphed into whatever fit into a microwave oven. But the coffee was still good and Iverson was looking forward to a cup.

Iverson and Numaga pulled off the road and into the store's puddle-pocked lot. They exited the Camry and surveyed the lay of the land surrounding Notch. The store sat at the base of High Pass Road. If you were headed to the coast, you had to scale the Coast Range and the climb started here. The varied landscape was kept green by eighty inches of annual rain and frequent, early morning fog. A small babbling brook coiled around the building, found its way under the road through a culvert and disappeared into a cluster of alders. The size of the area's conifers revealed the history of logging but a sizable stand of old growth timber anchored in ancient sediment encircled the store. The logger's concession to their mealtime oasis.

The store itself was outwardly in good shape. The porch had been recently rehabbed and its red metal roof provided stark contrast to the mossed green shingles of the main building's crown. The brown paint casing the store had been recently applied, a task made frequent by the dampness and wind endemic to life in the Coast Range. The scent of coffee wafted through a slightly opened window and caught Iverson's attention.

"Let's see who's home," he suggested.

"After you," Numaga insisted and gestured toward the door.

Iverson and Numaga stepped onto the porch, walked past an anachronistic pay phone and opened a creaky screen door. As the empty parking lot had hinted, they were the only patrons at the Notch General Store. They approached the elderly woman who was stocking a short shelf next to the checkout stand.

"Good morning," Iverson greeted.

"Mornin' folks," the lady replied. "I'll be right with ya." She took the last bag from a carton of Fritos, placed it on a shelf and repositioned herself behind the counter.

"There, now. How can I help you?" she asked pleasantly. She was a short woman with close cropped, curly gray hair and a plump face. Her left eye drooped and Iverson figured the old scar that creased the eyebrow above it had something to do with the wilt. Her wide-framed glasses helped hide the wound and were secured to her person by the silver linked chain dangling over her ears.

She wore a bright orange blouse atop loose fitted Levi's. Coast Range work clothes.

Iverson took a step back from the counter and moved his gaze to the Fritos. Numaga read his body language correctly and initiated the conversation.

"My friend here badly needs a cup of coffee and I'd like to ask a few questions."

"I know I got the coffee, but I'll have to hear the questions before I can promise any answers." Her words were accentuated by the sharp snapping of a large wad of vigorously worked gum.

"Fair enough," Numaga replied. Nodding toward Iverson, she added, "Can we get the coffee before he goes through withdrawal?"

"Sure," the woman replied. "It's serve yourself and the pots are over there." She pointed to a small counter that had two large thermoses of coffee stationed on its surface. One was labeled regular, the other ethyl. Iverson filled a large paper cup with the high octane ethyl and added milk from a pitcher sitting in a bowl of ice cubes. He stirred slowly and listened while Numaga talked.

"Mr. Coffee over there and I are private investigators," she explained. "We're looking for a family by the name of Tremaine. I know it's probably not your custom to give out information on neighbors but we have reason to believe they might be in harm's way. We'd like to make sure they aren't."

The woman's cheery demeanor left the building. "What makes you think they live in these parts?"

"We were given what we believe is reliable information," Numaga responded.

"By who?" the woman questioned.

Numaga didn't want to give the clerk Blakely's name so she offered, "Someone that knew them a ways back."

The old lady wavered. Numaga could tell she was struggling with whether or not to break an unwritten rule. Country folks choose their lifestyle for a reason. They want to be free from the constraints of city life and they resent any urban based laws that adversely affect their rural based lives. They distrust city dwellers and have a visceral disdain for anyone poking around in their affairs.

"Look," Numaga continued, "I know I'm asking you to go against an ages old grain. But there's a real chance that the Tremaines are in trouble, or are about to be. We're hoping to help them avoid that."

"We don't abide folks interfering out here, Missy," the clerk asserted.

"We aren't here to interfere in anybody's business, ma'am," Numaga assured.

"The Tremaines have been good neighbors. They ain't cookin' meth or growin' weed like some others out here. They mind their own business and keep their noses clean. You don't need to be hasslin' them."

"We're trying to keep them from being hassled, ma'am."

The woman walked out from behind the counter and over to the store's front window. Numaga followed. They stopped next to a counter of canned goods and the woman extended an arm and pointed an arthritic finger toward the uphill grade in the road. "Bout' a quarter mile up the hill on the north side of the road is a dirt driveway," she told. "The Tremaine place is another quarter mile in." She walked back behind the counter, turned her back to Numaga and began to stock more shelves.

"Thank you, ma'am," Numaga offered. "We won't mention how we found them."

"No matter," she said miserably. "The deed is done."

Numaga headed out the door and Iverson followed her to the parking lot.

"Well done, Detective," Iverson praised.

"I'm glad I got what I got, but I don't feel that great about the gettin'," Numaga said.

Iverson knew the feeling, knew he couldn't make it better so let the statement die. He lowered himself into the Camry and changed the subject to the task at hand. "Let's go find the Tremaines," he urged. "I'm hoping they're not all dead."

"A little optimism might look good on you, Stan," Numaga said sarcastically.

"Optimism is overrated," Iverson countered.

Chapter 28

Kralj Kovačić called a meeting. His two remaining vitezovi had been summoned to outlay their plans to rid the Kralj of his concerns. The meeting was held in the basement of a pool hall in an old part of Portland.

"Vitezovi," the Kralj began, "please tell me you've made progress with silencing the two detectives."

"I apologize, Kralj Kovačić," Jurić replied dutifully, "but we have not yet made them quiet."

"Tell me why Vitez Jurić?"

Jurić considered telling Kovačić about the dog and the subsequent heightened state of awareness of Iverson and Numaga but thought better of it. "They are intelligent Americans," he offered instead. "They know we are onto them and have made adjustments."

"Are they more intelligent than you and Marić?" Kovačić baited.

Neither Jurić nor Marić responded. They hung their heads and waited for Kovačić to continue.

"Tell me of your new plan to finish them," Kovačić demanded.

"They follow the bodies so we will provide them bodies to follow. We will wait. When they come, we will complete the task, Kralj Kovačić."

"And what of Horvat?"

"Horvat will not talk," Marić assured Kovačić. "He will not talk ever again."

"Is he dead?" asked the Kralj.

Silence again from the two vitezovi.

"I asked you if he was dead," Kovačić snarled.

"We think so," answered Jurić.

Kovačić glared at the men. "Have you seen Vitez Babić?" he asked.

The vitezovi looked at one another then back at Kovačić. "We haven't," answered Marić.

"Do you know why you haven't seen Babić?"

The men shook their heads.

"You haven't seen Babić because he is dead," Kovačić revealed. "I slit his throat with an Uskoci blade and had him cut into pieces and ground into garbage."

Silence again struck the wide-eyed vitezovi.

"Do you want to know why?" Kovačić taunted.

"Yes, Kralj Kovačić," the men said obediently.

"Because he failed me!" Kovačić bellowed.

"We won't fail you, Kralj," Marić declared nervously.

"You have little time to prove it," Kovačić warned. "Now get the hell out of here and eliminate our problem."

The vitezovi left hurriedly. Kralj Kovačić lingered and made a call to Croatia.

Chapter 29

Dulles and Frantzen awaited a Skype call from Houston, Texas. The two men sat nervously in their bargain priced suits, adjusting their ties and adjusting them again. Small droplets of sweat crept down Frantzen's temples and he dabbed them with a handkerchief he pulled from a pocket. Dulles stared at his partner with disgust.

"You sweat like a pig," Dulles grunted.

"I can't help it," Frantzen protested. "My nerves tap directly into my sweat glands."

"You'd better cap off the well before we're on screen or we'll both look like fools."

Frantzen dabbed more intently. He finished off his face and moved to his hands which could have shaken off the moisture with their tremors. He was gulping some water when the call rang through.

"Good morning, sir," Dulles greeted.

Dulles spoke to a man in his late fifty's. The monitor showed him from his shoulders up and revealed an intense, round face set atop a rigid carriage. He had short-cropped greying hair, thick eyebrows and a clean shaven face. Deep set, penetrating eyes peered back at the two men sitting anxiously 2,000 miles away.

"I need an update, gentlemen," the man prompted.

"We met with the Croatian yesterday and informed him of your concerns," Dulles reported.

"And what was his response?"

"He acknowledged that his group had made some mistakes but that they were the result of specific individuals having failed in their assignments."

"And what has been done with those individuals?"

"They're Croats, sir," Dulles pointed out. "They are merciless, violent men. I think it's safe to assume the offending individuals no longer breathe."

The Houston man asked, "Have you located the family killed by Kovačić's man?"

"We have not, sir," Dulles replied. "The Croat Babić isn't answering his phone and he controlled the guy who killed the family. It's a Croat loop and we're not in it."

"No help from our man inside?"

"He is unable to assist us with a location," Dulles explained. "He said . . .

"Frantzen," the man interrupted, "you look like you need a doctor. What's your problem?"

Frantzen mopped his forehead with his hanky. "I'm fine, sir," he responded. "Just some bug I've picked up."

"Well, you look like shit," the man barked. He was angry and frustrated. His problems were mounting.

"Sorry, sir."

"Get some air."

"Sir"?

"I don't like looking at you. Go get some air."

Frantzen got up clumsily, walked out of the room and closed the door behind him.

"Dulles!" the man commanded.

"Yes, sir?"

"I want this Croat problem brought under control. I'm giving them a short leash. They've been helpful for many years, but if they're not able to control their own men, it might be time to find another contractor."

"How would you like to proceed, sir?" Dulles inquired.

"I want closer tabs on Kovačić. I want daily progress reports on how he's solving our problem."

"He doesn't like to be bothered, sir."

"I don't give a fuck what he likes. He needs to know he'll be bothered until he does his job."

"Yes, sir."

"One other thing, Dulles."

"What's that, sir?"

"Get rid of Frantzen."

"Get rid of him?"

The man in the screen glared at Dulles and the icy look in his eyes clarified his words.

"I understand perfectly, sir," Dulles confirmed.

Chapter 30

Iverson and Numaga found the dirt driveway described by the clerk at the Notch General Store, turned onto it and drove toward what they hoped would be the Tremaine farm. Dappled sunlight splashed the rutted road and both driver and passenger were pitched about as the car made its way slowly over the potholes. As the clerk had estimated, the farm was about a quarter mile off the main highway. Numaga spotted the farm, pulled the car into a short pullout and together they surveyed the property before driving up to the knot of buildings.

"Nobody milling around," opined Numaga.

Iverson checked his phone's clock. "Maybe it's lunch time," he offered.

"Hoping for an invitation, Sergeant?"

"Yup."

"Shall we proceed?"

"Yup, again."

Numaga eked the Camry forward, circled the house and parked it facing back toward the road. She killed the engine and Iverson opened his door. Numaga followed suit and, like she'd done at Blakely's place, took a position at the front of the vehicle. Iverson walked slowly to the house, stepped onto the porch and knocked briskly on the aluminum frame of the screen door. No one came out to greet him so he opened the screen and knocked again on the wooden door behind it. Again no response. He looked back at Numaga who shrugged her shoulders and moved toward the south end of the building. Iverson stepped off the porch and moved to the north. They both drew their weapons.

Iverson walked slowly around his side of the house, pausing briefly to scrutinize pastured bovines and mesh-fenced chickens. Neither provided the ex-cop with any hint of disruption so he moved forward. He peered into a window and saw a small plank table in the middle of a large kitchen. Bowls and plates set on the table were filled with food but the only one partaking of the meal was the horde of flies buzzing about the room. He moved to the next window, looked in cautiously and saw two motionless bodies folded onto one another. He stepped back and continued around the house. He met Numaga at the west corner.

"Find anything?" she asked.

"Probable cause," answered Iverson.

"So they're dead?"

"At least two. You see anything?"

"No bodies . . . dead or alive," Numaga reported.

Iverson nodded toward a back entrance. "I'll go in here. After I'm in, you get the front."

"Got it," Numaga said.

Iverson tried the door. It was dead bolted but there was play in the bolt and a substantial gap between the door and the jamb. He took out his jackknife and stuck the long blade through the crack and worked it into the strike box and behind the bolt. He leveraged it slowly until it cleared the strike plate then pulled the door open.

"Okay," he told Numaga."

Numaga walked to the front of the house, scaled the porch and pushed open the front door. She followed her gun into the building. She cleared the kitchen, a bathroom and one bedroom. Iverson cleared another bedroom and a back pantry-washroom. They met in the living room where the dead Keepers lay.

"Family of two?" queried Numaga.

"I'm thinking three," Iverson said, "if Kant told the truth."

"There's a door off the kitchen," Numaga revealed.

Iverson and Numaga knelt over the Keepers and Iverson put his hand on their flesh. Cold and clammy. He picked up the shotguns lying on the floor next to them, cracked them open and checked their loads.

"They didn't fire," he revealed.

"Kant did," Numaga said. "And at close range. How long ago you figure?"

"I'm no M.E., but by the feel of the bodies I'd say forty eight hours or so," Iverson guessed.

Numaga shook her head silently. "Better check that door."

Iverson nodded his agreement and they rose up and walked to the kitchen. They readied their weapons and Numaga opened the door to a narrow staircase leading to a dimly lit hallway.

"Down the rabbit hole," quoted Numaga, trying to lighten things up. "You think we'll find Alice?"

"Doubt it," Iverson replied. "More likely the Mad Hatter."

They shared a quick smile before returning to their sober reality. Mini Maglites were drawn and they accompanied the sidearms as Iverson and Numaga descended the stairs. Their beams revealed the hallway had two side doors. One open, one closed. There was also an open doorway at the end of the hall and a large washtub and toilet beyond it. They made their way cautiously down the hallway to the closed door. Numaga opened it and cast her beam inside.

The room was a pantry stocked with an assortment of canned goods. Labels stuck to jars identified their contents and the year they'd been sealed. Peaches, nectarines, plums, beans and a variety of other fruits and vegetables had been preserved for the future. Iverson looked at Numaga, raised his eyebrows and indicated they should move on.

The open door room held a small bed and a small table with a small lamp. The lifeless body slumped on the bed was that of a young boy. *I didn't kill the boy,* Iverson recalled Kant saying. Numaga walked over to the bed, placed her hand on the boy and closed her eyes.

"There's been a lot of sadness in this house," Numaga said. "This boy had most of it."

"He has to be the boy Kant told me about."

"What did he say?"

"He told me the boy killed himself because he didn't want to be like Kant."

Numaga examined the boy's head wound and the gun in his hand. "Certainly appears possible, Stan. Forensics will tell us for sure. I guess we'd better let APD in on our little discovery."

"Let's think about that, Numaga," Iverson posed.

"They have to be called," Numaga insisted.

"Oh, they need to be called," Iverson agreed. "I'm just not sure we should do the calling."

"Please explain, Sergeant," Numaga beckoned. Iverson was noticing Numaga's tendency to use his former rank when she was irritated with him.

"Well, there are a couple of things to consider," Iverson reasoned. "One, you've recently spent a few hours at APD justifying one shooting. You call and report three more dead people and you're definitely on somebody's radar. You're a cop. What would you be thinking?"

"I'd be thinking I don't believe in coincidences."

"Exactly," confirmed Iverson. "And I don't think we need to be wasting our time sitting around APD all day answering questions so some detective can look good on a report."

"So what do you suggest, Sergeant?"

"That we make an anonymous call."

"It'll take APD all of four hours to figure out who made it," Numaga protested. "The clerk at the store will tell them about a man and woman snooping around and after she describes us, APD will know who it was. Hell, Stan, they'll think we killed these folks."

"They might consider that, but the M.E. will dismiss it. These three were killed long before we got to the Notch General Store."

"Still, Stan," Numaga argued, "it puts us in a bad light. Maybe even on the wrong side of the law."

"And there's the difference between being an APD cop and being a private cop. We get to make that choice . . . to take that chance."

Numaga paused to consider Iverson's argument. She wasn't totally comfortable with it. "You said there were two things to consider," she recalled. "What's the second one?"

"Two is related to one," Iverson explained. "If we get bogged down with APD, we lose valuable time working this case. And I think this case is about to blow open, Numaga."

"Why is that, Sergeant?"

"Because I found Kill Book II last night in Horvat's hotel room. This operation is far bigger than we thought and people are being killed to protect it."

Numaga left the boy's room and walked back up the stairs. She opened the front door, exited the house and stood on the porch deep in thought. Iverson traced her steps but remained silent while Numaga pondered her options.

"You're making the call," she finally said.

They walked past a shed on their way back to the Camry and Iverson noticed it had been padlocked in three different places. He walked back to the house and retrieved a key ring he'd seen sitting on the kitchen table. He returned to the hut, found the keys that sprung the padlocks and swung open the door. The shed was lined with one-by-six shelving and the shelves were covered with canvas tarps. Under the tarps was an arsenal of weapons. Handguns, rifles, semi-automatics and dozens of other armaments.

"An odd set of farm tools, wouldn't you say, Numaga?" asked Iverson.

"More than odd, Stan," Numaga answered. "A lot more."

Chapter 31

Dulles didn't particularly like Frantzen, but he didn't want to kill him either. He'd killed before, numerous times. But he killed as part of the job and the victims had all been people he'd not known. He considered Frantzen a bumbling idiot but he was also someone he'd spent significant time with during the past year. Killing him would mean looking at him. That would be uncomfortable . . . even for Dulles. He called a vitez.

The call rang through but was answered by an unfamiliar voice.

"Give me Babić," Dulles demanded.

"He is not available," the man on the other end of the call said.

"Who is this?"

The man paused and then answered, "I am Vitez Jurić. Who are you?"

"This is Dulles. I need to speak with Babić."

"Babić is gone," revealed Jurić.

"Gone where?"

"Just gone."

Dulles got the drift. He wouldn't be talking to or seeing Babić again . . . ever. "So you're now in charge?" he inquired.

"I will be answering this phone."

"Fine," Dulles consented. "I have a job for you."

"We already have a job."

"Not the right answer, Jurić."

"Meaning what?"

"Let me tell you how this works. I call you, give you a target and you send out one of your trained boys to take care of it. Simple. That's our arrangement. Are you telling me you wish to change the arrangement?"

"We have other problems now."

"So you *do* want to change the arrangement."

Jurić hesitated. He didn't have the authority to answer Dulles' question. If he told Dulles he wouldn't do the job, he'd most likely piss off the Kralj. Not a good idea. He was already pissed off. Jurić didn't wish to share Babić's fate.

"What's the job?"

"The target's name is Frantzen. I'll call back with a time and location."

"Will it be today?"

"It'll be when I tell you," Dulles barked. "That's the arrangement, Jurić. Get used to it." He ended the call.

Jurić put the phone in his pocket and smiled to himself. He'd never met Frantzen but he knew who he was. Now he knew *what* he was. A gift. Frantzen would be the bait with which to entrap the two detectives he had to kill. The Kralj would be happy. Things were looking up. For him, anyway.

Chapter 32

Iverson and Numaga made their way back to the Notch General Store and Iverson used the archaic pay phone on the porch to make his anonymous report to the Ashton PD. He muffled his voice with a red handkerchief pulled from a pants pocket. Numaga watched and listened with a mixture of curiosity and apprehension. The old clerk inside the store glared at them through the window but didn't come out to the porch to ask them what they'd found at the Tremaine farm. The call completed, they got back in the Camry and headed to Ashton.

"Let's head back to the farm and regroup," suggested Iverson.

"So I get the facilities tour after all, huh?" jostled Numaga.

"The short version."

"Why the short version?"

"It's a short house."

Numaga laughed. "You got food and beverage?"

Iverson grimaced. Both his refrigerator and pantry were near empty. "We need to make a food stop," he conceded.

"Figured as much," Numaga teased. "Good thing I asked."

Damn her, Iverson thought, but he was more embarrassed than angry. Numaga was making a habit of being right.

They stopped at a small, locally owned grocery store ten miles outside of Ashton and bought a frozen pizza and a six-pack of locally brewed beer and headed back to Iverson's farm. They road in silence for a few minutes before Numaga asked, "Are you a religious person, Stan?"

"Those dead people having an effect on you, Detective?"

Numaga stared at the road in front of them. "Seeing death up close has a way of re-focusing the big picture."

"Exactly what big picture are you referring to?"

"You know. Life, death, what comes after."

"Not my area of expertise."

"So you're ducking the question."

"What question?"

"The one I just asked."

"If I'm religious?"

"Yeah, that one."

Iverson mulled the question for a ten count before answering. "I hold a healthy respect for the right to believe as you choose," he finally said.

"That's still doesn't answer the question," Numaga disputed.

Iverson reconsidered the question. "I'm not religious," he submitted.

"So you don't believe in anything?"

"I said I'm not religious," Iverson asserted. "I didn't say I didn't believe in anything."

"So you believe in God?"

"No, actually, I don't," Iverson clarified.

"Then what do you believe in?" pressed Numaga.

Iverson considered his answer before tendering it. "I think human beings have a spiritual aspect to their existence and a capacity to use it. A large portion of the world's population channels their spirituality into religion. I personally think it could be put to better use."

"Put to use how?"

"By working towards a better world instead of praying for one. By being less concerned about supremacy and more concerned about equality. By being tolerant and respectful of the views of others rather than dismissing and denigrating them. The bullet points are endless, Numaga."

"So how does your concept of spirituality compare to your concept of religion?"

"Apples and oranges, Numaga. Spirituality is an internal quality unique to the individual. Religion is an external influence. It's chosen, inherited or imposed. Its configuration is corporate; it's structure hierarchical. There are strict policies and penalties for not following those policies. Religions and corporations have the same goal: to control people. Religion, however, has a more insidious methodology to achieve that goal."

"Which is?"

"Death manipulation. The heaven or hell option and the fear connected with both."

"Not all religions focus on our fear of dying, Stan," Numaga contended.

"That's true. Some religions focus on the life at hand and the importance of that life being well-lived. But most of those religions also script their system to achieve the ultimate end of controlling those who subscribe to it. I'll concede that for some, it works positively."

"But you find them unappealing as well?"

"If they include the concept of God, yes. I don't buy into an all-powerful entity in charge of this place we call the universe."

"You can't accept a higher power; something greater than yourself?"

"No, I can't. I can't accept that an all-powerful, all-loving deity would casually watch this world we inhabit, take notice of its many afflictions, and not feel moved to lend a helping hand."

"So hypothetically, Stan," Numaga coaxed, "if there was a God, and if you could have a conversation with him or her, what would you suggest that God fix?"

Iverson paused briefly, creating a short inventory. "Poverty, hunger, war, child abuse. I guess I'd start there, but the full list would make for a long conversation."

Numaga specifically noted the last item on Iverson's list but decided to forego its exploration. *Maybe another time*. "That'd be a good start," she concurred.

"But," Iverson added, "there's no conversation because God's apparently left the building."

"So definitely no God?" Numaga tested.

"That's my take," Iverson replied, "and I think it holds equal plausibility with those who believe God exists. The concept of gods is an ancient human contrivance. Gods have explained things we didn't understand and provided us with comfort in times of distress. Many religions, however, exploit those human vulnerabilities. But I can understand the comfort in believing that a crappy life on earth can be followed by a glorious afterlife. For a lot of folks, it's what gives them a reason to live, even if life is a struggle. Religions do offer their adherents hope. Not a bad thing. It's the exploitive and exclusionary methods employed to sell that hope that I find deplorable."

"So why then is the world so overwhelmingly religious?" asked Numaga.

"Humans need hope, Numaga," Iverson stressed.

"An interesting take on religion, Stan," she observed. "I guess we won't be rolling out a prayer rug for you anytime soon?"

"Most likely not, Numaga," Iverson agreed. "But I don't think I'm too rigid to learn something new."

"I don't see you as rigid, Stan," Numaga said. "You're not warm and fuzzy, but you're not rigid either."

Iverson liked the compliment though he was unsure what to do with it. He sidestepped it by turning the conversation to his partner.

"How about you, Numaga?" Iverson asked. "Do you pray to a god?"

"Paiutes pray each morning to the sun for buha."

"Buha?"

"Buha is power and it can reside in any natural object but mostly lives in the sun, moon, thunder, clouds, stars, and wind. We believe ancestral ghosts remain in this world and that they either plague us or help us. Buha helps keep their effect in balance. Anybody can seek buha for their own purpose but only a shaman can call on buha to help others."

"Who gets to be shaman?"

"Shamans acquire their first power in a dream. Additional powers can be developed spontaneously or as requested. Powers are highly specific to individual shamans but the primary purpose of a shaman's power is to benefit others."

"I thought the wave of early missionaries extinguished all that."

"It did, at least much of it. Catholics, Mormons, Presbyterians, Shakers and a host of other folks wanting to save us savages showed up with the miners and ranchers in the mid-1800's. The tribes offered a large new population to convert and the church folks set out to civilize us with their God. They did it harshly and, in many cases, successfully, at least by their account. Our history tells a different story."

"Did the Paiutes resist?"

"Of course, but resistance was short-lived and futile," Numaga answered sadly, "for the Paiutes and all other native peoples."

"You never hear much about the Paiutes. Why is that?"

"We were spread over a lot of territory and confused with a lot of other tribes. The original Paiute Nation was in Oregon, California and Utah. We were the Great Basin's nomads. Most Americans get their knowledge about Indians from movies and nomads don't make for interesting flick characters unless you've got Lawrence of Arabia hanging around. But we made a living where nobody else wanted to . . . until silver was discovered."

Iverson extended the cinematic analogy. "So Peter O'Toole didn't save the day?"

"No O'Toole, but we did have Wovoka," Numaga boasted.

"Who was he?" Iverson inquired.

"Wovoka was a shaman from the Walker River Paiute band who founded the Ghost Dance religion. Wovoka experienced a powerful vision during a solar eclipse and, in his vision, the earth was returned to a natural state."

"A natural state?" Iverson queried.

"No more white men."

"That had to appeal to more than a few Indians."

"It did, and within a few years the Ghost Dance religion had spread to angry and frustrated tribes throughout the West. Some tribes, like the Sioux, interpreted the Ghost Dance as a call for renewed violence against whites. The U.S. government banned it and ultimately the Sioux suffered the massacre at Wounded Knee."

"Does it still exist?"

"No. Indians have accepted the fact that white men aren't going away. We're just trying to preserve the remnants of our cultures the best way we can."

"How's that working out?"

"It's difficult, especially for the young people. They're caught in between two cultures and are conflicted by the choice of white money vs tribal tradition. Unfortunately, many never figure it out."

The discussion took them to the graveled driveway leading to Iverson's farm. Numaga turned up the track and Iverson directed her to the pullout a hundred feet in.

"Let's sit here for a few minutes."

"Any particular reason?" asked Numaga.

"Constructive paranoia."

Numaga nodded her understanding. She killed the engine, reached into the back of the Camry and pulled her laptop onto her lap. She lifted the lid, tapped the on button and waited for the machine to power up. The screen readied, she located an unsecured Wi-Fi signal and played the keyboard and touch pad to her e-mail account.

"Damn!" Numaga exclaimed.

"Problem?" asked Iverson.

"My APD e-mail account is down."

"Any explanation why?"

"No. There's no notification as to any problems with the server or that maintenance is being performed."

Numaga stroked the keyboard rapidly, stopped and read a few messages before keying in more information. "What the hell?" she asked angrily.

"What exactly is the problem, Numaga?" questioned Iverson. His PI enterprise had forced him to understand what computers did, but he was still in the dark regarding how they did it.

"Not sure yet. But it appears my APD account has been taken off-line."

"How does that affect us?"

"The APD account was my primary account. It's where any responses to my requests for information on unsolved homicides would have gone."

"You said primary account. Do you have a secondary one?"

Numaga didn't answer but instead resumed her frenetic key tapping. Iverson watched her intensity grow and decided to let conversation wait. Five minutes later, Numaga restarted it.

"Got em'!" Numaga exclaimed.

"The e-mails?" asked Iverson.

"Yup," Numaga replied, "thanks to you."

"What the hell did I do?"

"You reminded me that I had a secondary account. APD replaced its old server with a new one a few years back. When they told us about the changeover, I mentioned to a geek friend that I had concerns I might lose the volumes of old e-mails that I'd accumulated over the years . . . e-mails that I'd kept for reference and potential evidentiary material. The geek created a software program for me that backed up all my e-mails separately from the APD server. I'd forgotten about it until you asked me if I had a secondary account. Then I checked to see if it was still active and still backing up my incoming e-mails. And it is."

"So you have some responses?"

"Yeah. Quite a few actually. And the date-time log indicates there's more than I thought I had when I first looked this morning."

Iverson looked at Numaga and she looked back at him. Their thoughts were synchronized.

"Two questions, right?" Iverson asked.

"Two immediate ones, yeah," Numaga qualified. "More will undoubtedly follow."

Iverson asked first. "So who do you think dumped your account?"

"If it was done inadvertently, it could have been any number of people."

"And if it was done intentionally?"

"A much shorter list," Numaga calculated. "Solaras would be at the top of it."

"Second question?" Iverson probed.

"Why?"

Chapter 33

Silvio Solaras was born in New York City into a family of cops. His two brothers, father and grandfather were, or had been, respected members of New York's Finest. The Solaras family was a proud family. Proud of their Italian heritage and proud of their service to their adopted homeland.

Silvio was the last of five children born to Elena and Stefano Solaras. He was picked on incessantly by the two boys and two girls that had been born prior to his arrival. Not an unusual state of family affairs, but for Silvio, it was pure torture. He'd come into the world with a chip on his shoulder and the constant ridicule he endured from his siblings only made the chip larger. His brothers were typically Italian. Tall, dark and handsome. Silvio was short, light complexioned and rather unattractive. The family joke was that Silvio's genes came cloaked in different jeans. He fought back but his small physical stature served only to transpose his emotional frustration into physical thrashings.

The transition from home to school provided little relief. He was bullied and ridiculed by his classmates and demeaned by his teachers. He dropped out of high school before the end of his senior year and packed himself out of the family home. He worked grunt jobs on the docks during the day and drank heavily at night at the bar adjacent to the sleazy apartment he'd rented. The drinking landed him in jail on numerous occasions and his embarrassed family reluctantly plied their influence to keep him out of more serious trouble. Silvio was headed nowhere and it was a destination the hard working Solaras family found unacceptable.

Stefano Solaras was a patient man . . . to a point. He gave Silvio what he considered sufficient time to become a respectable Italian and when that didn't materialize, he gave his son a choice. Either join the NYPD or be shipped to Italy. Silvio begrudgingly opted to remain in the country whose language he understood. He joined the force and worked the pavement of Brooklyn. For five years he harangued the neighborhoods he was assigned to. He had no particular prejudices. He treated Puerto Ricans, Poles, Jews and all other ethnic groups alike . . . badly. He used his badge to exact revenge for the way he perceived life had treated him. Citizens complained and Solaras was cautioned. To no avail. He was finally removed from the streets and given a desk in a Staten Island precinct; a punishment disguised as a promotion. He accepted it without complaint but his bitterness burned.

Silvio's problems came to a head when he publically questioned the virtues of the Police Commissioner's young daughter. His insults had their intended effect: they embarrassed the entire Solaras family. Captain Stefano Solaras was called into the Commissioner's plush office to explain the actions of his wayward son. It was explained later to Silvio that he once again had a choice to make. Apply for work in distant places or be terminated for a cause that the force would contrive. NYPD would provide unlimited letters of positive reference as long as they approved the destinations.

Silvio wasn't a fool. The NYPD was a powerful force and could quash any future he had in the city. He crafted and submitted his resume to law enforcement agencies around the country. He received scant replies. One was from Ashton, Oregon. They had an opening for a mid-level officer in their Narcotics Division and were excited to interview a detective from New York City. The East Coast native took a West Coast flight the next day and was hired the next week. It was 1994 and Silvio Solaras's address had changed. He hadn't.

CHAPTER 34

Numaga moved out of the pullout and continued on toward Iverson's farm. They reached the house and Numaga parked the Camry aside Henry. Max came out from behind the barn and circled the car before settling down on the porch. Iverson noted the dog's calm demeanor, grabbed his satchel and the beer and exited the car. Numaga slung her laptop and purse over separate shoulders, collected the pizza and walked with Iverson to where Max waited.

Despite Max's apparent calm, Iverson inspected the area around the porch. The damp ground around the porch, however, had been trampled by the Bomb Squad so finding evidence of fresh footprints was impossible. He checked the door frame for tampering, found none and unlocked and pushed the door open slowly. He walked into the house but motioned to Numaga to wait on the porch. Max pushed his way past Iverson and ran to the kitchen while his master checked the other rooms. Satisfied the house was safe, Iverson summoned Numaga.

"All seems well," Iverson said. "Come on in."

Numaga walked in and surveyed her partner's ménage. "Early Spartan?" she asked.

"I don't get much company," Iverson explained.

"I can see why," Numaga quipped. Seeing only one chair, she waited for directions.

"Take a seat," Iverson said pointing to the distressed lounger. "I'll find another one."

While Iverson headed down the hall to find additional seating, Numaga sauntered into the kitchen, dropped the pizza onto a counter and inspected Iverson's culinary quarters. The open-faced cupboards were mostly empty and the counters, save for a bag of coffee, the machine that brewed its contents and an antiquated toaster, were barren. She thought about inspecting the refrigerator but decided against it. *Not ready for that, yet.*

Iverson returned with a crosshatched lawn chair from the 1950's. He planted it across from Numaga's assigned seat and joined her in the kitchen.

"Beer?" Iverson asked.

"Absolutely," replied Numaga.

Iverson pried open two bottles of Cascade Lager, handed one to Numaga and took a long pull from the other. "Take a load off in the other room and I'll put the pizza in the oven."

"Are you sure it works?"

"It works," Iverson assured, "unless the propane tank is empty."

Numaga chuckled, headed to the living room and lowered herself into the embrace of the thickly padded recliner. She opened up her laptop and checked her backup e-mail account again. Iverson joined her a few minutes later. "Food in twenty," he announced.

"Great, I'm starving," Numaga said. "Do you have Kill Book I in that pack over there?"

"Yeah. Why?"

"I've received a good number of names from my e-mail query and I want to start comparing Horvat's initials to the names."

Iverson retrieved his satchel, dug into its depths and pulled out Horvat's kill log. He offered it to Numaga who told him to keep it. After she extracted and organized the names and dates from the e-mails, they could cross-compare them to the initials and dates in the Kill Book. She massaged her data silently and announced she was done at the same time the pizza was.

"It appears we have eighteen unsolved homicides in the Sea-Tac area, fifteen in Portland metro, and another ten in the Bay Area."

"That's thirty-eight total homicides," Iverson calculated. "What window of time did you ask for?"

"I used the years you provided . . . 1995 to 2011. That *was* what you told me, right?"

Iverson checked the Kill Book. "Yeah," he confirmed. "That's the year range listed here. But Horvat's log also has fifty-five total entries. We're seventeen short of that."

"We haven't heard from any rural PD's yet," Numaga reasoned. "The three that responded have technological resources and IT personnel. My e-mail was probably forwarded to an IT geek who ran a data search addressing my specific request. The computer spit out the result and it was sent along to me. Probably a fifteen minute piece of work. That's not going to be the case with the rural departments. They might maintain a database, but they won't have personnel dedicated to its maintenance. If we get information from them, it'll be when somebody has the time. My request won't be considered a priority. But that's fine, we have a good start and I'm thrilled to have what we have and to have gotten it this quickly."

"Despite someone's effort at subterfuge," Iverson qualified.

"Yeah," Numaga acknowledged, "but we can work on that problem later."

"A reasonable approach," Iverson agreed. "Did the PD's provide the dates of the homicides with the names of the victims?" Iverson asked.

"All but a few," reported Numaga.

"Great," Iverson said. He sat back in the plaited lawn chair and opened Kill Book I. "Ready when you are, partner."

Iverson and Numaga spent the better part of the next hour comparing information between slices of pizza and swigs of beer. The food quelled their hunger and the data yielded an astonishing thirty matches.

"Wow," exclaimed Numaga. "This is one hell of a coincidence."

Iverson laid Kill Book I on the floor, moaned out of his chair and stretched his aching back. "And I think we have the same theory regarding coincidences, right?"

"I think we've established that, yeah," Numaga agreed.

"So what do you figure the chances are that our thirty have a common thread?"

"I'd say pretty good but we obviously need more information on the thirty."

"Any ideas how best to accomplish that, and by best, I mean quickest?"

Numaga thought about it. "I could go at it two ways. I can e-mail these PD's back and ask them for the case jackets. They'll have them somewhere . . . most likely in a closed but unsolved cases file. But it's not like checking a database. It would require leg work for each department and it would be a while before we got anything."

"A long while," Iverson opined. "Squad detectives aren't going to be overly motivated to help a couple of PI's work a case they couldn't solve. You know how the collar system works."

"I could use my APD position to cajole and coerce," Numaga added. "But even if that proved successful, they'd send the jackets to APD, and right now, I'm not sure we want to do that."

"We don't," Iverson affirmed. "You said you could go at our problem two ways. This one has issues. What's the other one?"

"Public domain. The thirty are from major metro areas."

"And?" Iverson asked impatiently.

"And, Sergeant," Numaga responded curtly, "they have major metro newspapers. Murder stories make news. The Seattle Post Intelligencer, the Oregonian and the San Francisco Chronicle should all have had some coverage on the murders. I'll bet if I Google the names of our thirty, or if I pull up a copy of those newspapers the day after our kill dates, I'll find a report on the crimes and with it, information on the victims."

Iverson retrieved his composure. "I think that's the place to start." He paused before adding, "Sorry about the gruffness."

"Apology accepted, Stan," Numaga responded. "And thanks for offering it. Let's grab another beer and go for a walk. You and Max can show me the back forty before I get back to the Internet."

Chapter 35

Adrian Dulles had never been a happy person. He was the singular offspring born to a woman afflicted with copious ills. Hope Dulles had little hope. What little she'd had, had been beaten out of her by a brutal stepfather and a succession of her own men who shared the same penchant for violence. She'd become pregnant at age fifteen and evicted from her mother's apartment the day her swelling belly forced her to come clean about her condition. She moved to the streets and bartered her body for food and shelter. Adrian was born a few months later in a Portland back alley, attended by no one and swaddled in a blanket mined from a dumpster. Mother and son were found by a garbage collector whose 9-1-1 call landed them in a hospital room. It was the finest accommodation of Adrian Dulles' childhood.

Hope Dulles' life didn't improve after the birth of her son. Foraging for drugs took precedent over finding food and Adrian was frequently left with unfamiliar people in unseemly places. The child welfare system eventually got involved and Adrian was placed with the grandmother who'd abandoned his mother. The husband who'd worked out his anger on Hope was gone but his many proxies weren't much better. But there was a roof over Adrian's head and food on his table. In the eyes of the Child Welfare system, his life was endurable.

Adrian was a small, chunky and unattractive boy. He was an easy target for other kids in his rough eastside neighborhood and he was the brunt of their jokes and their inherent cruelty. When he reached fifteen, he'd had enough. He left his grandmother's household, lied about his age to an overzealous recruiting officer and enlisted in the Army. He was an angry and undisciplined kid, traits that quickly got him into trouble in the regimented lifestyle of the military. Two tours in the brig didn't extinguish his anger and after a third encounter with the MP's at Fort Sill, Kentucky, he was summarily and dishonorably discharged.

Dulles tried his hand at myriad occupations for the next thirty years. He found occasional success but more frequent failure. He spent time as a mechanic, a cook and a logger; jobs that earned him a paycheck but little else. His anger kept him in conflict with both himself and his coworkers. Work usually offers opportunities for friendships. With Dulles, it provided the likelihood of enemies.

Dulles finally caught a break with the onset of Desert Storm, the first U.S.-Iraq engagement. He heard about a company recruiting private soldiers to provide oil field security, followed the lead and talked himself into a job. He was shipped to the Middle East and spent two months guarding a barbed wire fence at a Kuwaiti oil field. It was far from the inspiring work he'd expected but it marked the start of his career as a mercenary.

Dulles eventually learned to temper his violence but the anger always simmered. He always had an edge . . . always sought an advantage. Mercenary work offered him an outlet for his anger and a focus for his frustration. Killing does that.

The years crept forward but the work never got easier. Dulles' temperament precluded advancement and the rigors of mercenary grunt work took their toll. Bad food, bad company and a bad back eventually forced him to consider a more sedentary lifestyle. He'd met a lot of people and one of those contacts put him in touch with some people in Houston; an organization that had a need for someone with Dulles' talents. He flew to Texas and met with the group's leader. They sat at a short table and had a long conversation. Dulles got a new job.

*****

Dulles got ahold of Frantzen at about 5 PM. "Where the hell have you been?" he demanded.

"Rethinking my future," Frantzen replied.

"You can do your thinking on somebody else's time," scolded Dulles. "We've got work to do."

"Not today, we don't," Frantzen argued.

"Really," Dulles admonished. "I didn't see your name on the vacation schedule, Frantzen."

"It's not a vacation. It's retirement."

"We don't retire, Frantzen."

Frantzen considered his response. "Call it what you want, Dulles. But I'm done with these guys."

"Fine," Dulles said, "but you're leaving me in an awful bind here."

"Not my problem."

"It could be."

"Why's that?"

"Houston has expectations."

"Meaning what?"

"Meaning they want this job finished and I've got it set up to happen."

Frantzen paused. "You can handle it alone," he said hesitantly.

"There's two of them and one of me. It'd be better if you were there."

"Not gonna happen," Frantzen insisted. "I'm done."

"Is that how you'd like me to explain it to Houston . . . that you walked out when we had this taken care of?"

Frantzen recognized the threat and the validity behind it. He reconsidered his position. "If you're talking about the two PI's . . ."

"I am," Dulles interrupted.

"Then I need to know your plan," Frantzen finished.

Dulles nodded and smiled on his end of the call. He had Frantzen. He never doubted that he would. "They'll be in Ashton at the old Burlington warehouse tomorrow at 10 AM."

Frantzen replied, "I'll be there."

"You sure?" Dulles asked.

"One last time, Dulles," Frantzen asserted.

"One last time," Dulles confirmed before ending the call. *One very last time,* he said to himself. He reset his phone and called Vitez Jurić.

Chapter 36

Numaga and Iverson walked a path on the west side of Iverson's farm. The trail wended through stands of fir and scattered big leaf maples buttressed by clusters of salal and Oregon grape. The sun's descent behind the foliated landscape created dappled shadows across their route. They stopped by a small creek bed, sat on a couple of andesite boulders and watched the gurgling water slope past them.

"Tell me about your childhood, Stan," Numaga coaxed.

Iverson stared intently at Numaga. "You have a need to get personal, Numaga," he assessed. "Why is that?"

"It's part of being human, Stan," Numaga reasoned. "We have socially inquisitive brains."

"Sometimes, too inquisitive," Iverson countered.

"Are you telling me to back off?"

"I'm telling you my childhood is not on the discussion menu."

"Maybe it should be."

"And you're the topic chef?" Iverson asked sarcastically. His irritation was obvious.

"That would be up to you, Stan," Numaga conceded.

Iverson moved his gaze to the creek. It offered respite, but not escape. He'd buried his past and the feelings that went with it. Numaga wanted to excavate them. "Why exactly do you want to know?" he asked.

"Because we have a similar if not identical history and I know that hiding my history was a mistake. In reality, I was hiding it from myself."

"Meaning?"

"Meaning that for a very long time, I refused to accept what happened to me. I was angry but didn't know why. I didn't trust other people and I didn't really trust myself. I couldn't make sense of it. I had a rough start but I ended up in a good home with good people. I should have been happy but I wasn't. I couldn't figure out why, so I blamed myself."

"And then a miracle happened?" Iverson asked cynically.

"No, Stan," Numaga answered. "There are no miracles. I was so unhappy suicide had become a viable option. I actually had a plan in place. I hoarded some pills; even drafted a few notes. It gave me comfort thinking I was strong enough to end my own life. How sad is that?"

"I don't want to kill myself, Numaga," Iverson disputed. His claim was true. He'd never really considered suicide. But he did understand the concept of being unhappy. His reaction had always been to work longer and harder. It had proven to be a successful formula. So far.

"I'm not saying you do, Stan," clarified Numaga. "And maybe you're the most emotionally healthy human on Planet Earth. But I know something of your past and I'm getting acquainted with your present. I see where you live and I see how you live. I gotta' tell you, Stan, I see some red flags."

"Because I live alone, you think I'm unhappy? That's bullshit, Numaga. Lotsa people live alone." Iverson's irritation had morphed into anger.

"That's true. And many of them are probably happy folks. But I don't know them. I know you. I like you. I'm starting to worry about you."

"That would seem to be your problem."

"It's not a problem, Stan. It's what people who care about people do."

Iverson's anger momentum stalled. He deflected Numaga's affection with a question.

"So what happened to your suicide plan?"

"It got ambushed . . . by me. I had a friend over one day for dinner and she found one of the notes. I have a feeling I subconsciously made it available . . . kind of a last call for help. We took a walk, had a long talk and she convinced me to try counseling. I did. And I kept trying it. I still keep trying it. I didn't want to die, Stan. I needed to figure out why I thought I did."

"So you've spent maybe thirty hours total hanging out with me and have determined that I need counseling. That's some great diagnostic work, Numaga."

"It's not about the hours, Stan. It's about getting a glimpse of how you live and realizing that our lives share a common trauma. Through counseling, I've come to understand how that trauma affects me. I'm simply sharing with you that gaining an understanding of cause and effect has been beneficial to me and suggesting that you consider the possibility that it might be useful to you as well."

Iverson rose up from his rock and headed back to the house. Numaga followed without further comment. They got back to the farm and Numaga buried herself in her laptop. Iverson took his folding chair and a fresh beer out to the porch and watched the sun move toward the horizon. He resurrected Numaga's words, inspected them thoroughly and put them away for future deliberation. Numaga interrupted his reflections an hour later.

"I've got information to share, Stan," Numaga declared. "Wanna' come in and see?"

"If it's a list of psychotherapists, I'm not interested," Iverson responded drolly.

Numaga dissected the comment, decided it had a measure of levity attached to it and moved on.

"No, Stan, no psychotherapists," Numaga replied, "but the short list I've managed to compile involves some other interesting possibilities."

Iverson refolded his chair, tucked it under an arm and joined Numaga in the warmer confines of the living room. He switched on the overhead light and two pole lamps before settling back down. "Okay, Numaga," he said. "What've you got?"

"Of our thirty names, I was able to find newsprint reports on twenty-one. Eight are from Sea-Tac, six from Portland and seven from the Bay Area. Of the twenty one, I found obits for eighteen which provided additional information so I'm using those eighteen as our sample."

Iverson was impressed. "Any common threads?"

"From the obits, it appears the eighteen were well-heeled. Though obits don't provide accounting figures, they do tend to list interests and accomplishments."

"And what were their interests?"

"That's where it starts to get intriguing."

"I'm all ears."

"They were all politically or socially involved. At least that's my first glance conclusion based on what their obits reveal regarding organizational involvement."

"For instance?"

"I haven't broken out the specific numbers yet, but I'm seeing involvement in hot topic issues like gun control, environmental causes and gay rights. It'll take a bit longer to extrapolate more specific data."

Iverson got up and looked over Numaga's shoulder and onto her laptop's screen. She'd created a spreadsheet with column A's cells dedicated to organizational names and the B through F column headings labeled with the eighteen names in the sample. An X had been inserted at all row-column intersections where a name matched up with an organization. Iverson wasn't quite sure what he was looking at, but he was seeing a lot of X's.

"Very impressive, Numaga," Iverson gauged. "But what the hell am I looking at?"

Numaga explained the spreadsheet as best she could. Iverson listened attentively, but was lost as to what the data was portraying.

"Let me plug in some math, Stan," Numaga offered. "That'll help the data make some sense to you and more sense to me."

"Sounds good," Iverson said. He moved his chair closer to Numaga and sat back down.

Numaga reset herself in her chair and went back to work. Iverson watched the cursor scoot around the screen as its master selected various options from a variety of menus and applied them to the data. Numaga inserted a sum function into the spreadsheet, applied it to the appropriate data and, when completed, she had tally numbers for each of the organizations she'd linked to the sample folks. She then separated out specific numbers associated with specific organizational type.

"Better," Numaga told herself out loud.

Iverson untangled himself slowly, sat back and asked, "What have we got?"

"We've got eighteen dead people. If I've got the organizations labeled correctly as to their political or social emphasis, eleven of the victims were involved in gun control efforts, eight in environmental causes and seven involved in gay rights advocacy. Eight of the eighteen were involved in two causes which is why the numbers add up to twenty- six."

Iverson twisted forward again and stared at the spreadsheet. He used his right index finger to trace the data and help him collect its meaning.

"What are you thinking, Stan?" Numaga finally asked.

"I'm thinking we have the most unlikely of coincidences," Iverson judged. "Great work."

"Thanks, Stan," Numaga offered. "What's next?"

" A beer to celebrate and then some sleep. I think you've earned both."

They drank their brews quickly and Numaga packed up her computer, gathered her purse and walked out of the house. She found Max on the porch and stooped to offer a few pets. Max allowed the affection and actually appeared to enjoy it. The two PI's agreed to check in by eight o'clock the following morning and Numaga and her Camry left the farm.

Iverson watched Numaga drive off, returned to the inner sanctum of his ancient house and fell into the chair his partner had vacated. He lifted the footrest, folded his arms behind his head and revisited the characters in his most recent play. His thoughts wended past Gabos Horvat, Jon Farrell and Helen Matkin and continued on to a man named Kant and a woman named Numaga. Numaga's character lingered longest and their conversations spoke loudest. She'd asked questions he'd long avoided asking. Maybe it was time to ask them out loud and maybe Numaga would be the right one to ask. They had strong and undeniable bonds: foster care and police work. Maybe she'd understand. Max liked her. That had to mean something.

CHAPTER 37

The man in Houston had gathered his four sector heads at his high rise office. It was past evenfall but the countless bright lights of Texas' largest city added a sparkled illumination to the otherwise shadowy room. The self-proclaimed "High Five" sat on Le Corbusier leather chairs and faced each other across an oval table made of fine-grained mahogany illegally exported from Belize. They sipped seventeen year old Glengoyne Scotch from Waterford Crystal tumblers and pulled Beluga caviar from a sterling silver platter and placed it on Tang Dynasty porcelain plates. There would have been black suited servers had the conversation not had a need for secrecy.

"What's the news from the Portland?" one of the sector heads asked.

The Houston man replied, "I've taken control given the potential fallout from the problem. I should hear something back from our operatives there by tomorrow morning."

"What's the concern color?" another sector head asked.

"Orange at this point but I'm anticipating that it'll go back to yellow after tomorrow's conversation."

"What exactly is the problem?" inquired another man.

"The main problem right now is a couple of nosy ex-cops who got a sniff of what's going on from a disenchanted tribe member. A Croat."

"And where's the Croat now?"

"He's no longer functioning," the Houston man replied. He didn't offer to explicate.

"Has the tribe lost its effectiveness?"

"I'll know more about that tomorrow."

"And if they have?"

"Then I'll deal with them like I've dealt with other contract tribes that failed us in the Four Sectors. We've been doing this for thirty years now. You know how it works."

"We've also been lucky at times," the West Sector's boss qualified. "I had to use a contact in Soledad Prison last year to eliminate a risk."

"We're still here, aren't we?" assured the Houston man. "As always, our worst enemy will be panic. If we stay focused, things will work out. They always do. We have powerful friends."

"Who will undoubtedly abandon us if we lose containment of this problem," added the West Sector's manager.

The Houston man sent a glare across the table. "Yearly report," he instructed sternly. "Midwest Sector first."

"Steady," relayed the Midwest Sector's boss. "Four terminations. No current problems."

The Houston man nodded and moved on. "West Sector?"

"Three terminations with no problems," the West Sector's supervisor reported. "We have the Portland issue that you're now overseeing but, other than that, we're fine."

"East Sector?"

"One termination. No problems," the East Sector's chief reported. "The new Cuban relationship, however, could produce a problem with the current tribe. If relations really open up, we might have to make some changes."

"Explain," instructed the Houston man.

"Changes in needs create changes in allegiances. Trust might become an issue with the expatriates."

All the men nodded with a unified comprehension.

"South Sector?"

"No terminations," answered South Sector's representative. "All's well. It's the South, remember?"

The High Five all smiled at the obvious. They sipped more Scotch and talked about myriad other things related to keeping their power and growing their money.

Chapter 38

Iverson woke up at his usual six o'clock, stumbled into the kitchen and pressed the brew button on the coffee pot. He took a quick shower, removed the stubble from his face and poured steaming hot coffee into a cup with an image of the Sisyutl spirit. Sisyutl guarded the house of the Pacific Northwest's other native spirits but Iverson had bought the cup from a thrift store for its design rather than its protective powers. He'd always been enamored with dragons and the serpents on the mug were a close, if not an exact, approximation.

Iverson lowered himself into the chair in the living room, took a few sips of his morning brew and turned on his phone. He had two messages. The first was sent at 10 PM the previous night and was from Helen Matkin. Gabos Horvat had regained consciousness briefly before falling back into a deep sleep. Matkin considered it a good sign. The second message was curious. It read: *Meet me at the old Burlington Warehouse in the Rail District – 10 AM today.* It was sent while Iverson was in the shower and was signed, *Frantzen.*

Iverson switched to call to mode and pressed the contacts icon before tapping Numaga's name. She answered after one ring.

"Good morning, Stan," she greeted enthusiastically.

Iverson wondered how she could be so cheerful this early in the day but didn't ask. He had another question. "Had your coffee yet?"

"It's brewing."

"Pull the plug," Iverson said abruptly. "I'll pick you up in twenty. We can get yuppie coffee."

"I'll meet you at the Coffee Hut. That'll get us to the yuppie brands quicker and then we can take my car to wherever it is that we're going."

"We should take Henry today," Iverson argued. "We used your vehicle yesterday."

"And we'll use it again today," Numaga countered. "Nothing personal against Henry, but he's not my type."

Iverson considered mounting a defense but the reality was, Numaga was right. Her Camry was better suited for two people and he had to admit he enjoyed being a passenger. "Okay," he said. "See you in ten."

*****

The Coffee Hut was already busy by the time Numaga got there. Ashton's working population was in need of a jump start and caffeine was the legal and time honored way to get it. Numaga got in line and eyed the breakfast morsels sitting on plates under a domed glass enclosure. An array of berry filled croissants offered a tasty breakfast along with the sugar hit to double-down the caffeine in the coffee. There was a thick slice of banana-nut bread sitting astride a similar sized slice of the cranberry-orange variety. A few brownies topped with almond slices and a few jelly filled donuts were also available, but it was the one remaining chocolate croissant that Numaga was hoping lasted until her turn at the counter. Chocolate caffeine merged with coffee caffeine. *Can't get much better.*

Numaga made it to the counter with her choice still available. She ordered a sixteen ounce latte and pointed at the croissant. She asked the clerk to heat it up for twelve seconds only, paid her tab and moved down the counter to await her breakfast. Iverson walked through the door as she waited.

"Good morning again, Stan," Numaga greeted.

"Ditto, Numaga," Iverson parried. He had not yet allowed himself to work Numaga's first name. The name being called by the barista.

Numaga gathered her breakfast and surveyed the room for a place to sit. She spotted a couple getting ready to vacate a corner table and motioned to Iverson that she was headed that way. Iverson got in line and watched as Numaga settled in. His approach to breakfast was simpler. He'd get his Americano from the large thermos on the counter and take whatever was left in the food case. He wasn't gastronomically attached to any particular food item. Food was mostly a necessity though sometimes a tasty one. He collected his coffee and a chunk of the banana-nut bread and joined Numaga.

"So where are we off to this morning?" she asked her partner.

"Horvat woke up . . . briefly, so I thought we'd run by Doc Matkin's place first and get an update."

"If that's first, what's second?" Numaga inquired.

"That's where it might get interesting."

"Interesting how?"

"I had a text from Frantzen telling me to meet him in the Rail District at 10 AM."

"Frantzen?" Numaga questioned. "What the hell does he want?"

"Good question. I've got a few more."

"I'm listening."

"I'm not sure the text came from Frantzen since there was no ID on the message. Frantzen may or may not be in the habit of using burners, but whoever sent it most likely is. If it was Frantzen, I don't know why he didn't call instead of texting. It would seem a better way to assure I got the message."

"Did you attempt to reply to the text?"

"I did. It was non-deliverable."

"Curiouser and curiouser."

"Back to Wonderland, Numaga?"

"Seems appropriate, doesn't it?"

"More so, every day."

"The Rail District covers a lot of acreage, Stan," Numaga assessed. "Where exactly are we supposed to meet Mr. Frantzen?"

Iverson bit off a large chunk of his bread and took a sip of coffee. "The Burlington Warehouse," he answered between chews.

"It's been abandoned for years, Stan."

"Yeah, I know," Iverson acknowledged. "Burlington-Northern walked out of there in the 70's if I remember correctly. They still own it but refuse to raze it so it's become a haven for transient layovers and drug deals. Ashton's zoning department has been trying to get it condemned for years but the railroads apparently still hold sway with local governments."

"It's a perfect place for a trap, Stan."

"And we'll approach it with that in mind, won't we?"

"As always."

The two finished the solid portions of their breakfast and carried the remains of the liquid part out to Numaga's Camry. Iverson provided Numaga general directions to Helen Matkin's house and they pulled out into traffic. They arrived at the Doctor's home ten minutes later. Iverson led the way up onto the front portico and pushed the center of a bright yellow daisy that rang the bell announcing their arrival. Doc Matkin opened the door a few seconds later.

"Well, it's Judge Iverson," Matkin exclaimed.

Numaga looked quizzically at Iverson. "Long story," he muttered.

"Can't wait to hear it," Numaga deadpanned.

Matkin waved her two guests into the house and Iverson made introductions for the two women. Formalities concluded, they discussed Gabos Horvat.

"How's he doing?" asked Iverson.

"Mostly unconscious but with intervals of wakefulness. The intervals are increasing in both frequency and duration, so I'm hoping that's a positive sign."

"Did you get any test results back?"

"No blood test results yet but I did get the x-rays and it's better than I'd expected. There's a lot of bruising and a few busted ribs, but there's no evidence of internal bleeding. He's a lucky man."

"I'm not sure he'd look at it that way."

"I'll make sure to explain it to him," Matkin offered.

"It's more than his current condition, Doc," Iverson explained. "You should probably know that when I first met your patient, he asked me to kill him."

Matkin stared intently at Iverson. "He asked you to kill him? Can you possibly shed a bit more light on that?"

"I was sitting in a bar, minding my own business, when I get a note from the only other customer in the place. Our man Horvat had sent it via the bartender and the note contained an offer. $50,000 to end his life."

Matkin looked at Iverson over the top of her wire rimmed glasses. "This sort of thing happen to you often, Judge?"

"First time, actually."

"Did you accept the offer?"

"No."

"Not enough money?"

Iverson was insulted but the insult was buffered with Matkin's smile. Iverson played the game.

"I was holding out for a hundred," he continued, "but we never made it to the negotiation stage."

Numaga watched the conversation carefully. Her partner was showing a playful side. It looked good on him.

"So this is where the shotguns became part of the story, right?" suggested Matkin.

"That would be correct, Doctor. The shotguns, the questionable actions and claims by VCH and more than a few other strange events that led to Horvat's present condition and our presence in your home."

Matkin asked, "Any idea why he'd want to end his life?"

"Numaga and I are working on that. We're hoping Horvat wakes up and adds some usable information to our cause."

"Did he tell you anything other than that he wanted to die?"

"He left a few leads, but most of them have led to dead ends," Iverson explained. Numaga noted both the irony and the deficiency of information in Iverson's response. He was protecting her. The less Matkin knew, the less she could be found guilty of covering up.

"Not much information there," Matkin lamented.

Iverson changed the subject. "We've got a fairly pressing appointment, Doc. Is there anything we can help you with here before we go?"

"Unless you're proficient with miracles, no. I'll text or call if things change with Horvat."

"Thanks, Doc. You are doing me one helluva favor."

"Always smart to be in the good graces of the judiciary," Matkin jested. She smiled slyly, turned and waved a backwards good-bye as she walked towards her mini emergency room. Iverson and Numaga left the house and returned to the Camry.

"Okay," Numaga said. "I need to know what the Judge Iverson thing is about."

"Long story," repeated Iverson.

"You said that," Numaga argued. "We have some time."

Numaga pulled away from Doc Matkin's home and headed to the Rail District. Iverson grudgingly recounted his previous meeting with the Doctor and how he came to be a judge. Numaga found the story both funny and revealing.

"I think the good doctor has you pegged, Stan."

"Meaning what?"

"Meaning she's perceptive and you're transparent."

Iverson decided against pursuing further insight regarding Numaga's assessment. He was still wondering about some of their other conversations. Besides, he figured, they had more pressing concerns.

Numaga drove slowly to their destination. She wanted time to think about the Rail District layout and to let the caffeine settle down. They passed Ashton's outer boundary and she took the old service road that paralleled the ribbons of iron tracks that led into and out of the city. They passed through the industrial area with its sheet metal buildings that housed machinists, welders, fabricators and an array of other vocations that provided products essential to modern cities. Their dreadful din, offensive odors and pernicious pollutants were not allowed within the city's limits. They were necessary outcasts.

Numaga continued past the cacophony of commerce and followed the iron trail into a green area set aside for the neighborhoods that delivered the labor to the sheet metal industries. A green meadow gift to the blue collar workers. The park's deep-green grass was fertilized and trimmed by large migrations of geese. A large gaggle honked their displeasure when Numaga pulled onto a graveled pullout a few yards from where they were feeding. A chattering of starlings lined the telephone wires above the Camry threatening to deposit little white bundles on its shiny black surface.

"I hate those little black devils," Numaga complained.

"Blame Shakespeare," Iverson said.

"Why would I blame Shakespeare?" queried Numaga.

"Because back in the late 1800's, an idiot named Eugene Schieffelin decided it was a great idea to introduce every bird mentioned in the Great Bard's plays to America. He mentioned a starling only once, in Henry IV, but it was once too many. The starling's importation has been an unmitigated disaster . . . particularly for farmers and, of course, for car owners.

"Amazing," Numaga invoked.

"I know," Iverson concurred. "Humans have a nasty habit of acting before they think."

"That's not what I'm referring to, Stan," Numaga explained.

"Then what *are* you referring to?"

"That you knew about Shakespeare and the starlings."

"Why would that surprise you, Numaga?"

"It just did," Numaga said. "But don't worry, Stan. It's a good kind of surprise. What's say we discuss our plan for the warehouse before we get there."

Iverson bit his lip and nodded his agreement. He opened the passenger's side door and swiveled his body to face out toward the area the geese had vacated. "Mind if I smoke?" he asked as he placed a cigarette between his lips.

Numaga considered the request and decided partnerships sometimes require compromise. "I mind that you smoke on general principle," she answered, "but I don't mind if you smoke right now if you keep the carcinogens to yourself."

Iverson touched a flame to his Camel, took a deep drag and blew an explosion of smoke forcefully away from the Camry's interior. "It's been a while since I've actually been in the Burlington Warehouse but I can't imagine it's been upgraded."

"I was part of an APD bust of some wannabe drug kingpins there a couple months back and it was still the same neglected fire hazard it was when you carried a badge."

"Anything different on the perimeter?"

"No. There's still a large, paved parking area encircling the main building and a few small storage buildings scattered about near the rails. The lot has more ruts and the building more rats, but that's probably the only change."

"Except for what awaits inside," Iverson added.

Numaga checked her watch. "If the meeting with Frantzen is set for ten and it's only eight-thirty now, there shouldn't be anyone waiting."

"And you're counting on that, Numaga?" Iverson questioned.

Numaga hesitated briefly. "I guess not," she answered. "If our meeting with Frantzen follows the pattern so far, I'll expect the unexpected."

Iverson pivoted back into the Camry. Numaga restarted its engine and they headed to the warehouse.

*****

The Burlington Warehouse sat on a ten acre parcel of land. Rail tracks bordered the northern edge of the building and one track spurred into and out of the building itself. The Burlington-Northern Railroad had constructed the warehouse in the late 1920's to shelter shipments of perishable products as they awaited the freight cars that would distribute them around the country. Washington apples and Oregon pears found their way to tables in Denver, Chicago and New York. The warehouse operations ceased when cheaper and better methods were found to ship the fresh fruit and vegetables. The rail district remained active in the shipment of lumber, but the downturn in forest farming affected the volume. The tracks that remained were occasionally burnished by iron wheels, but mostly they served as a graveyard for cars at the end of their line.

Numaga pulled off the service road and turned the Camry onto the graveled area adjacent a double set of tracks. She slowly drove along a string of stationary, rusting railcars that bore the multi-colored tags of graffiti artists. A number of the cars had open doors and no doubt served as overnight accommodations for some of Ashton's homeless population. A few of them scattered as the Camry approached.

Numaga continued on. She and Iverson continually scanned the area as they approached the warehouse. They didn't speak until Iverson pointed at something behind one of the railcars. "There," he said.

Numaga braked the Camry and followed Iverson's extended finger. A dark sedan was parked behind a rusty railcar with the remnants of Burlington-Northern inscribed on the side.

"That's Dulles car," Iverson said.

"I thought you said we were meeting Frantzen?"

"I did," Iverson answered. "The text was signed Frantzen but maybe they both came."

"But why park over here? And why are they early?"

"Good questions," gauged Iverson.

Iverson studied the warehouse and the surrounding area. A fifty yard swath of open space surrounded the building on all sides. There was no way to approach it unseen. The warehouse had two floors and multi-paned windows interspersed the lower level and encircled the top one. If anybody was inside, they had a good view. They already knew they had visitors.

Frantzen had been an FBI agent and Dulles most likely had similar training. They'd understand strategic positioning. They'd be proficient with their weapons. If their intent was to kill Iverson and Numaga, they only had to wait for their guests to get stupid. They'd be ducks on a pond if they approached on foot. Dead ducks. Iverson didn't like it. "This looks like a bad idea," he said.

Numaga had been doing her own assessment. "So you're not thinking surprise party, then?"

Iverson relaxed. Numaga's humor wasn't only good, it was useful. "Uh, no," he managed. "Got any suggestions?"

"Trust in the buha."

"Buha?"

"Damn, you've forgotten already," Numaga admonished. "Very discouraging, Stan."

Iverson pushed a pout from his lips and taxed his memory. *Buha, what the hell is buha*? "Buha is power for your tribe," he finally announced proudly.

"Good job, Stan. There may be hope for you."

Iverson continued. "So you want me to trust in the power. Sounds very Yodaesque."

"I want us to think this through. It's either that or go get some more coffee."

"I'm all ears, Numaga."

"Okay," Numaga started. "I'm sure you've eliminated the walk up and get shot by a sniper plan, right?"

"Definitely."

"So how about I drive up to that set of double doors over there and park the Camry tight to the building. That should eliminate the sniper aspect and maybe get us in a door that isn't covered."

Iverson considered the plan. "And if the door's padlocked?"

"When I was here for the bust, the doors were open. No locks anywhere. Burlington-Northern apparently has no interest in spending the money to keep people out. They know people will find a way in if they want to."

Iverson digested Numaga's plan. "Got a plan B?" he asked.

"It's still percolating."

"Okay," Iverson said. "Let's go with Plan A. Any recollection as to what's behind the double doors?"

"Thirty feet of open space with piles of clutter and a row of partitioned offices beyond that. If I was the only bad guy in there, I'd station myself in one of those offices. If we're dealing with *both* Dulles and Frantzen, there's probably one on each floor."

Iverson said, "They'll know our access point by where we put the Camry."

"They'll guess the obvious."

"Did Plan B finish brewing?" queried Iverson.

"It did," Numaga affirmed. "There's varied access on all sides. Some easy, some not. Doors and busted out windows. I'll park the Camry by the double doors, but instead of making our entrance there, we split up like we did at the grange, straddle the sides of the building under the eaves and enter simultaneously from opposite points."

"Timing?"

"We don't move in until we text agree that we're both ready."

"Let's do it," Iverson said confidently.

They silenced their phones and synchronized their phone clocks before Numaga put the Camry in gear. She covered the ground to the warehouse and parked as close to the building as she could. She and Iverson slithered out the passenger's side and hugged the sheet metal siding. They drew their weapons, nodded to each other and moved cautiously in opposite directions.

Iverson worked his way around to the north side of the building, found a door cracked slightly open and held his ground. He texted Numaga: *set on north. e z access. ready when u r.* Numaga responded sixty seconds later: *set on south. go on 8:55 xactly.* Iverson texted back: *ok.* He stared at his phone. It read 8:54. When the four became five, he opened the door and stepped into the warehouse. Numaga did the same.

CHAPTER 39

Kralj Kovačić made a decision. It was time to go. He'd already cleaned out the house he'd rented in Portland and he was now in Ashton looking for his vitezovi. The house had been his home for fifteen years but the furnishings he left behind would not be missed. Neither would the people he never took the time to know. He didn't say goodbye to the neighbors because he'd never said hello. He'd never spoken to any of them. He didn't know their names and had no clue if they had children or pets. He never allowed himself to get close to people or attached to places. His past had taught him that everything in life was transient. Nothing lasts. Don't invest time in the hope that it will. Hope was for fools.

Kovačić tried but failed to get in touch with his vitezovi. They weren't at the Ashton house and they didn't answer his calls. He figured they were either dead or afraid. Or maybe they'd simply concluded they didn't want to work for Horvat's successor. They had, after all, been allied with Horvat back in the homeland and maybe they felt more loyalty to the traitor than they did to him. If that was the case, they could all rot in hell. He would not rest his fate on the misplaced allegiance of underlings. He had no idea that Vitez Jurić and Vitez Marić had simply silenced their phones.

Kovačić had one more task to complete before he headed to the Ashton airport and the flight that would take him back to Croatia. It was a personal task for personal reasons. Something he had to do. A score to settle. A wrong to make right. He picked up his phone and tapped the name of a contact.

"It's Kovačić," he announced to the man answering his call.

"I told you not to call me at work," the man said peevishly.

"You've told me many things," Kovačić replied. "Most of it rubbish."

"What do you want, Kovačić?"

"We need to talk."

"I'm busy."

"Get unbusy."

"What's your problem, Kovačić?"

"It'll be your problem if you don't meet me in thirty minutes at the garage."

"That sounds like a threat," the man jeered.

"That's because it is, asshole." Kovačić tapped the end icon on his phone and headed to a downtown parking garage. He knew the man would show.

*****

Kovačić backed his car into a slot at the east end of the garage. He got out, propped up his muscular body with the vehicle's hood and waited for his contact. He showed up ten minutes later.

Lieutenant Silvio Solaras drove up to Kralj Kovačić and opened the passenger side window. The Croatian eyeballed the vehicle's interior. Satisfied the Lieutenant was alone, Kovačić leaned into the open window. "Follow me," he ordered Solaras.

"Why would I do that?" Solaras asked gruffly.

"Because you're a greedy bastard," Kovačić replied. He turned his back on Solaras and got back in his vehicle.

Kovačić drove out of the parking garage and Solaras followed. They navigated a series of back city streets to an old cemetery in the hills above the university where they parked in the bulky shadows of garryana oaks. Kovačić got out of his car and moved to the back seat of Solaras's vehicle.

"All right, Kovačić," Solaras demanded, "what the hell is this about?"

"It's about honor, Solaras," the Kralj answered, "and you don't have any. You disrespect me and my countrymen. You disrespect our ability to survive. Simply put, Lieutenant Solaras, you need to be exterminated."

"Full of bullshit, as always, Kovačić," Solaras ranted. "You Croats are a piece of work . . . a piece of shit work. Get the fuck out of my car."

Kovačić pulled a Glock 17 with a silencer out from under his jacket and fired one close range round into Solaras's brain. He casually wiped the weapon clean, clasped his victim's hand around its grip, and fired one more round though the driver's side open window. Lastly, he dropped the unregistered Glock on the bench next to Solaras's blood stained lap before taking a last look at the man he despised. "Fucking asshole," he said. His last task completed, he returned to his car and headed home. *All the way* home.

Chapter 40

Police work is testosterone driven and Francis Frantzen pursued it to prove he possessed his share. He'd struggled with gender identity for as long as he could remember and law enforcement seemed like the perfect vocation to prove his manhood to himself and any others who might question it. It didn't work out that way.

Frantzen began his cop career with the New Mexico State Police after completing Big Hat training in Albuquerque. He was assigned to an office in Taos but spent the bulk of his time in a four-by-four cruiser plying rutted out roads in washed out canyons. The crimes were mostly petty, the criminals frequently ghosts. In rural New Mexico, visions outnumber victims.

After eight years of tedium, Frantzen secured a position in Santa Fe as a detective. America's oldest capitol city is divided into two cultural camps: rich white people and poor brown people. Frantzen's work frequently fixed on the friction in the space between them. He settled into the job but remained troubled in his life. His identity eluded him and he avoided serious efforts to find it. He might not like what he found.

Frantzen eventually decided that New Mexico was not where he should be. He was born there, but he didn't belong there. Machismo oozes in all police departments, but in the Old West, the viscosity is thicker. A culture of guns, trucks and horses does something to men; something good and something bad. It offers fellowship but it also breeds intolerance. Frantzen, a man afflicted with an uncertain self, feared both.

Frantzen left Santa Fe for a low-level job at the FBI branch office in Portland, Oregon. He hoped the liberal leanings of a large Northwest city would be a better fit for who he thought he might be. He worked the job but never fit in and never advanced. The Northwest had machismo too. Lots of it. His frustration grew; both professionally and sexually. He recused himself from a personal life and adopted a hands-off persona at work. The approach got him labeled as uncooperative and dim-witted. He looked elsewhere for a place to belong.

In 2008, Frantzen met Adrian Dulles at a bar in Portland's east side. They discussed the vagaries of life and the complex notion of fairness. Dulles had a proposition and Frantzen was willing to listen. Dulles was practical; the job doable. He mulled the idea and made a decision. He resigned his position from the FBI.

Frantzen slid into the new job effortlessly. It was easy work if you didn't talk to your conscience. He maintained his dumbed down façade because he'd grown comfortable with the benefits it provided. Less expectation. Less interaction. Less rejection. Francis Frantzen didn't have to explain himself to anyone anymore. He didn't have to explain the person he didn't really know.

CHAPTER 41

Numaga was right. Iverson's entrance into the warehouse had him planted on the edge of a large open area pocked with puddles fashioned by a leaky roof and landscaped with the remnant debris of the building's past. Islands of pallets dotted a gray cement sea and the rusting remains of machinery stippled the spaces between them. Piles of plaited metal strappings had created a rodent township and their musty odors hung thick in the air. A rusty, charred oil drum anchored the center of the space and was surrounded by blue milk crates and broken pallet shards. A warm respite from a cold, hard life.

Iverson quickly realized he was an easy target for anyone hunting humans. He shuffled left and swung his Colt from side to side, searching for a threat. He saw Numaga on the other side of the room. She was doing the same thing. His busy eyes eventually fixed on a man sitting in a metal chair in front of one of the hollowed out offices. Frantzen! He moved his inspection to the right and saw another man sitting on the floor next to Frantzen. His arms were stretched out behind him and he was manacled to one of the many stanchions that supported the building's upper level. His head was bent forward towards his chest. Dulles!

Iverson looked over at Numaga. She nodded toward the two men and then gestured her intent to scale the stairwell next to her entry point and see what lurked on the second level. Iverson held up his hand, backed himself into a position offering a panoramic view of the front end of the second floor and then gave her a thumbs-up. He then turned his attention to Frantzen.

"Show me your hands," Iverson commanded. Frantzen immediately complied.

Numaga ascended the stairs. Iverson kept the Colt trained on Frantzen and moved his vision between him and Numaga's destination. He cocked his ears and listened for sounds indicating she'd encountered trouble. A few minutes later she leaned over the upper level's rusty metal railing. "Clear up here," she reported.

Iverson moved toward Frantzen. "Is it just you and Dulles?" he asked sternly.

"That's it," Frantzen replied.

Iverson continued his approach and Numaga descended the stairs and covered her partner's back. Iverson reached Frantzen and the shackled Dulles and circled them cautiously. Numaga backed her way over to the three men and acquired her own take on the situation. "You were right, Stan. It's not a surprise party."

Iverson broke a half-smile but kept his attention on Frantzen and Dulles. "Where're the sidearms?" he demanded.

"Mine's under my jacket and I tossed Dulles' over there." Frantzen answered. He nodded toward a far corner of the room. Numaga spotted the weapon, walked over to it and tucked the Smith and Wesson M&P into the small of her back. Iverson stepped behind Frantzen, reached over his left shoulder and under his jacket and a pulled Beretta 92 from its holster. He pushed it under his belt buckle. He checked both men for secondary weapons and found a small .22 caliber pistol harnessed to Dulles' left ankle. Frantzen didn't have a back-up. The two PI's stepped back from the situation and took a deep breath. Dulles didn't stir. Whoever took his consciousness, took it all. Frantzen waited silently for someone else to initiate the dialogue. Iverson accommodated him. "Start talking," he told Frantzen.

"Start where?"

"You can begin with the text," Iverson answered. "Did you send it?"

"What text?" asked Frantzen. His perplexed look answered Iverson's question.

"If you didn't send me the text, why are you here?"

"Dulles set it up," Frantzen explained. "What'd the text say?"

"To meet you here," Iverson said. "*Just you.*"

Frantzen considered the message. "I guess I was the bait," he surmised.

Iverson looked at Numaga. They were thinking the same thing.

"Why you?" Iverson asked Frantzen.

"Because they think I'm stupid," Frantzen reasoned. "They're wrong."

Numaga asked, "If you were the bait, who was the catch?"

"I'd assumed it was only me," Frantzen described. "But now that you're here, I'll have to alter that assumption to include the two of you."

"Why us?" Numaga asked.

"You've become a problem," Frantzen answered. "Dulles and I are supposed to solve problems."

"It appears your partnership went south,' Numaga assessed. "Care to explain why your buddy's counting sheep while handcuffed to a pole?"

Dulles stirred as Frantzen worked up an answer.

"When he called me about meeting you here, I told him I wasn't interested; that I was done with this work. He leveled a not-so-subtle threat about the folks in Houston and how my life wouldn't be worth a plug nickel if I walked away. I knew he was right, but I also suspected that the order to dispose of me had most likely already been given; that this warehouse meeting was only about filling that order. I didn't expect to see the two of you."

"That doesn't explain Sleepy's current position," Numaga insisted.

"Like I said, they think I'm stupid. I got here early, before when I figured Dulles would arrive. I watched, waited and thumped him when he came through the door. I considered using a bullet but decided things might work out better if I gave him a chance to sing. I knew Dulles would give up Houston to save his own skin and when he did, there'd be some panic in Texas. I'd have some leverage. I thought he was lying when he told me you'd be here so I planned on letting you know that *he* was. My present to the two of you; wrapped up and ready to talk. But then you actually showed up so I sat down and made myself comfortable. And here we all are. An odd bit of irony, isn't it? I guess the next move is yours."

"Tell us more about Houston," Iverson instructed.

Dulles moaned from the floor and grabbed everybody's attention. He opened his eyes and rolled his head back. Frantzen had hit him hard enough to leave a grapefruit sized contusion on the left side of his head. He was wobbly, blurry eyed and pissed off.

"Frantzen, you fuck," he squawked.

Frantzen gave him a quick look and then reset his gaze on the door behind Iverson. Two men had entered unnoticed and they both had their weapons trained on the two PI's.

"Guns on the floor," ordered the taller of the two men.

Iverson and Numaga looked at each other. Iverson's gun hung at his side and Numaga had holstered her weapon. Numaga nodded and Iverson dropped the Colt. She slowly opened her jacket flap, removed her Sig Sauer from its holster with her thumb and her forefinger, and dropped it on the floor. Iverson remembered she carried a back-up on her right ankle and hoped she still had it. The intruders eliminated that hope.

"Back-ups," demanded the shorter man.

"No back-ups," Numaga claimed.

Vitez Marić fired a round into Dulles' chest. The ex-mercenary's eyes filed with shock for an instant, then closed for the last time.

"Back-ups," the short man commanded again. His expression showed no emotion.

Numaga lifted her pant leg, ripped open the velcroed harness that secured the .22 caliber and its holster, and dropped it to the floor. She hitched up her other pant leg to show she carried no other guns. Iverson followed suit and revealed only white, skinny legs.

"The one in your belt," said Marić while glaring at Iverson.

Iverson pulled Frantzen's gun from under his belt buckle and dropped it on the floor.

"Back up slowly," instructed Marić. He waved his gun in the direction he wanted Iverson and Numaga to go. The two PI's did as they were told and the two Croatians approached Frantzen.

"Get up," Jurić ordered Frantzen.

Frantzen complied and Jurić patted him down. He found no weapons and told him to sit down again.

"Dulles call you?" Frantzen inquired.

"Dulles lacked balls," Marić answered harshly. "He wanted you dead but needed us to do it. He deserved what he got."

"What about them?" Frantzen asked and nodded toward Iverson and Numaga.

Marić laughed wickedly. "We've been hunting them for a while. The hunt ends here."

"*You* sent me the text," Iverson reckoned.

"I did," Marić admitted proudly, "And now we're all here. A good day . . . for some of us."

"We're on the same side," Frantzen said.

"Are you Croatian?" asked Marić.

"No," answered Frantzen.

"Then you are not on our side."

Frantzen took a deep breath and considered his options. "Am I on your list?" he asked.

"What list?"

"The list you get from your Kralj."

Marić and Jurić looked at each other quizzically. "We have no list." Jurić said.

"But you have orders," Frantzen reasoned. "If I'm not part of the orders, the Kralj will be unhappy. A vitez always pays the price for his unhappiness."

"Dulles wasn't ordered," Jurić argued.

"But Dulles was a coward. You said so yourself. The Kralj will be happy he's dead."

The vitezovi backed away to discuss Frantzen's logic. Iverson gave his partner a subtle nod of his head and Numaga moved her hand to the gun parked on her back. She fingered the weapon to make certain the safety was off and then grasped the grip firmly in her hand. Then waited. Timing is everything. The vitez's increasingly heated discussion provided the opportunity. When Marić raised his arms in exasperation, his weapon rose with it. Numaga saw the opening and whipped Dulles' Smith and Wesson around her torso and pointed it at the two men. When they turned toward her and leveled their guns back in her direction, she fired two quick shots. One hit Marić square in the chest, the other hit Jurić in the right shoulder. They both went down to the concrete floor. Iverson retrieved his Colt took a bead on the intruders and walked with Numaga to the two Croatians. Iverson stood above them while Numaga cleared their weapons. Jurić lay writhing in pain but made no sound. Numaga checked two pulse points on Marić, looked at Iverson and shook her head. They looked back for Frantzen. He was gone.

CHAPTER 42

"You okay?" Iverson asked Numaga.

"I'm unhurt," Numaga replied meekly. She was describing her body, not her spirit. The body count was climbing. Never a good thing. But it was made worse for Numaga because she'd now put two on the list herself. It's rare that cops fire their weapons. It's even more uncommon to have it result in a death. Numaga had been forced to kill Kant and now she'd killed Marić. Both were necessary shootings . . . lives taken to save lives. But despite the legitimate rationale, the deaths would linger in her psyche. Ending a life stole something from you.

"Never easy, is it?" Iverson comforted.

"Never should be," Numaga reflected.

Iverson understood completely. He knew there was nothing he could say to lessen the impact so he worked the scene while Numaga regrouped. Iverson moved the Croatian's weapons to a safe place, being careful not to leave his prints on them. He located a suitable length of electrical cable amid the floor's rubble and ordered the still mute Jurić to a post next to Dulles. He hobbled the Croatian's feet, secured both his arms and his legs to the stanchion with multiple wraps of the wire and checked the hole Numaga's bullet had left in his shoulder. The round had cleared and the bleeding had ebbed to a trickle. Jurić was in pain, but not in danger of dying.

"Tell be about the Kralj," Iverson prodded. The Croatian spat in his face. Iverson wiped the spittle from his cheek and tried again.

"Who's in Houston?" he asked sternly. Jurić tightened his lips and fixed his gaze on the ceiling. He wasn't coughing up information and there was nowhere to stash him for a later interrogation. Iverson abandoned the effort. He took Jurić's phone and walked back to Numaga.

"We need to go," Iverson announced.

"I know," Numaga replied. "I'm ready."

They returned to the Camry and Iverson made a 9-1-1 call with Jurić's phone and then tossed it as they pulled away from the warehouse. He then returned to the business at hand.

"What do you suppose a kralj or a vitez is, Numaga?" Iverson asked. "Kant used the term vitez as well, but I assumed it was somebody's name."

"I believe I left my Croatian dictionary at home, Stan," replied Numaga.

Iverson was happy to have her sarcasm back.

"On the English side," Numaga added, "what about Houston? Frantzen was as worried about Houston as much as the two Croatians were worried about this Kralj character."

"So we have two new leads we know nothing about," Iverson lamented. "Better than no leads, I guess."

Numaga pulled over to the side of the road. "You drive," she told her partner. "I'll fire up the laptop and do some research."

"And where would you like me to drive to, Detective Numaga?"

"Somewhere quiet where I can get Wi-Fi," Numaga instructed. "No traffic, no people, and most of all, no guns."

They traded positions in the Camry and Iverson shifted into gear while Numaga powered up her computer. Iverson had no clue regarding Wi-Fi hotspots, but he figured altitude would be a plus. He followed the tracks back into Ashton and turned uphill past the old granary that the railroad had serviced in years past. The serpentine road took them through a narrow corridor of lanceolate cedar boughs to the summit of Jasper Butte. The sylvan peak was a favorite spot for adolescents working on romantic refinements, but Iverson figured noon would be too early for its unskilled practitioners.

The lot was empty and Iverson parked between two jagged and weedy fault lines in the pavement. He got out of the car, walked over to the three-foot cement safety barrier and lit up a Camel. Numaga stayed in the Camry and searched for a connection to the Internet.

Iverson calmed his nerves with the cigarette and took in the view of his city. The morning's early cloud cover had relinquished its grip to a few scattered patches of blue and the sun was playing peek-a-boo high in the sky. An unsteady breeze worked its way through a copse of firs and carried their procreant pollen to the city below. Ashton's asthmatics had a love-hate relationship with trees.

Spring in Oregon is always unpredictable. Often volatile. Rain is a given. But in spring, the liquid can be frozen and leave dents on your car. Thunder and lightning make sporadic appearances and often arrive with take-shelter winds. Oregon's forests were thinned mostly by loggers, but Mother Nature had not been averse to periodic clearcutting.

Iverson paced along the wall and tried to make sense of the past few days. Horvat, Kant, Dulles and Frantzen were dots. How were they connected? Two of the dots were dead. Add in the Tremaines and the total was five. It could easily have been larger. And what of the names on Numaga's spreadsheet? And the initials in Horvat's Kill Books? This was a tremendously deadly enterprise. Who was running this lethal operation? And why? Iverson was hoping Numaga was finding some clues. She summoned him ten minutes later.

"Clear your brain, Stan," Numaga suggested. "I've got a lot to share."

"You've discovered what kralj means?

"Yeah, and much more," Numaga relayed.

"Ready when you are," Iverson advised.

"Let's start with Lieutenant Solaras."

"Not what I would have expected, but, sure, go ahead."

"I had a text from the Lieutenant to come in to the station. He mentioned Notch, so I figured somebody at APD had a conversation with the old woman at the store."

"We anticipated that," Iverson said.

"Yeah, we did. But not the next item. I called Solaras to set up a time but the switchboard routed me to Captain Stroud instead. He told me Solaras was dead. He was found at the Masonic Cemetery by a groundskeeper a couple of hours ago. Prelims say it's either a suicide or a staged one."

"Think there's a connection?" asked Iverson.

"Definitely," Numaga replied. "There are no coincidences, remember?"

"What else?" Iverson prompted.

"Do you play chess, Stan?" asked Numaga.

"Occasionally. Why? Are we moving on to board games?"

"The online translator informs me that kralj and vitez equate to king and knight in English. Sounds to me like an adapted, military style hierarchy."

"But why chess?" Iverson asked. "Do Croatians play chess?"

"By the Numbers, an online trivia bank, lists chess as the number one board game played in the Balkans."

"The Balkans?" Iverson questioned.

"The countries on the Balkan peninsula," Numaga explained. "Albania, Croatia, Kosovo, Serbia, Slovenia and a few others I can't remember. I found another reference to a band of sixteenth century Croatian guerrilla fighters called the Uskok that fought the Ottomans. They likened their warfare tactics to the game of chess."

Iverson considered the new information and applied it to the characters they knew.

"So if the two Croatians at the warehouse were knights," Iverson reasoned, "who might the king be?

"And where?" added Numaga.

They added the new knowledge to the old, attached labels to the characters they knew and looked at what they had.

"Let's assume the Uskoks are running this enterprise," Iverson began. "We don't know the Uskok king but we've just met two Uskok knights. Upper level pieces on the board and both possessing Croatian backgrounds and training. Kant and the Tremaine boy must have been pawns. They weren't Croatian, but maybe pawns aren't supposed to be because they're infantry. They're expendable. Like in chess, they're sacrificed for the good of the king. In chess they don't get replaced but in real life, you need replacements. You lose the war when you run out of infantry. Kant told me the Tremaine boy killed himself because he didn't want to become him. I think that boy was being trained to be a killer just like Kant. If I play this out over the time frame provided by Horvat, I can imagine a need for a lot of pawns."

"For what purpose?" Numaga asked.

"Go back to your spreadsheet."

Numaga recalled the eighteen unsolved homicide victims she'd put in her database. Her research into their histories had produced some interesting common denominators. Iverson watched as the light went on in Numaga's brain.

Chapter 43

The High Five were spending a comfortable afternoon as guests of an oil company executive. It was hot in Houston and an occasional dip in the pool while they sat around offered a welcomed respite from the unrelenting sun. The mansion's host had considered their every need. The tables next to their padded lounge chairs offered an assortment of catered food items and their glasses were kept full with the finest of spirits served by bikini clad women. Business was discussed briefly but mostly the conversations centered on the Cowboys, the Longhorns and oil. The alpha male's leisure was disturbed by his phone. The Caller ID told him it was Dulles.

"What the hell do you want, Dulles?" the man barked.

"Dulles is dead," Frantzen said. "You'll have to deal with me now."

The alpha recognized Frantzen's voice. "What happened to Dulles?" he demanded.

"The Uskoks killed him," Frantzen revealed. "And then the PI's shot the Uskoks. Unfortunately for you, I'm still alive. All in all, you've had a bad day, asshole."

The alpha said nothing. He was thinking. Thinking about what this meant. Nothing good, was his first take.

"Cat got your tongue?" Frantzen goaded.

"Where are you?" the man asked.

"Somewhere safe."

"What do you want?"

"Ten million dollars."

"No chance, Frantzen. Who the fuck do you think you are?"

"I'm the guy you told Dulles to kill. Your mistake. I'm also the guy who knows how you got rich. I know what you've done and I know where you live. They do lethal injections in Texas, don't they?"

"I don't have ten million dollars."

"I'm not going to play that game," Frantzen warned. "If you continue to play me for a fool, you'll do so at great risk. You have the money, we both know that. All that's left for you to do is gather the ten million and make whatever arrangements are necessary to transfer it."

"Transfer it where?"

"I'll share that information when it's time to transfer the money. You have twenty four hours to get it together. After the twenty four hours is up, I'll call and give you an account number. You will then transfer the ten million into that account. If I sense you are stalling, or if the money is not transferred to my satisfaction, I will end the transaction and send my journals to the nearest FBI office."

"Journals?"

"Names, dates and recordings; more than a few of the video kind. They have you as the star. You really should bone up on the dangers of technology."

The man paused, examining his options. "What do I get in return?" he finally asked.

"If I get what I want, you'll get the journals and you'll never hear from me again.

"What guarantee do I have?"

"None. You know as well as I do guarantees are worthless."

"What are you getting out of this, Frantzen?"

"Ten million dollars and a lot of years of looking over my shoulder. I figure it's worth it."

The alpha paused again, considering his options. "I'll have to talk to the partners," he said.

"Talk all you want," Frantzen replied. "I'll be calling at exactly 3 PM tomorrow; Texas time. You have one opportunity to get this right. There'll be no second chances." Frantzen ended the call. The alpha placed a conference call to the men who paid him. He placed another call to his accountant. A third call was made to a man in Portland. His name was listed under: "Emergency Contacts."

Chapter 44

Numaga decided that she needed to stop by APD and check in with the Solaras situation. She worried that she might be pulled in off her leave, but felt a measure of responsibility to be available for the investigation that was most certainly gearing up. If the preliminary findings concluded his death was a homicide rather than suicide, the squad would be on high alert. But a visit to APD would also provide Numaga an opportunity to explore any connection between the Lieutenant, Dulles and Frantzen. Numaga would play two ends of the same case. Not easy.

Iverson drove the Camry back to where Henry was parked. "How long you figure you'll be at APD?" he asked Numaga.

"I'll spend the rest of the day shift poking around and asking questions. Nobody liked Solaras, but we'll all have to spend some time talking about what a great guy he was. It's the blue brotherhood's way. You know how it works, Stan."

Iverson nodded his understanding. Law enforcement is a high stress, high risk profession and he'd been a badge carrying member of the cop fraternity for many years. He didn't make friends on the force, but he always knew who his friends were.

The partners exited the Camry and walked over to Iverson's truck. Iverson flipped a Camel out of its package and stuck it between his lips and placed a flame to the end of it.

"You know the City Council is considering a ban on smoking within the city limits," Numaga jibed.

Iverson shook his head, took a long drag from the cigarette and offered a measured response to his partner. "I've heard that rumor," he stated petulantly, "and my compliance with that law will coincide with the enactment of bans on car emissions and the carcinogens in our food supply."

Numaga shook her head and moved on. "Where are you headed while I'm at APD?"

"I have a few more questions for Grace Johnson at CPS and then I thought I'd check on Horvat again."

"Great," Numaga said. "Let's check in every hour or so."

Iverson nodded his agreement, flicked his cigarette butt down a curbside rain gutter and walked towards Henry. He stopped, paused, and then turned back toward Numaga.

"Hey partner," Iverson yelled.

"Yeah?" Numaga answered.

"Thanks for sharing your buha."

"My pleasure . . ., partner."

Iverson turned around, opened Henry's door and lowered himself into the truck. He wrote down some notes while Numaga drove off and then headed to CPS. He hoped Grace Johnson was still at the office.

*****

Grace Johnson met Iverson in the CPS lobby. The visitation room was occupied by a sad looking woman and two small children so Grace led him through a locked door, down a maze of corridors and past a labyrinth of high-walled cubicles. They settled into the confined space Grace called home for eight hours a day. Grace's long CPS tenure hadn't translated into plush workspace, but she was separated from the main hive that buzzed outside her door.

"What's up, Stan?" Grace asked. "More questions?"

"Nothing specific this time, Grace," Iverson explained. "Just some questions as to how the Child Welfare System works in general."

"Fire away, Stan."

"How many kids are in the system at any given time?"

"Kids under the Juvenile Court's jurisdiction, or just kids in out-of-home placements?"

"I'm looking for the number of kids actually in foster care . . . kids not living in their parent's home."

"Countywide, about eleven hundred," Grace calculated. "Statewide, it's close to eighty- five hundred."

"Where are those kids placed?"

"The majority are placed with relatives. CPS certified foster homes serve the next largest share and we also have kids in pre-adoptive placements and in treatment programs that we tag as out of home placements."

"That's it?" Iverson questioned. "Are there any other placement possibilities?"

"That's pretty much the spectrum of options for out-of-home placements."

"Are all the providers screened?"

The scowl on Grace's face showed her offense at the question. "Of course," she said irritably. "What are you getting at, Stan?"

Iverson figured he'd better share the reason for the inquisition. He briefly outlined his case and provided Grace a sketch of his theory. He disclosed the Tremaine family's fate and that they'd had a boy living with them who'd also been killed. He was cautious about laying culpability on CPS's doorstep but Grace Johnson didn't feel exonerated.

"So you think our foster care system is a factory for criminals?" Grace responded peevishly. Her body language spoke even louder than her words. People employed in Child Welfare are often maligned. Usually, unfairly. Caseworkers are charged with a difficult task: protecting vulnerable children from dysfunctional parents. And in a culture that holds sacred the rights of parents more than the rights of the children they bear, it's a job rife with frustration and anger. The anger Iverson was seeing and hearing from Grace Johnson was the manifestation of those emotions.

"I'm just thinking out loud, Grace," Iverson explained. "I'm not blaming CPS for anything . . . really. I'm just trying to connect some dots. The Tremaines are part of the puzzle and it appears they were training the boy for more than just farm work."

"So what do you want from me?" Grace asked. She was still angry.

"I know you think I'd indicting CPS, but I'm not. I just want to understand what's going on and I'm hoping you can help me with that."

"How?" Grace asked. Her posture remained defensive but her tone softened slightly.

"If my theory holds water, then someone is filtering young children into families like the Tremaines. Those families are then provided the resources to raise these kids a certain way . . . to do the bidding of whoever is behind this. I know that sounds like something out of a bad movie, but it's not unheard of. Children are exploited all over the world. To think it can't happen in the United States is to have your head in the sand."

"You're preaching to the choir, Stan," Grace admonished.

"I know," Iverson admitted. "That's why I'm here. I need help from the choir."

Grace Johnson considered what she knew of the man sitting across from her and then what she knew of herself. She relaxed back into her chair, took a long, deep breath and did what good caseworkers do. She offered to help.

The next hour was spent on a voyage through the complicated Child Welfare System. Iverson owned some experiences, but they had been either as a child victim or as a peripheral enforcement official in his role as a cop. He had little clue as to the day to day workings of the agency charged with maintaining the safety of children.

Iverson listened attentively, questioned frequently and took copious notes. He underlined twice one particular point. Whenever a CPS involved family moved to Oregon from another state, the state of origin sent the paperwork first to the local PD. The PD ostensibly received the paperwork first for the purpose of assessing and tracking potential sex offenders. The files were reviewed by PD management staff and then forwarded to the local CPS agency.

Iverson plugged Lieutenant Solaras into this process and a potential piece of the puzzle slid more tightly into place. He'd considered Solaras a player when Numaga's e-mails had mysteriously disappeared. And now he'd discovered that Solaras had opportunity. If Solaras was murdered, that would add even more fuel to the conspiratorial fire. Too much to ignore.

Iverson thanked Grace for her time and for the education she'd provided. He apologized sincerely if he'd offended her and offered to assuage any residual bad feelings with lunch at her favorite eatery. Grace negotiated the deal up to a dinner and they parted as the friends they'd been.

Iverson returned to the quietude of his truck and placed a call to Numaga. He was late by their prearranged schedule, but so was she.

"How are things at APD?" Iverson asked.

"Bustling," Numaga replied. "Solaras's murder has everybody on edge."

"So they're calling it a homicide?"

"Definitely. They're still working forensics but the early returns indicate either an amateurish or hurried attempt at a staged suicide. That Solaras was murdered is not in question. Why he was murdered, still is."

"I think I can help with that," proffered Iverson.

"Please do," Numaga urged.

Iverson laid out his theory of Solaras's involvement in their case. The enterprise needed a way to identify potential candidates for their school of assassins and Solaras was in the perfect position to do that. He'd only have to come up with a new student every few years or so who fit the criteria of having dysfunctional parents who could be easily manipulated. There was never a shortage of that demographic and the protocol of PD review for out of state offenders provided Solaras the opportunity to filter candidates. He provided the crack into which these families fell. The local CPS never knew they existed because Solaras never forwarded their paperwork. His risk was reduced by the fact that many of these parents had histories of choosing drugs over their children. Their hard core addictions were what got them in trouble in the first place. He could offer desperate parents a carrot of methamphetamine or a stick of incarceration. It would be a compelling choice.

"Interesting theory, Stan," Numaga adjudged. "But why would he do it?"

"The usual reasons, I'd imagine," Iverson supposed. "Plus you said he was just plain mean. Maybe it's as simple as that."

"Well, mean met its end in the Masonic Cemetery," Numaga concluded. "But you didn't say why."

"I think this thing is falling apart, Numaga. Solaras was probably deemed a liability and silenced before he could do any damage. They tried to kill Horvat, killed the Tremaines and probably would have killed Kant had he not done it himself. Whoever they are, they're feeling pressure to clean things up."

Iverson's phone announced he had a text. "Hang on a minute," he told Numaga. He switched his phone to the messaging function and read a script from Helen Matkin. *Gabos wants 2 c u.*

"Gotta go," he told Numaga. "Horvat's talking."

"Terrific," Numaga replied. "Let me know what he says."

Iverson told Numaga he'd call again in an hour and tapped the end icon. He was looking forward to his next conversation.

*****

Doc Matkin opened the door before Iverson knocked on it.

"How is he?" Iverson asked.

"Conscious but weak," Matkin reported. "I'll give you fifteen minutes with him and I'll be monitoring him while you talk. If I sense he's stressed, you'll have to leave. Understood?"

Iverson nodded his acceptance of the arrangement. "Let's do it," he said.

Gabos Horvat was propped up on the bed with a bevy of pillows. Doc Matkin had cleaned and mended him the best she could but he still looked as though he'd been repeatedly run over by a truck. His blackish-blue face carried a resigned look. An intravenous drip line tapped into a vein in his right arm and carried the clear fluid slowly draining from the bottle hanging from a bedside pole. An archipelago of gauze dappled either side of his neck and extended downward to the top of his chest. Iverson's questions were stalled by his damage inspection so Horvat initiated the conversation.

"I guess I saved myself fifty grand," he said drolly.

"Yeah," Iverson replied. "Now you can take that trip to the Bahamas you were planning."

Horvat managed a smile and asked, "Been busy, I hope?"

"Very," Iverson answered. "You left me with a lot of unanswered questions."

"I was tired, Mr. Iverson."

"And now?"

"Even more tired."

Iverson looked at Doc Matkin and she nodded to the side of the bed. She had taken precautions by securing Horvat's arms, legs and torso to the bed's metal rails with soft restraints. It would be extremely difficult, if not impossible, for him to access any of Matkin's menageries of doctoring tools for the purpose of self-destruction. Horvat acknowledged their concerns with a glance at the restraints and then continued the discussion.

"Progress report?" Horvat requested.

Doc Matkin lurked so Iverson offered Horvat an abbreviated update. His story included Horvat's fellow Croatians, chess pieces, Kill Books, Dulles and Frantzen, APD insiders and the concept of schools for assassins. Horvat was impressed. Iverson had been a good choice.

"Too bad about the pjeseks," Horvat said. He identified Kant and the Tremaine's boy as the pawns. "They are the innocent ones."

"How many are there?" Iverson asked.

"I don't know how many total," Horvat answered. "There were three active pjeseks in the West."

"The West?"

"The West Sector," Horvat explained. "One of four."

Iverson's eyebrows went up and he sucked in his lips. His thinking face.

"And you were the King . . . the Kralj of the West?"

"I ruled the Croatian Uskoks. Another ruled the Sector."

Iverson knew his time was running out and that Doc Matkin would probably hold him to the limit she'd set. He prioritized his questions and fired them off.

"Is Houston the center of this operation?"

"It is."

"Who's in charge there?"

"I never had names. I was too low on the ladder."

"What did you have?"

"A phone. They called me with targets and when there were problems."

"Do you still have the phone?"

"No."

"How'd you get paid?"

"Wire transfers paid me. I paid the Uskoks."

"Times up," Doc Matkin announced. "You can come back tomorrow if his progress continues."

Iverson looked at Helen Matkin, hoping for a window of negotiation. He didn't see one. He still had a litany of questions cycling through his synapses but they'd have to wait. He turned and walked dejectedly towards the door leading out of the room.

"Iverson," Horvat called after him.

Iverson spun around. "Yeah?" he replied.

"Frantzen's now the key," Horvat said. "He's smarter than he lets on. He'll take you to the High Five."

Chapter 45

Iverson called Numaga per their schedule. She told him she'd be spending another hour or two at APD helping to pull together the Solaras investigation and picking up some of the slack his death had created. Iverson shared the highpoints of his brief conversation with Horvat and what he thought it meant.

"We have three priority items on our agenda," he told Numaga, "and I think we can split the first two."

"Which one do I get?" Numaga asked tentatively.

Iverson explained the need to locate Horvat's bank records. They had to find the source of the funds that Horvat had been wired from Houston. In theory, there should be records tracking those deposits.

"And what will you be doing while I'm sipping cold coffee with cranky bean counters?"

Iverson heard the irritation in Numaga's voice. "I'll be looking for Frantzen," he explained. "You're still with APD and thus empowered to access bank records if you can convince a judge to sign a warrant. That's iffy for you but impossible for me. I'm counting on your powers of persuasion and your skills with the computer. I'm sure you'd agree I'm lacking in both areas."

"No argument there," Numaga granted. "What's your plan for finding Frantzen?"

"Good question. I've got people I want to talk to but beyond that, I'm not sure. I'll talk to Horvat again tomorrow. Maybe he can help me pull the rabbit out of the hat."

"What's the third item on the agenda?" asked Numaga.

"A trip to Texas," Iverson disclosed.

"I'll have to buy boots," Numaga quipped.

"And a hat," Iverson added.

"Already got the hat."

"Pink?"

"Nope. Red."

"I was thinking low profile."

"You're messing with my style, Stan," Numaga teased.

Iverson considered critiquing his partner's style but thought better of it. "I'm thinking Northwest casual will work fine for our purposes."

Iverson didn't get a response. "Numaga?" he searched.

"Hang on, Stan," Numaga replied. "They've just brought our Croatian friend into The Pen."

Iverson waited and imagined the scene. Numaga would busy herself trying to see while staying unseen. The longer he waited, the more anxious he got. Numaga finally returned to the phone. "That was interesting," she said.

"What happened?" asked Iverson.

"He saw me as soon as he walked in the door. I didn't have time to move out of view so we just stared at each other as he walked through the room and down the hall to the IR's."

"Did he say anything?"

"Not a damn thing. Gave me a bit of a nod and then just stared at me with a sinister smirk."

"Did you get a chance to talk to the arresting officers?"

"They didn't stop to talk to anybody. They walked our guy straight into IR-1 and closed the door behind them. After we made the 9-1-1 call, I figured he'd end up in the ER and held under guard at VCH until he got stable."

"Maybe he did," Iverson said. "Was he still wearing his bloodied shirt?"

"Nope. Cleaned up and confident."

"There's got to be a connection between the hospital and Houston," Iverson assessed. "Maybe it's time I revisited that."

"That's probably a good idea," Numaga agreed. "Most perps in his situation would be pointing fingers and hollering police brutality. Not this guy. He's quietly confident for some reason."

"Could be he figures he's got protection," Iverson suggested. "Maybe he hasn't heard about Solaras yet."

"That would certainly explain the attitude."

"But, so far so good as far as you're concerned, right?"

"It appears so."

"Still," Iverson persuaded, "the sooner you're out of there, the better. If APD connects the two of you, you'll be there a lot longer than we can afford."

"I couldn't agree more," Numaga said. "I'll process a warrant for the bank records and head over to court and try to get a signature. Anyone besides Horvat I should be looking at?"

"I don't think so. Horvat said he paid the others."

"How about Dulles or Frantzen?"

"Most judges limit the scope of warrants. They want one person per warrant."

"I can process single warrants for all three and hope for a generous judge."

"Then sure, process warrants for Dulles and Frantzen as well."

"Any particular financial institution I should be targeting?" asked Numaga.

"Start with Confederated Bank since that's where Horvat had the safe deposit box. They appear to function on the slack side of protocol. If that comes up empty, you'll have to work your way through Ashton's myriad banks, credit unions and brokerage houses; any institutions that offer wire transfers."

"Tall order, Stan," gauged Numaga.

"Large crime, Numaga," responded Iverson.

"Let's talk later tonight," Numaga suggested. "Hopefully I'll have something positive to report."

"Same here," Iverson said. "Good luck with the judges."

"Good luck finding Frantzen."

"Thanks," said Iverson. "And one more thing, Numaga," he added.

"What's that?"

"No red boots, either."

*****

The conversation with Numaga prompted Iverson to make a return visit to Valley Christian Hospital. He wanted another conversation with the doctor who'd showed some concern for the hospital's lack of accountability.

Iverson parked Henry and walked into the VCH Emergency Room. He asked the woman at the reception desk to page Dr. Jenkins and took a seat in a hallway chair. The doctor stepped out from behind a curtained room, initiated a hushed but intense discussion with the nurse who paged him, and ambled disgruntledly over to Iverson.

"Find those records yet, Doc?" probed Iverson.

Jenkins' eyes searched the space between his shoes. Iverson surmised he was looking for the least incriminating answer.

"I've been busy, Mr. Iverson," the doctor eventually said.

"Of that, I have no doubt," Iverson conceded. "But I have an idea that some of your business was pondering how to keep your career."

Jenkins' reluctant eye contact confirmed Iverson's suspicions. The doctor tried to change the direction of the conversation. "How's your head?" he asked Iverson.

"The head's fine," reported Iverson. "How's your conscience?"

"What do you want from me, Iverson," Jenkins demanded.

"I want some answers."

"What are the questions?"

"You've already heard the first one."

Jenkins' shoulders slumped and he took a long, deep breath. "I didn't find the records you're referring to. As far as I can see, they never existed and neither did the patient."

Iverson examined both Jenkins and his claim. "Do you get paid for your lies?" he asked.

"I don't appreciate the inference, Mr. Iverson," Jenkins said irritably.

"I'm not concerned with what you don't appreciate, Doctor," Iverson responded harshly. "Since I left this hospital, seven people have been killed. Seven! If you take any inference from me, I'd like it to be that both the killing and the killers need to be stopped. If you can help make that happen, I'd strongly suggest that you do."

Jenkins scanned the nurse's station uneasily. Iverson sensed he wanted to talk but couldn't, at least not there. "Can you take a break?" he asked.

"Breaks don't exist in ER," Jenkins said, "but my shift ends in thirty minutes."

"I'll meet you wherever you want," Iverson offered.

"Grosvenor Park in an hour," Jenkins said. He turned abruptly, walked quickly away from Iverson and disappeared back into the curtained room.

Iverson worked his way back to Henry. With an hour to burn, he'd have time to collect his thoughts, organize his questions and down some coffee before heading to Grosvenor Park.

*****

Numaga arrived at the courthouse at 3:30. It was the tail end of the judicial day but she was hopeful of finding a judge with a brief opening in their schedule. Judges have a penchant for well-defined order. It's a favorable and necessary attribute in their line of work. But it conflicts with the helter-skelter dynamics of police work where predictability is sought but rarely achieved. Successful criminals are those that employ and exploit ambiguity. Though the police and the courts are often perceived as a unified force, in reality they are frequently at odds. Judges want the cases presented to them to be rooted firmly in law. They loathe lazy cops and scorn sloppy work. Warrants are their tools to control both.

Numaga checked with three clerks before finding a judge in chambers and who would grant her the few minutes it would take to review her warrant requests. She had readied three authorizations. All three named Confederated Bank. The first one granted access to all financial records held by that institution in the name of Mr. Gabos Horvat. The second warrant request granted the same action for Adrian Dulles. The third for Francis Frantzen. If the judge refused to sign the warrant, or if Confederated Bank didn't have records for any of the three men, she would face long days of tedious leg work. Something she and Iverson couldn't afford. Numaga was hoping for miracles. One in the judge's chambers and another one at Confederated Bank.

Numaga pleaded her case quickly and efficiently knowing that that in itself would be a plus with the judge. Judge Aileen Stepnoski listened attentively, if not passively, asked a few germane questions and signed one sheet of paper before handing the entire warrant portfolio back to Numaga.

"Officer Numaga," the judge added.

"Yes, Your Honor?" Numaga replied.

"I've signed but one warrant and that only because you have evidence that the individual in question has history at the institution listed on the warrant. The other two requests present no such evidence. They are ill-advised and an insult to this court. Are we clear, Officer Numaga?"

"Yes, ma'am," Numaga answered contritely. "Very clear."

Judge Stepnoski turned her attention elsewhere and dismissed Numaga with a wave of her hand. Numaga took the queue readily, rose from her chair and headed toward the door.

"Thank you, Your Honor," she said respectfully before walking out. She received another muted wave and escaped to the lobby outside the courtrooms. She rifled through the warrants, looking for the signature and found it on the Horvat-Confederated document. *Better than nothing*, she told herself and hurried back to the Camry. Banker's hours didn't leave her much time.

*****

Iverson acquired a coffee and arrived at Grosvenor Park at exactly 4:22 PM. It was a familiar venue. Iverson had worked hundreds of cases in his career and he was always amazed at the serendipitous recurrence of places.

Grosvenor Park was often the location of choice for cloistered conversations and anonymous activities.

Hubert Grosvenor was the first Park Superintendent for the city of Ashton. The city had been incorporated in 1862 and the fledgling township was growing quickly along the banks of the river. Grosvenor, a trained biologist, approached the city fathers with a plan to preserve tracts of land on the waterfront. The "allure of Ashton," Grosvenor claimed, "would be ground into sawdust" if preservation efforts weren't taken up. The city agreed with one condition: that Grosvenor himself implement the plan. The English expatriate accepted the task and worked diligently to secure and develop selected parcels of riverfront property for public use. His tireless efforts resulted in the town bestowing his name on the first of the many parks he'd created. He would have sought a name change had he toured the acreage now.

Iverson sipped his Americano and looked out at the park. Years of governmental budget cuts had left park maintenance at the bottom of the prioritized spending list and Grosvenor Park exposed the consequences. Uncontested blackberry had overwhelmed the perimeters and blocked both the view and the path to the river. The manicured lawns had lost their battle to the inexorable march of weeds and arriviste seedlings were staking vertical claims to the sun. The remnants of walking trails and bike paths were barely discernible beneath the moldering remains of countless autumnal molts. Weekend picnickers had been replaced by weekday drug users. Most of them scattered when Iverson arrived.

Iverson's reflections ceased when a silver sedan came through the park's open gate. He watched as the vehicle drove slowly through the parking area before turning towards where Henry was parked. Iverson removed his weapon from its holster and placed it on his lap. Given the events of the past few days, he wasn't taking any chances. As the sedan drew closer, Iverson could see the driver was Jenkins. He relaxed, but kept his weapon in place. Nobody could be trusted at this point.

Jenkins parked alongside Iverson and they both lowered their windows.

"There's a table over there," Iverson said and pointed to an old, weathered slab.

Jenkins didn't answer. He pulled his car forward, killed the engine and got out. Iverson sheathed his Colt and did the same. They walked separately and silently to the table and sat on opposite benches.

"I'll give you ten minutes," Jenkins said. He scanned the park nervously.

"It's all we'll need if I get some answers," Iverson asserted.

"Then start asking questions," Jenkins said anxiously.

"Expecting company?" queried Iverson.

"There's a lot you don't know, Iverson."

"I'm here to be educated, Doc."

"It's your dime and the clock's ticking," Jenkins maintained.

"Okay," Iverson agreed. "I ask, you answer."

"You ask, *maybe* I'll answer," corrected Jenkins.

Iverson was getting irritated, but realized it was because Jenkins was acting like he would. He started at the top of his question list.

"Did you actually look for the records on Gabos Horvat?"

"Yes."

"And did you actually not find them?"

"Correct."

Did you ever see Horvat?"

"No."

Gonna be a quick interview, Iverson thought. "Was he at VCH?" he explored.

"More than likely," Jenkins replied. His body language indicated his flight response was developing.

"Who hijacked Horvat away from VCH?" Iverson asked.

"I don't know. I wasn't there."

Time to change directions. "Is what happened to Horvat a single event or one in a pattern?"

Jenkins looked at his watch and scanned the park again before answering. "There've been other incidents," he admitted.

"How many?"

"Maybe six in my time in ER."

"Which is how long?"

"It's a twelve month rotation. I've got two months left."

"What types of incidents are we talking about?"

"Uncharted admissions or discharges. Missing records. A few others."

Iverson upped the ante. "Any dead people involved?"

Jenkins glared at Iverson. "I won't answer that one."

"Doctor," Iverson said sternly, "very soon you're going to have to answer to someone and it will definitely matter who's asking the questions. Murder makes people nervous. On both sides. You may not be hands-on involved in what's going on at VCH, but you're aware of it. That makes you an accessory to the good guys and a liability to the bad ones. You're wedged quite tightly between the proverbial rock and a hard place, Doc."

"Are you threatening me, Iverson?"

"I'm explaining the threat, Doctor. A threat you apparently don't see."

"To my career?"

"To your life, Doc," Iverson stressed. "These people are killing anyone they perceive as a threat and you, Doctor Jenkins, could easily be assigned that label."

"Then why am I talking to you?"

"Because it's too late to talk to them."

Jenkins went silent, spinning his situation around in his head. Iverson had the feeling he'd abandoned the conversational time limit. He pushed on.

"How many VCH people are involved in this?"

Jenkins looked up at the oak leaf canopy looming above them and did a quick calculation. "It's the ER that's involved at the functional end," he said. "That's maybe a dozen people spread out over two shifts. With a few exceptions, we're all just starting our medical careers. Our proving ground is ER."

"Who's in charge of ER?"

"The ER Administrator."

"Name?"

Jenkins paused before answering. "Susan Kincaid," he eventually divulged.

"And Kincaid runs this illicit enterprise at VCH?"

"She informs us of when to go 'off record'."

"How long has she been at VCH?" Iverson asked.

"Not sure," Jenkins said. "She was there when I started my internship. I was told she'd previously worked at a corporation in Texas."

"Texas?" Iverson repeated.

"That's what I was told," Jenkins confirmed.

Iverson changed gears. "Ever meet a man named Frantzen?"

"Yeah, a few times," Jenkins admitted. "He'd show up in ER and then we'd get a call from Kincaid. He was there when you and your friend Horvat were admitted."

"I thought you said you weren't there?"

"I was there when he came in, not when he left. That, I believe, was your question."

Iverson thought back and decided Jenkins was right. He moved on. "Did you ever treat Frantzen as a patient?"

"Not me personally, but he was treated for a gunshot wound a few months back by another doctor."

"I don't suppose there'd be a record of that?" Iverson asked sarcastically.

Jenkins pondered the question. "Not in ER, obviously, but maybe in the pharmacy. He was most likely prescribed pain medication and they probably took his personal information."

Iverson hiked his eyebrows at both the new possibility and the fact that Jenkins had contributed it. *Maybe some hope for the doctor.* "One last question," he said. "Who owns Valley Christian Hospital?"

"The parent company is called Global Solutions," Jenkins revealed.

"Based where?" Iverson queried.

"Houston, Texas," answered Jenkins.

"Bingo!" Iverson exclaimed. He gave Jenkins a small task and they left Grosvenor Park.

******

Cassie Numaga presented her warrant at Confederated Bank to the Accounts Manager. The woman checked with someone on her in-house phone before leaving Numaga in her office and disappearing into a different room. She returned ten minutes later.

"This should satisfy the warrant," Janet Hardwick said as she set a portfolio of papers in front of Numaga.

Numaga examined the contents of the folder carefully. She was more than surprised at what she found. Gabos Horvat had made no effort to obscure his money trail. On the contrary, his deposit and withdrawal records were clear and concise. Deposits of $20,000 had been recorded from January through November, 1995 through 2011. Sixteen additional deposits, each in December, and each in the amount of $50,000, had been made during the same time frame. Withdrawal amounts varied but at no time did they exceed $10,000. The Federal Government requires notification for any withdrawal exceeding that amount, so Horvat was obviously trying to keep under the radar. The current balance in the account was $50,000. Numaga recalled that that was the amount Horvat had offered Iverson to end his existence.

"I'm sorry officer," Hardwick interrupted, "but the bank is about to close."

"May I take these with me?" Numaga asked, holding up the folder.

"Those are your copies, officer," Hardwick explained.

"Great. Thank you," Numaga said. She rose from her seat, tucked the folder under her arm and walked out of Confederated Bank. She resettled into the Camry and continued reading through Horvat's bank records. The last page was a compilation of all the data associated with the money transfers. Dates, times, amounts, and various banking codes that Numaga didn't understand. It was the last two columns that caught Numaga's attention. They were headed "Transfer Agent" and "Originating Account." The agent was always Bank of Texas. The account was always Global Solutions.

Numaga called Iverson and they agreed to meet back at the farm. They were both starving. They both had a lot share. Things were heating up.

Chapter 46

Francis Frantzen busied himself cooking the last dinner he would eat on U.S. soil. He threw a steak on the griddle, a potato in the oven and returned to his living room to find a movie to watch while he ate. He felt safe. Only Dulles had known of this residence. Dulles was dead.

Frantzen had packed his only suitcase with an assortment of clothes and a few items he'd collected on the road of his life. His gloomy rental in Portland held nothing of personal importance and he kept the few cherished items he had at his apartment in Ashton.

Possessions reflect identities and Frantzen had few possessions. There was a photo of a tall, dark-haired woman he'd once dated and a small print of a painting by Georgia O'Keefe. The painting depicted a solitary deer skull resting on an expanse of hot, desert sand. He'd always felt kinship with the skull. He never knew why. He had a collection of artifacts he'd unearthed in the webbed canyons of New Mexico during his Big Hat days and a few pieces of pottery given to him by the dwellers of pueblos. The pictures and collections were the only memories he packed. They were the only ones he wanted to keep. The rest were not needed. Not wanted. He would leave them behind to be lost in the wind.

Frantzen's plane ticket showed Spain as his destination. He'd considered the move before but never mustered the courage. It was hard enough being a loner. It had to be worse if you couldn't speak the language. But isolation involves scant conversation so what did it matter. It was time to go. No turning back. His threats to the man in Houston assured that. He knew that.

Frantzen found a movie to watch and returned to the kitchen to check on his food. He flipped the steak and turned the potato. A salad was constructed with things green and things red. Some nuts and dried berries completed the ensemble. He clanked some ice into a tall glass and filled it with Coke. After turning the steak one more time, he returned to the living room to set up his chair. The man sitting in it held a very large gun.

Chapter 47

Numaga arrived at the farm fifteen minutes after Iverson did. Max had already been in the house and was back outside when the Camry was parked in front of the porch. He waited for Numaga to exit the vehicle, sniffed her briefly and then headed out to the western pasture in search of whatever it is that dogs search for. Numaga had had the forethought to stop at a grocery and carried a six pack of longnecks and a bag of food under her arm. Her partner, as Numaga suspected, was unprepared for the hunger they both claimed. He sat at the living room table munching stale chips from a shredded bag and reading barely discernible notes in a tattered notebook. Iverson looked up at Numaga as she cleared the doorway and offered a welcoming smile.

"Hey, partner."

"Hey yourself," Numaga replied tersely. "I brought food. You can do the cooking."

Iverson rose quickly, grabbed the bag and bottles from Numaga, and toted them to the kitchen. Numaga took his chair and buried herself back into Horvat's bank records. She highlighted a number of entries and jotted notations in margins. She excavated a calculator from her purse, tapped its keys vigorously and added its computations to the paperwork. Her report was fully ready when Iverson returned from the kitchen with an array of cheese wedges, salami slices and sections of fruit. Upon his return from a second foray into the kitchen, he set a sleeve of crackers and two bottles of Hefeweizen on either side of the food tray. The food distributed, he unfolded the lawn chair and plopped himself across from Numaga. They dug into the victuals with tenacity and delayed their reports until their hunger was sated.

Iverson washed down his last mouthful of food with the last swallow of wheat beer, brushed a few remnant cracker crumbs from his shirt and initiated the post meal report. "Time for the main course," he said. "What've you got?"

Numaga took a sip from her longneck, pushed the food tray aside and laid Horvat's portfolio in its place. "You were right about Confederated Bank," Numaga began. "Horvat kept his financial records there. Records he obviously wasn't trying to hide."

"Meaning?"

"Meaning there was no effort whatsoever to hide the trail of the money. I can't help but think that Horvat had been planning his exit from this enterprise ever since he got into it."

"How much money are we talking about?" Iverson asked.

"Deposits for the sixteen years, 1995 to 2011, totaled $4,320,000."

The amount didn't shock Iverson. "What about withdrawals?"

"All but $50,000."

Iverson's eyebrows rose up. "Now that's interesting," he appraised.

"I thought so, too," Numaga agreed. "I guess you were supposed to be the final expenditure."

"You think the rest went to the Croatian crew?"

"That's a ton of money, Stan. Horvat probably paid his crew well, but there had to be other expenses. Housing, vehicles, food, weapons, etc. Maybe the Keepers and Solaras were paid out of this pot, too."

"I doubt we'll ever know the full breakdown of who got what. Maybe it doesn't matter. What else have you got?"

"Two institutional names. The bank of origin for the wire transfer and the corporation listed as the funding source."

"They're both in Texas, right?"

"You're spoiling my fun, Stan," Numaga warned.

Iverson broke a grin. "Sorry, partner. Please continue."

"The Bank of Texas wired the money. It came from an account registered to Global Solutions."

"Thank you, Gabos Horvat!" Iverson exclaimed.

"For what?" questioned Numaga.

"Global Solutions came up today in my conversation with Doctor Jenkins."

"Doctor Jenkins?"

"Long story, Numaga," Iverson clarified. "I'll explain on the plane ride to Houston."

"So, we're still going to Houston?"

"Right after I talk to Frantzen."

"And that will be when?"

"Right after the pharmacy opens."

Numaga tilted her head and stared questioningly at Iverson. He stared back. "On the plane, Numaga," he promised. "It'll all make sense on the plane."

"So will some sleep, Numaga added. "I'm planning on catching up during the flight."

"Likewise," Iverson added.

Numaga collected her possessions and headed out the door. Max pushed past her and followed his nose to the leftover salami sitting on the table. He sat on his tail and looked over at Iverson hopefully.

"Where're you going?" Iverson asked Numaga.

"To the red boot store. And then to bed. Call me when you have our flight schedule."

Chapter 48

Iverson woke up early and placed a call to the travel agency he used for the occasional flights he booked. The agency hadn't yet opened for business, so he left a message explaining his ticketing needs and preferences and an approximate time that he'd come by for pick-up and payment. His personal information was on file at the agency, but he left Numaga's cell number in case there were questions or problems regarding her ticketing information.

Iverson had tried processing flight tickets on the Internet but found he didn't have the patience required to sift through the myriad schedules and itineraries. All he needed were tickets, not an increase in frustration. He had plenty of that in the work he did. If paying a commission to Worldwide Travel meant avoiding additional angst, he'd happily pay it.

Iverson showered and shaved before wolfing down a breakfast of burnt toast, sloppy eggs and gritty coffee. He went out to the barn and made sure Max had plenty of food and water available for the time he anticipated he'd be spending in Texas. He returned to the house, packed a small duffel and headed to Ashton. It was 8 AM. His first stop was Doc Matkin's. He was certain she'd already be awake and busy with work. He wanted to check on Horvat's progress and have another conversation with him if Matkin would allow it. Matkin answered the door with a scowl on her face.

"You really should call first, Sergeant," she complained.

Iverson wasn't accustomed to be on the receiving end of grumpy and he struggled for a response. "Uh, sorry, Doc," he managed. "Next time, I'll call first. I promise. Mind if I check in on Horvat?"

Matkin answered with a dismissive wave of her hand. Iverson left Doc Matkin's mood and walked into her patient's room. Horvat was sitting up in bed looking at a magazine. His restraints had been removed. He looked up over the rim of his glasses to see his visitor.

"Good morning, Iverson," Horvat greeted. "I'm surprised to see you. I thought you might have taken a vacation."

Iverson recognized the game. "And where would I have gone?" he asked.

"Somewhere with answers."

"Any recommendations?"

"Someplace hot," Horvat suggested. His mouth broke a wry smile.

"Which would be where?" Iverson queried.

"I think you know where, Iverson."

"I'm thinking Texas," proposed Iverson.

"Excellent choice."

Iverson moved away from the game. "I found your bank records," he revealed, "and you knew I would. From the minute we met in the bar it was your goal to get me to Texas, wasn't it?"

Horvat set the magazine aside and smiled again. "You are very smart, Iverson," he said. "This is why I chose you."

"What are you after, Horvat?"

"I already told you. In the letter."

"Tell me again. This time in person."

"I want the insanity to stop. I couldn't stop it."

"What's the insanity, Gabos?"

"The killing is the insanity," Horvat explained. "And I'm insane because I created the killers. I wanted to stop it but they wouldn't let me. So I ran. For years I've been running. I got tired. I found you."

Doc Matkin entered the room with two cups of freshly brewed coffee. She handed one to Iverson and sat down with the other. She held up her hand and splayed out its five digits. Iverson had five more minutes.

"You mentioned the High Five yesterday," Iverson said to Horvat. "Who are they?"

"Houston divided the U.S. into four sectors," Horvat explained. "West, East, South and Midwest. Each sector has a head. That's four. The heads have a head. That makes five. The High Five."

"And you worked directly under the West Sector head?"

"Correct."

"His name?"

"No name. He called me with instructions."

"And you said you dumped the phone, right?"

"Yes. It was traceable. I didn't wish to be found."

Iverson paused before continuing. "Tell me about the instructions," he said.

"Always simple. A name, description, date, time and location."

"And it was understood that it was an order to kill the named person?"

"Correct."

"And after the kill?"

"I would receive another call asking for the outcome."

"And the Kill Books record those contracts?"

"Correct."

Iverson paused again, collecting his thoughts. "What changed your mind?" he finally asked.

"About killing?"

"Yeah," Iverson said, "about killing."

"Not really sure, Iverson," answered Horvat. "Maybe I reached my limit."

"Of killing?" Iverson asked.

"Yes," Horvat answered softly. "I guess I reached my limit of killing." He lowered his eyes and stared blankly at his hands.

Doc Matkin rose up and Iverson took the queue. He lifted himself from his chair, straightened his back and stepped toward the door. He turned at the threshold and spoke to the man in the bed. "I'll see you in a few days," he told Horvat.

"Maybe sooner," Horvat replied.

*****

Iverson left Doc Matkin's and drove back to Valley Christian Hospital. He parked Henry at the back end of the lot and walked to the hospital's main entrance. He avoided the ER entrance as a consideration to Dr. Jenkins. Houston was downsizing their Oregon operation and their risk assessment probably included Jenkins. Another Iverson sighting in the ER might confirm his termination. There'd been too many deaths already.

Iverson walked through the large automated front doors of VCH and headed to the main reception desk. The woman working the counter was an effervescent beauty.

Her long blonde hair framed an angelic face and a hint of make-up emphasized her sky blue eyes. Iverson wished he had more time. Old fools always do.

"Could you point me to the pharmacy?" Iverson asked pleasantly.

"I'll do better than that," the cherub replied. "I'm headed in that direction and would be happy to escort you."

"Perfect," Iverson said. He stepped aside and allowed the woman to take the lead. She slowed her pace and allowed Iverson into the space adjacent hers. He made a brief attempt at conversation. It failed miserably. The pharmacy sign appeared at the turn of a corner and Iverson was more than relieved.

"Thank you," Iverson told the woman.

"My pleasure," the woman replied as she continued down the hall. Iverson watched her walk away. *Not in any lifetime,* he said to himself.

There was only one pharmacist on duty and he was too busy counting pills to notice Iverson lingering at the counter. Iverson cleared his throat to announce his presence but the white coated worker kept counting. Iverson assumed he'd been heard and checked his phone for messages while he waited for the pill-count to be completed. Numaga had left one message. *Got red boots. red e for texas.*

"Can I help you?" the pharmacist asked.

"I hope so," replied Iverson. "Did you by chance get a message from Dr. Jenkins regarding information on a patient named Frantzen?"

"I have the information but I'll need to verify identity before I can release it."

"Sure, no problem," Iverson said. He pulled out his wallet and opened it up for the pharmacist to examine his driver's license.

"Your license corresponds to the name Dr. Jenkins left on his message, but I'm still not sure how ethical this is. There are laws that govern the confidentiality of our patients."

"There're also laws that govern murder," Iverson rebutted, "and those are the laws I'm seeking to uphold right now. You get to choose which ones are most important."

The pharmacist tapped his fingers rhythmically on the counter, trying to decide what to do. After a few seconds of internal debate, he handed a twice folded slip of paper to Iverson.

"I hope you're legit," the pharmacist said.

"I hope your patient's still alive," responded Iverson. He abruptly turned away from the counter, navigated a maze of hallways and left the hospital. He didn't look for the blonde.

*****

Iverson parked Henry a block away from the address listed on the pharmacist's note. He killed the engine, lit up a Camel and took a long look at the landscape. The two-storied apartment complex sat at the western most edge of town. It had been constructed in the late 1970's and, despite pockets of weathering from Oregon's harsh climate, was still an appealing place to live.

The location was relatively secluded and quiet. *A selling point for Frantzen,* Iverson thought. The compound's architect had the artistic foresight to wend the pod array around and through a stand of ancient Sitka spruce. The synergy served both the human and sylvan residents. A well-traveled road flanked the property's eastern perimeter but its remaining three boundaries were open acreage. Two margins had been preserved as wildlife habitat and the third was owned by a family who'd shown an impressive resistance to development disease.

Iverson crushed out the Camel, exited Henry and walked to the facility's center courtyard. He checked the numbers on his note and located Frantzen's apartment; first floor, end of a pod and adjacent a parking area. *Strategic,* Iverson assessed. He cautiously approached number 124 and knocked on its door. No response. He knocked again. Same result. He left the doorway, walked past a curtained window and moved around the corner of the building. The back end of the pod was fenced with a six-foot high row of faded cedar slats. Iverson craned his neck to acquire a view of Frantzen's back yard. Nobody there. He returned to the front entry and knocked louder. Again no response. He grasped the door knob firmly and turned it. No resistance. He took out his weapon and pushed the door open slowly. A television droned in the room to the left of the entryway and he stalked in its direction. He stepped through the room's threshold and saw Frantzen slouched in an overstuffed chair. He had two vacant eyes and a hole in between them.

Iverson cautiously approached Frantzen and, out of reflex, checked his pulse. No blood pumped through Frantzen's veins. His body was cold and rigor mortis had claimed it. Frantzen's life and the person who took it were both long gone. Iverson holstered his weapon, left the body and checked the house for clues to his death. He found none. What he did find was a slackly packed suitcase, an uneaten meal and the remnants of a Spartan existence. The apartment was austere and unadorned. No comforts. No keepsakes. It was cold and lifeless. Just like its occupant.

Iverson texted Numaga to meet him at the airport and then used the burner phone he found in Frantzen's pocket to make another 9-1-1 call. It was his third in three days. A trend he'd like to end. After one last look around Frantzen's apartment, he walked briskly back to his truck and drove to World Wide Travel. It was time to get the hell out of town.

Chapter 49

Numaga was waiting in the airport lounge when Iverson arrived. Her beer was half empty, so Iverson guessed she'd been there awhile. He checked the clock above the bar, ordered a Hefeweizen and joined Numaga at her table. He drained half the beer in one long gulp before detailing his conversation with Horvat and describing what he'd found at Frantzen's.

Numaga shook her head. "Eight dead," she lamented. "Been a helluva week, Stan."

"And it's not over yet, Numaga," Iverson cautioned. "I'm hoping we can bring this to a close in Texas."

"What's your plan for Horvat?"

Iverson knew the question was coming sooner or later. Gabos Horvat was a murderer. By his own admission, he'd facilitated or participated in dozens of killings. Iverson had developed a sense of compassion for the Croatian. He actually liked him. But the fact remained; he was a murderer by both legal and ethical definitions.

"He'll have to be handed over to APD as soon as he's healed."

"And when might that be?"

"It'll ultimately be up to Doc Matkin, but he was looking better this morning."

"How're you feeling about that?"

Iverson took a moment before responding. He wasn't totally sure himself. "There's really no choice," he finally said. "I know we've discussed the choice making difference between PI's and cops, but there's no choice to be made here. Horvat needs to be judged for his crimes."

"I think he knows that, don't you?" Numaga rebutted. "I mean he asked you to kill him, right?"

Iverson sloshed down the last of his beer. "Yeah, he did. But I don't think he gets to be his own judge and select his own executioner." He pointed to the clock. "Time to go, Numaga."

Iverson handed Numaga a boarding pass and briefly detailed their itinerary. A one hour flight to Portland, an hour layover, and then a three hour flight to Houston. Their luggage was carry-on so they headed to the line wending its way through the security area. They both had unloaded handguns in their luggage so they were pulled aside and thoroughly searched and questioned. Numaga's badge expedited the process.

The Boeing 727 was full. One hundred and fifty passengers crammed like sardines into a narrow fuselage. Iverson and Numaga walked slowly past the First Class section and settled into row eighteen. Center wing seats.

"Great," Iverson mumbled. "Fuel seats. At least if the damn thing explodes, we'll be the first ones out."

"A little queasy about flying, Stan?" Numaga asked gingerly.

"If I was supposed to fly, Numaga," he said with a glare, "I'd have been born with wings."

Numaga backed off. Iverson's body language conveyed borderline fear. They stowed their gear and settled into their cramped space and watched the remainder of the herd board the plane. Iverson sat in the window seat staring out at the green fields surrounding the airport. *One last look at home,* he thought. He really did hate flying.

The flight to Portland was uneventful. The aircraft took off easily, landed smoothly and didn't explode in between. Their next flight was scheduled to depart two gates down from their arrival gate. There was a lounge planted in between the gates and Iverson found it, plopped himself on a bar chair and ordered a beer. Numaga followed suit. They drank in silence, focusing instead on the breaking news broadcast on the television above the bar. The Ken Doll anchor was describing the latest in a string of murders in the Ashton area. It had been reported at 10 AM by an anonymous 9-1-1 caller and was being labeled by APD as an apparent contract killing. The announcer was attempting to make a connection between this murder and the others that had occurred in the past few days. He offered a number of potential theories as to who might be behind the killings and why. None of them came close to what Iverson and Numaga knew to be the truth. The two PI's looked at each other, shrugged their shoulders in unison and walked to their next gate.

Iverson took an aisle seat. Numaga wanted to catch the sleep she'd promised herself but decided keeping her partner busy with conversation was more important.

"I notified the Houston PD that we'd be in their area doing some investigative work," Numaga announced.

Iverson wasn't particularly happy with Numaga's revelation but he knew it was what she had to do. It was universal protocol to notify any local PD of your presence and intent if you were conducting an investigation on their turf. Cops are competitive. Collars are contested. Numaga was still a cop. "Who'd you contact?" he asked.

"Sergeant Joseph Parker," answered Numaga. "He's a twenty-year Houston PD vet and has worked homicide for the last ten."

"Sounds like you know Mr. Parker."

"I do," Numaga confirmed. "We all know each other."

"We?"

"Natives in law enforcement. We actually have our own organization."

"Seriously?" Iverson responded. "What's it called?"

"Natives in Law Enforcement," Numaga said with a smile.

The plane taxied out to the runway and Iverson's grip on the seat arms tightened. His knuckles whitened and his facial muscles stretched taut. Numaga could see him taking long, deep breaths in a quest for self-control. She studied the tough old cop briefly, gently patted his arm, then lightly grasped and held it. He didn't remove her hand. They both stared straight ahead as the Boeing 737 thundered down the runway and achieved airborne status. *No going back now.*

When the plane leveled out at 32,000 feet, Numaga flagged down a flight attendant and ordered two drinks, one for herself and one for Iverson. She gave the uniformed woman a subtle shift of her eyes in Iverson's direction and the attendant's nod indicated her grasp of the message. She returned quickly with two small bottles of vodka and offered a choice of mixes. Numaga chose for both of them, paid for the beverages with a credit card swipe and blended an elixir for herself and her partner. The drinks were both a stabilizer and a conversation re-starter.

"What tribe does Joseph Parker belong to?" asked Iverson.

"He's a Wichita."

" A Texas tribe?"

"Originally in Texas, but now with recognized land in Oklahoma."

A brief pause in the conversation was ended by Numaga. "I lied about the organization," she said.

"So there's no Natives in Law Enforcement?"

"No," admitted Numaga. "But there *is* a Native American Foster Care Association. Sergeant Parker and I are members." Iverson looked uneasy, but this time it was related to the conversation, not the altitude. "NAFCA was chartered shortly after the Indian Child Welfare Act of 1978. ICWA gave Indian families a voice. NAFCA gives Indian children a voice."

Iverson tried to alter the mood of the conversation. "I can't imagine you needing a voice, Numaga."

"All kids need a voice, Stan," Numaga replied, "particularly kids in foster care. You know that better than most."

"I had no problems in foster care," Iverson insisted.

"Bullshit," Numaga responded.

Iverson slumped back into his seat. His body language said the conversation was over. Numaga ignored it. She had a thoroughly captive audience. An audience in need of a diversion. "How old were you?" she asked.

Iverson kept his gaze focused forward but managed a response. "How old when?"

"How old were you when you first entered foster care?"

Iverson took a deep breath and stared at Numaga with intense eyes. She returned a kind and gentle look. A welcoming look. A look that said she understood.

Iverson exhaled. "I'm not sure," he said. "Around two, I guess. Maybe earlier. There was a lot of back and forth."

"Lotsa different families?" Numaga asked.

"*Always* different families," Iverson emphasized. He said it to himself more than to Numaga.

"Any worth remembering?" Numaga probed.

Iverson paused, examining his past for an answer. "I can't recall any," he eventually said, "so I guess the answer is no. I never wanted to know the foster parents or the other kids. I just wanted to go home."

"I know," Numaga said. "I felt the same way. Most foster kids do. No matter how crappy home is, that's where we want to be."

"Weird, huh?" Iverson judged.

"Not really, Stan," explained Numaga. "We were kids. We were emotionally bonded to our parents like all kids are. We wanted their love regardless of the form it came in. That they were incapable of providing it in a healthy way, was not our fault."

"That little bit of helpful analysis somehow escaped me when I was two-years old," Iverson said cynically.

Numaga could feel the anger in Iverson's comment. "What was the hardest part for you?" she asked.

Iverson thought again before answering. "At first, the hardest part was being taken from home. But eventually, the hardest part became *going* home because home didn't last. It wasn't real. It didn't exist. I'd go home filled with hope that my mother had changed. She never did. Her demons were too powerful. Eventually, I gave up the hope. It caused too much pain. I'd just wait for the social worker to show up and take me away."

"And this went on for how long?"

"She died when I was six."

"That's a lot of hopeless years, Stan," Numaga said. "That's devastating at that age."

"I survived," Iverson assured Numaga.

"Yeah, you did," Numaga concurred, "but what was the cost?" Iverson didn't answer because he didn't *know* the answer. He'd never asked the question.

Numaga flagged down the flight attendant, ordered another round of drinks and moved the conversation to lighter fare. She'd hoped to give Iverson something to think about besides flying in a tin can at 32,000 feet. Mission accomplished. They landed in Houston at 4:00 PM, CST.

Chapter 50

Six different flags have flown over Texas: Spain, France, Mexico, the Republic Of Texas, the Confederacy, and the United States. The state draws its present-day identity from each of those standards as well as from the ancient cultures that preceded the first explorers. Comanche, Apache, Kiowa, Caddo and Mexican traditions figure prominently in the state alongside the imported cultures of the European settlers who arrived later.

Europeans were interested in Texas as early as 1519, when Spanish conquistadores searching for the fabled cities of gold navigated the Gulf of Mexico and landed on the shores of Southeast and South Texas. Although no gold gilded cities were ever found, the Spanish established numerous missions in South and West Texas, including the state's earliest towns. In 1685, the French, still convinced there was treasure to be found, financed a colonizing expedition to the Gulf Coast led by Sieur de La Salle. The weather, Indians, and an unhappy crew kept La Salle from succeeding. The French abandoned their claim to Texas.

The Spanish continued their missionary efforts through the 18th and early 19th centuries. The territory was cultivated as ranchland under the auspices of the Spanish government. Colonization continued as political winds shifted farther south, forever changing the face of the region. Mexico, which had won its independence from Spain, enticed settlers to the Texas territory with offers of land grants. When disputes over ownership and religion exploded between the Texan population and the Mexican government, another fight for independence was on, this one for independence from Mexico.

On March 6, 1836, Mexico's dictator, General Antonio Lopez Santa Anna, led his troops into San Antonio and massacred a small band of Texans at the Alamo mission. Santa Anna went on to defeat the Texans at the Battle of Goliad shortly afterward. The Texan troops, however, marched valiantly on. Finally, in a military blunder that cost him the war, Santa Anna marched his troops straight into a surprise attack led by General Sam Houston at San Jacinto on April 21, 1836. Texas gained its independence in a battle lasting only eighteen minutes.

The new Republic of Texas named Sam Houston its president and the republic lasted almost a decade. In 1845, it became the 28th state in the Union. The new state was deluged with adventurers, fortune seekers and settlers. After a short period of peace, Texas found itself embroiled in another war. It seceded from the Union and joined the Confederacy in 1861. Unlike most of the other combating states, the Civil War rejuvenated the Texas economy. Longhorn cattle became prized for their robust nature and over the two decades immediately following the war, cattle drives were a common site. Nothing in Texas' past, however, prepared it for the change that transpired when the Splindletop oil well roared on January 10, 1901.The race for the black gold and the power that went with it was on.

The traditional Euro-American culture of Texas was heavily influenced by the plantation culture of the Old South. It was dependent on African-American slave labor as well as the patron system prevalent in northern Mexico and South Texas. In these societies, the government's primary role was seen as being the preservation of large scale social order. Individual problems were seen as local problems with the expectation that individuals should resolve their own issues. These attitudes continue to affect Texas today. Texans are fiercely independent and highly resistant to outside influences. They will go to great lengths to demonstrate their individuality and their eccentricity.

*****

Iverson and Numaga were greeted at the airport by Joseph Parker. Introductions were made and the usual post-flight banter was shared. The Houston detective suggested a beer at a nearby bar while debriefing the case that had brought the Oregonians to Texas. Iverson readily agreed. Walker grabbed Numaga's small piece of luggage, shook out its wheels and led his guests to The Longhorn Lounge. He chose a large booth with red Naugahyde seats. A small chandelier constructed of intertwined cow horns loomed above them and all the other booth sitters in the lounge. A bar menu, a beer list and oil derrick salt and pepper shakers were enclosed in a miniature corral in the center of their table. *Definitely in Texas,* Iverson thought.

Joseph Walker was a striking man. Numaga had suggested that Walker was in early fifties, but he looked younger. Iverson guessed his height at around six-four; his weight at about two-twenty. He wore suede cowboy boots, tight blue jeans and an olive plaid shirt stretched tight by the muscles concealed beneath it. His Wichita heritage was proudly displayed in a strong-boned face and dark, deep-set eyes. His long, black hair was harnessed in a ponytail and the few grey streaks wending through it provided an aura of dignity to an already impressive man. Joseph Walker was the perfect cop. Iverson was impressed. Numaga was enamored.

They all ordered beer. Walker ordered a Lone Star, Numaga a Bud-Light and Iverson a Hefeweizen. The pert and pretty waitress presented a bewildered look to Iverson so he simplified his choice to a Budweiser. They settled into case-talk while waiting for the beverages.

"So what's your investigative itinerary?" asked Walker.

Numaga looked at Iverson and he nodded for her to take the lead. It made sense. She knew Walker.

"We only have one lead," she admitted, "so I guess that's where we'll start."

"And that would be where?" Walker asked.

"Global Solutions," replied Numaga. "Do you know much about them?"

"I know where they're located but not much else. They've never been on my radar."

"So no prior legal issues as far as you know?"

"Nothing has come across my desk with their name on it," answered Walker. "But as you know, that doesn't mean anything. Global Solutions could be spit-shine clean or they could simply be good at the crimes they commit."

"We're pretty sure they're involved in the killings back in Oregon," Numaga said "It's just a matter of figuring out the who and why of it all and then making a case that will hold up in court."

"That's always the problem, isn't it?" Walker lamented.

All three nodded in unison. Evidence, even really solid evidence, was often not enough to convict someone of a crime. Sometimes, it wasn't even good enough to get an arrest. Cops could work diligently collecting physical evidence and have it dismissed or disallowed on any number of technicalities. Relevance, possession, tampering and chain of custody are among the many issues that plague physical evidence. Judges don't allow anything into their courtrooms that might end up being the cause for an appeal. Judges hate appeals. Appeals are judges passing judgment on other judges. They do everything in their power to avoid an appeal that could refute or rebuke their decisions. Control of admissible evidence is their most useful tool in achieving that goal.

Iverson took a turn. "How's the Child Welfare agency here in Texas?"

"In what regard?" asked Walker.

"Are they pretty clean in terms of operations?"

Walker took a long drink from his longneck. "They've had their problems. The overall problem of child abuse has blown up with the increased use of methamphetamine. It's a real plague down here."

"It's a plague everywhere," stressed Numaga.

"Anything out of the ordinary?" asked Iverson.

"Homicide doesn't normally have contact with CPS, but we've had a few cases lately that crossed over with them. A couple of deaths involving foster kids and one that involved a foster parent that we got involved in."

"Separate cases?" Iverson queried.

"Yeah," confirmed Walker. "We never found a connection between them."

"Were they all resolved?"

"Yeah," Walker said again. "Two quick trials and a plea bargain."

"You sound surprised by that," Numaga gauged.

"To be honest, I was surprised," Walker said. "You guys know how slowly the wheels of justice turn. They probably turn a little faster in Texas due to the judicial mood here, but all three of those cases were moved through the courts with uncommon speed."

"How so?" asked Iverson.

"Arrests and arraignments occurred within two weeks of the crime and the two trials were docketed within a month of the arraignments. And the verdicts for both were rendered within a week of opening remarks."

Iverson bit his lower lip and nodded slowly. Texas justice was obviously quick justice. Either they took the right to a speedy trial unusually seriously or something else was in play.

"Who went to trial?" Iverson asked.

"The two individuals indicted for the kids' deaths," reported Walker.

"Charges?"

"Voluntary manslaughter and depraved indifference."

"Sentencing?"

"Two years each."

Iverson's eyebrows elevated slightly. "Tell me about the plea bargain," he continued.

"A foster parent killed a man he claimed was an intruder. Evidence was sketchy and the only weapon found was the foster parent's gun. Plus the victim was a non-citizen. We couldn't find any information on him and found no evidence connecting him to the foster parent."

"The plea?"

"Voluntary manslaughter with mitigating circumstances."

"Sentence?"

"Two years," Walker revealed. "Suspended."

Iverson's tilted head and furrowed brow revealed his bafflement.

"I know," Walker said frankly. "Not quite right, is it?"

"Did you work any of the cases, Joe?" Numaga asked.

"I didn't," Walker answered. "All three cases were handled by Detectives Colton and Stroik."

"Still in the department?" asked Iverson.

"Stroik died in a car wreck about six months ago. Colton left the force shortly after Stroik died and had a heart attack about a month later. Died at the hospital."

"How about the D.A. who prosecuted the cases?" asked Numaga.

"That would be Andrew Burleson."

"And what's happened to Mr. Burleson?"

"Also gone," Walker informed. "Early retirement."

Iverson's eyes met Numaga's and they understood each other's look. *No such thing as a coincidence.* They charted the information and moved on.

The cop, the ex-cop and the one in between decided they were hungry and Walker insisted that the airport lounge was an unacceptable place to sample genuine Texas cuisine. The Texan paid for the beers and led his guests and their wheeled luggage through the maze of walkways and escalators and out to the car rental area. Walker left to retrieve his own vehicle while Iverson filled out the paperwork to secure theirs.

Iverson and Numaga walked out of the airport and exchanged its air-cooled environment for a wall of suffocating heat. They located their silver Ford Escort among a long line of baking rentals. Walker pulled up alongside them in a double-cab Dodge pick-up as they were tossing their suitcases into the Escort's small trunk. He instructed them to follow him and promised to drive at a speed that would enable the rental to follow. Just to be on the safe side, he hollered an exit number as he pulled away into traffic.

Detective Walker wended his way expertly through George Bush Intercontinental Airport and worked his way onto I-45. He followed rush hour traffic to a mid-town off-ramp and exited behind a line of slow moving commuters headed home from work. The Escort followed two cars behind. Numaga was driving; Iverson sightseeing.

Downtown Houston was a high-rise jungle. Iverson lowered his window, craned his neck upward and stared with amazement at the mirrored buildings soaring from the pavement into the bright blue sky. Though not quite summer, the air was stifling and Iverson's view was distorted by slowly rolling waves of heat seeking an escape route from the wall of buildings. Numaga reached over and cranked up the AC to counter the heat coming through Iverson's opened window.

Walker drove slowly, keeping the visitors close behind him. After navigating through a series of traffic lights, he turned off the main thoroughfare and into a less developed area of the city. A few blocks later, he crooked into a small, crowded parking lot next to a semi-dilapidated building with a sign above the portico that read "Jake's." Numaga slid the Escort into the slot next to the Dodge and they exited their vehicles in unison.

"Houston's best," Walker announced.

Iverson's skepticism was obvious. With his hands on his hips, he surveyed Jake's and the surrounding area with the eye of the detective he was. The neighborhood was old and littered with ramshackle storefronts. Many were shuttered closed and appeared to have been that way for some time. Foot traffic was sparse, unhurried and indifferent. In many ways, it reminded Iverson of The Brubaker area back in Ashton. The favorable comparison narrowed his concerns.

"What's on the menu?" inquired Numaga.

"Really good food," replied Walker briskly. "I'll order, you eat."

They walked into the eatery and Walker was immediately greeted by name by a harried waitress. She was a tall, fair skinned, red haired beauty. Two large, silver hoops dangled from her ears and a much smaller one protruded from her left nostril. She had a tattooed star on one arm and a dragon slithering down the other. Her green eyes twinkled despite her frazzled demeanor. The smile she presented Walker was bright and genuine.

"Your table for three is ready, Mr. Walker," she declared. "Good thing you called when you did."

"You called ahead?" Numaga asked Walker.

"At a stop-light stop," Walker described. "This place is always busy so I figured I'd better get us a table."

"Looks like you made the right decision," Numaga said as she surveyed the room and the line forming behind them.

The waitress herded them to an area in the far back of the dining room. She sat them at a well-worn table that had four unmatched chairs. Salt, pepper and sugar containers sat on the table-top and were accompanied by an array of hot sauces in multi-shaped bottles. No menus. The waitress waited; pencil and pad ready for work.

"We'll have the big tray," Walker said.

"Dirty rice and bread?" asked the waitress.

"Absolutely," Walker replied enthusiastically.

"Beer or Sweet Tea?"

Walker looked over at Numaga and Iverson for their preferences before ordering three longneck Lone Stars. The waitress finished writing the order, smiled appreciatively and walked to another table of hungry customers.

"Big tray?" Numaga inquired.

"Patience, Cassie," Walker appealed.

"Will I have to kill it before I eat it?" questioned Iverson semi-seriously.

"Maybe a few," Walker teased.

They sat and discussed the weather and a few other mundane topics before the Lone Stars arrived. The "big tray" arrived shortly thereafter. It was hefty platter holding an enormous mound of bright red crayfish. Two bowls of liquid, a basket of sliced French bread and a bowl of rice mixed with kernels of corn and diced peppers were also placed on the table.

"Smallest lobster I've ever seen," Iverson quipped. "I thought everything in Texas was supposed to be big."

"These here are Texas shrimp, Detective," Walker retorted. He winked at Numaga.

"Seriously?" Iverson asked.

Numaga stepped in. "These are crayfish, Stan," she explained. "AKA crawdads."

Walker grabbed a handful of the clawed cuisine and dropped them on his plate. Numaga did the same. Iverson examined the miniature lobsters carefully and took one. Walker then spooned some rice onto his plate and offered the bowl to Iverson. "Dirty rice?" he asked.

"Not without an explanation," Iverson qualified.

Walker smiled broadly, set the bowl down and offered a verbal rendition of the recipe. "Boil up some chicken livers, set the meat aside and cook up some rice in the liver juice. Throw some diced onions and peppers along with some corn on the finished rice and, voila! Dirty rice."

Numaga watched Iverson's reaction with interest and amusement. He had listened attentively and was now deciding whether or not to merge his new knowledge with his palate. *To eat or not to eat . . . that was the question.* After a few moments of deliberation, he grabbed the rice bowl, took a small scoop of its contents and tapped it onto his plate. He then took one crawdad from the tray and laid it gently next to the small rice mound. Lastly, he snatched three pieces of bread from the basket. *Just in case,* Numaga figured. She grabbed herself a handful of crawdads, a large helping of rice and a chunk of bread.

"Just how does one eat a crayfish?" Iverson asked.

"Fortunately," Walker announced, "Crawdad 101 is in session." He lifted one from his plate for Iverson to see and then bent the critter's tail downward before realigning it and jerking the tail and a bundle of trailing flesh away from the hard-shelled body. He sucked the crawdad's body cavity loudly and discarded it into a large empty bowl. He dipped the tail into one of the two bowls of liquid, put it to his mouth and pulled out the meat with his teeth. The tail's husk then rejoined its shell in the debris bowl.

"What's in the bowls?" asked Iverson.

"Butter and vinegar," Walker said while pointing to each as it was identified.

Iverson grabbed his crawdad and mimicked his Texas host. His effort wasn't perfect, but he got a small morsel of meat and a large ration of flavor. He grabbed another one and repeated the effort. Then another. And still another. He put a trace of rice into his mouth, moved it over his taste buds and swallowed it. Without comment, he added a larger portion to his plate.

The meal was consumed quickly and accompanied by brief snippets of predictable conversation. Getting acquainted dialog. The meal completed and their hunger sated, the discussion returned to the case.

"What's our responsibility to you?" Numaga asked Walker.

"I'd like a daily update," Walker specified. "It's more so that I know your safe, but I also need to cover my ass with my bosses."

"Who all knows we're here?" asked Iverson.

Detective Walker listed his squad's Lieutenant and Captain as those he'd been required to notify of Numaga and Iverson's presence and intentions. Neither PI had a problem with the arrangement. They both were familiar with departmental politics and protocols. They also understood that they were fortunate in being granted formal investigative privileges in a city where Numaga's badge held no jurisdiction and Iverson held nothing at all. Iverson was certain that Walker's and Numaga's shared heritage had been instrumental in making that happen.

Walker changed the conversation's direction. "Cassie tells me you're a member of our tribe," he said to Iverson.

Iverson looked over at Numaga who busied herself with an extraneous bite of bread.

"Which tribe might that be, Detective Walker?" Iverson asked.

"The tribe of foster kids," Walker answered.

Iverson glared at Numaga. She glared back. Iverson returned to Walker. "Numaga did mention that the two of you belonged to some organization."

"NAFCA," Walker replied. "Got any Indian blood in you, Sergeant?" he asked.

"Not that I know of. Why?"

"We're always looking to enhance our membership."

"Thanks, but no thanks," Iverson said. "I don't play well with others."

"No argument on that," Numaga teased. "It's getting late, Stan," she added. "I think we should locate our accommodations."

Iverson checked his watch and nodded his agreement with Numaga. Walker flagged the waitress and a minute later she arrived with the check. They each laid enough cash on the bill tray to cover the charges and add a generous tip.

"Thanks for meeting us at the airport and for taking us to Jake's," Numaga said once they got outside. "It's nice to have a familiar face in a strange town."

"My pleasure," said Walker. "I was glad you called. I'm available to help as much as I can."

"You could start right now if you'd like," Iverson interjected.

"Uh, sure," Walker responded. "What can I do?"

"Two things," Iverson said. "One, tell us how to get to the Alamo Inn."

"That one's easy," Walker said and pointed down the street. "Take a right at that light and your hotel should be about ten blocks down. There'll be a large Alamo Inn sign on the right side of the road. Can't miss it. What's number two?"

"I'd like an address for District Attorney Burleson."

*****

Iverson and Numaga found the Alamo Inn without difficulty and Numaga parked the Escort under the large awning that shaded the main entryway. They left their luggage in the car and walked together into the three story hotel. An array of stuffed animal heads greeted them and the glass eyes of sacrificial deer, elk and pronghorn stared vacantly at them as they made their way to the reception desk. Aside from the taxidermy, the building's interior was typical of all corporate owned hotels catering to transient and weary travelers. It had a well-appointed foyer with a comfortable sitting area and a computer station set off to the side for those not carrying their laptops on their journey. Reproduced scenes of Texas landscapes hung from the small sections of wall space not adorned with dead animals. Iverson didn't see the breakfast nook frequently found at these overnight stops but he did see a sign labeled "Restaurant and Lounge" and an arrow pointing down a hallway. Breakfast wouldn't be complimentary. Numaga left Iverson and followed the sign and Iverson set off to secure the two rooms his agent had booked for them. The desk clerk looked up from her computer screen and greeted Iverson with an agreeable smile.

"Good evening, sir. How may I help you?"

Her accent was subdued, but unmistakable. She was tall, thin and more cute than pretty. Her dark hair matched her eyes and its shoulder length style flipped upward as it gently touched her shoulders. Her blouse was low cut and the blue-stoned necklace she wore drew Iverson's eyes to the clear, smooth skin it lay upon. He kept his glance brief.

"Two rooms in the name of Iverson," Iverson said. "There were special requests with the reservation."

The clerk scanned her computer briefly before responding. "Here it is, sir," she said pleasantly. "I'll just need identification and a credit card."

Iverson produced both, signed the paperwork the clerk presented him and gathered the rooms' key cards. Numaga re-joined him as he was completing the process.

"How's the bar look?" he asked.

"Like the perfect place to de-brief today and plan for tomorrow," Numaga answered.

"Great," Iverson said. "Let's dump the luggage in the rooms and meet back in the bar in fifteen minutes."

"Perfect," agreed Numaga.

They retrieved their luggage from the Escort and rolled it back past the reception desk and down the hallway to their rooms. Iverson had requested adjoining first floor rooms with a common internal access door. He handed Numaga her key card and used his on the door next to hers. He threw his gear on the bed and checked out his room before knocking on the common door. Numaga opened it.

"Why, Stan," she said. "I hadn't realized our relationship had made the leap." Her tone and look both told Iverson she was teasing, but his face still flushed.

"I, uh . . .," stammered Iverson.

"Just kidding, Stan," Numaga disclosed. "But you should know that you're actually kind of cute when you're vulnerable."

Iverson wasn't sure what to make of the comment so he left it alone and recalibrated. "If it's okay with you, Detective Numaga," he said, "I think it's best if this door remains unlocked."

"Will I be safe?" Numaga asked, keeping her foot on the tease peddle.

"From me, yes," Iverson assured stoically. "I'm pretty sure I'm still one of the good guys. It's the bad guys I'm worried about."

"Okay, Stan," Numaga relented. "We'll keep the door unlocked. I understand and agree with the serious context of what you're saying."

Iverson gave Numaga a nod, closed the door and returned to the hallway outside their rooms. He paced the building's lower level and mentally mapped its floor plan and the location of its exits. He then walked out of the building and over to the Escort. He plucked his set of the Escort's keys from a pocket and backed the car into a slot directly across from a driveway that accessed the main road in front of the Alamo Inn. He returned to the hotel lobby, spun into the lounge and found a vacant booth with a view of the same driveway. He sat down and waited for Numaga. She appeared five minutes later. They debriefed the day and talked about their approach to the next one until jetlag caught up with them. They left the lounge and separated at their hotel room doors. Their beds and sleep welcomed them.

Chapter 51

Iverson woke up earlier than normal. He attributed his restiveness to the two hour time change, but it had more to do with the heightened flow of adrenaline he always experienced when he felt a case coming to a climax. He took a quick shower, bladed off the graying stubble protruding from his face and threw on some wrinkled clothes he extracted from his hastily packed suitcase. He pressed his cell phone on to check messages and debated what would be an appropriate time to buzz Numaga's room with the hotel phone. The first text message he read ended the debate. He called Numaga.

Numaga answered her phone after two rings. "Good morning, Stan," she said without Iverson uttering a word.

"You awake?"

"Nope," Numaga retorted. "I'm having a sex dream and a fairly handsome old guy just called me."

Iverson appreciated the comment but ignored it. "Ready for breakfast?" he asked.

"Biscuits and gravy?"

"Not a chance, Numaga."

"C'mon, Stan," Numaga chastised. "We're in Texas. Enjoy the moment."

"I'm still enjoying the crawdads and dirty rice, Numaga," Iverson replied cynically. "My intestines need something familiar this morning."

Numaga laughed heartily. "Okay, Stan," she allowed. "Whatever keeps you off the porcelain."

"Downstairs in ten?" asked Iverson.

"See you there," Numaga approved.

Iverson took the same booth he and Numaga had occupied the previous evening. Numaga arrived a few minutes later and slid in across from him. A tired looking waiter came over and laid two breakfast menus on the table and asked if they wanted coffee. His question was answered quickly, affirmatively and in tandem. He scribbled on his note pad, swiveled and left to retrieve their start-up beverages.

"Really hungry or just eager to get started?" Numaga asked her partner.

Iverson ignored the question. "I got a text from Doc Matkin this morning."

"Is Horvat okay?" Numaga asked seriously.

"Horvat's gone."

"Gone?"

"Matkin checked on him when she got up and he wasn't there. He'd disconnected his IV and walked out."

Numaga sat back into the cushions. "Wow, Stan," she appraised. "What do you make of it?"

"I'm not sure, Numaga," Iverson said. "Could be he's bent on finishing the job of dying or maybe he's had some other plan all along. I really don't know what to think."

"He's got to know he's got no future. He'll be wanted in this country and I can't imagine he'll find any quarter back in Croatia after he quit on his countrymen here."

"He's not stupid, Numaga," Iverson assessed. "He knows his options are limited."

The torpid waiter appeared with their coffee and inquired as to their food preferences.

"Biscuits and gravy and a large OJ," Numaga announced quickly. Iverson scanned his menu for a few more seconds before ordering oatmeal and an apple juice.

"That's definitely safe," Numaga teased.

"The crawdads are still swimming in their butter," replied Iverson.

The waiter walked away and Numaga moved back to work talk. "I got a text from Detective Walker this morning," she said.

"Anything we can use?"

"D.A. Burleson's address."

Iverson looked up, pushed himself back on the vinyl bench and took a swallow of hot coffee. "So much for that early skinny dip in the pool," he said. Numaga smiled. Stan Iverson had a sense of humor. Who knew?

*****

Numaga used her phone for directions to the address Walker had provided. Burleson's home was in an upper middle-class neighborhood. It was a two story, red brick Tudor style home that sat about 150 feet back from the road. The frontage was landscaped with a manicured lawn dotted with an assortment of well-trimmed shrubbery. The crown of a tall silver maple spread its heavy limbs over the back side of the roof and the morning's sunlight was stippling its way through its shiny leaves.

The house wasn't a mansion but it was certainly large. Iverson guessed four bedrooms, three baths minimum. A recent model, cream colored Land Rover sat at the end of the long driveway and in front of a closed garage. A black Toyota Avalon was parked next to it. Iverson looked over at Numaga who was slowly shaking her head. He didn't need to ask her what she was thinking. He was thinking the same thing. Early retirement worked well for D.A. Burleson.

Numaga drove slowly past the house, turned around and parked in the street directly across from Burleson's home. She made a quick phone call while Iverson watched the house. It was 7:30 AM. Early. A good thing. They got out of the car.

Numaga approached the front door and Iverson stood ten feet behind her. There shouldn't have been any reason for Burleson to expect them, or to present a threat if he did, but they weren't taking any chances. Not with the body count where it was. Numaga pushed the button in the middle of an oxidized sun ornament and heard a low-toned cascade of notes thrumming beyond the door. She waited approximately fifteen seconds before repeating the signal. A sleepy looking man opened the door. He was clad in red and white striped pajamas and a light blue, terry-cloth bathrobe. He stood about six feet tall and the loose fitting sleep wear failed to hide his substantial paunch. He was hairless except for the small patches of gray hair lingering above his ears and the meager eyebrows perched above his worried eyes.

"Andrew Burleson?" inquired Numaga.

The man looked beyond Numaga, saw Iverson with his hands folded over his chest and returned his attention to the woman in front of him.

"Do I know you?" he asked Numaga.

"We've never met," Numaga replied, "but I have a feeling you knew we'd show up here sooner or later."

Burleson looked around Numaga again and stared at Iverson. "I'll need some identification," he said calmly.

Numaga produced her badge and Iverson stepped forward and handed Burleson his business card. He studied them both carefully.

"You have no jurisdiction in this state," Burleson said matter-of-factly.

"You're absolutely right," Numaga conceded. "But we do have the local authorities' permission to conduct our investigation."

"And what is it that you're investigating on this fine Texas morning, Detective?"

Both Numaga and Iverson noted the Texas reference. Burleson wanted to remind the two Oregonians where they were.

"We're actually here to do you a favor, Mr. Burleson."

"Really?" Burleson asked cynically. "What favor might that be, Detective?"

"We're here to provide you a path to a long life."

"You've lost me, Detective?" Burleson said.

"It's early and you're probably still a little fuzzy," Numaga said, "so I'll make this quick and simple."

"Make what quick and simple?"

"We know about the High Five, Burleson."

Burleson paused briefly, took a step backwards and then responded. "I have no idea what you're talking about," he claimed.

"And we had every expectation you'd say that."

Burleson said nothing so Numaga continued. "The High Five is in trouble, Burleson. They're scrambling for cover. Their West Sector operation has collapsed. The Croatians are either talking or permanently silenced. I'm sure you think I'm lying, but consider this, Mr. Burleson: we're on your doorstep. How'd we get here? I'm betting your next visitors won't ring the doorbell first."

"I still have no idea what you're talking about," Burleson repeated. "I've got nothing more to say to you."

"As I said, Mr. Burleson, it's early, " Numaga replied calmly. "Have some coffee and digest this conversation thoroughly. Make some calls. Check my information. You'll find that the High Five is nervous. Real nervous. Eight people have already been killed and they'll surely not hesitate to kill more to protect themselves. And you, Mr. Burleson, are more liability than asset. Help us and we'll help you. Stand pat and you risk your life and the lives of the others inside this beautiful home of yours. The choice is yours. Choose wisely, Mr. Burleson. Choose quickly."

Numaga turned and walked down the steps to where Iverson stood. She heard the door slam behind her.

"Helluva bluff, Detective," Iverson appraised.

"Let's hope it works," Numaga replied.

Iverson and Numaga returned to the Escort and Numaga drove for a few blocks before pulling over to the curb. She snatched her phone from a pocket and called Detective Walker.

"Okay," Numaga told Walker. "We just left Burleson's. You can put your phone company contact to work."

"Is he worried?" Walker asked.

"I hope so," answered Numaga. She ended the call and looked over at Iverson. "Where to, Sergeant?"

"Global Solutions. It's time we took a look at the who part of what we're dealing with."

Numaga put her attention back on her phone. She Googled Global Solutions, typed the company's address into her phone's GPS system, tapped a few icons and finally handed the phone to Iverson. "I'll drive, you navigate," she said as she pulled away from the curb.

Iverson studied the map on the small screen. "Looks easy enough," he said hopefully.

"The satellite will keep us on track," Numaga explained. "You just tell me what streets to turn on."

Iverson did his job and the map directed them to the center of Houston's commercial district. They made three passes past their destination in an effort to find street parking. No luck. Numaga turned down a cross street and spotted a parking garage located in the center of the block. Iverson asked her to circle the lower level until a spot was vacated. Numaga honored his request and she eventually found an open slot. She didn't question her partner's constructive paranoia. She was learning to see its value.

Both Iverson and Numaga checked their weapons before exiting the Escort. They decided that Iverson would attempt to find someone from Global Solutions to speak with and Numaga would reconnaissance the building. They followed the Global Solutions signs to an access door, walked through it and stepped into an enormous lobby. Thirty foot windows separated by narrow slats of copper encircled the room. A polished marble floor anchored a wooden staircase that led up to a railed walkway and a series of double doors. A sitting area ensemble consisting of a long, white couch, two matching chairs and a glass and chrome table sat unoccupied at the base of the staircase. A uniformed man sat at a reception desk in the lobby's center and beyond him was another panel of doors, two of which were elevators, another two restrooms. Hallways flanked the panel and illuminated exit signs were posted above each access way.

Iverson and Numaga approached the guard. His well-muscled body sat uncomfortably on a long-legged, short-backed chair. He eyed them suspiciously.

"Can I help you?" he asked soberly.

"We'd like to speak to someone from Global Solution's administration," Iverson said.

"Do you have an appointment?" the guard asked.

"Nope," Iverson replied tersely.

"Then you won't be meeting with anyone from the company," the guard said unsympathetically.

Iverson watched the man check something below the counter and presumed it to be a monitor. He had already assumed that he and Numaga were being watched by any number of cameras that were placed in and around the building. They had most likely been tracked from the moment they exited their vehicle. The guard's action only confirmed it.

"Can I assume you have a camera back there as well as the monitor?" asked Iverson as he nodded towards the back of the counter.

"Excuse me?" the guard asked gruffly.

"It wasn't a hard question, Bubba," Iverson baited sarcastically.

Numaga broke in. "As much as I'd love to chat with you boys," she said, "Mother Nature beckons me elsewhere." She strode confidently past the desk and headed to the restroom. The guard watched her briefly before returning his attention to Iverson.

"This building is fully secure, sir," the guard explained. "We have cameras and monitors in many locations."

"So there's one right in front of you?" Iverson queried again.

The guard pondered the question and the consequences of either of the two possible answers. "Yeah," he finally said, "there's a camera." He pointed to a spot behind the counter Iverson couldn't see.

"I don't need to see it, Bubba," Iverson said caustically. "I just want you to put something in front of it."

"What?"

Iverson extracted a business card from his wallet and handed it to the guard. "Put that in front of the camera so that the boys upstairs can read it."

"What?" the guard asked again.

"Do I need to speak more slowly, Bubba?" Iverson taunted. The guard's face flushed red with anger but he understood his role. He was a replaceable part. He took the card from Iverson, examined it carefully, and held it in front of what Iverson presumed was a closed circuit camera. The phone on his desk buzzed thirty seconds later.

"Take the elevator to the sixteenth floor. Somebody will meet you there."

"See, Bubba," Iverson said mockingly, "that wasn't so hard." He walked to the elevator and pressed the up arrow.

"What about your lady friend?" asked the guard.

"Hell, Bubba," Iverson answered, "she could be in there for an hour. Send her on up when she surfaces." The elevator door opened and Iverson stepped in. He pushed the number sixteen button and gave Bubba a wave as the door closed between them. He figured he might have fifteen minutes with whomever it was that Global Solutions sent to meet him. Numaga probably had less.

The cameras undoubtedly would be watching both of them. *Fair enough,* he told himself. We're watching them too. He checked his Colt again and waited for the door to re-open.

Chapter 52

Numaga cracked open the restroom door and looked for the blue-clad guard. She located him sitting at his station paging mindlessly through a magazine. She wasn't sure what the subject matter was, but from their brief encounter, she figured it had to involve either scantily clad women or guns . . . or both. She opened the door wider, tested the brass hinges for complaints and found them to be pleasantly muted. She closed the door, connected a charge cord to her phone and plugged it into the wall socket above the sink. After the charging icon appeared, Numaga tapped up an app that she'd paid her geek friend handsomely to tailor to her personal needs. Its icon was a video camera encircled in, and crossed over, with a thin red line. *No video*. The app opened with a request for the user's ID and a password. Numaga entered both with a quick sequence of keyboard taps, pushed enter and activated the software that recognized any video equipment running off the same electrical circuit she was plugged into. Numaga was banking on the building's wiring being designed to incorporate a unique circuit for each of the building's levels. She anxiously waited the few moments it took for the software to search the circuit and was relieved when a list of eight cameras flashed onto her screen. A column immediately to the right of the list presented "Enable" or "Disable" options for each camera. Each camera was currently enabled so Numaga carefully scrolled down through the list and checked the box that disabled them. She unplugged her phone from the wall socket, returned to the door and cracked it open again. The somnambulant sentinel was still vicariously immersed in his publication. Numaga removed her shoes, eased her way out of the restroom and walked slowly toward the hallway at the west end of the lobby. She turned into the honeycombed passage and out of the view of the rent-a-cop.

Numaga wasn't exactly sure what she was looking for. She tested each of the doors she came across. Some opened, some didn't. Her lock-picking skills assured access to all of them. Cleaning supplies, unused office furniture and outdated electronic equipment populated many of the rooms. Nothing of interest. She found a back stairway, took it to the second floor and plugged her phone into an outlet at the top of the stairs. After tapping her way back to the video app, she located the second floor cameras and froze them. Moving slowly through the hall, she continued checking doors and examining contents. Still nothing. She came to a door secured with two locks rather than one. She heard a dead bolt shift in the door, jumped back and looked for a place to hide. She didn't find one. She quickly stashed her pick-kit in a pocket and greeted the startled man who opened the door.

"Perfect timing," Numaga stated brusquely. "I was just about to knock."

The nerdy looking man was taken aback by Numaga's presence. "Uh, who are you?" he managed.

"I'm from the security company contracted by Global Solutions," Numaga replied. "We got a call from management about a problem with the video monitoring system."

"What problem?" the nerd asked.

"If I knew that, I wouldn't be here, would I?"

The young man took a step back. "No one called me about a problem," he said meekly.

"Maybe you're not on the need to know list," Numaga suggested haughtily.

The nerd took another step back and Numaga moved past him. The room had a bank of computers abutting the far wall and a maze of cables tentacled between them. Laptop work stations, shelving, a full sized refrigerator and a microwave oven occupied the remaining space.

"Look," Numaga pressed, "I'm supposed to check all of the computer installation locations in the building and it looks to me like this room fits that description. Would you like me to call the CEO and tell him that my work is being impeded by an IT lackey?"

The nerd's shoulders slumped and he pushed his glasses up the bridge of his nose. "I just don't understand why I wasn't notified," he complained.

Numaga read the nerd's body language and ushered him into the hallway. "I'll need thirty minutes," she said rigidly. "Get yourself some coffee or whatever it is that nerds drink. Knock when you return."

The subdued geek moved slowly down the hall. Numaga dead bolted the door and took a seat by the largest computer screen in the room. She navigated to a file index and scrolled through the file folders until she found two that looked promising. The first was labeled "Accounting," the second, "Sector Records." Numaga checked their byte size. They were fairly large. That meant it would take some time to do what she wanted to do if she could find a way to do it.

Numaga needed to locate an e-mail server on the system that would enable her to attach the folders to an e-mail and send them to her account. She assumed, given the computers location and the multiple locks on the door, that the operating system's outside server had been disabled for security reasons. But she also knew geeks would never be stuck in a room for eight hours a day without Internet access. She ran a quick search for application files and scrolled through the file names looking for something familiar. She found a Foxfire file a quarter ways down, double clicked it and found herself in the Internet. She opened the create-mail window and inserted her e-mail address into the send-to box. She then clicked on the attach-file icon and attached both the Sector Records and Accounting folders. She hit the send button and a message box popped up telling her it would take seven minutes to complete the file transfer. She sat back and nervously watched the progress bar.

The green bar finally disappeared and Foxfire notified Numaga that her files had been sent successfully. She backed out of the system, returned the monitor to its original screen and answered the knock on the door. She brushed past the nerd, walked to the end of the hallway, stopped and waited for the dead bolt to shoot home.

Hearing it, she plugged in her phone, re-enabled the video cams and repeated the exercise when she got back to the first floor.

Numaga navigated back down the hall and peeked into the lobby. No guard. She strolled over to the seating cluster, lowered herself onto the couch and waited for Iverson. *Sure hope he shows.*

Chapter 53

The elevator reached the sixteenth floor and settled in after a slight hiccup. The door opened and a burly, granite jawed man awaited Iverson. He wore a short-sleeved, light blue work shirt and tight fitted, boot cut Levis. His lizard skin belt matched his footgear and was anchored by an enormous silver buckle shaped like a cowboy hat. His steely eyes studied the ex-cop carefully and his shoulder holstered weapon offered a no-nonsense message that Iverson clearly understood. He summoned Iverson out from the elevator with a wave of his meaty hand and Iverson moved into the hallway to await further instructions. He didn't wait long.

"There," the man said and pointed to a small alcove ten feet down the hall where a small glass table and cushioned chair sat beneath a stained glass window.

Iverson complied without comment. His escort's actions were actually a good sign. He was being treated as an unwanted visitor rather than an intruder.

The chiseled man followed Iverson into the recess and added some directives.

"Empty your pockets and put the contents and your weapon on the table."

Iverson took some time to fully consider giving up his gun. *They'd have killed me already if that was their intent,* he thought. He hoped he was right. He placed his Colt, a small box of cartridges, his phone, a half empty pack of Camels, a book of matches and the Escort's second set of keys on the table.

"Arms up," the man commanded.

"Excuse me?" Iverson said.

"Put your arms up . . . high," the man repeated. He spoke without expression.

Iverson complied again. The burly man pulled a twelve inch, rod shaped device from behind his back, clicked a button on the handled section and waved it over Iverson. The wand was searching for anything metal or electronic. Whoever Iverson was going to be talking with, didn't want their conversation recorded. Another good sign. They wouldn't be worried about tapes if they planned on killing him. He took a deep breath.

The man finished his scan and pointed down the hallway. "That way," he said gruffly.

Iverson lowered his arms and stared questioningly at his phone and revolver.

"Not a chance," the guy grunted. He pointed again to a double door at the end of the hall. "Move."

Iverson walked to the door and awaited his next direction. His chaperon instead left him at the door, returned to the alcove and took a seat in the padded chair. The doors in front of Iverson swung open and he was greeted by the man who opened them.

"Hello, Sergeant Iverson," the man said. "I've been looking forward to meeting you."

Iverson's host was an average looking, older man. He was about five-foot eight, had thinning gray hair and wore wire rimmed glasses. His round face had more than a few wrinkles and crow's feet were beginning to form at the corners of his eyes. He was clad in a tailored blue suit and the red tie adorning his starched white shirt bore a Confederate flag for a tack. Iverson gauged his age to be in the mid-sixties. His confident air spoke of power and success.

"You have me at a disadvantage," Iverson claimed.

"My apologies, Sergeant," the man offered. "My name is Austin Dodge." He extended his hand but Iverson ignored it. "Shall we sit?" he asked and waved his retracted hand toward a grouping of dark leather chairs.

Iverson walked over to the cluster and stood silently. Dodge sat down. Iverson followed suit. A young man appeared from a side door, walked over to where Iverson and Dodge sat, and asked them if they wanted coffee or another beverage. Iverson said he didn't and Dodge waved him away.

"So, Sergeant Iverson," Dodge began, "what do you want to know?"

Iverson was both surprised and delighted with the lack of foreplay. "How much are you prepared to tell me?" he asked.

"I have nothing to fear from you, Sergeant," Dodge said confidently. "You and your lady friend downstairs will never be able to make a connection between my people and the fools you've been chasing in Oregon. This is Texas. We do things differently here."

Iverson wondered if Dodge's words were rooted in false bravado or well-placed confidence. *Doesn't really matter,* he decided. He figured his time was limited so he steered to the questions he'd been asking himself.

"Why the foreigners?" Iverson asked.

Dodge reached over and plucked a high end cigar from a box on the table between them. He clipped off the tip with a silver cutter, lit it with a butane torch and sat back in his chair.

"Well, first off," Dodge began, "they're willing to do the work. Desperation will make a man do almost anything, Sergeant. I'm sure you've noticed that in your line of work. Fortunately for us, the world has a never ending supply of desperate people. As with all businesses, we match skills with the job. We discovered a long time ago that conflict zones provide the best pool of recruits. Soldiers are obedient and loyal. War removes their principles. We don't consider morality a job requirement."

"I take it recruiting has been successful?"

"Immensely," Dodge boasted. "There's no shortage of conflict in our world, Sergeant. We view human suffering as opportunity. In a way, we're helping people achieve a better life."

"By causing more suffering," Iverson said cynically.

"That's your opinion," Dodge retorted. "I work for those who hold a different point of view."

"And that would be . . .?"

"That the world is controlled by those willing and able to control it. And we, Sergeant Iverson, are both willing and able."

Iverson moved on. "How does the recruitment work?"

"We identify suitable situations, assess potential and make contact if and when we need people."

"The Croatians?" Iverson baited.

"A perfect example," Dodge replied. "The Balkans were ripped apart by war. Its population was ravaged. Borders had crumbled and alliances disintegrated. Thousands of soldiers were searching for a new home. They had skills, but not the type utilized by Fortune 500 companies. We made contacts. We targeted a few specific individuals. We offered U.S. citizenship and plenty of U.S. dollars. It's a deal that's hard to turn down. Nobody does."

"Nobody?" Iverson asked.

"Not yet," Dodge replied. "You do know how the world works, don't you, Sergeant Iverson?"

Iverson did know. His naivety had disappeared a long time ago. For much of his life he'd witnessed the exploitive nature of his fellow human beings. Dodge was simply engaging it on a large and different scale.

"Why foster homes?" Iverson asked.

"I was wondering when you'd get to that," Dodge said.

"You can stop wondering," Iverson responded. "Why did you choose the foster care model for training your killers?"

"This is a long term operation, Iverson," Dodge explained. "Like any business, we occasionally need to replace workers. However, in the one facet of Global Solutions that you have interest in, we can't advertise for the employees we seek. Using the Croats as an example again, their core, like all the immigrant groups we use, is small. Small by design because small is discreet. But because it's small, we can't use them for our real work. Attrition would quickly eliminate their ranks."

"By real work, you mean killing people," Iverson asserted.

"That's one way of looking at it," Dodge replied.

"And you have a better way?"

"We're eliminating barriers to a better world."

"Really?"

"Really," Dodge maintained. "We're doing the American people a great service."

Iverson shook his head. "Are you going to answer the question about foster care?"

"I believe I was doing that, Sergeant," Dodge chastened. "I simply assumed being an ex-cop, you'd be partial to details."

Iverson sat back in his chair. "By all means," he said, "continue."

"Our work requires strict obedience and unquestioned loyalty from everyone, but it's especially important at the lower levels. The *real work* level. I believe the Croats called them pjeseks. The best way to assure those traits is to instill them at a very young age. Children. We need access to children to train for the real work. The Child Welfare System in this country provides that access. Not willingly or knowingly, of course." Dodge took a puff from his cigar and smiled a self-satisfied smile.

"Why Child Welfare specifically?" Iverson asked.

"Given that you're a product of that system, I wouldn't have thought I'd need to explain that to you."

Iverson was taken aback by Dodge's knowledge of his personal life but didn't skip a beat. "Humor me, Dodge," he baited. "Tell me how it works."

"Child Welfare is tasked with treating an ever growing social malignancy that will never be cured. All across the country, those agencies charged with protecting children consistently make matters worse with tactical, procedural and personnel blunders. They are dependably dysfunctional. That dysfunction, however, works to our advantage. We identify the agencies with repeated infractions and track the families and the foster parents attached to those agencies. That's our recruiting base."

"So you have Child Welfare people on your payroll who identify child and Keeper candidates?"

"Well done, Sergeant," Dodge said. "Your deductive reasoning rivals Sherlock Holmes."

Iverson asked, "Does that include judges and attorneys?"

"I think I'll leave that for you to figure out, Sergeant," Dodge teased. "I can't tell you everything, can I?"

"Why tell me anything?"

"Why not?" Dodge replied mockingly. "I told you, we don't fear you. You've gone as far as you're going to go. You're in Texas now. Your ability to impact our operation ended once your plane landed in Houston. You caused us some grief back in your home state, but we've cleared out of Oregon and won't be going back. You've actually done us a favor by identifying a weakness and assisting us in eliminating it. We appreciate that, Sergeant Iverson."

"Who's the money behind this?"

Dodge got up from his chair, walked over to an intricately carved wooden bar and poured himself a glass of amber colored liquid from a leaded glass decanter. "I'm afraid I've shared as much as I'm willing to, Iverson," he said.

"As a matter of fact, I've shared more than I'd anticipated. It's time for you to leave. Please collect your friend down in the lobby, get the hell out of my building and then get the hell out of Texas."

Iverson knew the change in Dodge's tone meant the information sharing had ended. Dodge had wagged his arrogance until he tired of the exercise. His ego was sated. Iverson rose from his chair and slowly walked to the door he'd come in through. He returned his attention to Dodge before opening it. "I'll see you again, Dodge," he said calmly. "Sooner than you think, I'd imagine."

Dodge cracked a cynical smile and hoisted his glass in a mock toast. "Fuck you, Iverson," he said.

Iverson walked through the door and over to the table still attended by the chiseled guard. He retrieved everything he'd left on the table. He checked the gun. It had been emptied of its bullets. He opened the cartridge box. Also empty. The guard gave him a sly smile and escorted him to the elevator. He punched the down button and when the door opened, reached in and pressed the lobby button before retreating back into the hallway. Iverson rode the car down and began wondering what Numaga had been up to. He reached the lobby and saw her sitting on the snow-white couch fully engrossed in her cell phone. She spotted him as he started towards her and she offered him a devious smile. *Must be something good.*

Chapter 54

Iverson and Numaga drove back to their hotel and filled each other in on the details of their separate adventures at Global Solutions. They were both pleased with their discoveries and impressed with each other's skills. The partnership was gaining momentum.

Numaga parked the Escort in the same slot and grabbed Iverson's arm as he was opening his door. "One more thing, Stan," she said.

"What's that?"

"I got a text from Sergeant Walker while I was couch sitting."

"Anything interesting?"

"Burleson called Houston PD."

"Definitely interesting," Iverson appraised. "What'd he have to say?"

"He wanted to know if there was an active investigation involving Global Solutions."

"What'd they tell him?"

"He was told they couldn't comment on *any* active investigations."

"So HPD basically confirmed the company was being looked at," deduced Iverson.

"In cop-speak, yeah, they did," Numaga confirmed.

"So he's worried. Good work, Numaga."

"It's only a possibility, Stan," Numaga cautioned. "But we'll see where it leads."

"It's another part of the puzzle," Iverson added, "and the puzzle's coming together."

The Texas heat was beginning to intensify and it was still only late morning. Numaga grabbed her laptop from the back seat and she and Iverson scurried into the Alamo's lobby and detoured immediately into the lounge. Iverson led them to his preferred booth and waved Numaga into the bench. He took up his sentry position and waved over a waitress. Numaga opened her computer and powered it up. Iverson ordered two coffees and Numaga waited for her screen to come alive. When it did, she immediately checked her e-mails.

"Bingo!" Numaga exclaimed.

"Everything?" Iverson asked.

"Looks like it," Numaga answered. She opened up both folders and partially scrolled through the files. "There's a lot of information here that would take days to siphon through. Got anything in particular you'd like me to try and find?"

Iverson considered the request thoughtfully. "How's the data broken out?" he asked.

"There's a separate sub-folder for each year going back to 1985," Numaga detailed. "It's the same organization for both main folders."

"Let's focus on the most recent year's data in both."

Numaga copied two 2015 folders, one from Sector Records and one from Accounting, moved them to her desktop and minimized everything else. She opened the Sector 2015 folder and found Excel spreadsheet documents labeled by sector name and month. She opened the first entry, January 2015, East Sector, and moved the laptop so that Iverson could see the screen. Iverson leaned into the computer and scrunched his eyes uncomfortably. Numaga zoomed in the data.

"Thanks," Iverson said. "New age print and old age eyes aren't a good match."

Numaga appreciated her partner's realistic appraisal. Older cops still working the squad would never have admitted to the diminishment of any body part. Some parts in particular. Numaga scrolled between sectors and months for the first six months of 2015 and then brought up the accounting files and repeated the process. They perused the documents and made non-conversant sounds as they digested the data. The limited examination complete, they pushed back in their seats and took a deep breath.

"What are you thinking, Stan?" Numaga asked.

"I'm thinking this is one arrogant collection of thugs. The American Oil Corporation, the National Firearm Association and the National Christian Coalition are large, wealthy and powerful organizations. I would have thought they'd have been more careful."

"They're Texans," Numaga reminded Iverson. "They have a different mindset."

Iverson considered Numaga's rationale. "My conversation with Dodge provided a hint of that," he said, "but to keep such detailed records is to ask for trouble. It's Caponesque."

"Capone's arrogance and penchant for detail led to his downfall," Numaga recalled. "Maybe we can craft the same ending for Global Solutions."

"I'm listening."

"If you can't beat 'em, join 'em. We need an inside look at their operation."

"You're suggesting we sign on with Global Solutions?"

"I'm suggesting *you* sign on."

"And just how do you propose I do that? Dodge and I didn't exactly hit it off today. There's no way in hell I can walk in there again and work my way into another meeting."

"We use an intermediary."

"And you already have someone in mind, don't you, Numaga?"

"Burleson."

"Why Burleson?"

"Because he's been put on alert that he's at risk. His call to HPD proves he on edge. I think he'd jump at the opportunity to put himself back in good graces with his bosses."

Iverson waived over the waitress again. He needed time to think and he wanted to do it on a full stomach. He ordered a grilled cheese sandwich with a side of fries and a large coke. Numaga said "ditto" when it was her turn.

"So what do we do with you while I'm hanging out with my new friends?"

"I head home," Numaga said nonchalantly.

"You're heading home . . . to Oregon?"

"Well, sort of."

"I need a bit more information, Numaga," Iverson insisted.

"We make them *think* I'm headed home."

"And how might we do that?"

"A very public, partners' quarrel might be a good start."

"So our partnership dissolves, you appear to head home to Oregon and I make an attempt to join the Dark Side."

"Exactly."

"Why didn't I think of that?"

"Sometimes it takes a woman, Stan."

It did this time, Iverson thought.

The sandwiches came and the partners ate quietly. They stared out at the distorted waves of heat rising from the asphalt parking area and watched the traffic coming and going from the Alamo Hotel. They finished the food and re-started their conversation.

"Any thoughts as to how you'd like to break up?" Numaga asked.

"Well," replied Iverson thoughtfully, "we'd want the Global Solutions folks to be aware of it and we'd want them to find it believable."

"So we need the appropriate audience."

"Precisely," Iverson confirmed. "And for that role," he added, "I'd like to nominate the two Global Solution lackeys sitting in the black sedan in the parking lot."

"The ones with binoculars and a proclivity for voyeurism?" Numaga asked.

"The very same," Iverson affirmed.

"Since they're watching," Numaga suggested, "we should probably stage Act I here. I'll get my gear during intermission and we can work Act II out by the Escort."

"Sounds good."

Numaga paused for a few seconds, reconsidering the plan. "What if you need a car?"

"Not sure," Iverson told Numaga, "but I'll think of something. Keep your phone handy."

"Okay," Numaga agreed. "Ready?" she asked.

"I should pay the check first."

"I've got a better idea," Numaga said.

"What's that?"

Numaga grabbed her water glass and threw its icy cold contents in Iverson's face. The look on his face almost caused her to bust out laughing but she quickly assumed her new character and began to loudly berate Iverson. She gestured wildly and added more than a few colorful words to her tirade before rising up, grabbing her laptop and stomping out of the lounge and down the hallway toward her room.

Iverson didn't say a word. Partly due to the shock of Numaga's performance and partly because she'd provided him no opening. He watched her storm away and then sat back in the booth, wiped his face with a napkin, and calmly finished his coffee. It was his turn to act for the black sedan audience. He rose from the bench, walked slowly to the bar and asked for the check. He saw Numaga out of the corner of his eye dragging her luggage and headed out to the parking lot. He finished up the bill and followed her out to where the Escort was parked.

Act II didn't take long. Numaga threw her gear and her laptop into the trunk, offered a few more choice words to Iverson and announced her new plans loud enough for their targeted spectators to hear. Numaga huffed into the Escort, slammed the door demonstrably and left a bit of rubber on the pavement as she left the parking lot. The scene was brief, dramatic and hopefully convincing. Iverson walked back into the lobby and took a quick, furtive glance back at the sedan. The car was still there. The men were not.

Chapter 55

Iverson walked to the reception desk in the Alamo Hotel's lobby and hailed the clerk who was occupied with an outgoing traveler. The man raised his index finger with the universal signal for, *just a minute*.

"I could be dead in a minute," Iverson said tersely. "Maybe you too, if you don't get over here."

The patron looked at Iverson, realized he wasn't joking and aborted his business. The clerk moved down the counter to where Iverson stood. His name tag identified him as Jerod.

"First," Iverson explained, "I need you to call me cab and have it wait at the building's south entrance. They need to get here quickly, so tell them it's an emergency."

The clerk looked at Iverson with uncertainty. "Is there a problem, sir?" he asked.

"There will be if you don't do exactly as I say," Iverson retorted. "In a few minutes, two men will walk in here and they'll ask you for my room number and then for a key. You'll tell them you're not allowed to provide that information and then they'll show you their guns and you'll give them the number *and* the key. You with me so far, Jerod?"

"Yes. Yes, sir," fumbled Jerod.

"All I want from you is that you take an extra moment or two to look up my room number before you give it to them. I don't need you to be a hero. Give them what they want. I only want you to delay the giving a few seconds. Got it?"

"Yes, sir," the clerk managed.

"Great," said Iverson. "Now call the damn cab."

Iverson walked briskly down the hall, slid his key card through the lock on the door and hurried into his room. He threw his belongings into the center pocket of his duffel and took out a full box of .38 caliber cartridges from the side slot. He reloaded his Colt and stuffed a handful of bullets into his left side pants pocket. After one last look around his room, he opened the suite's common door, moved into Numaga's flat and secured the dead bolt. He pressed his ear to the door leading to the hallway and heard advancing footfalls. They stopped outside his room. He heard his room's door open, then close. He cracked open Numaga's door and peered down the hallway. No one there. He loped to the exit at the south end of the building and hopped into the waiting taxi. He called Numaga as soon as the cab cleared the Alamo Hotel's parking lot.

"Good to hear your voice, Stan," Numaga said.

"Had you any doubts that you would?" asked Iverson.

"Of course not, Stan," Numaga answered. "You have positive buha."

"Always wondered what kept me alive all these years."

"Buha and your constructive paranoia."

"Not sure how to take that, Numaga."

"You can decide later," Numaga said. "Where're we at?"

"I just left the good old boys at the hotel and thought I'd swing by Burleson's place and see if I could make a new friend."

"You've been doing a lot of that lately," Numaga evaluated.

"Yeah," Iverson countered. "Deep down, I'm a real charmer."

Numaga laughed out loud. "What do you want from me?" she asked.

"Transportation would be good. I'm in the back seat of a cab at the moment. Switch out the rental and meet me at the first cross street north of Burleson's place in an hour. It won't take me long to make my pitch."

"It might take me longer to get a new car," Numaga reasoned.

"Then I'll be the one sitting on the curb smoking a cigarette."

"The neighborhood watch might call you in as a vagrant, Stan."

"Then pick me up at the county jail." He ended the call and gave his driver directions to his destination. He knocked on Burleson's door fifteen minutes later. The ex-D.A. had changed his clothes but not his disposition.

"What the hell do you want?" he asked gruffly.

"I want to talk," Iverson responded evenly.

Burleson stepped out beyond the door and looked past Iverson and down the street. "Where's the bitch?" he asked.

"On a plane back to Oregon," Iverson revealed. "We had irreconcilable differences."

Burleson returned to the doorway, leaned against the jamb and eyeballed his visitor. "What kind of differences?"

"The money kind."

Burleson tilted his head to one side and scrunched his narrow eyebrows. "So I'll repeat, what the hell do you want?" he demanded.

Iverson readjusted the duffel slung over his shoulder and scanned the neighborhood. "I'm not real comfortable talking about this in public," he said. "Mind if I come in for a minute?"

Burleson considered the request for a five count and then waved Iverson into his house. He led his guest past a well-appointed living room and into a spotless kitchen. He opened the refrigerator door, extracted a beer and opened it. He didn't offer one to Iverson.

"Okay," Burleson said soberly, "You've got sixty seconds to interest me."

"I want another meeting with Dodge," Iverson said bluntly.

Burleson cackled. "I heard the first one didn't go well. Why do you want another one?"

Iverson guessed that Burleson had called Dodge after his phone call to HPD led him to think there was an investigation in play that might involve him. His attitude seemed to exhibit that Dodge had assuaged his fears.

"As I'm sure you're aware, D.A. Burleson, most initial meetings are about fact finding. I got facts earlier today. Now I'd like to make a proposal based on those facts."

"What proposal?" Burleson demanded.

"You're not high enough on the food chain for that, Burleson."

Burleson's face flushed red. "What do you know about the food chain?"

"I know you're close to the bottom."

"Get out," Burleson yelled. "Get the fuck out of my house."

Iverson turned and walked back through the house. He could hear Burleson's heavy steps and labored breathing behind him. He reached the entry, opened it and slipped outside. The door slammed behind him. *Mission accomplished,* he hoped.

*****

Numaga was waiting for Iverson in a dark green Toyota Camry at the designated pick-up point. She wore dark shades and a wide-brimmed, red hat.

Iverson tossed his duffel into the back seat of the car and slumped into the passenger seat next to Numaga. "Nice hat," he panned.

Numaga smiled. "It's all me," she said. "Like the new ride?"

Iverson looked around the Camry. "Looks familiar," he said dryly. "I thought you'd be late."

"Siri found me a Hertz outlet in midtown."

"Who?"

"Siri."

Iverson remained perplexed. "Who's Siri?"

"She's in my phone," Numaga explained.

Iverson shook his head. "Never mind," he said. "I don't need to know."

"How's your new friend, Burleson?"

"He's totally pissed at me, no doubt. But I'm pretty sure he'll call Dodge."

"Why's that?"

"Because he's feeling vulnerable right now. Being a good worker bee will help him demonstrate his loyalty."

"How long do you want to wait on him?"

"Iverson looked at his watch. It was 1:30 PM. "Let's give him until four. If he doesn't contact me by then, he probably won't. In that case, I guess I'll just head back to Global Solutions and see what happens."

"What would you like to do with the wait time?"

"How about finding a new hotel?"

"We could ask Siri," Numaga teased.

"Ask whoever you want," Iverson responded. "Just make sure they don't send us to the Roach Hotel."

Numaga pressed the button on her phone and Siri inquired as to what she needed help with. Numaga voiced her request and Siri responded with a list of ten hotels within a two mile radius. She handed the phone to Iverson and told him to choose the one he wanted. "Let's splurge," Iverson said. He chose the Radisson in Midtown Houston.

Numaga plugged the Radisson's address into her phone's GPS, put the Camry in gear and headed downtown. She took a circuitous route to make sure they hadn't acquired a tail and arrived at the hotel with half of the sweltering Texas afternoon in the books.

The Radisson was palatial compared to the Alamo. Vaulted ceilings stretched above the cathedral sized lobby. Scattered knots of luxurious seating, a wide screen TV and multiple computer stations dotted the landscape that was anchored by a polished plank floor. No dead animals festooned the walls. The Radisson had better taste.

Numaga and Iverson approached the walnut veneered reception desk and Iverson requested the same room arrangement they'd enjoyed at the Alamo. They received their key cards and walked down the first floor hall toward their rooms. Halfway there, Iverson's phone signaled an incoming text. He dropped his duffel, took the phone out of his pocket and tapped the message icon. The dispatch was from Burleson. *meet dodge at girardi's restaurant. 7 PM.*

Chapter 56

Iverson and Numaga dropped their luggage in their rooms and met back in the hotel lobby. They'd decided it would be wise to study Girardi's Restaurant before Iverson's 7 PM dinner date. Numaga's phone provided an address and directions, and they hopped back into the new rental and headed to Houston's south side.

The large sign outside Girardi's advertised "Traditional Italian Food." The smaller sign on the door told the two PI's that the restaurant only served dinners and that it was open from 6 PM until 1 AM. Their hopes for a walk-through dashed, Numaga drove slowly around the perimeter of the building and the two PI's gathered what information they could from the car.

The building was of older vintage and smallish for a restaurant. Through its windows they counted four booths and eight four-chair tables. A small bar sat back from the tables and, adjacent to it, a set of swinging doors which they both assumed led to the kitchen. Numaga spotted a short set of steps leading to an unseen room toward the back of the building. Their perimeter scrutiny of that section revealed no windows.

Three doors provided entry and exit to Girardi's. The main entrance door sat under a green and red awning attached to the building and supported by two large, gilded poles. A second access door was located off the kitchen. It had a screened outer door and opened to a small area enclosed with slatted fencing and a gate leading to two large dumpsters. The third door accessed the windowless room and was unadorned with the exception of a stenciled message: "Private."

"I don't like it, Stan," Numaga cautioned. "It may be a public place, but I'll bet it's *their* public place."

Iverson had the same feeling. "Well," he reasoned, "it's either go for it here or go back home."

Numaga slumped behind the wheel. "Damn, Sarge," she lamented. "I'd sure like to see these assholes pay for their crimes, but I'd also sure as hell miss you if you were dead."

Iverson swiveled a bit and looked directly at his partner. "Thank you, Numaga," he said sincerely. "That may be the nicest thing anybody's ever said to me."

Numaga blushed, her face now coordinated with the hat she wore earlier. "So what do we do?" she asked.

"How about a beer?" Iverson asked.

"Seriously?"

"Seriously," confirmed Iverson. "Let's get a beer at the hotel and review what we've got. After that, we can decide our next move."

Numaga agreed to Iverson's proposition and pointed the car back to the Radisson. Iverson peered out of the

Camry's windows deep in thought. Texas might be the last place he'd see. He didn't much like that idea.

The bar at the Radisson was beginning to get busy. Many of the travelers staying at the hotel had already checked in and were in the mood for a cold drink in the air conditioned comfort of the lounge. Iverson spotted an open booth in the rear of the room and was walking toward it when he saw another couple headed in the same direction. They arrived at their common goal simultaneously and stood silently, eyeballing one another. While Iverson waited, Numaga slipped in behind him and sat down on the black vinyl seat. She ignored the stink eyes from the other couple, opened her laptop and powered it on. The other couple gave Iverson a disgusted look before huffing off while muttering something about Texas hospitality.

"Nice move, Numaga," Iverson said sarcastically.

"Got us a seat, didn't it?" Numaga rebuked.

Iverson couldn't argue with the result even if he didn't particularly care for the method. He moved on. A sandy haired waitress with round blue eyes arrived at the table and took their order. Two cold beers from a tap. Her choice. She smiled and left to select their order.

"Let's start with direct evidence, okay?" Iverson suggested.

"Starting with eyewitnesses?" Numaga asked.

"Sure," Iverson agreed. "Who back in Oregon had knowledge of the operation that we could list as a potential witness in a trial?"

"Your friend Horvat would qualify."

"He would. But my money's on Horvat being either dead or long gone," Iverson gauged. "Next."

"What about the other Croatians?" asked Numaga.

"We eliminated one and the other doesn't appear to be the witness type," Iverson said. "And I'd lay good money on the Kralj and any other Croatians also being long gone. Dodge told me they got out of Oregon. I'm sure they either packed up or buried any remaining operatives."

"Frantzen and Dulles would have been helpful," Numaga suggested.

"True, but they're definitely not available."

The waitress arrived with two tall, foamed glasses of beer and laid two small bowls on the table. Salted peanuts and trail mix. Make-you-thirsty snacks. She inquired as to whether they wanted to order dinner and, after being told no, left to attend other customers.

"Solaras is dead, too," Numaga continued.

"So are the Tremaines, including the boy."

"And Kant," Numaga added.

"Yeah, and Kant," Iverson echoed sadly.

"Well, Stan," Numaga said, "that's ten potential witnesses and they're all dead, presumed dead or mute. I think that's it for known Oregon connections. Did I miss anybody?"

Iverson thought about Numaga's question for a few moments. "There's Doctor Jenkins," he finally offered. "But I'm not sure how much he really knows or if he'd even be willing to testify. I'm fairly certain his main focus is preserving his career."

Numaga set aside the witness list and moved on to other direct evidence possibilities. "How about physical evidence?" she asked.

"No clue," Iverson replied. "That would all be in the hands of APD and we've been working peripheral to them. At times, in conflict with them. I'm sure they have print, DNA and blood evidence but, for our purposes, I think we need to assume they have nothing that would seal a conviction."

Numaga changed directions. "Since we're not doing too well in the direct evidence category, let's try the indirect route."

"Circumstantial evidence?"

"That's all we've got left, Stan."

Iverson was not enthusiastic. No law enforcement official is. Circumstantial evidence is weak evidence. But Numaga was right. It's all they had left.

"Okay, Numaga," Iverson said. "Tell me what we've got."

"We've got the files I lifted from Global Solutions' computer and the eighteen person, Kill Book spreadsheet that demonstrates a pattern of murders starting in 1995. Those two pieces of information can be tied together.

My spreadsheet demonstrates that the eighteen people killed were involved in gun control, environmental or gay rights causes. The Global Solutions data clearly tells us that their funding has predominantly come from the National Firearm Association, the American Oil Corporation and the National Christian Coalition. I see a pretty clear relationship, don't you?"

"Of course I do, Numaga," Iverson said, "but I'm prejudiced. A Texas jury won't be and that evidence will undoubtedly be presented in a Texas courtroom. And after Global Solutions' high powered attorneys spin their tale, that Texas jury will probably be singing their praises."

"How about the other Global Solutions data we pilfered?" Numaga asked desperately. "The Sector Records data shows a history of payments to groups like the Croatians?"

"One very large obstacle there, Numaga," Iverson stipulated, "and the key word is pilfered. All of those documents were obtained without a warrant. You know they'd never make it into *any* courtroom. Texas or Oregon."

Numaga deflated back into her seat. "How about the Kill Books?" she asked feebly.

"It would be weak evidence at best," Iverson replied, "and without Horvat, no evidence at all."

"So we've got nothing," Numaga said angrily.

"Nothing we could go to trial with," clarified Iverson.

"So what's next, Stan?"

"I don't know about you, Numaga," Iverson said, "but I've got a hankering for Italian food."

Chapter 57

Iverson and Numaga lingered in the Radisson lounge for another hour before taking some alone time in their rooms for rest-up and clean-up. They met back down in the hotel lobby at 6:30 PM. Their plan was simple. They would navigate a one block radius around Girardi's until they established a suitable vantage point for Numaga to watch and wait. Iverson would call a cab to meet him at their chosen location and then take history's shortest taxi ride to the restaurant. If Iverson didn't emerge from the building thirty minutes after he'd walked in, Numaga would contact Sergeant Walker and they'd go in after him.

They found a reconnaissance position for Numaga and Iverson made a call to Metro Cab. The hack arrived at 6:55 PM and Iverson hopped into the back seat and pointed to his destination. Numaga could see the conversation in the cab was strained, but the driver stopped quibbling when his passenger handed him a twenty dollar bill. Iverson looked over at Numaga and gave her a crooked smile and a thumbs-up. She hesitantly returned both. The cab moved forward, stopped twenty seconds later in front of Girardi's and its fare stepped out. He walked under the polychrome canopy and disappeared behind the restaurant's front door.

Iverson was greeted first by the ubiquitous scents of Italian cuisine. Waves of garlic, basil and oregano all sailed past his olfactory system on an ocean of freshly baked bread. His mouth watered and his stomach growled. *Should've had a bigger lunch.*

Iverson's second greeting was more sight than smell. The granite jawed man from Global Solutions' office approached him wearing cargo pants, a muscle revealing T-shirt and the same emotionless face he bore earlier in the day.

"This way," the man grumbled. He turned and led Iverson toward the rear of the building. Iverson scanned the restaurant's patrons while he walked and saw people happily occupied with food and conversation. He anticipated something different in the back room where he was headed. They entered a small vestibule and his chaperon turned and held up his hand.

"Same routine as before," Dodge's personal bouncer ordered.

"Seriously?" Iverson asked with feigned disbelief. His minder's reply was a finger pointed at the table standing next to him. He cleared his pockets, laid his weapon and phone on the table and raised his arms upward. They played the wand game again and the guard added a full body frisk for good measure. Satisfied, he led Iverson into the main room.

The chamber was dimly lit and Iverson could barely make out the faces of the five men seated at the table across the room. He looked at his escort for direction and was waved forward. Iverson strolled to a point where two chairs were stationed and stopped. The men behind the table faced him. The High Five holding high court.

Iverson recognized the man in the middle of the group. Dodge. The others he hadn't seen before. They were all clean shaven and dressed in top shelf business suits. Dodge was the smallest of the five; the others appearing equal in physical stature. The table was littered with the remnants of a just completed meal and they were now sipping after dinner drinks. A lanky, white clad waiter was scurrying about filling glasses with a golden liquid poured from a cut-glass carafe. "Sit down," Dodge instructed.

Iverson lowered himself into one of the two high-backed, slatted chairs. His minder receded to the back of the room and took a seat on a wooden bench.

"I decided to grant you another audience, Mr. Iverson," Dodge began, "so that my co-workers could face their enemy." His tablemates stared intently at their guest. Iverson offered each a smile and a nod.

"Would you mind doing introductions, Mr. Dodge?" Iverson asked.

"That won't be necessary, Iverson," Dodge replied. "There's no need for you to get to know one another. Suffice it to say these are the Sector Heads I'm sure you've heard about."

Iverson knew immediately that Dodge was planning to kill him. He needed to stall until Numaga could bring in the posse.

"Actually, Mr. Dodge," Iverson said, "I'd like to talk to you about what I've heard. I've been listening and watching for a while now and have a plan that I believe would benefit all of us."

"Seriously?" Dodge asked sarcastically. "How could you possibly help us?"

"Well," Iverson began, "I could start by burying what I know in a very deep hole."

"That's it?" Dodge asked disparagingly. "We think we can accomplish that without your assistance."

Okay, Iverson thought to himself, *bad choice of words.* "There's more," he said hurriedly. "You told me you were packing up and moving your operation out of Oregon, right?"

"Go on," Dodge baited.

"You wouldn't have to do that if you'd put me in charge of that area."

"Why the hell would we do that?" asked the Sector Head to Dodge's right. His question provoked laughter across the table.

"Because I already have the connections in place to make it work. And since you have knowledge of my history, you know I have no great love for the local PD."

A dark skinned man entered the room via the same door Iverson had passed through. He spoke briefly with the brawny guard on the bench and then left. The guard stood, nodded in the direction of the High Five, and sat back down. Dodge and his group huddled up and whispered amongst themselves for a few minutes before Dodge re-visited the conversation.

"What about your girlfriend?" Dodge asked. "Won't she be a problem?"

""No," Iverson replied. "Not a chance."

"You sure?" Dodge asked.

"Absolutely," Iverson said confidently.

"Maybe we should ask *her*," the man at Dodge's far left posed.

Dodge looked directly at Iverson and smiled mischievously. "What do you think, Iverson?" he inquired cynically. "Should we ask Ms. Numaga if she's going to be a problem?"

Iverson wasn't sure what was going on but he knew he didn't like it. "Well," he said hesitantly, "I personally think that's a bad idea, but if that's what you need to do, by all means, go ahead, call her. Her plane should have landed in Portland by now."

"So she's back in Oregon?" lured Dodge.

"That's where she told me she was headed."

"Then that would make both of you liars, wouldn't it?"

"Pardon me?"

Dodge signaled the sentry in the back of the room with a wave of his arm. He disappeared into the foyer and returned a few seconds later. Numaga was with him.

"Sit her next to Iverson, Victor," Dodge instructed his pawn, "and secure them together."

Victor pushed Numaga forward and roughly pressed her down into the chair next to Iverson. He took a set of Cobra Cuffs out from a cargo pocket and ordered the two PI's to put their arms behind their chairs. He pulled Iverson's left wrist and Numaga's right wrist through their chair's back rails and fastened them roughly together with the cuffs. The captives winced but made no sound.

Dodge and his cohorts watched the proceeding silently. They all had a look of sadistic appreciation on their faces, but Dodge in particular appeared to be taking in the scene with unfettered amusement.

Victor completed his task and moved back to his assigned seat by the door. Dodge convened another whispered conversation and the four Sector Heads leaned in towards their leader and listened attentively.

"Sorry, Stan," Numaga whispered to Iverson. "I guess I got careless."

"Save it for later, Numaga," Iverson said. "We've got bigger problems. Did you manage to alert Walker?"

"No," Numaga answered quietly. "Didn't have time."

"Did Victor take your weapons?"

"The two guys who jumped me in the car took the Sig, my back-up and my phone. They turned everything over to Victor when he came out to get."

Iverson looked up at the men who had now become their judges and, most likely, their executioners. They were still involved in conversation. He strained against his restraints and felt the plastic cuffs cutting into his skin. Maybe he could break the slats, but then what? He scanned the room. The back entry was held down by Victor. The private entrance at the back corner of the room was a long way away and dead-bolted. Victor's bullets would have a clear path. There was a single-swing door that probably led to the kitchen, but they'd have to get past the High Five to get to it. Iverson saw nothing that offered a glimmer of hope. *Nothing. Nothing at all. Shit!*

Numaga was conducting her own assessment. "Is Victor the only one packing?" she asked.

"We're in Texas, Numaga."

"Sorry, Stan," Numaga said. "Dumb question."

One of the Sector Heads, the one at Dodge's far left, pushed himself away from the table and stood up. He then abruptly sat back down and clutched his abdomen. The other panel members eyed him curiously. The man seated to Dodge's far right walked over to the afflicted man, stooped down and examined him closely. Even in the dim light, Iverson could see the alarm form in his eyes. He walked over to Dodge and whispered something in his ear before gripping his own stomach. Ten seconds later, another Sector Head grabbed his gut. All three stricken men collapsed off their chairs and onto the floor. The first one affected had fallen into convulsions.

Dodge's amused demeanor morphed into a visible state of confusion and panic. He glared at the remaining seated Sector Head with eyes demanding an explanation. He received none and when his visual target grasped his mid-section, he turned his attention to Victor. Victor left his station and tentatively approached the High Five's table. When he saw the fourth judge collapse to the floor, he came to a full stop, made an about face turn and fled the room.

"Victor!" Dodge screamed. Victor didn't look back. Iverson heard two doors slam and was certain Victor would not be heard from again.

Two of the Sector Heads lay still and the other two were experiencing full-on seizures. Dodge sat wide-eyed in the midst of the havoc. Numaga saw that he'd placed an open palmed hand over his stomach and that sweat was dripping profusely from his forehead and down the channels of his furrowed face. His color had turned ashen and his free hand twitched. But it was steady enough to lift a Smith and Wesson revolver from a shoulder holster and point it at the two people seated in front of him.

"You did this, didn't you, Iverson?" Dodge accused angrily.

"Afraid not, Dodge," Iverson corrected. "But whoever did, has my full gratitude."

"A smart fuck to the end, huh, Iverson," Dodge huffed with the little breath he had left. He grimaced with pain and squeezed the revolver's handle to control it. He took his left hand away from his gut and used it to steady his aim."

"Kick backwards with all you've got," Iverson told Numaga.

"When?" Numaga asked.

"Now!"

Their backs hit the floor as the shot rang out. Iverson waited for the pain to reach him. It didn't. He lolled his head to the left and looked over at Numaga. She was staring up at the ceiling wondering where the bullet had found a home.

"Numaga?" Iverson asked calmly.

"Yeah?"

"You all right?"

"It appears I am. How about you?"

"I'm good," Iverson advised. He craned his head up from the floor and looked around. Dodge was slumped over the table and the other four men lay still on the floor. He relaxed back down and reported his findings to his partner.

"What the hell happened, Stan?" Numaga asked.

"Good question," Iverson responded. "Let's figure out a way to right ourselves and maybe then we can get some answers."

They started to work the chairs in hopes of returning to an upright position when they heard footfalls. They halted their efforts and craned upwards in search of the source. They saw a man clad in white. White pants, white shirt and a tall white chef's hat. He also had a Glock 19 in his right hand. The man leaned over Dodge, lifted his head and studied him briefly. He dropped the head carelessly, squatted down and eyed the four lifeless bodies laid out on the floor. Pushing himself up from the floor, the man turned around and walked towards Iverson and Numaga.

"Stan?" Numaga questioned.

"Yeah, I see," answered Iverson.

Gabos Horvat stopped a few feet short of the tethered PI's.

"Nice to see you again, Stan Iverson," Horvat said calmly. "And you as well, Ms. Numaga."

Iverson suppressed his surprise. "Are you responsible for that?" he asked and nodded toward the table.

"I am, yes," Horvat answered unemotionally.

"How?" inquired Numaga.

"You kill rats with rat poison, Ms. Numaga."

"So what now?" Iverson asked.

"Now," Horvat said, "it is finished."

"What's finished?"

"The killing."

Iverson and Numaga both knew what Horvat meant. Neither needed to know why he'd killed the men at the table. The fact that they were alive because he had, didn't escape them.

"What about Numaga and me?" Iverson asked.

"When Victor left, he alerted the restaurant's customers that they should leave too. They took one look at his panicked state and emptied out. But one of them will certainly call the police and I suspect you will be freed from your bondage shortly after I leave."

"You're leaving?" asked Numaga.

"Of course," Horvat said. He turned and started toward the private entry door at the rear of the room. He reached the portal, slid the dead bolt free and put his hand on the tarnished brass handle. He looked back at Iverson and Numaga.

"Not how I imagined our last meeting, Stan Iverson."

Iverson looked back at Horvat from the floor. "Me either," he admitted.

"Stan Iverson," Horvat said.

"Yeah?"

"Thank you."

Horvat pulled the door open, walked through it and disappeared into the hot Texas night. Iverson knew it was the last time he'd see him.

CHAPTER 58

Iverson paced the white linoleum floor in his kitchen. He was busy pretending to be the cook he wasn't and anxiously anticipating his role as the host he'd never been. He'd invited Numaga to his place for dinner. His confidence was high at the time, but with her arrival fast approaching, it was wavering. Social grace had never been associated with Stan Iverson.

Iverson and Numaga had been back from Houston for two weeks. They'd taken some time away from one another to decompress and to get some distance between themselves and the bloodshed. At least thirteen people had been killed in less than a week and Iverson and Numaga had been involved in all the deaths. Unless you're a sociopath, there's a price to pay for that kind of carnage.

Iverson had taken calls from the Houston Police Department after he'd returned home, but sleepless nights and listless days convinced him he needed to take a break from humanity's dark side. He turned off his phone and spent long hours on his rickety porch and taking long walks with Max. It didn't help his mood. He felt himself sinking into depression. Max was a good companion, but he didn't talk much. Iverson needed a human friend. He called Numaga.

Iverson's four burner stove had only three working burners and three cast iron skillets were perched on top of them. He ignited the functioning burners and added a small amount of olive oil to each pan. He threw chopped peppers and onions into one pot, pineapple slices into another, and marinated steak strips into the third. He adjusted the burners, grabbed a beer from fridge and keyed it open. He finished a long pull as Numaga knocked on the door.

Iverson opened the screen door for Numaga and she entered holding a six-pack of beer and a bouquet of flowers.

"Flowers?" Iverson queried.

"For your sensitive side, Stan," Numaga teased.

Iverson cracked a controlled smile. He'd thought he missed Numaga. Now he was certain.

Numaga took the beer into the kitchen, pulled one from its slot and put the rest in the refrigerator. She looked over at the stove top and took a deep, nasal breath. "Sure smells good, Stan," she commented. "Old family recipe?"

"More like an old fart recipe, Numaga," Iverson countered.

They sipped their beers and made small talk while Iverson sautéed and browned their dinner. He eventually announced his culinary work was completed and he scraped the skillets' contents into three bowls and put them on the table. He returned to the kitchen, grabbed an array of bottles and a stack of tortillas from the counter and laid them next to the bowls.

"Voila!" Iverson announced.

They ate quietly until Numaga broke the silence.

"You doing okay, Stan?"

Iverson expected the question. A few weeks ago, he would have put her off with a dismissive answer. Not now. He answered her with as much honesty as he had available to him. Numaga listened. He knew she would. They discussed what had happened and how it had affected them. Numaga revealed her own distress and that she'd dealt with it by escaping to the Coast. "Essentially," Numaga said, "I let the ocean wash away the bad buha."

They talked briefly about the fallout from the case. Detective Walker, from the Houston PD, had informed Numaga that both the FBI and the IRS were actively investigating the National Firearm Association and the American Oil Corporation. The National Christian Coalition had thus far fended off any attempts to open their books. They were apparently claiming the constitutional separation of church and state precluded them from having to do so. Court dates were being negotiated.

Numaga also told Iverson that the autopsies on Dodge and the four Sector Heads had determined that all five had died as a result of ingesting Monofluoroacetate, a compound commonly used in rat poison. The Houston PD had not yet located Gabos Horvat nor did they have any leads as to his whereabouts.

Numaga had filed a written report with the Ashton Police Department, chronologically detailing the events of the entire case. In a separate report to APD, she detailed what she believed to be the level of involvement in the case by the late Lieutenant Solaras.

Iverson's update included a letter he'd sent to Valley Christian Hospital detailing his knowledge of the nefarious and illegal workings of the hospital's Emergency Room staff. He didn't incriminate Dr. Jenkins. Iverson figured he could make that choice on his own. He did mention Susan Kincaid, the ER Director and his thoughts as to her connection to Global Solutions. Iverson cc'd the letter to the County Health Department, the Oregon State Health Care Regulation Board and APD. He also told Numaga that he'd sent a letter to the Oregon Department of Child Welfare describing the Houston operation and the possible link between it and the department's personnel. That letter was cc'd to Oregon's State Attorney General's Office as well as the Office of the Governor. He had contacted Grace Johnson to provide her a heads-up before mailing the document.

Numaga and Iverson agreed that the end result of their work may very well exact no change. "Real change," Iverson posited, "rarely happens."

Numaga agreed it was an uphill battle filled with frustration. "But," she reasoned, "to abandon the effort would be to desert those who need it most." Iverson nodded his agreement.

Numaga helped Iverson clean up after their fajita feast and they retired to the porch for an after dinner beer. They watched a white-tailed doe stroll across the yard with a couple of spotted and leggy newborns. A few minutes later a gaze of raccoons waddled past Numaga's Camry, inspected its wheels and moved out into the pasture. Max returned from wherever he'd been, sauntered over to the porch and joined them for a glimpse of the setting sun. When it finally tucked itself beneath the horizon, Numaga checked her phone and announced it was time to head home. She rose from her chair and instructed Iverson to do the same. He complied and Numaga encircled him in a warm embrace. Iverson hugged back.

"Thanks for the wonderful dinner, Stan," Numaga said. "Next time, my place, okay?"

"Definitely," Iverson replied.

Iverson watched as Numaga walked to her car. Max followed her and as she bent down to pet him, Iverson remembered something. "Numaga!" he yelled.

"What?"

"Hang on a minute. I forgot to give you something."

Numaga leaned against the car and waved her okay. Iverson hurried into the house, returned a few moments later and walked over to Numaga.

"Here," Iverson said as he handed her a small box. "You might need these."

Numaga opened the box. In it was a stack of business cards. She plucked one out, flipped it over and read it. "**Stanley B. Iverson & Cassie Numaga - Professional Investigations**."

CPSIA information can be obtained at www.ICGtesting.com
Printed in the USA
BVOW06s2359300916

463884BV00023B/64/P